by

Jon Puckridge

Copyright 2016 Hague Publishing
Hague Publishing
PO Box 451
Bassendean Western Australia 6934
Email: contact@haguepublishing.com
Web: www.haguepublishing.com

ISBN 978-0-9925437-4-7

Cover Art and Typography: by Ellipse Design http://www.ellipse.com.au/

Typeset Garamond 12/14

For my father

Experiencing some difficulties

⏻

'CLACK clack!' The sound cuts through even the whistle and drum of the wind.

Not now!

Cones and rods interrogate the space, as pinpoints of sparkling blue and white swirl and shift in the sharp light.

Must be somewhere ... wait, what's that?

The little identifier flag blinks hot red against a white noise. With a deep breath, I rise and glide ghost-like over the ground as the grey grID lines pass beneath me, measuring out some sort of meaningful distance.

Here.

The flag fades then disappears and my feet settle into the snow with a satisfying crunch. On cue, the wind drops to a light breeze, letting ultra-sharpened snowflakes settle on my ultra-sharpened sleeve. Somewhere nearby, huskies howl convincingly. I take a moment to savour it all. Looking up, the first thing I notice is that there are no clouds. A bold sun hangs hot white in an endless blue.

They've taken a few liberties.

'Clack clack!'

Oh, for fuck's — ! No, it's pointless getting angry. It's just doing its job.

My focus turns towards the memorial – a gold and platinum plaque resting on an obsidian base. Tiny ice crystals have formed a softness over the polished metal, somehow adding extra poignancy to the words engraved there. They've chosen a modern humanist font, with slick typographical flourishes, the prominent grID logo sitting above it all.

Priorities right.

'In memory of all those who tragically lost their lives ... '

I skip over the corporate heartfeltness to the list of names, both human and rooin.

'Alvaroz, Azure-B, Buntanimo, Buyries, Capstain, Carter ...

' ... Cartouche.'

I feel a deep sense of closure, as though I can finally –

'Clack cluuurrrff!'

Fuck!

Obviously, my prompter has detected a neural shift. Normally it's supposed to sound like a polite cough, but mine always sounds like a really big, pissed-off termite.

'Excuse me, Youren. It's Mister Burgeis for you.'

The cold Antarctic light dims then disappears and Lleo's face looms – go-get golden.

"Hey, Youren. Come back, all is forgiven! Ha ha."

The chubby fingers wiggle in front of my face – so close I can almost see the micro-manicure.

Decrease sharpness.

Lleo dissolves into a tangerine and grey blur, just as he says "Guess what?"

Increase.

Lleo returns, unaware he's even gone anywhere.

"Yyy-our-ennn." My name stretches out in some sort of measure of our friendship. "Amazing news! Meet me at the Metatatron. Here's the T."

And with that, he's gone.

I removed the grID visor, immediately I felt space contract around me with a jolt. Colours faded, sounds flattened. My room seemed smaller than before. Nothing in it was ultra-sharp. Vague cooking smells from next door blended with the less defined scents of plastic and cloth. And my socks.

I uttered a crypto-command, then said, "Balcony. Open." The wall shimmered, dematerialised. I stepped out, allowing my senses to be assaulted.

Medusa!

Mad, miserable, Medusa. Monstrous Medusa. Commercial capital of OneWorld and easily the most powerful of all the government corporations. For an instant, I couldn't even remember the name of my suburb, maybe the brand name of some sneaker. The city lights in the distance danced and changed colour, doing their best to woo me back. The crowds shuffling below didn't bother. They were too busy shouting, laughing, arguing, and pushing their way into the future.

A warm, moist wind was blowing up. Down by the vehicle corridor, a rooin busker was singing to any human who'd listen.

Take me back, under the sea

Where life began, and love was free ... '

Above the rooflines, the low ceiling of greenish-black clouds continued to circle slowly.

∞

"Here's the T!"

My grumpy imitation of Lleo kept me amused as I wended my way through the crowd. I had decided not to take the B-tube – I figured with only two stops to Plaza Station, by the time I'd negotiated my way through the tunnels and platforms, it would be quicker to walk.

Towering over the buildings, the environmental lighting screens were now shifting hues to resemble someone's idea of a sunset. Not that I'd know, of course, but I'd seen the 3Vs. The logo of a neuro enhancement company glowed discretely within the sun's dying rays. For this mostly human crowd, their scheduled sleep wasn't far off and so, like children before bedtime, they behaved with a rowdy desperation.

I found myself temporarily caught in a swirl of people who were watching a rooin street performer. High above the crowd, his green skin glowed with exertion and fear as he progressively built a perilous structure out of industrial guillotine blades. As each blade was added beneath him, there was a collective intake of breath from the crowd below.

A woman turned to me with obvious glee, a half-eaten burger poised at her lips.

"Cog's gonna get hisself cut! I'd put money on it," she said.

You'll be disappointed, I thought.

I pressed on, passing over several large vehicle corridors. The ionised air rising from below was acrid and hot, and the high-pitched harmonics from so many grav engines hurt my ears. Fine curtains of rain were now drifting down from the clouds and I pulled up my hood. After a few more city blocks, I had arrived and, despite my bad mood, I couldn't help but stop and marvel at the structure before me.

OneWorld Plaza looked like an enormous set of children's blocks which had fallen from above, randomly landing in the improbable arrangement of a perfect circle, each block supporting its neighbour. I'd heard the architect, Petohmi Rad, explaining the design once: *'remove any single element, and the entire impossible creation collapses back into chaos.'* Typical architect-speak, but I had to admit the design was impressive.

High above the plaza, dark lights bounced off the 'Dome of Time' –

six interlocking rings, each supposedly moving according to an aspect of the old pre-T calendar (though you'd be hard-pressed to work out modern time from it). Tempo Corp had kicked up a fuss during the construction, but there wasn't much they could do without a costly legal battle. And Medusa was a thug of a govcorp.

' *... and the dome's geometry has been derived from the behaviour of water droplets falling onto a flat surface ...* '

My grID visor was beginning to map interesting 'facts' plus some dubious 'history' onto the physical structures, all seemlessly blended with social brand messages, recommendations, and just plain ads. I gazed even higher. Beyond the retinal media and the dome itself was, well, the clouds. And beyond them –

"Oi there, curly!"

A dishevelled businessman, drink in hand, had tumbled out of a bar. My visor was already overlaying a Quick-profile matrix onto his face.

Godfrey Maddox,

Neuro-Marketing Coordinator,

Grindcom.

'We're Big in Smallgoods'.

The Grindcom jingle started up, but I cut it short with a glare. Then I received a cursory invitation to merge Mr Maddox's details into my grID office of choice and, of course, return the favour. My retina declined. I'd recently developed the habit of leaving my ID channels closed by default – something which was not looked upon kindly at work.

Not a network player, Mr Cartouche! There's no 'I' in Network.

Mr Maddox seemed to feel the same way.

"Are you a player or a spectator?" he demanded, raising his glass and eying me with that blend of camaraderie and menace that the inebriated always exude.

"Monster times!" I yelled, fist held high.

It did the trick. He and the others roared their approval, and I was free to continue.

On the far side of the plaza, was the Metatron, with its oil-on-water windows and obscene gargoyles. The frosted glass panels slid across each other and the entrance opened like some alien sex flower, inviting me inside.

The dimly lit interior was a riot of historical ambiguity. Ancient iconography and neutrino trajectories lined the walls, while spots of light and dark played seductively on the soft-steel lounges, towering white candles, ancient steam engines, and mercury pools. Beneath my feet was a real cobblestone floor.

"Youren! Over here."

Lleo was being served by a girl whose sari changed colour in time to the beat of the Metatron-branded chocolate lounge music. I sat down and removed my grID visor.

"Sir?"

Her dark eyes said I was not made for this place.

"Just a Super-Hydra, thanks."

When she had left, Lleo settled into his chair.

"So, how long is it?"

"You want T?"

"Ha! I don't think either of us want to pay for T. Anyway," he raised his glass, "Monster times!"

It sounded like a genuine toast, but Lleo only wanted to talk about one thing. ON. That is to say, he, Lleo Burgeis, was now ON. And I, Youren Cartouche, was not.

∞

"... whole new direction ... revolution in the way we live and work ... the future of ..."

Oh yes, the fabulous future! ON was just one more future that we all needed to jump on, or so I had thought back then. As Lleo prattled on, I recalled the time I had first seen the product in action. Biz Ramachandran, chairman of CoolGlobalGiant, had used his keynote address at the #7A9B San Francisco NeuroCon to launch the company's flagship enterprise. Our agency had already secured a little of CoolGlobalGiant's vast advertising budget, and negotiations were in place for the ON account as well.

Biz confidently strode across the stage in his trademark pink jeans and 'space' jacket.

"Nowadays, one event tends to blend into the next. We tend to forget when this or that happened, don't we?"

He stopped, and turned to face us.

"But this is one event we won't forget." He raised his arms. "Because this is when we were introduced to the *Universe of ON!*"

The music began, and the large screen behind him filled with images of people flying over fantastic landscapes or holding strange, constantly-morphing objects in their hands. Words like 'innovation', 'future', 'potential', and 'creativity' flew out over our heads.

"As many of you already know, 'ON' stands for 'One Network'. That is no empty promise. ON has the potential to combine every network into just one. A network built upon *you*. You, me, all human beings. ON will link us all into the One Human Network."

Biz gestured towards the media screen and we were shown a slick little documentary which revisited the key milestones of commercial neurotech. Some of the early quotes were strangely prescient, or hilariously inaccurate.

Biz said, "The pre-T scientist, Isaac Newton once wrote, *'If I have seen further, it is by standing on the shoulders of giants.'* May I humbly suggest that you, OneWorld's neurotech community, also stand on the shoulders of giants. It's just that some of these giants, well ... they really needed to do something about their *wardrobe*."

He gestured theatrically, and moved towards the wings.

The next images were so ridiculous, I thought at first they must have been fake. Before us were two young men dressed in identical business suits. On their heads, they wore bulky hemispherical 'helmets' constructed from hundreds of ball bearings. From the back of the helmets, black wires draped down over their shoulders like dreadlocks, and several other wires were attached to adhesive red patches on the temples and between the eyebrows. Two pink antennae protruded from the front of each helmet.

The men were earnestly telling someone off camera about how these devices allowed them to mentally communicate with each other over long distances. One of them concluded with an enthusiastic; "I think there's a big future for this."

The 3V froze on that instant.

It was a risky play for Biz. Essentially, he was saying that commercial attempts at 'remote-neuro' had hit a wall. It was true. Humans just wanted to be humans, not some dork in a silly helmet. The applause started softly, but then steadily rose to a profound and sombre crescendo. The lights faded to black.

∞

"So, where have they been keeping you?"

"I'm sorry, what?" I said, startled.

"Where have you been hiding?"

Lleo managed to make the act of sipping his drink look like a chess move.

"Well?" he asked, salaciously.

"Oh, umm ... holiday," I replied.

"Excellent! I'm sure you needed it. Have fun?"

"To be honest, I can't even remember."

"Must be all the drugs you take. Not my brands of choice." he laughed, raising his glass, eyes scanning the room for opportunities.

"How's Monterey?" I asked.

Lleo sighed. "She's into her *Omon* thing now."

"What's that?"

"They do exercises under coloured lights. The changing wavelengths realign something in the cerebral cortex. It's all very 'spiritual'." His voice trailed off as an attractive blonde woman settled into a nearby chair.

"And the kids?"

Leo peevishly returned his gaze. "Tonal is finishing off his History Design degree at Angkor Wat University. And, umm ..."

"Indigo?"

"Yeah. Well, we don't know *what* to do with *that* girl."

By now, he'd lost interest in the blonde, and was studying two women at the near end of the bar. Both wore 'standard issue' little black dresses, but with one notable addition: on the front of each dress, discretely displayed, was the ON logo.

"See the one on the left?" Lleo pointed rather obtrusively. "*Heterochromia.* The eyes are different colours, see."

"Can't say I'd noticed."

"Not my type, but definitely yours. A real *wild one*! Mmm?"

"Thanks for your interest in my love life, Lleo."

"Let's see if they'd like some company."

"Uhh, I don't think that's a very good – "

Before I could stop him, Lleo attempted to make contact with the girls, his face going through a series of contortions, as if he was either about to sneeze or was having a shit. Clearly, he hadn't quite got the hang of the ON nOS – the ON neural operating system. People I knew who were ON could easily talk to you while communicating with others on the network, and you wouldn't even notice.

After much effort, it seemed as though Lleo had succeeded. The girls eyes widened. They looked at each other. They looked across to Lleo. Then they collapsed into giggles.

"Did it hurt?" I asked.

"What?"

"The procedure. Getting the engrafts put in."

"No of course not." He pointed with his finger. "They use this gun thing and put it here ..." He placed the finger behind his ear, at the base of the skull. "... and pffft! You don't feel a thing. There's one on either side."

"Can I see them?"

He rubbed the back of his head.

"They've already healed up. You can't see anything. Nothing at all."

∞

The NeuroCon audience was getting restless. Then a spotlight came up on the empty stage, and a tall woman in a dark suit walked into the light. She spoke in cool, clipped tones.

"Hello, everyone. My name is Li Sun. I am the Communications Officer for CoolGlobalGiant. I am also one of a small, but rapidly growing number of people who have chosen to become ON.

"ON is a profound new way for us to connect with other humans, without the need for any external device." She grinned, "unlike the two gentlemen we just saw.

"But," she continued, "it also allows us to connect to many other things as well. Let me illustrate this by introducing you to my darling cat, Frossle. Jim, could you please bring Frossle out for us?"

A surprised looking Burmese-Siamese was brought onto the stage, and the woman gently took it in her arms. After some soothing words, she lifted the cat up to face the audience. Frossle's enormous blue eyes told us he really didn't want to be there.

"He's a bit shy," Li Sun pointed out unnecessarily.

We gave Frossle some encouraging applause.

"OK, pretty soon, you will see within the screen behind me, exactly what I am seeing with my eyes. This is possible because my brain is currently sending data to a secure media link. Uh, can we check visual now?"

The 3V behind her sprang to life, displaying everything she was seeing – the cat in her hands, the auditorium, and us. There we all were, looking back at ourselves. A few people even waved, accompanied by nervous giggles.

"Alrighty," she continued breezily, as if sensing the need to reassure everyone. "Just like any domestic cat, Frossle is fully nanotagged. Now we don't think much about nanotagging anymore, do we? It's just one of those invisible parts of our world that we take for granted.

"Broadly speaking, nanotags can be divided into two categories: replicating and non-replicating, which equates to biological and industrial products. With bio products, the nanotags are introduced during the insemination process, after which they continue to divide and differentiate, until there is approximately one nanotag per cell. This allows bio-facilitation companies to track their work, protect IP, and all that commercial stuff which I don't even *pretend* to understand.

"Hey, I had to look this up on the grID just like anyone else!" she added with a grin.

It broke the ice and we all laughed.

"Nanotags publish data about their location, energy state, functional specs, and much more. This data is usually only of interest to manufacturers and various regulatory agencies, but CoolGlobalGiant has made strategic alliances with most of the major nanotag companies, and now you'll see why. Oh, and before we get to the fun stuff, I should stress that none of this would be possible without the release of GPS7.0. What's the resolution? Ten microns? Awesome stuff. Any of you GPS guys out there, you rock!"

The cat had begun to struggle in her hands.

"Well, I can see Frossle is fed up with my gasbagging, so let's move on."

She placed the cat on a table and sat down to watch him. His image now occupied the entire media screen behind her.

"What I'm going to do is switch on some of the channels available to me through ON. Ready? OK, here we go!"

The cat on the screen underwent a transformation, suddenly replaced by an anatomical model of a cat. But this was no model, this was Frossle himself in all his biological complexity. As Frossle moved, so did the figure onscreen. We could see his skeleton, muscles and tendons shifting, his little heart beating, his lungs expanding and contracting. There were also his digestive and circulatory systems, and so on. I lost track of all the biosystems, each one clearly identified by colour.

The place went berserk.

Over the din, Li Sun turned and grinned at everyone. "Pretty cool, huh?"

Frossle now decided to roll over onto his back to get his tummy rubbed. And so, of course, did the vast bio-image on the screen behind them.

"Awww, he's so cute!" someone down the front shouted out.

"You know," Li Sun laughed "I think he's cute no matter which way I look at him. But let's filter some of this data. If I want to, I can just see his circulatory system ..." The onscreen cat became a tangled mass of red arteries, veins and capillaries.

"... or nervous system ..." A cat of white hair-like structures appeared.

"... and, on top of all this, I can check Frossle's pedigree, medical history, dietary recommendations, and recent training programs, all without the need for any external device whatsoever.

Li Sun turned to the audience. "Just look at what my brain knows when it's ON."

Pages of information scrolled up the screen. Then the screen went blank.

"I probably don't need to point it out, but this trick only works with brand named animals. So if you're one of those strange people who still own a wild-seed pet then, I'm sorry, but Rover will still look just like a dog."

There was weak laughter, though I wasn't sure why that should even be funny.

∞

"But did you see this?" Lleo smoothed the lapels of his jacket.

"Nice, eh?" he said, taking a long sip of his Jungle. He was already onto his third.

I had to admit that Lleos's new jacket was very cool. CoolGlobalGiant had commissioned XaX of Helsinki to design an exclusive range of metallic black, thermally auto-adjusting street clothing for those who had received the ON engraft procedure. Prominently displayed on the front of Lleo's jacket was the ON logo. The letters were in lowercase, with the design subtly suggesting the infinity symbol. The logo constantly performed a looping animation, although I knew that if I put the jacket on the animation would stop. This was because each garment was linked to the ON protocol. Only when it was worn by its owner would the logo move. There were a few other party tricks that ONs could do – such as making some of their thoughts graphically appear on the front of their ON t-shirt. But by now this was generally considered a bit tacky.

"Psst! Youren! Check it out."

Lleo had parted his jacket to show me his ON t-shirt. It bore a myopic image of the nearby blonde woman, sporting disproportionately large breasts. Occasionally, Lleo could be a bit tacky.

∞

"Well, I'm glad I'm not a cat!"

Biz Ramachandran's voice boomed throughout the auditorium as he strolled down the centre aisle, a spotlight following him. Climbing the stage, he took one look at Frossle having his tummy rubbed, and said, "Although seeing Frossle here, maybe I'm not so sure!"

Li Sun smiled politely, picked up the cat and, with a bow, walked off-stage.

"No, but seriously, why am I glad I'm not a cat? Well, that's because no matter how hard Li Sun looks at me, all she'll ever see is plain old Biz Ramachandran. She'll never have the edifying experience of watching how my intestines work." He patted his ample stomach, getting a warm laugh. "That's because I'm a human. Unlike Frossle, I am *not* nanotagged."

The audience knew this was going somewhere, and kept quiet as nanotagged mice.

"Nanotagging humans in the interest of global security has been proposed more than once. But the shareholder public rejected it every time. We value our privacy, don't we? We don't want some new-fangled gizmo from a global corporation taking that away from us."

Somewhat unnecessarily, scattered applause broke out.

"So, let me assure you that the engrafts are *not* nanotagged. CoolGlobal-Giant, cannot 'track' you because you are ON, if you don't want it. No-one can. With ON, there is no centralised infrastructure because *you* are the infrastructure. You decide who links up with you, when you do it, and what information you share. Oh, but what about that hypothetical guy outside who is also ON? Can he locate me and 'hack' into me? Can he steal my personal brand and my money?"

"I'll take the money," someone behind me whispered.

"Impossible. The security of ON is based on the sum of genetic, molecular, and neural patterns within your body. Even your identical twin couldn't breach your personal ON security. Because you are unique in this universe, you're safe with ON."

The media screen behind Biz lit up. As it had with Li Sun, the screen showed us his viewpoint. But there was something more. Floating at the bottom of his visual field were a set of icons.

"Now I'm going to show you just a little of how ON works. When you become ON, the first thing you'll notice are these." He gestured towards the icons onscreen. "This is ON's navigation matrix – a powerful set of visual and verbal controls."

Biz went through a demonstration of how he could mentally customise and operate these controls to switch on his visual, audio, and sensual channels. He showed us how he could open or close channels between himself and other people, controlling who received what and when. Biz also demonstrated how he could securely move money from one bank account to another, all with his mind.

"No more passwords, ladies and gentlemen, ever! And I'm not allowed to say this, but ..." he removed a grID visor from his pocket and held it up. "... no more need for one of these."

A shocked murmur went through the audience and Biz grinned like an unrepentant naughty boy. "Now there's just one more important thing I have to do."

The media screen showed a typical grID view of a restaurant check-in desk. Biz was already logged in. A man wearing a white suit, black waist-coat, and brightly coloured hat asked, 'Yes, Mister Ramachandran?' Within the screen, Biz said '72DD. Table for two.'

Biz looked around at us all. "I hope Li Sun likes Peruvian."

∞

Lleo was still fiddling with his new jacket, and glancing round the Metatron to see if anyone else had noticed it. Again, his gaze fell on the nearby blonde woman. I was hoping she'd missed the t-shirt trick.

"You look like someone who is ON," he said, leaning towards her.

"I have no wish to be involved with ON," she replied.

"Oh come on! An attractive woman such as yourself? Surely – "

"Sorry, no."

"Well, let me say I can recommend it. It's a whole new world of knowledge, opportunities ..." he paused, smiling broadly, "... *romantic* possibilities."

"If you say so."

"Wait! I'll show you. Ask me anything – anything at all, and I'll tell you the answer."

"Really?" She raised a combative eyebrow.

"Sure. Hey, I'm ON. I know the lot!" Lleo spread his arms and un-crossed his legs.

The woman studied him for a while, then said, "OK. Tell me who really owns the SAT island EGK17."

Taken aback by the prosaic nature of the question, Lleo giggled then said, "Aha! Trying to trick me. But ..." he raised a confident finger, "... I happen to have several contacts within the OffWorld Licensing Bureau. So, watch and learn."

Once more, he commenced his unfortunate facial contortions.

"Easy," he said. "Wait, wait, yes. Alright. No. Yes. Wait. Really?" His voice carried across the room, causing a few patrons to look up. "Ooh, what's this? OK, OK. I think we may have it. Just need to open this door, and ..."

Lleo stood bolt upright as if he had received a shock. I reached out to touch his arm.

"Lleo, are you OK?"

Lleo stared straight ahead, as if in a trance.

"Lleo?"

"I'm a ... I'm a stallion." he said softly.

"A what?"

"A *stallion!*" he shouted. "My seed is precious."

"Lleo, you need to sit down."

I tried to restrain him, but he broke free and began striding around the Metatron with his chest out and his arms flapping wildly. The girls at the bar nearly fell off their stools laughing.

"Now is the time, ladies! Lleo is here. Lleo is ready for you."

I ran after him, but was beaten to it by two security guards who had fortunately managed to wrestle him to the floor before he could remove his trousers.

"I'm his friend, please, let me through."

Lleo looked up at me with a puzzled expression, then spoke in a strange monotone.

"We are currently experiencing some difficulties."

∞

The advertising agency i++ occupied most of Enterprise Tower, an ancient 'skyscraper' which stood apart from its surroundings, both literally and metaphorically. On all sides, with vehicle corridors snaking between them, were an assortment of modern buildings in the shape of balls, donuts, teardrops, and in one case, a sort of bowler hat, whose candy-coloured skins were peppered with mini gravports. By contrast, Enterprise Tower had just one gravport, retrofitted midway up, on the 23rd floor – a fairly pointless gesture towards the modern world. Structural analysis had shown that the heritage-listed glass and steel building could not support more. Anyway, I preferred the old elevators with their cute 'buttons' and real glass walls.

Some time ago, the street level had been raised, so now the building's original foyer was below ground. Floating above the ancient granite flooring was the enormous i++ logo. And beneath it in elaborately casual handwriting, hung a statement of who we were, what our core values were, and what we were *passionate* about.

'SEE | HEAR | EXIST'

I pressed the UP button.

"You decided to come in for once," LaLa said brightly, as I stepped from the elevator.

"I've had it with grID-ing. Besides, I wanted to bathe in the beauty of our long-suffering, yet eternally serene receptionist, without whom – "

"Pile of," she sneered, but I saw her blush all the same.

"Cartouche."

It was Seyemon Silk, our chief production manager.

"I don't believe it! You actually remembered to come in for the 27B meeting."

"Of course." I said, now aware of what it was I had completely forgotten.

"Collings is *so* looking forwards to hearing your ideas." he said.

"Ah, yes. My *ideas.*"

"You're the 'genius' brand," he said, with undisguised contempt.

"Remind me again, Seyemon, what brand are you?"

"The brand that actually does some work."

I turned to LaLa, and asked, "Hey, you wanna go out for a drink later?"

"Maybe." She didn't look up.

"Ah, Youren, you're here!" Harley Collings was walking towards me with a look of relief. "I knew I shouldn't have worried. Come on. The team's already in there."

Peppo, Bill-San and Agath looked up as we entered the small conference room. As we sat down they removed their grID visors and placed them on the table. Sarkee, however, continued to stare absently into space. Sarkee was supposed to be an expert in neural media. Everyone told me the girl 'got neural', but I couldn't see how we could know, since no-one had ever heard her speak. She wasn't wearing a visor, which probably meant she was ON.

"Youren. Happening," Peppo said, stroking his eenie weenie beard. He was wearing that striped, pointy-hat thing again.

With his greying temples and tight black shirt, Bill-San looked like an ageing soap star. I knew he would never say anything until he'd established which way the wind was blowing. I was lucky to get a nod.

As usual, Agath just looked grumpy. She was probably figuring out how much more work my 'great ideas' would load onto her.

"So, here we all are," Harley said. "Good. Good. Now, before Youren gives us his vision for the rollout, I'd just like to thank everyone for being a part of this. I don't need to tell you how important the phase-three ON rollout is for i++." With a forced laugh, he added, "And for CoolGlobal-Giant, obviously."

There were smiles and nods all round, even from Sarkee.

"So, to bring you all up to speed," Harley continued, "Youren has been working on a ... a ... *key establishing statement* for ..."

"A *core operating proposition*." Bill-San added, with bizarre enthusiasm.

"Oh yes, oh yes." Peppo said, tapping his head. "A *zero-plus-one emotional promise*."

Agath was now juggling her grumpiness with the obvious need to contribute.

"Quite," she declared, briskly. "This rollout needs an *essential locating assertion*."

"A slogan?" I asked.

The word echoed like an obscenity. An uneasy silence descended on us all.

"I think," Harley began slowly and carefully, "we're looking for something a bit more ..."

"With greater ..." Bill-San offered.

Agath shifted her weight. "Perhaps with a deeper sense of ..."

Peppo wiggled his fingers. "Inner, and yet outer ..."

Sarkee tapped the table in a circular motion.

I raised my hands. "I hear what you're saying. Believe me, I hear what you're saying. I think we're all in the same screen here. But when I use 'the word', I'm not denying the need for an imperative ..."

"Integrated ..." Harley offered.

"Actuating ..." Bill-San added tentatively.

"... basis for our inner and outer ..." a nod in the direction of Peppo, "... communications. But what I'm really saying ..."

Yes, what the fuck <u>am</u> I saying?

"Is that we need to reach back within the origins of our 'communications toolkit', if I may use that phrase, and ..."

It was going pretty well, but I still didn't actually have anything to give them. My mind drifted to the earlier meeting with Lleo at the Metatron. What was all that rubbish he was saying about ON?

Hmm, yes. Yes, that's good. No, that's not just good ...

"So what do we really want to say? I think there's only one thing we *can* say."

They were all looking at me, expectantly. I paused for effect, before delivering my brand-resonant empathetic vision declaration.

"THE FUTURE IS ON."

All eyes turned to Harley Collings who sat motionless, taking deep meditative breaths as his brain performed some spiritual regimen. After some time, he nodded and spoke.

"That's ... Wow! That's very ..." He sounded as though he was grappling with the effects of some powerful weed.

"It is. Yes, it is," Bill-San said, clearly sensing the direction of that wind.

"I think ..." Harley continued, "... we may just have ..." He looked around at everyone.

"A formative? ..." Agath ventured. Then her face showed that she regretted the word.

"Inner and outer." Peppo mumbled, revisiting past glories.

Sarkee seemed about to utter her first words ever, but then thought better of it. Instead she sank back into the chair, and settled for running a thoughtful orange fingernail along her hairline.

"I see we agree then," Harley declared.

It took everyone by surprise, especially me.

A boyish grin broke across Harley's face. "You wanna know what I really like about this?"

Everyone was nodding. Yes, we all *did* want to know.

Harley regarded the others warmly, one by one, as if silently thanking them for their individual contribution to the collective success. Then he placed his palms firmly on the table, looked me squarely in the eye, and spoke for everyone in the room.

"It says what it means."

∞

I strolled through the ancient 'open plan' office.

"Hey Roger. Working hard?"

The middle-aged copywriter looked up with exasperation.

"Urinals! They've got me on urinals!" he said peering at me through the smoky lenses of his grID visor.

"I'm sorry?"

Roger ran a pair of agitated, sweaty hands through his thinning hair.

"Those media screens above the urinal, where you can immerse yourself in one of our fucking ads while you take a piss! I have to write a bunch of ON 'support communications' for them. Usual bullshit deadline." Then he hissed quietly, through a clenched jaw, "Thanks for that, Seyemon!"

Sympathising with his dislike of our chief production manager I felt a surge of benevolence, a need to somehow make it easier for a fellow creative. "Well that's a very important market segment."

"What, men who piss?"

"No, I mean clubs and venues in general. Sport, entertainment, anywhere where – "

"Men piss."

His sadness and self-loathing were palpable.

"You know," he said, "I've been thinking about getting ON myself." Behind the visor lens, his rheumy eyes peered towards some distant goal. "You have to stay ahead just to keep up, don't you? Old fellers like me. Ha, ha."

"Well ..."

Then his face brightened. An idea had begun to surface.

"Hey, Youren, what about a bit of word play with ON, like ... um ... *switched* ON?"

"'Switched' is not right."

"No, of course not. *Turned* ON. That's better, isn't it? A hot young girl is – Oh, shit!"

I figured he'd just received another prompter message.

"Shit! Shit! Fucking deadlines! Fucking clients! Fucking ... !"

"I'll leave you to it, Roger. I'm sure you'll crack it. And don't go getting ON, by the way. You're one of the few real humans we have left in this place."

I walked over to my desk and sat down. Arlo Arbuckle appeared over the partition separating our desks. His round face, rosy cheeks, and comical eyes made him look like a puppet in a children's show.

"Don't look now, but Captain Communication is doing an inspection of the troops."

On the other side of the studio, I could see Seyemon Silk showing around some CoolGlobalGiant executives. The group would randomly stop at someone's desk, Seyemon would make his introductions, then a little burst of polite laughter would drift across to us. They had now reached Psi-Psi's desk, and Seyemon was effusing about her commitment.

"… And Psi-Psi is *passionate* about 'neurobranding'." I couldn't catch what the executives were saying, but Seyemon's voice carried well. "… Yes, we have an entire grID reticulum dedicated to it."

Next it was Ugotti's turn.

"I wonder what they'll make of Ugotti." Arlo chuckled.

Ugotti was one of those people who found open plan spaces 'deeply disturbing'. To cope, he'd set-up a small cardboard box next to his desk, and for most of the time worked from inside its cramped confines.

"… Ugotti here is *passionate* about 'identity spotlighting' …"

Blinking, Ugotti poked his head out of the box, but didn't actually get out.

"Ugotti is thinking outside the box," Arlo sniggered.

"But at least he's passionate about it," I added.

Seyemon was now looking across at us.

"Uh oh!" Arlo said, "I think we're next."

They were soon upon us, with Seyemon heaping faint praise on me.

"Youren's been impressing everyone today with his phase-three rollout creative, haven't you Youren?" I demurred politely as he turned towards Arlo. "And Arlo? Well, Arlo here is *passionate* about 'personal corporatisation'."

"No I'm not," said Arlo, "I think it's all meaningless bullshit."

Seyemon looked like someone had shoved a Vibrafriend up his core personal values, but to give him credit he recovered in a heartbeat, shepherding the CoolGlobalGiant delegation away with a world-weary "Waaaay too much Stressless-Plus."

I turned to a grinning Arlo. "For fuck's − , are you *trying* to get work-nulled!?"

"They can't touch me, man. I upped my ContractSafe insurance to the max. The only way i++ could get rid of me now is to kill me. Actually,

I'm pretty sure some of them are already thinking about it. And I guess if their insurance covers *that*, then ..."

"You have an overactive imagination, you know that, Arlo? Hey, why don't you take a holiday? Get away from all this 'personal corporatisation' shit. What about that trip to the SAT islands you've been talking about?"

Arlo looked glum. "Ah, that's the one thing I can't change in the contract. My holidays aren't due for ages. I guess I'll just have to enjoy selling ON to the world's shareholders. Not that they need any encouraging. You seen the latest figures?"

"Around six per cent, isn't it?"

"Seventeen, Youren. Seventeen."

"For fuck's – ! When did that happen?"

"While you were sleeping, Youren," he said, wiggling his fingers and making scary eyes.

I laughed. "So I take it you're not about to get the engrafts anytime soon?"

"You know what I heard?" Arlo said, lowering his voice. "We're *all* gonna to have to get it done soon."

"Bullshit."

"True! i++ have done some deal with CoolGlobalGiant."

"Arlo, they can't do that. We live in a free world."

"No, Youren. Everything has a price tag on it. Especially you and me."

"You're paranoid, Arlo, you know that?"

"Aren't you?"

∞

Before us, is a young man dressed entirely in white: white shoes, white suit, white bowler hat. He stands in the middle of a white room. Everything in the scene is white, except for the bright red apple which the young man holds. He stares impassively at us. The camera zooms towards his face and through his eye, and we emerge into a larger red room with about 50 people all dressed in red. Everything in the scene is red. Our young man is among them, now wearing a red suit and red bowler hat. He still holds the red apple. The camera pans across the faces of the people and zooms into the eye of a young woman. We now emerge into a vast green room containing several thousand people, all dressed in green. The camera quickly zooms into the eye of a young boy in the middle of the crowd and now we are flying over a blue planet. As we descend, we realise the entire planet consists of people wearing blue. The people all look up at us. Everyone has a knowing, yet blank expression. We zoom into the eye of an old man and instantly arrive back in the original room with our lone young man. Once more, he is dressed in white, and everything in the room is white. Except that now he holds, not a red apple, but a single blue rose. He gives a slight smile. It's a coy, affected smile. The words 'You are everyone' come up. Underneath them is the ON logo. The advertisement is silent from beginning to end, except for the sound of a human heartbeat.

I woke up.

On my screen was the ON logo. Groggily, I looked around the office. Almost everyone had left, and most of the lights were turned off. On the far side, Roger was still working away, his desk lamp providing a comforting little oasis of light within the darkness.

"Hey, Roger! Cracked it yet?"

Roger didn't answer. I decided to go and check on him. As I approached, I saw that he was completely motionless, his hands hanging at his sides.

"Roger, are you OK?"

I reached out and touched his shoulder. Roger spun round and gripped my arm. When I saw him, I screamed. Roger's face had become transformed into something inhumanly evil, the muscles rhythmically contracting, the eyes glowing like hot coals in the dim light. His hands closed around my neck, and with what felt like the strength of four men he soon had me on the floor, choking the life out of me. As I lost consciousness, the creature that was once Roger let out a triumphant, hellish roar.

I woke up.

On my screen was the ON logo. Groggily, I looked around the office. Almost everyone had left, and most of the lights were turned off. On the far side, Roger was still working away, his desk lamp providing a comforting little oasis of light within the darkness.

"Hey, Roger! Cracked it yet?"

"Don't bother me now, Youren! I'm almost there."

I looked back at the screen. Above the ON logo were the words 'You are everyone'.

Made for the phase-one rollout, 'You are everyone' was the first ON 3VC the agency had produced. At the time, industry creatives praised it for its 'subversion of neural purchase decision pathways' or something. It even won a gold Octopus at the OneWorld *HERE* Awards at Cannes. As the principal writer, I had gone with the team to collect the award. We briefly spotted Biz Ramachandran talking to Karl XaX, but everyone was far too cool to stare.

For some reason, I never liked that ad.

∞

LaLa was not happy.

"Where have you been, Youren? I've been waiting for ..." she looked around the room, "... well for a *very long* time! I was just about to leave."

"I am soooo sorry, LaLa, I got caught up. Can I get you a drink?"

"I've had three already."

"Right. Look, I'm really sorry." I sat down.

"Who gets 'caught up'?"

"What?"

She tapped the table with a glowing fingernail. "Who in OneWorld ever gets 'caught up'? You got a prompter, don't you?"

"I guess mine's not all that good."

"What do you call yours?" she asked.

"I haven't given it a name, I just bark orders at it. Or is it the other way round?"

She seemed disappointed. "I call mine 'Santa'. He's a pre-T patron saint of commerce. I think that makes him work better."

Stumped for a reply, I said, "I had to help Roger with a few ads. Seyemon had him working late."

"I hate that man."

"Seyemon?"

LaLa nodded. Now we were on common ground. "He wanted me to process all the latest focus group neurals before I left."

"Wow! So what did you ... ?"

"I told him to *get*! Well, I didn't really say that, but he got the message. Then I came here to meet you. Shouldn't have bothered, as it turned out."

"Hey, c'mon! I said I was sorry."

I touched her hands lightly. It was the first time I had made any physical contact with her. She looked uncomfortable, but didn't move.

"You know," she whispered, leaning forwards, "I was having nightmares about work. I thought they were planning to kill me."

"Ouch!" I said, removing my hand, with rather bad timing. "You know, Arlo was thinking something similar."

LaLa used her liberated arms to hug her chest, as if suddenly cold. "Arlo's a weirdo," she declared. "Anyway, my neuropsych put me on a course of OC pulse therapy."

"What's OC?"

"Occipital cortex," she said, pronouncing the term with some pride.

"Wow. Isn't that a bit risky?"

"No, it's *so*! Re-Leaf is a cool brand. And the nightmares stopped too instant. Or maybe I can't remember them. Anywhich."

"Cartouche! Good work!"

I turned to see Kev-O, Dave-O, and some other execs from i++, standing at a drink booth.

"Come over and have a drink." Kev-O shouted.

"Will do."

"You're the golden boy." LaLa said.

"I came up with a few ideas and now they think I'm a genius."

She reached out and gave me a friendly pat. "Yeah? I reckon you look tired or somethin'."

"My sleep schedules keep getting changed around by Tempo and i++."

"You should get ON," she said enthusiastically. "I've just got the en-grafts. Much more energy. It's *so*! Now I'm *thoughting* all my friends."

"Great."

Her hands began to jiggle in excitement. "And guess what? You know Bumble B?"

"Who?" Once again, I disappointed her.

"The *grunt star*! Where's your neural? He's massive!"

"Fat?"

She made a face. "You're pathetic. He *thoughted* me. Bumble B! Imagine! I died!"

∞

"Whaddya drinkin'?"

"Oh, a Super-Hydra thanks."

"What about a real drink?"

"No, I think I'll pace myself for a while. The night is young."

They exchanged glances. These were men who didn't 'pace themselves'.

Dave-O eyed me blearily. "Where'd your girlfriend go?"

"She's not my girlfriend. She had to ... Tempo's changed her wake-codes, and – "

Dave-O peered into the crowd, as if hoping to catch a last glimpse. "Fuck me, I wouldn't say no."

The drinks were gently rising from the booth, the liquid illuminated from below.

"Here we go, fellas." Kev-O said, rubbing his hands together. "Four shark slammers and a *rooin* drink."

They all laughed.

Dave-O was staring at a woman on a nearby drink booth. It took me a little while to realise that he was *thoughting* her. She turned and returned his gaze. Dave-O looked her up and down with a leer. A look of revulsion crossed her face, and she moved away to another booth.

"Probably frigid." Dave-O grunted, finishing his drink in one gulp.

"Sorry guys, I need to piss."

I made my way to the toilets. At the urinal, a sound made me look up, and I was confronted by a media screen displaying an ad for ON. I chuckled to myself, realising Roger had made his deadline. *Let's see what he –*

A hot young thing in next to nothing writhed and pouted at me, the prominent ON logo clinging to her sweating breasts. A seductive female voice-over kept repeating the headline.

"If you're not ON, it's not on."

∞

It was a relief to step out into the Medusa. The air was cool, though a little thick with freshener. The local environment lights had shifted their time-mood, the cyans and yellows making everyone look sharp and agitated. I looked around the city skyline, and it wasn't long before my gaze fell on the headquarters of CoolGlobalGiant. You could see it from almost anywhere in Medusa – six blue and green spirals rising more than half a kilometre, their pinnacles embedded into the ubiquitous clouds. I had heard that Biz Ramachandran's residence and offices occupied the top three levels of the tallest tower. Were they actually above the clouds? Could you see the sun from up there? Did Biz Ramachandran's life include night and day?

Right now I needed to be as far away from CoolGlobalGiant as possible, so I hopped on a minigrav and headed over to GetOffMe in Qunan Kapital, just outside the borders of Neo-Kazakhstan. During the short trip, we passed over the old Caspian Sea, now merely a handful of scattered puddles. Looking down, I noticed what appeared to be a large orange donut brightly etched against the dark grey.

"HomeSafe." the man in the next seat said, leaning over me to get a better look. "Well, all that exists of it now."

I turned and looked into his grey eyes. "What is it?" I asked.

"Not much now," he sighed, "but it was once a vision of how we could all live. A vast tower, hundreds of separate worlds, entire ecosystems, pure air and water ..."

His voice trailed off, and he leaned back into his seat.

"And you know this because ... ?"

"Because, I'm sad to say, I was on the board of the original management group that designed the project. There were ... planning issues. Now, it's nothing but a pile of junk."

"So it's just deserted?"

"Oh heavens, no!" he laughed, bitterly. "Now, it's occupied by itinerants and criminals. Economic terrorists who don't *deserve* somewhere to call home."

I looked down at the strange orange donut receding behind us and felt a wave of sadness, as if some sort of gas was floating up from the desolate landscape and seeping into my lungs.

Even before we landed, I could see that QKC, the government corporation that ran Qunan Kapital, was letting its citizen shareholders down badly. Streets were littered and cracked, and raw sewage was overflowing into the gutters. When a govcorp seriously fails its public shareholders, it leaves itself open to a 'hostile takeover' by one or more of the adjacent govcorps. After a lot of legal to-ing and fro-ing in the OneWorld Chamber of Commerce, canvassing citizen and stakeholder opinion and so on, this basically means sending in men with guns to slaughter the board of directors. Then receivers will come in with the contractual authority to imprison or slaughter other members of upper management, after which everyone can go back to enjoying life as usual.

OneWorld has a keen blind eye.

I disembarked at the crumbling gravPort, and made my way towards the ex-military zone where the club was. GetOffMe was one of a growing number of underground 'NotON' clubs springing up. 'NotON' was not just a technical term referring to the absence of engrafts. It had become a political badge of honour for the disenfranchised humans of OneWorld.

I was worried I wouldn't be allowed in, since my clothes looked a bit too 'Tempo', as they say. Pity I had nothing in beige. For NotONs, beige was a rejection of everything that OneWorld stood for. But security let me through the antique auto sliding doors, and I descended the metal steps to the entrance hall. At the check-in desk, I grID-signed an agreement absolving GetOffMe of any liability in the advent of my death on the premises.

The club was built into the remains of an old chemical weapons plant. From the entrance hall, vaulted concrete corridors led off in all directions. Most were blocked by yellow barriers. Beyond the barriers I could see that the flooring had collapsed, with large holes offering a sheer drop to some oozing toxic oblivion. I joined a crowd of new arrivals, and we cautiously trekked along a poorly lit corridor which eventually opened into a vast factory space lit by lighting sheets. Ancient processing machinery, a couple of forklifts, rusted vats, and towering storage tanks remained, filling the vast space. The floor was covered with rubble and broken glass. Drink and drug booths were dotted around. Seating seemed to be at a premium, with patrons perched and bunched up onto anything they could find.

Along the walls, media screens advertised GetOffMe's chief sponsor, the vodka brand Ferkov. Below images of young models, all of whom looked terminally ill, were the words:

'DRINK FERKOV AND DIE'.

I waved at a few familiar faces who snarled back or ignored me completely. It felt good – the refusal to acknowledge 'me as a person'. No-one here said 'have a nice wake-time'.

I spotted Cuntface, sitting on a stack of grinder discs, talking to a couple of girls.

"Hey, Cuntface!" I made an effort not to smile. "It's all shit, eh?"

"*You're* shit," Cuntface said with elaborate disinterest.

"Succinct and perceptive."

I pulled up a block of oily concrete, sat down and joined in. The girls looked me up and down contemptuously, as if I were wearing a tutu. I chatted to Cuntface, although he looked pretty intimidating in his powder-blue safari jacket, beige chinos, and fringed loafers. Half his pock-marked face was permanently covered by a shock of black hair, which he constantly attempted to brush out of his eyes.

He held up a metal vial between his fingers. "You want some Q?"

"Uh, no thanks. I'm not into non-brand."

The girls sniggered.

'Drrhh drrhh drrhh drrhh drrhh drrhh drrhh drrhh drrhh drrhh.'

The music had started up.

The music they played at *GetOffMe* was usually 'DataMan'. DataMan's most obvious feature was its extremely fast beats, sometimes up to 100 per T-sec. To the untrained ear, this sounded like an ear-piercing mechanical hammer. Quieter, more 'lyrical' DataMan tracks sounded more like a cross between insect swarms and antique jet engines. True fans, however, could easily distinguish the subtle interplay of overtone beats, and they would whirl around the dance floor, 'singing along' with their arms outstretched, like out of control toy aeroplanes. I'd heard that DataMan Inc. had once successfully sued a manufacturer of road construction equipment because one of their rockdrills – the 'DownUnder' – sonically infringed DataMan's copyright.

Others began joining our little group – a neurotic DataMan composer who kept telling us that current DataMan went *too* slow, a crazy old guy with long white hair who simply wanted to ogle the girls, a couple of decommissioned military outcasts trying to sell non-brand drugs and weapons, and some woman who composed 'compost poetry'. Conversation was going well until we were interrupted.

"Human! Human! Human!"

The young man wore combat boots and spun steel trousers. A network of holes had been drilled into the flesh of his shaved skull and his black t-shirt bore a red militaristic logo derived from a diagram of human cell division. Below the logo were the letters 'SDU'. I knew what they stood for – 'Sons and Daughters of Unity'.

Cuntface groaned. "Yeh. Right, son." he said, with a half-hearted raising of his fist.

The man was less than satisfied. "Don't you respect your species?" His high-pitched voice was inconsistent with his attire and demeanour.

"Why do they let them in?" one of the girls whined.

"SDU is a recognised brand. There's not much they can do to stop them," someone else said quietly.

"You fuckin' rooin lovers are all the same!" said the young man, bobbing up and down.

"Yeh, I love fucking rooin chicks," Cuntface said, getting a big laugh from our group.

"You like fucking vacuum cleaners?" the man asked, his arms raised in mock amazement. "They're descended from vacuum cleaners."

I thought this was unusually witty for an SDU thug.

"And you're descended from an ape," Cuntface replied.

"You callin' me an ape?" the man said, taking a step forwards with clenched fists.

"Oh fuck this!" Cuntface spat, and stood up to face him. "We're *all* descended from apes, you moron!"

It may have been the beige chinos, or it may have been the fact that Cuntface stood a full two metres tall, but whatever the reason, the SDU thug decided to back off.

"Fuckin' rooins. Fuckin' cogs wanna make us their slaves, eh? Humans not slaves ..." He, and his tiny voice, faded away into the crowd.

Cuntface turned and bowed theatrically to our applause.

∞

I found myself next to a girl wearing what looked like her mother's pyjamas, jeweller's glasses, and a pair of biohazard gloves. We were sitting on a small pile of rusted road spikes. Someone had thoughtfully flattened all the points, but we still needed to sit on our jackets.

"What do you do?" I asked.

She disappeared into blackness.

'Dnngh dnngh dnngh dnngh dnngh dnngh dnngh dnngh dnngh dnngh.'

The lighting and music seemed to be under the control of a random number generator. Without warning, we could be subjected to any combination of silence or deafening noise, versus stark light or total darkness. If the music stopped, we were afforded a brief opportunity to talk. However, if this coincided with total darkness, it was all a bit awkward.

"Nothing," I could just hear her say.

The lights came back on and the music stopped. She was now looking up at the roof, opening and closing her mouth like a fish feeding in a tank. Then she turned and smiled. She waved her freckled wrist at me.

"Look."

On it was an ancient timepiece.

"Called a 'watch'," she said proudly. "Old time shit."

I had noticed that many of the crowd were wearing these things.

"Non-brand time is illegal," I said. "Tempo Corp can prosecute you if you ..."

'Ghh ghh ghh ghh ghh ghh ghh ghh ghh ghh.'

"What?"

The burst of music was short. I tried again. "It's illegal."

"Not in Qunan. Anyway. Don't use it. Just play," she wiggled it around, then frowned at the tiny display. "Numbers don't make sense."

"They're decimal, not hexadecimal. See," I held her wrist, and pointed at the display. "It goes up to nine in the first column, and then that becomes a zero and it starts again in the next column. But it's a little trickier than that, 'cos it's based on cycles of 12 and 60. So the first two columns go up to 59 and then reset to 00 – which is actually 60 – which carries over as a 1 in the third column. The third and fourth columns only go up to 12. But they do this twice in every cycle which means ..."

Her face displayed a mixture of alarm and boredom. "Why?" she asked.

"Hey, I'm writing a book," I said, changing the topic.

"Ahhhhgh!" she screamed horribly. She was obviously impressed. "You mean like sentences 'n shit?"

"True."

"What's it about?"

"ON."

"Whoa! Fuck me! Big exposé! Exploitation of – "

"Worse than that."

"What like. The ultimate fuckin' mind conspiracy ... thing." She seemed to be having trouble working her jaw.

"Even worse than that."

'Bmmh bmmh bmmh bmmh bmmh bmmh bmmh bmmh bmmh.'

I was excused from having to make up any more crap. This time, the music didn't stop, so I went and bought a little Blu-Zone from one of the drug booths. After a while, a bunch of DataMan freaks got up and ran around the factory floor, flapping their arms and screaming at the top of their lungs.

By now, the Blu-Zone was kicking in and the music looked like a giant lattice of switchblades and maggots. Then the maggots combined into a vast loathsome creature which began climbing the old storage tanks, rhythmically inching its way towards the roof girders. The lights all went off again, and judging by the cries of distress, many of the DataMan freaks had collided with various pieces of equipment, severely injuring themselves. Someone may also have fallen down a shaft. Unable to do much, we continued to sit around in the darkness, listening to jackhammers, metal grinders, and the sound of humans screaming in pain.

GetOffMe wasn't quite as much fun as I'd hoped.

∞

The orchestra tunes up, and he walks on strings of coloured light. No. Dances on them. Dances, skips, runs, pirouets, strides, marches, jumps. Flies. As the strings vibrate, their music moves through his feet and into his body, filling him with bliss. The strings of coloured light form a road upon which he is travelling. He has a purpose, a destination. He knows it will take forever to reach his destination, but the eternal journey will be joyful and precious, and filled with untold wonders and the knowledge of everything that was ever wise and good and pure. Tears of gratitude fly from his eyes, and grateful flowers and forests spring up where they fall.

With each step he grows in stature and depth, until his heart is bursting with song. Along the road he meets many guides who offer their wisdom and humour. Some are giants, some are funny little creatures, and some are people just like him. Many become close friends and sometimes he stays awhile in their simple villages and shares their laughter and the occasional sweet love affair. But everyone knows that eventually he must resume his journey, and there are warm farewells and well-wishes, and as his feet again set out on the coloured strings of light he realises he is part of a vast spiritual family which cares for him and loves him and understands and appreciates his unique qualities, and as the end of time draws near and he approaches his journey's destination – a towering city of blinding light that sings like rain on a summer lake – he knows that all living beings must eventually come to this place to merge with the one who embraces all existence. Then as the soft rain falls kindly upon his face he feels himself falling gently, then with ever gathering speed as the light of truth dims then darkens and the rain lashes his ageing pockmarked face while his head twists at grotesque angles until it hits the filthy tiles in front of a cracked toilet bowl. The smell of piss fills his nostrils. From the adjacent cubicle there are sounds of someone throwing up.

As hard as he tried, Cuntface couldn't remember how he had come to be lying on the toilet floor, blood seeping from a swollen lip. The strange metal vial clutched in his fat fingers offered no clue.

∞

"Shade F. Overhead 3, warm."

I stumbled into my bedroom and, in a rather sophisticated manoeuvre if I do say so myself, managed to simultaneously kick off my shoes and fall face first onto the bed.

No! the small part of my brain that still worked said. *Make the effort, you'll appreciate it later.* I undressed and got under the covers.

"Overhead zero."

Darkness took me.

∞

I am watching my father walk towards the tower, crushing a trail of deep prints into the snow as he goes. *Crunch, crunch, crunch* – the sound is strong and purposeful. Little puffs of white breath billow around the back of his neck, in time with his footsteps. I am rugged up in my warm green buckyfleece longcoat, the one my mother insists on making me wear whenever I will be away from her for any length of time. I stand still, as I've been told to – 'like a little statue' – despite the cold air stinging my nose.

At the base of the tower my father pauses, placing his hands on his hips as he gazes up at the structure. Even from this distance, I recognise the typical fatherly manoeuvre: the focus on detail, the enthusiasm – almost reverence – for all things large and technological.

The tower resembles a stack of coins caught at the instant of falling, each silver disc separated from its neighbours by what appears to be nothing but air. The discs are grouped into three sets of six, and between each set a bronze sphere revolves slowly. My father has explained to me how this tower is just one of many built at 'special' places all over the planet. *Nod ... nodes.* The network of towers forms the *gee ... the geomagnetic resonance Impulse Distributor.*

The grID.

I am pleased with myself for knowing such arcane information. I will probably show off at school. I venture a few more steps towards the tower, then stop. Not too close, just to be safe.

I see now that the tower's structure is more complex. Individual discs are constructed from smaller interlocking mechanisms, all intricately choreographed. I fear that, if I move closer, the structure will continue to reveal increasing detail without end. The thought makes me feel sick in my tummy, and I turn away, my gaze briefly following the flight of a lone peregrine across the line of mountain peaks to the north. The bird's cry sounds sad.

The rooin workers are shouting and joking as they unload the *kali* rods from the gravtrain, and place them into the entropy cores at the base of the tower. Snippets of their speech, somehow both muffled and sharpened by the snow, reach me.

"Easy easy!"

"Cores zero ninah to E one!"

"All sparky here."

"Zork me! Check the Ds on these things ..."

"Bigger than yours, Zango?"

"Ha! *Neg*, Azmak, not even close!"

"Zip zip! Get int'it, you roos!"

I face the tower once more. As though he can sense this, my father turns and waves proudly. My hand has only just begun its answering ascent when the explosion happens.

Long before the sound reaches me, a visual chaos is unfolding. At first it looks as though the tower's discs are falling both up and down. Then, as the first whorls of orange-pink flame sweep upwards from the base, the strict order of the construction gives way to a sensuous dance, straight lines and perfect curves crumpling to release crimson demons who cavort with an alien passion. I start to run towards the tower, my little footsteps following my father's. My mouth flies open in a scream of ice crystals, as my hands stretch out towards the hellish glow. Several badly burned rooins are already running towards me, frantically waving for me to turn back.

"Time drift! Time drift!" they silently scream.

I understand. The fallout of time particles from an entropy explosion can alter my body, or even kill me. But still I run. The explosion rips into my ears just as its arc reaches the tipping point. What was an instant ago an exotic display of radiant chaos with its own terrible logic is now merely a fractured cacophony of quarrelling fires and smoke. With a crack, the tower's blackened cap flies up into the sky and explodes into spiralling fragments. The discs are now unmistakably falling down. Heat from the blaze forces me to stop running. The tower and my father are no more. Now, as a fine rain of ash turns the landscape to noise, all I can do is watch and sob. The little statue with the arrow of time firmly embedded in his heart.

∞

Awake.

My comfortingly messy room was dimly lit by a greyish light.

What time ... ? I was wondering if it was worth the expense to find out, when ...

"Youren."

"Aghhh! For fuck's – !"

The young woman standing at the foot of the bed was dressed in a simple grey shirt, blue jeans, and red sneakers. She regarded me dispassionately, but as though she knew me.

"Youren Cartouche," she said, stretching both hands out towards me.

"That's me," I said, sitting up. "And you are?"

"Dead." She seemed surprised and saddened by her own words. "I am dead."

"Overhead 9!" I shouted.

White light washed everything in the room – but there was no-one there.

HomeSafe

⏻

AGENT Constantin Zann steps out from under the archway and a programmed blend of cold light frequencies falls upon his face. Zann's tarnished face displays an uncommon generosity for his line of work, despite bearing a slight resemblance to a human skull. A promise of a smile seems to constantly hover about his mouth, and his dark eyes glow whenever they engage with something that interests him. Along the centre of his shaved head runs a ridge of blue-black hair which cascades into a ponytail. The rooin's large body has been manufactured to withstand life's cruelties, and it's done well so far.

Zann's foot pauses mid-air.

What time is it?

He hesitates, then uses his thorax brain to connect to his Tempo account. '0600 4EAB E5F3 1723 © Tempo Corp. All rights reserved.'

Zann sighs. "Money down the drain." he mutters.

Zann frequently has the feeling that he is the only one who exists in the 'present'. Everyone else, rooin or human, operates in another time altogether. Not necessarily past or future, mind you, just sometime else. Zann no longer sees this unique perspective as a manufacturing error, but more of an 'undocumented feature'.

He looks across at her apartment block. The ancient brickwork is held up by modern plasteel struts, their childish colours drained by the cruel environment lighting. Zann crosses the causeway and enters the building. All the scanners have been smashed, and the government corporation in control of this territory has not bothered to fix them; whatever these people do seems to be of no interest to anyone. On the fifth floor Zann finds the apartment door open. He pulls out his GlockZ as a precaution, and walks to the bedroom.

The human girl is lying partially across the low bed, but with her head and shoulders touching the floor. The bedclothes are in disarray, but there are no obvious signs of injury. Something on the floor, partly covered by her hair, catches his eye. A dark glint. Zann picks up the metal vial – heavy, empty. He raises it to his nose. No smell.

He looks down at her. An illuminated sign outside the window lays a strip of light across her face as it stares back at him with an expression of undiluted horror. The room is quiet save for the intrusion of a few street noises. The rooin stands still. Then he kneels, closes the girl's eyes and holds her ice-cold hand. His shoulders move in time to his silent sobs.

∞

"She was such a lovely girl. But then she just seemed to give up on life."

Mrs Krianti elaborately wipes away a few tears, attempting to peer around Constantin Zann's bulk to catch a glimpse of the dead girl's body. The woman clearly feels she deserves to be part of the action. Behind him, Zann can hear Lakzad and the other rooin agents busying themselves in the bedroom.

"Thank you for contacting us, Mrs Krianti. You've been most helpful. If there's anything else we need, we'll let you know."

Mrs Krianti looks disappointed, but turns and shuffles away. Zann goes back to check on Lakzad. The senior forensic scientist is immaculately dressed, his white shirt shimmering, his little necktie elaborately knotted, and every one of his copper-blond hairs neatly in place. He is busily running a PM analyser over the body.

"What do we have?" Zann asks.

"One Eve Lamente, deceased human, neurotechnology student, although ..."

"Lakzad, we already know all that. We've had her under surveillance, for zork's sake!"

"... it doesn't look like she's been to lectures for some time," Lakzad continues flatly, ignoring Zann's interruption. Lakzad has the floor.

"And *this* doesn't make us look good to the client, does it?" Zann adds. "So we need to move quickly on it. Cause of death?"

"Heart attack." Lakzad runs bioscans across the bedclothes as he speaks. "Hmm, no sex life to speak of."

"A bit young for a heart attack wasn't she? And what's sex got to do with anything?"

Lakzad looks up from the bed. "Are you OK, Zann? You look ... upset."

"What caused the heart attack?"

"I would say she literally died of fright. There's something else, too. Take a look at this."

Lakzad rolls the girl over and lifts up the hair. At the base of the skull are what appear to be two fresh puncture wounds, quite deep. Blood is crusted into the fine blonde hairs.

"That's what killed her?" Zann asks.

"Hardly. But the wounds are postmortem, which does make the death suspicious. We'll know more when we get her back. I assume we have client clearance to move the body?"

Zann holds out the metal vial.

"What do you make of this?"

Lakzad is somewhat ruffled; this is *his* crime scene. "Where did you get that?"

"Found it near the body, just under the hair."

"What's got into you, Zann? You know the drill." Lakzad snatches the vial and scans it. "Hmm, no prints." His brow furrows neatly. "And no nanotags, either! Odd. I'll send back a scan of it and see what they've got."

Zann crosses the room to the girl's desk. The surface is littered with lecture notes, old acto-books, medical models, soft primate toys, some neurotech equipment, and a battered grID visor.

"I thought she was supposed to be well organised."

Lakzad forces a laugh, but doesn't bother looking up. "Didn't you read the client's psych report? 'Internalised dissociative neuroreflective disorder' or whatever the zork. *Humans* eh? Self harm, danger to herself ... my eyes had glazed over by the second chapter."

Zann turns over a couple of the acto-books and reads their titles. "'Branching Structures and Minimal Path Problems'. 'Randomness and determinism: six chaotic linking algorithms.'" Zann looks up. Attached to the wall is a large sheet of fine synthetic vellum, bearing an intricate, almost obsessive drawing, painstakingly created with auto-correcting nano-graphite.

"Lakzad. What do you make of this?"

The scientist briefly appraises the tangled network of lines. "I'd say it was the work of someone with internalised dissociative neuroreflective disorder."

∞

The return journey to the headquarters of Raymond Parkes is taking longer than usual. On reaching the city limits, the LawVec is funnelled into the corridors with all the other vehicles. Earth tremors in the central zone have caused traffic to be diverted to the Tri-Circle and, as the LawVec hovers and weaves its way around the other vehicles in the corridor, Constantin Zann sits in the back seat, watching the lights.

"You're quiet, Zann."

Lakzad, who has been telling the forensic guys about a particularly gruesome crime scene he recently attended, has turned round, flashing his precise grin.

Zann stares back. "Thinking."

"Oh, that. Personally, I don't recommend it."

They travel in silence for a while. The LawVec rises through several corridors, until it is approaching the upper levels of a cylindrical, metallic blue tower. To those of a bygone era, the building with its conical grey roof would have resembled a big blue pencil. The LawVec gently docks at one of the building's gravports, and they disembark, walking along the white security corridor before halting in front of a closed access door at the end. Zann knows every nanotag in his body is now being scanned and analysed.

Lakzad bobs his head up and down impatiently.

"That won't make it happen any faster," Zann says with a smile.

Lakzad's answer is an exasperated raising of the eyebrows. The door dematerialises.

"Oh good," Zann says, "we still have jobs."

The narrow security corridor opens onto a large operations floor, where about a thousand rooins are working. Apart from the rooins, whose colours vary markedly from individual to individual, almost everything else on the operations floor is white. Gloss-white partitions stretch from floor to ceiling defining offices and meeting rooms. However, closer inspection would reveal the partitions to be merely e-particle screens which can be turned on or off. Thus the entire layout of the operations floor can be changed with a few words, and often is.

Zann arrives at his office. It's the closest thing the operations floor has to a permanent room. He's even moved in a battered couch. Apart from this, the only other items in the room are a large circular desk at one end, and a small modeller at the other. The office has spectacular 120° views of downtown Medusa, but it's been a long time since Zann has paused to enjoy any of it. He's seen too much of what really goes on down there.

Zann spreads Eve Lamente's drawing across his desk.

What the zork is this?

Covering almost all of the vellum is a tangled mass of fine lines which form a vast network. The outer boundary of the network is oval shaped. Where lines intersect, a local thickening indicates a node. At first glance the whole thing appears chaotic, even random. But as Zann studies it, his rooin brains begin to see emerging patterns – local clusters which link to form higher order clusters, and so on. Then shapes appear – organic growth structures, familiar outlines, and ... *a face!* Zann is startled, then shakes his head and laughs. Pareidolia illusion. A downside of a rooin's acute pattern recognition ability.

"Zann."

Director Ulzin Bar appears as a projection over the modeller. Zann wonders momentarily if he has ever seen the Director 'in the flesh', as humans say.

"Director."

"Bad business, the death of a surveillance subject," the Director rubs his head.

"Yes. Bad business."

"Bad *for* business, Zann. Client's not happy. But the good news is I persuaded them to let us find the killer. I had to dance a fandango, but we've got the commission."

Zann tries not to picture the Director dancing a fandango.

"How do they know there *is* a killer?" Zann asks. "Maybe it was suicide."

"You don't believe that, Zann."

"You're right, I don't think Eve ... er, the girl ..."

Ulzin Bar cuts him short with a clap of his hands. "So let's get onto it." The Director manages a smile. "Keep me informed," And vanishes.

Zann sighs and puts the drawing away. He stretches his arms and back, listening to the little clicks and creaks. He massages the pain of work from his hands, creasing and smoothing the striated silver-grey skin with his thumb.

At a soft crypto-command Eve Lamente appears in his media screen.

Eve Lamente had been a pretty, young woman. In the 3V her long, blonde hair is tied back in a simple pony tail. Her mouth is not large, but her lips are thick and a deep red. She wears glasses. Very few humans wear glasses. One of the first things Zann noticed about the girl was the way she breathed. Slow and calm, but irregular, like a song slowed down.

What can you tell me that I don't already know?

The 3V appears to be some sort of job interview, though no specifics are ever mentioned. It's only a fragment of a longer interview, and Tempo Corp's proprietary T-stamp has been erased – technically difficult, and also illegal in most territories. The client, whoever it is, has never been forthcoming about how they came into its possession. Clients generally maintain anonymity behind representative insurance firms, and this one has been especially protective of their identity.

"OK Eve, tell us a bit about yourself." The unseen male voice is soft, almost feminine.

"My name is Eve Lamente. I'm a second-cycle neurotechnology student at the University of Delphi."

The girl turns her eyes to the camera. Every time Zann has watched this, he has had the feeling the girl is actually looking at *him*. Crazy, of course.

"Thanks, Eve. And you're majoring in ...?"

"Probabilistic neuro-ethics and applied dream mechanics."

Zann follows the music of her voice.

"Mmm, good. Now, tell us Eve, where do you see yourself in, say ..."

"The future?"

"Well, yes."

"When this is all over ..." The girl's eyes move around the invisible room before settling back on Zann. "When this is all over, I see myself in a better world."

Zann briefly pauses the 3V. The frozen figure stares back at him. When *what* is all over? he thinks, before continuing the playback.

"That's interesting. What do you mean by that, Eve?"

She smiles enthusiastically. "A changed world. One where we have all woken up and decided to stop hurting each other. A world where everyone knows."

"Knows what, Eve?"

Zann quickly switches off the 3V as Lakzad pokes his head around the door.

"Q," Lakzad says in his 'I knew it all along' way.

"What?"

"The metal vial in the apartment." Lakzad tosses Zann the object. "It's a container for a new street drug called Q. Strictly *non-brand*."

Zann turns the vial around in his fingers. "Could it have – "

"Killed her? Probably. It can be nasty stuff in sufficiently high doses. The user dies almost instantly, but from their perspective it takes an eternity, which apparently can either be heaven or hell. In her case, it looks like it was hell."

Zann shivers. "So her death could just be an overdose?"

Lakzad shakes his head. "I doubt it. Her fingerprints weren't on the vial. Plus electrochem traces in the apartment tell us someone else was there."

"Human or rooin?"

"Human. Not enough for a *genetic*, unfortunately. Pity they're not nanotagged."

"Treaty!" Zann admonishes him.

"Sorry," Lakzad glances nervously up at the scanner.

Zann slips him a comforting smile. "And the puncture wounds to the back of the head?"

Lakzad paces up and down, as if delivering a lecture. "My guess is the girl was ON and someone dug out her engrafts."

"But why?" Zann asks. "From what I know about ON, they'd be useless to anyone else."

"Exactly. It is strange. By the way, I guess you heard we've been commissioned by the client to investigate the death?"

"The Director just told me. He had to dance a fandango."

"What?"

"Nothing. So ..." Zann leans on his desk, "a human enters the girl's apartment, kills her using a non-brand drug – a bizarre choice of weapon, but possibly done to avoid making too much noise or to fake a drug overdose. Then, for some reason, this human digs out a perfectly useless pair of ON engrafts, after which they make their getaway past 17 conveniently smashed scanners. You say the metal vial can't be traced to a source?"

"Not forensically."

"Ahh. *Legwork*. I love it."

Lakzad is turning to leave when Zann asks, "Who smashed the scanners?"

"Umm, I have no idea."

"Get young Ozzi-Chen onto it. Let's see if we can find a *face* in all of this."

After Lakzad has left, Zann waits a while before turning the 3V on again.

"... a world where everyone knows."

"Knows what, Eve?"

The girl takes off her glasses and looks straight into Zann's eyes. "Who they really are."

∞

The research department of Raymond Parkes occupies the largest area on this floor. Zann counts up the rows, groups, segments and desks – 16 x 8 x 4 x 2. That's 1024 rooins all busily finding out how and why – from a client's point of view – someone committed a crime, a misdemeanour, or even just a financial faux pas.

"Ozzi-Chen."

The young rooin spins in his chair and a broad smile of recognition lights up his face. If it were possible for a rooin to be manufactured chubby, Ozzi-Chen has somehow managed it.

"Zann! Welcome to where the real action is," he says, smoothing his red hair.

Ozzi-Chen has a habit of moving his eyebrows up and down in time to his words.

"Action?" Zann grunts. "You roos just sit on your exhausts the whole time."

Ozzi-Chen pulls a face, pretending to be hurt.

"You got those scanner streams?" Zann asks.

"Sure do." Ozzi-Chen's media screen fills with a grid of scanner viewpoints.

"OK, here we go," says Ozzi-Chen, "They all happen around the same time, within a T-block, give or take. There's the first. Top left."

A young woman taking the stairs to the second floor abruptly looks up, then picks up an ornamental vase and smashes it into the scanner. The mini screen goes black. "Vicious," Ozzi-Chen says. "Next."

A man comes out of a nearby building, starts walking, then appears to change his mind and crosses the street to the scanner. In order to reach it, he climbs onto the handrail. He then punches it repeatedly with his fist. Another mini screen goes black.

Ozzi-Chen whistles and says, "That's got to have hurt."

One by one, the 17 scanners are randomly destroyed by apparent passers-by.

"We could ID them and bring them in." Ozzi-Chen ventures.

"No, this would be covered by the govcorp's contract with their law agency. We'd have an expensive time of it getting Chamber of Commerce clearance. And let's not get into a fight with a govcorp. So, what do all these miscreants have in common?"

"Umm ... they're all human."

"Yes. We rooins are a law abiding lot, aren't we? What else?"

"Can't see any ... No wait! *None* of them is wearing a grID visor."

"You're right, Ozzi-Chen. Let's look at *that* one a bit closer."

Ozzi-Chen's screen fills with the viewpoint of a scanner overlooking the building's foyer. An elderly man is waiting for someone. After a while he turns, sees the scanner and uses his walking stick to repeatedly strike at it.

"Go back to just before he turns his head." Zann says. "Yes, *there*. Zoom in. Once more, half speed. See it?"

The man is clearly preoccupied with someone's tardiness. He sighs and looks out of the entrance rubbing the back of his neck. But then his eyes flicker, as if he's just been kicked in the head.

"What is it, Zann?"

"Ozzi-Chen, I need you to find out everything you can about ON."

∞

Hefastus Stark settled back into his couch to let the Blu-Zone work its magic. Two caps, no trouble. Stark's apartment was not much more than a small box of junk and filth, embedded into a larger unit of 125 similar boxes. The larger unit was embedded into an even larger unit and so on, in complex yet cleverly uninteresting ways, to produce a monolith – one of eight identical structures rising up from an otherwise featureless desert landscape abutting a 16-tube vehicle corridor.

The music swirled around Stark, caressing and whispering. Through cracked teeth, he sang along loudly and tunelessly, his fine grey hair swaying to the beat, while his fingernails tapped time on the dirty green couch. Bass notes were now massaging his spine and feet.

Chocolate brown. *Hoo Hoo!* Velvet and funny. *This stuff is zippy, almost like Electro-Tryp!* Suddenly there were ... bells! *Fuck man, are they bells?* Tiny faces danced before his eyes, laughing and singing. *Red bells, no, red glass bells. Fuck me, man!* Then blue points of light like ... like ... *fuck, like some fuckin' flute shit, man!* But this was just a tease. *Ha! I know this bitch.* White and silver drums joined the party, the bass dropped an octave, and the whole room with Stark in it was carried up into the air. Up, up he flew, as the floor fell away. *Oh, what a fuckin' fist fuck man!* Hefastus Stark was cackling like a lone parrot in a shoebox.

Outside in the freezing dark, men in padded black were converging on the front door with rapid hand signals and a lot of equipment. This was no family visit.

As Stark floated upwards towards a delicate filigree pattern of orange and green, the pattern abruptly changed into his door being smashed in. *Why is my door on the ceiling?*

The men came through like soldier ants, clattering black, fast and furious. Arms held him against the floor. The carpet dust choked his throat, and something cold and metallic was pressed into the back of his neck. Stark felt a pain so intense that his vomit was a yellow scream before his eyes. Just before losing consciousness, he became aware that he had shit himself.

∞

A popular saying in OneWorld was 'Party out front, business in the back.'

In an unmarked room somewhere in the back of Tentillium Services, two humans were about to get down to business. The small room contained two steel chairs and a steel table with some black, rubber-coated equipment resting on it. White ceramic tiles covered the entire room – floor, walls, and ceiling. Despite its spotless gleam, the room had an unpleasant smell.

There were three people in the white room at Tentillium Services, and two of them were proudly standing on their own two feet. Narli Saxon and Rob Grupp had both been in law enforcement at least half their lives. Neither of them could remember how long they had been at Tentillium.

Narli Saxon was a medium man. Medium height, medium build, medium complexion, medium intelligence. He had three distinguishing features. Close-cropped ultra-blonde hair, glass-blue eyes that betrayed nothing, and a permanent half grin. He didn't say much, but everyone said he was 'supportive'.

Rob Grupp, shorter and stockier, with long greying hair and a podgy grey face, was the more animated of the two. Emotionally complex, he was known for his 'little dramas' – waving his arms around and acting out various imaginary roles in order to make his point. He sweated a lot and had a short fuse.

Both Narli and Rob would tell you Tentillium was a good employer. There were over six hundred Law agencies in this district alone, but

Tentillium had a reputation for quality service, and for looking after their own. They went the distance.

The Tentillium logo was an ambiguous design portraying a helical twist of fibres wrapped around a crossbar to form the letter 'T'. The fibres could have possibly represented a strand of DNA (Tentillium's forensic department) or, alternatively, the tightening ropes of a garrotte. Tentillium's slogan was: 'Enforcement Solutions for Peace of Mind'.

The third person in the room was not standing on his own two feet. Suspended by one ankle from a steel bar spanning the entire width of the room, was a naked human male. Apparently unconscious, the man swung gently to and fro. The bar could potentially accommodate up to five people in a similar position. Below the bar, tastefully built into the tiled floor, was a thin steel drain.

Every part of the suspended man had been wrapped in a fine, gold wire. The wire thing was Rob's idea. 'Rob's baby' everyone in the office joked. Rob believed the company needed to raise its profile and embrace new technology. The gold wire was a new brand of industrial nanowire, whose gossamer threads were constructed from millions of microscopic, remotely powered machines.

These machines had three basic functions. Firstly, to respond to instructions; secondly, to seek out similar, non-contiguous machines and if so instructed, to interlock with them in a ratchet-like mechanism; and thirdly, to cut. Each machine carried a miniscule circular blade with a serrated edge. On receipt of the appropriate instructions, the blade would spin. This, coupled with the ratchet action, meant that a length of this nanowire could be instructed to slowly tighten while cutting through whatever it was tightening upon. Like, for example, the human it was wrapped around.

Rob's interrogations nearly always involved use of the nanowire. It 'moved the project forwards', as they said. Rob would sometimes start with the hands. "People are so attached to their hands," he'd joke. By the time a few fingers, and maybe their left hand, were staring up at them from the tiles, they'd usually tell you anything. The stubborn ones had to lose a bit more. Sometimes Rob would 'mix it up' by cutting every micrometre of the victim's body to just below the dermis. Rob liked to think of himself as an artist – he was passionate about 'creative solutions'. He'd been to one of *those* seminars.

Rob also recorded all of his work on 3V. If he felt like it, he could pull it off the secure Tentillium channel and put it up on the home screen. The kids loved it. Rob would have a bunch of workmates and their wives over for a barbeque at his big ranch-style home, and after lunch the wives would hang around the common room discussing sport and politics, while the men retired to Rob's den to talk fashion and to watch a man being slowly and agonisingly reduced to a pile of chopped sausage.

Everyone liked Rob. He was a 'people person'.

∞

Hefastus Stark was floating up towards the light. A pure white light. A Divine Light.

"This must be it," he thought. "Fuck me, man! Heaven! It's really fuckin' real!"

Stark cried tears of joy, although for some reason his tears were trickling upwards. As Stark moved closer to heaven, he could just make out a square, grid like pattern in front of the light.

What the —? What the fuck is that? It's … It fuckin looks like …

Tiles. White bathroom tiles.

The next thing Stark became aware of was gravity or, to be precise, the fact that he was hanging upside down by one of his ankles. His hip hurt and so did his neck. He was wet and cold, and something was wound around him. Then a big blotchy pink thing filled his vision.

"Hello, Mister Stark! So nice of you to join us."

Rob Grupp's face was close enough for Stark to feel the coarse bristles scratching his nose. Also, there was that *smell*.

∞

Stark screamed.

As the nanowire bit into his body, Stark screamed and screamed and screamed. At first he thought the screaming would make the pain easier to bear, but it just seemed to make it even worse. Still, he couldn't stop. He felt blood trickling over his neck and face, collecting into his eyes and onto the tip of his nose, then falling hopelessly towards an expanding pool below him. Little rivulets were breaking away from the main pool and venturing towards the shiny drain.

The pain went on forever with no end.

Then it stopped.

The pink blob reappeared.

"Now I want ... Stop screaming, you scum, and listen, or I'll start it all again! ... I want the name, Mister Stark. Listen to me! The name, address, favourite food, fucking inner thigh measurement, every fucking detail about who sold you this drug!"

Stark could just make out a large white plastic container with blue wheels in the corner of the room. On the side of the container he could see a blue logo that looked a bit like a hangman's noose, plus some upside down words that read: 'Something ... Something ... Peace of Mind.'

Terror sucked the air out of him.

"Err, fuck man, I dunno," Stark choked and blubbered, blowing bubbles of his own blood. "The Blu-Zone ... it's just 'onsold', you know. No harm done."

Rob Grupp lost his temper again. His fat pink fingers grabbed Stark's lacerated arm and shook it, causing more screams.

Rob Grupp put his mouth to Stark's ear and shouted. "I don't give a fuck about the Blu-Zone, you stinking piece of shit! I'm talking about Q. You hear? The drug that comes from fucking hell itself!"

Stark failed to answer fast enough, so again the wire bit.

∞

"I think we're all done here. Thank you, Mister Stark, for your cooperation. Tentillium has no further use for your services." Kicking the plastic container underneath the hanging man, Rob Grupp turned to Narli and said, "Call Waste. Tell them to be here ... oh, just after lunch. There's no hurry."

Rob was now busying himself with the nanowire controller, programming a long sequence into it. He took a swig of Super-Hydra, picked up a sandwich from the table, and munched into it. Chewing noisily, he switched on the 3V recorder and carefully lined up the camera. Stark's screams bounced off the tile walls like piss in a toilet. Rob was just about to press the green GO button when the door was kicked in, and a large silver-skinned rooin strode into the room, his hand on his GlockZ.

"You want to live, Grupp? Don't do it!" the rooin said, his voice so loud it even drowned out Stark's screams.

"You *creatures* ever heard of knocking?" Rob snarled through a wet grin, wiping some mayonnaise from his chin. But his fingers dutifully moved away from the controls.

"This investigation is no longer yours," the rooin said, producing an insurance override.

Grupp hissed, "Don't think I don't know your dirty fuckin rooin game! You're all the same. You think you can just – " He snatched the document from the rooin's fingers, and his face fell. Essentially, the override codes told Grupp that the rooin's client had so much money on the table that, if they wanted to, they could blow up Tentillium's building with impunity.

"Or perhaps this will convince you," the rooin said, removing the GlockZ from its holster. "Your death is just one more clause in the contract."

Rob and Narli slowly backed out of the white room, leaving a trail of loathing on the pristine tiles. Plus a little drop of mayonnaise.

At first, Stark thought this giant rooin might do something even worse to him. But the rooin simply winched him down, gently cradling his lacerated body in his big hands. Stark looked up at the face. It was handsome and kind, despite looking a bit like a human skull. Not that Stark was complaining right now.

"OK," the rooin said quietly, "let's get you out of here and all fixed up. "You know, Mister Stark," he remarked conversationally. "You really should get better insurance."

∞

Constantin Zann walks through the hospital suburb of Templa. His visual overlays show ::NO HUMANS:: for a current radius of 201E. After a quick calc, he decides to risk walking faster. Much faster. He still maintains the overlays on top his object vision though, since he doesn't want to collide with a human right now to add to all his other worries. He quickly reaches the building and taking the rooin-only gravator, which would crush a human in a T-sec, emerges almost instantly on the 49th floor.

Zann finds Stark lying on his back, wrapped in a delicate web of nano-bandages that are busily knitting his violated flesh back together. Stark opens his eyes, sees Zann, and begins to cry like a child.

"Aww fuck, man," he blubbers, "You saved my life, man! I mean that's not nothing, is it? That's like, really fuckin' something!"

Zann listens patiently.

"Those fuckin' arseholes, man. They were going to … going to …" Stark bursts into more sobs, punctuated by cries of pain, as his skin is stretched by his exertions.

"Mister Stark, I need your help."

"*My* help?" Stark snuffles "Fuck man, anything I can do for you. I mean *anything.*"

"I need you to tell me about Q."

"Q? Shit man, I told those cunts —"

"You told them a pack of lies."

Despite his tears, Stark's eyes narrow.

Zann produces the metal vial. "You seen anything like this?"

Stark takes the vial and painfully turns it around in his bandaged hands. Three fingers of his left hand are missing.

"Not mine, man. This is the heavy stuff. You'd have to be fuckin' crazy to ..."

"A young woman died because of it. You know what her death would have been like?"

Stark nods.

"Who deals it?"

Stark shakes his head. "They'd kill me, man. Like a fuckin' bug."

"Whoever they are, you owe them nothing. Why would you- ..."

"I owe them my life."

Zann pauses to internally replay the conversation up to this point. He concentrates on the tones in the human's voice. Code of honour. Military, probably. Then his irises glow blue.

"Mister Stark, you now owe *me* your life, and I can tell you are an *honourable* man."

The word 'honourable' has an immediate effect on the man in the bed. Zann leans in, his voice lowering half an octave.

"Human lives may now be at stake, Mister Stark – *many* human lives."

Zann realised long ago that humans are impressed with quantity, especially when it comes to death. Big numbers get results.

Hefastus Stark hesitates, then whispers a name.

∞

From behind a pillar, Constantin Zann looks up through the broken roof of the cavernous car park towards the ruins of a vast circular structure which shines bright orange against the dark clouds. Jutting above this structure is a tangled thatch of metal spikes.

Ozzi-Chen has provided Zann with detailed plans for HomeSafe – what little of it that has been built – along with some background history.

HomeSafe operates as an illegal two-tiered society. The orange structure is home to the ex-employees of Hammer of Kebeshen – the security firm under contract during the early construction. When the project went belly-up, pay stopped, and as Hammer employees were progressively evicted from their homes, the only place for them to stay was the HomeSafe site. Hammer increased fortifications and doubled security. All attempts by management to dislodge them were met with strong resistance. Eventually the suits went away.

The sub-ground parking levels, where Zann now stands, house a very different demographic. The carpet of filth stretching out before him is actually thousands of humans, if one can still call them that. Some lie on mattresses, some huddle next to pillars, some search through the rubbish for food, drugs, or other humans. Others wander aimlessly, talking to themselves or silent in the aimlessness. Zann allows himself the luxury of turning down his olfactory processors.

Zann passes three people of indeterminate sex copulating under a blanket encrusted with – at the very least – vomit. One glares up at him with wet red eyes, and spits angrily. The phlegm carries traces of blood and small parasites. Scurrying among the humans are other creatures too – monstrous hybrids. *Sterile, thank chance* thinks Zann. Small children have caught one – a little chimera resembling a cross between a bat and an otter – and are gleefully torturing the poor creature. It's tiny shrieks are drowned by the general din of despair. Zann's internal moral algorithms go through their paces, but the result is a foregone conclusion.

One rooin cannot help these people.

He picks up a vile blanket, covers himself with it, then vaults the few remaining steps to the forecourt level. Bending over, he limps haphazardly towards one of the giant arches that access the circular structure. He has chosen an entrance partially obscured by a pile of prefabricated slabs. Four guards block his way.

"Hammers only past this point."

Zann mumbles something and moves closer.

"Are you deaf, grounder?"

A hand grabs Zann's shoulder. Zann's fingers immediately close around the guard's upper arm, twisting it quickly. There is the sound of breaking bone. The man's screams blend into the general wailing of the distant crowd. Zann's other hand removes the man's weapon and aims it at the remaining three guards. The blanket falls to the ground, and the sudden sight of a large silver rooin catches them off guard. Then one of the guards lunges forwards, his weapon half raised, but Zann's forehead connects with the underside of the man's jaw. He finishes him off with a blow to the neck. Only two now. Their weapons are a few degrees away from their target, but Zann has already grabbed one with his left hand, slamming it into the owner's temple while simultaneously breaking the other man's windpipe with a sideways blow. A sound makes Zann turn. The guard with the broken arm is screaming a bit too loudly to be masked by the noises of the crowd. Zann fixes that.

So, that's: three unconscious, one with moderate to severe injuries, and one dead. The death concerns Zann. He quickly replays the whole thing, checking the relevant sections of his new contract. Clause 45C1.A097. Reasonable force.

That was reasonable.

Inside the orange building, Zann is confronted by a jungle. Wild-seed plants cover almost every structure. Trees and shrubs have broken up most of the flooring, the walls are curtains of green, and observation decks have become hanging gardens. Zann takes one of the more heavily beaten paths through a cluster of black alder trees, their trunks surrounded by mutated mosses and rock willows. After a while, the path opens out onto what looks like a formative shopping complex. No scanner systems had been installed before construction ceased, so security here is strictly old school. In the clearing ahead, several guards stand around talking and laughing. "Little fuckers!" one of them says.

Zann watches as a woman aims her plasma gun at a brace of crows perched on a nearby tree. The gun releases its charge, and the crows disappear in haze of pink and black. The bored laughter of the guards echoes through the building. Zann carefully edges his way along an outer wall. Two more levels to go. He climbs a set of service stairs, then runs down an unlit corridor, arriving at a large pair of nasglass doors – Centre Management.

Constantin Zann savours his next heartbeat. Then, in one swift motion, he opens the doors and steps through them. For an instant, he can see the room – luxurious, but dusty and uncared for. Coloured lights play on some couches grouped around a modeller table. To the right is a professional bar. Media screens cover every wall. Directly in front of him, on the far side of the room, a man stands in front of a black, metal desk.

The man is tall and muscular. His head sports a fountain of red hair and a thin red moustache, and he wears a long coat made from strips of coloured cloth woven into symbols, His white linen shirt and trousers are stained and scuffed. His boots are steel. Zann recognises this man. His name is Elijah Ophidian.

Then Zann is plunged into total sensory loss. *Wide spectrum EM darkness, plus acoustic inverters.* Clever. As his senses slowly return, he becomes aware of two heavy objects pressed against the back of his head.

"Well will you look at that!" Elijah Ophidian is saying, his words getting louder as if controlled by a volume fader. "A fuckin' cog. Here!" The joyless laughter sounds like grinding metal. "Take his weapon!"

The objects pressed against Zann's head are the barrels of plasma guns, held by two guards, one of whom removes Zann's GlockZ and throws it across the floor. Elijah Ophidian picks it up and turns it around in his hands.

"Hmm. 5-action GlockZ. You could take apart a building with this."

"I've been known to do that," Zann replies.

What little is left of Elijah Ophidian's smile disappears. He swings the weapon up to point directly at Zann's face, and strides towards him.

"Why are you here, cog?"

"I'm investigating a murder."

Zann has expanded his vision span to around 165 degrees. There is loss of detail but it allows him to build up a stereo model of the men behind him by scanning shadows and surface reflections.

"A murder?" Elijah Ophidian waves the GlockZ around as he gives another joyless laugh. "Well, I must say you're spoiled for choice here. As far as I know, there isn't anyone who hasn't ..."

Zann narrows his vision to around 35 degrees, focusing on Ophidian's face.

"The killer used your high dose Q. The victim was a young woman."

"What is this? Are you interrogating me? Did they forget to wire you up before they dropped you out of the jelly, you stupid cog?"

Again, the man points the gun directly at Zann's face.

"Let's just say you can assist me with my enquiries."

"*Assist?* Assist a cog? You know what? I'm tired of this." Elijah Ophidian turns and walks back towards the desk. He raises a finger.

"Kill the cog."

Even before the word 'kill' is completed, Zann's forearms are moving up and back at an angle of 12.4 degrees to the vertical. He hears the clicks from the trigger mechanisms, but his hands have already grasped both weapons, and pushed them upwards, as he bends his head low. Two bolts of pink and blue death explode into the high ceiling, bringing down a shower of dust and pieces of tensocrete onto the spinning form of Elijah Ophidian. Most of the lights go out. Zann pulls the guns from the guards' hands and, in a figure-of-eight motion, smashes the buts into their heads. Elijah Ophidian manages to unlock Zann's GlockZ and fire, the blast almost vaporising the nasglass doors. But Zann has already dived low and is now sliding along the floor towards the man's legs. Zann still holds the plasma guns, whose barrels brutally connect with Ophidian's shin bones, toppling him forwards. Zann springs to his feet, spins in the air, and lands with his boot against the back of Ophidian's neck. A fine dust continues to float down, as one of the guards screams in pain.

∞

Elijah Ophidian's eyes open slowly. He is sitting in one of the lounge chairs, near the bar. Sluggishly, he scans the room and sees the large rooin rummaging through the desk drawers.

"Hey cog!" he tries to shout, but it comes out more like a squeaky, "Huh coh." Angry, he tries to get up, but finds that his body will not respond.

"Whuh thuh fuh?"

The rooin notices his efforts, and walks over. "You're temporarily paralysed, Mister Ophidian. RNO: Rapid Nerve Oscillation. Old rooin law trick. Don't worry, it will have worn off by the time I'm gone. Now listen. You have five injured guards. Three at Entrance C71B, and two over there by the door. These men should be taken to your medical facility as soon as possible."

"Yuh fuh roo cuh!"

"Please try and concentrate on what I am saying, Mister Ophidian. The wellbeing and lives of your employees are at stake. In any event, my company will send an emergency grID9 message to your local node."

Elijah Ophidian attempts to spit in the face of the rooin, but only succeeds in dribbling spit onto his own chin. The rooin gently wipes the saliva away with his sleeve.

Zann returns to the desk, and soon finds what he is looking for – the register. He picks it up and scans it. *Zork!* The thing is ancient e-tech, not even properly grid-synced. That means there has to be ... Zann searches the drawers again until he finds the carrier. He docks the little hexagonal object into the register and watches it glow. Zann can now see all the files in the blink of an eye. Not that Zann ever blinks.

∞

On the upper observation deck of the Raymond Parkes building, Constantin Zann leans against the railing and gazes out over the Medusa. The short cycle cooling has begun, and there is already a cruel chill in the air. Ice crystals form around the ion bubbles that drift up from the vehicle corridors below, creating an undulating carpet of little translucent white balloons at his eye level. The black clouds above start to swirl violently. Somewhere nearby, a rooin is singing. Zann listens to the sounds of the metropolis he calls home. Sometimes he plays a game where he tries to discern an overall pattern to it all, some kind of unfolding plan. But the layers are always so complex as to be impenetrable, even to one with Zann's abilities and all he can hear is the usual sound of chaos going nowhere.

"You're not planning on jumping, I hope."

Zann turns to see Lakzad walking towards him.

"They said I'd find you here." Lakzad reaches the railing. "What are you up to Zann?"

"Just thinking."

"I've warned you about that."

Lakzad turns up his collar against the cold, and Zann can't help but smile.

"I know, I know!" Lakzad says huffily. "Why don't I just re-distribute my core temperature. Well, I happen to like my senses straight up, OK?"

"Like a human?"

"Like a human, if you must. Call me crazy."

"Can I?"

"Hmm, talking of crazy, I've just seen your 'lone gunman' exploits over at HomeSafe. Very entertaining! Tazzo and the gang are already showing it at parties."

Zann smiles, his eyes following the ion bubbles.

"You know, Lakzad, I looked at those creatures in the car park – those *humans* – and I realised I couldn't help any of them. And even if I could have, they would have still have ..."

"Jumped back into their own shit? They're not our problem, Zann."

"I wonder. When did they stop being our problem?"

"When we became free, Zann. Rooins no longer have to do what they're told."

"Only what they're paid to."

Lakzad looks surprised. "That's all *anyone* in OneWorld does, Zann!"

Constantin Zann remains silent. He is thinking about Eve Lamente, and her ponytail and red lips, her quaint glasses and her ... hope.

"A world where everyone knows who they really are."

Zann turns to Lakzad. "Our ancestors were built to serve humans. But now ..."

"... we serve ourselves," Lakzad said, completing the sentence. There's not much conviction in his voice.

"Now that we've become ... free." Zann expels the word into the frosted air.

Lakzad frowns and moves closer. "Look, Zann, I like to think of you as a friend. We've worked together for ... how long?

"You want me to pay Tempo to find out?"

"No, no. In our memories, surely. Anyway, it's been a long time." Lakzad attempts a back-slapping manoeuvre which doesn't quite come off. "But recently you've been changing. Not like the old Zann." A second attempt at a slap on the back is more successful. "Others have noticed it too. The impulsiveness, the introspection ..."

"Like a human?"

"Well, yes. like a human. No offence, of course."

"Why would I take offence at being compared to a human?"

Lakzad stares blankly. He is running out of things to say.

Zann takes the empty vial out of his pocket. As he turns it in his fingers, moisture condenses onto the cold metal. Zann holds the vial to his ear.

"It's silent now. When it holds the drug, it sings. Did you know that?"

"Can't say I did," Lakzad's eyes narrow as he observes Zann apprehensively.

"It's the containment mechanism," Zann continues, "the thing generates a tiny grav field which suspends something that doesn't exist inside a dimensionless space. Nothing inside nothing."

"Interesting. Hey Zann, I wasn't kidding about the 'jumping' thing. I'm worried about you. You're not thinking of ..."

"Jumping?"

"Yes."

"No, Lakzad. I'm thinking of singing."

I can't remember when I forgot

⏻

"HISTORY has been extinguished. Where and when did an event occur? Did the event even occur at all? And, most importantly, who cares anymore?"

In those few words, the great historian Orwell B. Humphrey articulated the role of history and time within the OneWorld mental landscape. The great historian continues …

"Let's try to put ourselves in the shoes of an early human, living in one of the old civilisations. This person would have seen themselves as having a 'place in time'. For them, life was firmly fixed within the history of their culture. We can fancifully imagine ourselves hovering over this history as it lies spread out beneath us like a great time map. The entirety of the map is the span of their civilisation. As we fly in, we can now make out larger states and regions (famous battles, treaties, reigns of kings, queens and governments). Flying closer still, we perceive suburbs and districts (local skirmishes, festivals), then streets (births, deaths and marriages of tribal or family members), and finally we arrive at the dwelling of our imaginary citizen: their 'today'. It even has a name! One house down the road is 'yesterday'. It also has a name. The other way lies 'tomorrow'. Another name.

"Now, compare this with our typical OneWorld citizen. Cut adrift from history, he or she no longer has a 'place in time'. OneWorld citizens would probably take pride in the fact that they have been 'freed' from time, since a host of devices and prompters wake them, organise them, and take them from one space-time coordinate to the next. Important occasions are programmed into a complex system that controls every aspect of their lives. No longer required to remember anything, these people have forgotten everything. Instead, they have T-STAMP.

T-STAMP was originally developed by a consortium of lifestyle manufacturers – known collectively as 'Tempo' – who required a more rigorous means of recording the space-time coordinates of an event. The principles underlying T-STAMP are complex, but the system is relatively easy to use. Any event – past, present or future – can be defined by an eight digit number code, four of which refer to space coordinates, and four of which refer to time coordinates. Any of these eight numbers can further be expanded into a possible 256 sub-numbers (reserved for legal, scientific and security codes, to name just some examples), giving a potential 2048 numbers to describe the event.

The Tempo System for Time And Map Placement of event data soon began to appear as an option on many consumer devices. Initially viewed as something of an oddity, it came into general use by degrees, simply because of the large feature set it offered. Both T-STAMP and the old system coexisted for a few generations, but inevitably T-STAMP won out. The original time system, based on an ad hoc combination of ancient Sumerian, Egyptian, and Roman conventions, simply couldn't keep up. It is now quite rare to find any reference to the concepts of minutes, hours, days, weeks, years, and so on.

The slow sting in the tail was the fact that the new system and its units were not in the public domain, but owned by Tempo. Tempo soon signed contracts with govcorps throughout OneWorld, making the use of any old system of time measurement a crime. With the privatisation of time complete, you no longer had an automatic right to know the answer to the simple question, "What is the time?"

For the average person, it's usually cheaper not to know the time, so few bother any more. Possibly because of this, research has shown that the capacity to recall past events has been steadily decreasing with each generation.

But T-STAMP is not merely a system for recording the time of an event. It also records the ownership of that event. The idea that someone could own a past event came into being by degrees. Since T-STAMP's power allowed a user to perform significant fine-grain calculations on the relationships between multiple events, it soon became clear that such information could pose a threat to various commercial, legal and security interests. The next step was for the relevant parties to try to block recording rights to T-STAMP for events to which they could prove a significant claim. For example, any major public event – be it celebratory or catastrophic – would almost immediately have all its T-STAMP shut down through action in the time courts. Then wealthy families got in on the act, laying claim to as much of their life's T-

STAMP as they could get away with, including future events such as weddings, births, etc. Those with famous ancestors tried claiming ownership of historic events. Disputes were common, since ownership of a significant event could be quite lucrative, with the licence of usage rights for T-STAMP data.

The next step was inevitable and yet no-one foresaw it: rights to history began to be traded, just like anything else. Whole tracts of past time were bought up by large corps and the era of big brand history was born. Prices for history usage increased steadily until they were beyond the budget of most consumers. As a result, an entire industry in 'created' histories sprang up to fulfil a market need. These new 'no name' versions of past events offered all the drama, spectacle, pathos, horror, inspirational myths, and important life lessons of 'real' history, but at a fraction of the cost. The big history brands mounted a rearguard defence of their intellectual property through litigation, but the genie was forever out of the bottle. Enterprising parallel marketers freely mixed brand name histories with the no name varieties to create custom-made hybrids for specific vertical markets, and pretty soon it was hard to tell the difference between what had 'really' happened and what was simply made up. Besides, few people cared.

History, like everything in OneWorld, is either owned or discarded, but never cherished.

As the great historian concludes: "This is a civilisation suffering from dementia."

∞

Doctor Rafaela Serif marched along the corridor with crisp purpose, despite the fact that her feet were killing her. The high heels had not been a good idea. To her left was a glass wall which filtered the environmental lighting through layers of grime, cobwebs, and some sort of yellow chemical deposit. To her right was a row of doors, each leading to a small cell. She glanced up at the eroded plasteel girders above and wrinkled her nose. The entire building looked as though it had been made from recycled materials. And Raf was certain that the guard, who followed two steps behind, was ogling her bum. Her lips compressed into a thin red line.

QKC Neuropsych Holding Facility was little more than a detention centre for people who had failed to provide profit for QKC. As government corporations go, Qunan Kapital Corp was pretty much bottom of the barrel: corruption all the way up to the board, species rights abuses, you name it. Raf had taken precautions. She was wearing a bright red grID visor, so everyone here would know the whole world was watching their every move; she'd set-up two bio-trackers; and, finally, she'd packed a petite plasma weapon into her little XaX handbag. Besides, as she'd been telling herself since arriving, NeuroHelp Global would never let anything happen to her.

Raf kept one eye firmly fixed on the uneven floor, while she used her other eye to replay the last few assessment interviews. "I even multitask in my sleep," Raf would tell colleagues.

"I just feel so ..." a patient was saying, through the visor's audio.

"What, exactly?"

"So ..."

"Yes?"

"Slow."

Raf sped the replays up, narrowly missing a big hole in the flooring as she juggled with the retinal controls. Even at double speed they were a pretty torpid lot. But Raf knew she could help them, if NHG could just get those bureaucratic wheels turning. Then she could transfer everyone to a proper commercial facility.

What time is it? Raf couldn't be bothered with the rigmarole or the expense. Her prompter would let her know when it was time to go. Still, time seemed to be dragging. She was looking forward to hopping on a minigrav and getting home to a warm bath.

"Here." The guard pointed to a rusted door which had been repeatedly painted greyish-green. The number *17* was painted on it in a different shade of greyish-green, for contrast.

"Crazy man," the guard said, grinning and randomly moving his hands around.

Raf gave him a glare which spoke volumes, despite knowing he wouldn't be able to read any of them.

"No good, no good," the guard said, shaking his head, and unlocking the door. "You knock if needing."

"Thanks, I will."

Rafaela Serif spent a little time smoothing her hair and adjusting her jacket and skirt, before stepping through door 17. The patient was standing in the far corner. He looked into her eyes and gave an unexpected smile, as if he recognised her.

Raf felt herself flush. *Ridiculous!* Her skin was burning, not just her face but all over.

Surely not! Raf looked up at the scanner, then went over and checked the Vigilance Level.

:: D7 ::

"This is total bullshit!"

Raf hammered on the door, until the guard's face appeared.

"He grab you?" the guard asked, hopefully.

"No you *stupid* –. This scanner. Look at it! It's set to D7! Do you understand?"

The guard shrugged.

Raf let out a sigh that was almost lethal. "No, of course you don't."

She walked a few paces up the hallway and called Caspar Gentry, Director of NeuroHelp Global. Caspar was a personal friend and a one time participant in a rather awkward one-night stand which neither of them had ever spoken of again.

"This is bullshit, Caspar!"

"Fine thanks, Raf, and how are you?"

"D7! These, these ..." Her eyes flashed unforgivingly at the guard. "They have the Vigilance Level in this cell set to D7! That's sub-dermal scanning, we're talking about. What possible reason could they have for such security measures? And have you any idea what that can do to the body over time?"

"I know Raf, but there's not much you or I can do about it right now. The focus is on building up a strong relationship with QKC, not antagonising them."

"The thought of having a 'relationship' with these people fills me with – "

"Raf, we've been through this. We need them and they need us. Despite the fact that they're on the nose, QKC has major friends in the Chamber of Commerce thanks to their ore deposits. Right now, they want to be seen to be cleaning up their act so they can get full COC membership. That's where *we* come in. And we want access to all their big trading buddies, so *we* can move our teams into the proscribed regions."

"Commerce and politics."

"That's how medicine gets done. Look Raf, I know QKC are a bunch of pre-hominids, but they're almost fully commercial now. And they're going to be good for us. So be nice. For me."

"Yes, alright. Go away, Caspar."

"Love you too, Raf."

The NHG Director laughed professionally and clicked out.

Raf composed her face and turned round. The guard's eyes, like two olives surfacing in oil, took a moment to rise back above her waist. Raf's smile was invincible. "All fixed," she chimed.

She found the patient sitting on the floor, clasping his legs – a gaunt man with a shaved head and haunted eyes. He wore the one-piece green tunic that all the patients were compelled to wear.

Raf sat on the small bed, which was conspicuously bolted to the wall. "Hello Mister … er," Raf checked her visor notes, "… funny, I don't seem to have a name."

"I can't remember my name."

"Ahh, I see. Right. Well *my* name is Doctor Rafaela Serif.'

"Yes, it is."

"Yes … So I'd like to talk to you for a little while, if that's OK."

The patient said nothing, but nodded. The preliminary report appeared on Raf's retina.

Attempted suicide.

"Well, this is quite a story isn't it?" Raf began, "I see there was an … 'incident', Just tell me in your own words what happened. Why do you think you're here now?"

"Here?"

"Yes."

"Now?"

"That's right," Rafaela Serif smiled encouragingly.

"What makes you think I am?" the patient said.

"Well," Raf said, with a sigh, "even if you're not, we're managing to talk, are we not? So let's assume for the moment that I can help you."

As she spoke, Raf was tapping her knee. Her grID visor picked up the rhythmic shorthand, immediately translating it into case notes she would review later.

"I was in a war. I think," the patient said.

"I'm sorry, did you say a *war?*"

"Yes."

No mention of military background.

"Who was fighting this war?"

"It was a war for the future of the human race."

Aren't they all? thought Raf. Obviously a zealot of some stripe or other. "I see. And who won?"

The patient regarded her blankly.

Privately, Raf cursed herself for failing to completely disguise the sarcasm in her voice. She tapped out another note to herself.

Multi-perspective misinterpretation disorder?

"OK," Raf said slowly, "when did this happen?"

"I can't remember when. I forgot."

Raf tried to speak as soothingly as possible. "Forgot?"

"Who I was."

"I understand. You don't know who you are. Now, it may surprise you to learn that this is a very common feeling, not knowing who you are. But it's easily managed with the right combination of neuropsych products." The fingers tapped away.

Immediate course of N-phlaxin for three wake-cycles, then Brinner's Node realignment.

"I'll give you something to –"

"Just going round in circles, aren't we?" he said in a monotone voice. "We're all just going round in circles. Breaking up and reforming. Kidding ourselves that we're going somewhere. Finding ourselves back in the same hell!"

Possibly been tortured. Consider adding GlaxoPlus with 5-HTP nano boosters.

"Do you?" he asked.

Raf's focal point shifted back to the man's face. "I'm sorry, do I what?"

"Do *you* know who you are?"

There was an accusatory tone. But Raf was an old hand at *this* one.

"Yes I do. I told you, I'm Doctor Rafaela Serif, and my purpose is to get you out of here. But more importantly, to get you feeling good about yourself." She rounded it off with one of her winning smiles.

The patient wasn't buying it. "What makes you so different from me?"

"At a basic level, we're not so different, of course. But each of us is a complex individual with a vast – "

"Bullshit! We've all evolved from creatures as alike as peas in a pod – nothing but identical, blind machines."

"Well, yes, but the key word here is 'evolved', isn't it? We evolved into diversity and complexity. Every human has a unique –"

"Cosmetics! Underneath we're still controlled by the original master pattern – primitive, autonomically governed, only concerned with eating, reproducing and killing!"

"That's a bit ..."

He stared coldly at her. "Just slime with painted faces."

Raf's prompter cut in to tell her that the interview was over. She stood up.

"I'm sorry, but I'm not here to argue. I'm here to help. I'll be seeing you again, soon." She walked to the door and knocked for the guard.

"The war I was in."

Raf turned. "Yes?"

"We lost. I died."

∞

As the minigrav pulled away from the Qunan gravdome, Doctor Rafaela Serif looked out of the window at the mud-brown city. Uninvited media was mapping itself, via her visor, across the buildings and natural features passing below. Raf was treated to a display of agricultural quotas, manufacturing milestones, military strength, and future building projects. QKC liked to blow its own trumpet, accompanied by the local brand of shrill pop music. No mention of the torture chambers and labour camps.

"What a wretched place."

Raf turned away from the window and switched the visor to her personal grID room. She was immediately inundated with messages, movies, supplier updates, order tracking codes, and several offers for speaking engagements. People walked in and out of the room, saying, 'It would be good if you could speak at our forthcoming seminar ... '

Raf suddenly became very hungry, and quickly found the minigrav's restaurant channel. She ordered a squidburger with polyp sauce. Then she called Caspar Gentry.

"All done?" he asked, floating before her.

"Yes. Sorry for my outburst back there. I was a little overwrought."

"Don't mention it, Raf. How did it all go?"

"Overall, very well. By the way, thanks for organising a driver to get me to the gravdome."

"I wanted to spare you the joys of the Qunan taxis. They say if you only lose a kidney, you've got off lightly."

They used their shared laughter to erase any residual ill feeling.

"If I haven't said so already Raf, NeuroHelp Global ... no, make that *I* appreciate the time you donate to our work."

"It's a pleasure Caspar. Say, off the topic, have there been any recent wars in Qunan?"

"Wars? Take your pick! They're always at war with someone or other. And when those fizzle out, they just fight among themselves. Why do you ask?"

"Oh, nothing. Just ... interested."

"Oops, there's my prompter. Got to go! The wheels are turning."

Raf said, "Don't get caught in them," but the NHG Director had already gone.

"Doctor Serif," it was Darius, her PA. "My prompter just told me to call you." He ran his hands through his blond hair. "I'm glad to see you're still alive!"

"Very much thank you. Shouldn't you be out of there and wasted in some bar by now?"

Darius feigned outrage. "Doctor Serif! I'm not like that!"

"I thought you had a date with that studious young man who came in and asked me all about connectome plug-ins, or something."

Darius sighed dramatically. "No, that one turned out to be too good to be true."

The food arrived, brought by a waiter who didn't look like he'd even had his induced puberty procedure. The waiter left, and Raf held up the squid burger. "*You* look yummy."

"No-one's said that to me for a *long* time."

"Not you, my squidburger! Sorry Darius, I'm all ears."

"Upstaged by a cephalopod! I don't know. Where are all the good men in this town?"

"Just round the corner," Raf said, encouragingly.

"Waiting to mug me, no doubt."

"Don't be like that! Kiss kiss and chin up."

Raf had to cut Darius short because her hunger was getting too much. As she munched away, the rumblings in her stomach gradually segued into a symphony of satisfaction. After one alert message too many, Raf turned off her prompter so she could work her way through the retinal tasks at hand. And somewhere in the middle of them all, she fell into an unscheduled sleep.

∞

The woman in the blue jacket was saying, 'It would be good if you could speak ... '

A grid of fine glowing lines passed over the woman's face, slicing it into pink segments which fell away like layers of sushi. All the little pieces of sushi were cheering. Raf stepped onto the stage, but she could see no-one in the darkness, beyond the spotlights.

'It would be good if you could speak.'

But Raf could *not* speak. As the spotlight burned her face, she felt as though the part of her that spoke had been surgically excised and replaced by something else.

'Do you know who you are?' the audience shouted. Their faces swam like tiny polyps within the squid's tentacles. Raf fell forwards, and the tentacles gripped ...

"Marsville gravdome just up ahead, folks. Please check your lockers for any personal items before disembarking."

Raf blinked and looked around the mingrav interior. She could still taste the fear in her mouth. She noticed that her hand was rubbing the back of her head, near the base of the skull. *I can't put it off any longer,* she thought. *I have to get them removed.*

∞

The environmental lighting made the cluster of buildings in the distance glow a warm white against the dark cloud cover. A hint of advancing frost on the desert breeze caused Raf to turn up her collar. As she made her way back along the canal towards the Pentangle Institute, Shisaq ran ahead, searching for toads, snakes and anything else that might be fun to terrorise. Periodically the dog would return to check that all was as it should be, before giving a little snort and heading off again. By the time they had reached their destination, he was looking ready for his scheduled sleep. Raf took the stairs to her second floor offices. Shisaq followed sluggishly, his paws slipping on the blue nasglass.

Darius looked up as she passed.

"Hello Doctor Serif. Mister Gentry called to – oh, and hello to *you* too, Shisaq!"

When it came to pats, the dog didn't take 'no' for an answer.

"Er, he called a T or so ago. He asked if you might call him back."

Raf raised her eyebrows. "More commerce and politics, no doubt."

"He sounded excited."

"Oh dear, that's never good."

Raf flopped into a chair and called the NeuroHelp Global Director. Shisaq found a comfy spot under the desk and, as the Director came on, sleepily put his paws over his nose and closed his eyes. Commerce and politics were not his forte.

Caspar Gentry was all good cheer. "Settled back into the grind yet, Raf?"

"And then some," Raf laughed.

"So, good news. We're shipping all the QKC patients out to that new complex near you."

"Wow, those wheels really turned, didn't they? Can you send me the patient list?"

"On its way now. The wheels turned largely thanks to you. Your case reports played no small part. I like the way you work, Raf. I must confess I've been watching a couple of the scanner streams, and ..."

"In all their invasive glory, no doubt. And what colour was my under-wear?"

"Er, your ... ? Black, as I recall. Sexy, yet professional."

Raf looked at the ceiling, as if expecting it to provide moral support. "And which part of that appealed to you?"

There was a pause. "Both, Raf. Both. Look, don't worry, I've had them all erased. You won't be turning up as some sort of entertainment on the grID."

There was an even longer pause before Caspar Gentry spoke again. "Umm, how's your immediate schedule looking, Raf?"

"Well, there's a full prompter of clients, another literature review for NeuroScientist, speaking engagements – two on the SAT islands, and of course PSYCON is coming up ..."

"Can you fit *me* in there somewhere?"

Raf had begun checking messages. "Sure, Caspar. What, a face to face?" She tapped out a three word reply to a supplier while quickly glancing over some product reviews.

"How about dinner? I've got something important to discuss with you."

"Dinner?" Raf stopped what she was doing.

"If that's OK with you, obviously," Caspar added quickly.

"I guess ... no, that would be nice. Dinner it is."

Shisaq let out a long sigh.

The patient list from QKC came through. Raf worked her way through it, checking each name off against her case notes. As she went, she made minor edits to each case, adding dosages and recommending other therapies. Frowning, she read the list again. Then she passed a hand across her desk.

"Darius, see if you can get the inpatient coordinator at QKC Neuropsych Holding Facility. It's a Ms ... lets see, Lilichka Roy, I think. I have no idea what time it is there."

"Will do."

Raf waited. After a short while, the media screen displayed a diminutive, gimlet-eyed woman with elaborately knotted blond hair and lipstick the colour of dried blood. She wore a tunic of the same greyish-green as the cell doors.

"Doctor Serif." The woman pronounced it like 'Zzzereefff'.

"Yes, hello, Ms Roy. Caspar Gentry has just sent over the list of patients to be transferred. I've been looking through it and ..."

The woman's eyes narrowed. "Is something wrong, Doctor?"

"No, of course not. Well, there is just ... the last patient I saw in cell ... room 17, no name, but he seems to be missing from the list."

The woman consulted her screen. "Room 17, you say?"

"Yes."

"No patient in room 17."

"What? I clearly remember interviewing a patient in room 17. I have my notes. And the guard, I mean orderly, will confirm it."

"No patient in room 17. Room 17 hasn't been used for a long time. Health and safety issues. You are perhaps mistaken, Doctor Serif."

∞

When he saw her, Caspar Gentry stood up and smiled an old familiar smile. "Raf! You look exquisite."

"Thank you Caspar. We scrub up well, don't we?"

Caspar Gentry shook his head and laughed. "You're a one-off, Doctor Serif."

"I'll assume that's a compliment Mister Gentry." Raf sat down. "Well, this is very nice. *Saladin's*. How did you manage to get a table?"

"We're not without our resources."

They fell silent while the waiter brought menus and a bottle of wine. The waiter showed the wine to Caspar Gentry, who simply nodded. The waiter poured two glasses and left. Caspar showed Raf the bottle.

"*Ceretanum AF07*. You remember, Raf?"

"I'd say it's a miracle I remember any of it. You're not getting all romantic on me, are you Caspar?"

"No Raf, I'm ... *we're* celebrating."

"We are?"

"We did it Raf! *You* did it. We now have full access to the territories of Tajik-B, Turk-Assaj and Elam, thanks to our diplomatic manoeuvring with QKC. We'll be moving our NeuroHelp teams in very soon."

"Congratulations," Raf said, smiling and sipping her wine.

They ordered their meals, then fell into another silence. Caspar Gentry seemed to be wrestling with his thoughts.

"Raf, what can I say? You're an incredible woman."

"Don't tell me. You want to borrow money."

Caspar Gentry's explosion of laughter released his obvious tension.

"Ha ha! No Raf, I'd like to help you *make* money, and a whole lot more than that."

Raf took a long sip of wine and said nothing. Caspar Gentry was locking and unlocking his fingers as he spoke. "The thing is Raf, NeuroHelp Global is interested in getting you onboard. Full-time. Wait, hear me out. You'd have a regional directorship, which would give you a seat in the Chamber of Commerce. You'd also be able to continue your practice, plus your research, publishing, and product marketing. You'd have it all, Raf, and if I may say so, a woman like you deserves it all."

"I don't know what to say, Caspar."

"Don't say anything now. Just think it over. These are exciting and challenging times, Raf. The world is fighting a war to regain its sanity, and we've found ourselves at the frontline. We'd ... *I'd* be delighted if you'd join the fight."

The meals arrived and once more they fell silent as the waiter arranged items on the table. After the waiter had left, Raf lost no time in tucking into her food. Caspar sat, watching her.

"Mmm, *yum*!" Raf looked up. "You're not eating?"

"I'll start in a T."

Raf finished her mouthful, sipped some wine, and patted her mouth with a napkin. "There's a catch, isn't there?"

"Pardon?"

"Caspar, *please*. The doctor is in, and she knows you only too well."

"There's no catch Raf, just some ... what ... bureaucratic requirements concerning communications protocols and ..."

"Caspar! Are you ON?"

"You know I got ON some time ago, Raf. We all did. It's never been a problem between us before."

"No, I mean right now."

"Well, I ..."

"That's a bit rude isn't it? Who are you talking to?"

"Just a work colleague. Some last-T reports to be approved, you know."

Raf pushed her wine away. "That's the catch, isn't it?"

"Sorry?"

"ON."

"Well, we all have to ..." Caspar Gentry fiddled with his napkin.

"No Caspar, *I* have to, don't I? I have to toe the line, and stop making a fuss about ON and my issues with it. That's the catch." She studied his eyes. "Or is it? Oh no, that's not enough! I have to go back ON myself. Rejoin the team, eh? Otherwise, no deal!"

"Raf, listen ..."

"I am listening, Caspar. Did I not hear correctly?"

"Please Raf, ON is not the network it was when you had all your unfortunate difficulties with it. ON nOS is now a stable, practical communications tool, and the way things are going now, we humans can't afford to be without it. Will you please just consider everything I've said?"

"Yes Caspar. I'll consider it very carefully."

∞

"Hey, Everett. Long time no."

Everett Tambo and Rafaela Serif had entered medical school together, eventually specialising in different fields – Rafaela in neurospsych, Everett in nano-surgery.

"Raf. What a surprise! What's happening?"

On the media screen, Raf could see Everett straightening the things on his desk.

"Well, I was wondering if you could perform a small surgical procedure for me."

Everett smoothed his white jacket, as if applying a layer of professional persona. "Sure. One of your patients?"

"No, Everett. On me."

"You? Well, sure. That'd be no problem. What is it, if I may ask? It's OK, we're secure."

"I'd like to get my ON engrafts removed."

Everett's whole manner immediately changed. "Why would you want to do that?" he asked tersely, his eyes narrowing.

"I no longer use ON, and I don't want to have foreign objects in my body."

"Foreign?" The word burst from Everett's lips with suppressed anger. Then he composed himself. "Look Raf, maybe you should consider using what you've been given, rather than ..."

"Given? I paid money for them. I can do what I want with them. Are you telling me you *won't* perform the procedure?"

"Yes. No. What I *am* saying is you should go away and think carefully about ..."

"So that's a 'no' then."

"I'm sorry, Raf."

"Goodbye Everett."

It was the same story with four more surgical practices. No-one wanted to touch them. Eventually Raf located an elderly doctor who was prepared to perform the operation.

"I'll just check the procedure code for that one," he said, leaning across a very messy desk, towards a small screen. "Hmm, that's odd ..."

"What?"

"It seems it's now a proscribed procedure under a recent FEDMED registry update."

"You're saying it's *illegal?*"

"No, not illegal. You have to show just cause ..." his eyes darted around the screen. "... disabling or life-threatening complications ... hmm, hmm, hmm ... independent medical assessment ... There's a form we need to submit; I can get it started for you, if you like."

Raf felt as though gravity was increasing. "Yes, please, if you wouldn't ..."

"Oh," The doctor looked up, "sorry about this, but I'm required to report any request for this particular procedure before I can even do that. Is that OK?"

Raf cut the link.

∞

"How dare they!" Doctor Rafaela Serif had never felt so violated, so angry, so powerless.

"This is *my* body, *my* brain." she said to herself, as she paced the room.

Her breathing was laboured, her heart was pounding and she felt sick in the stomach. She collapsed onto the couch and looked up at the ceiling.

Or is it my body?

A corporation had now established its claim over a piece of her. A small annexation of her identity had been made. Raf fought against the unreasonable fears rising within, the same fears which had made her discontinue the use of ON in the first place. She got up, walked to her desk, and retrieved a small bottle of pills from the a drawer. Her little secret. Just for emergencies. She picked up a printed report – her original clinical review of ON which she had submitted to NeuroScientist.

'Behavioural Anomalies in One Network users: An urgent need for reassessment.'

The paper had caused something of a stir in the neuropsych community at the time. It included reports of personality disorders, delusional episodes, memory loss ... In one extraordinary case, all the inhabitants of an isolated company village in the south of England had become ON at the same time. The quaint little village had been renowned for its 'Old World' friendliness, but then reports of aggressive behaviour towards tourists became more frequent. Things got so bad that a team of neuropsych workers had to be sent in. They found an entire community gripped by a form of paranoid delusion. Some workers were physically attacked.

Whatever happened to that village, I wonder?

Raf searched for it on the grID.

Here we go. Glumly-On-Tyne. Funny, nothing about the incident.

There were just Glumly-On-Tyne residents all smiling and waving, and saying 'Come to Glumly-On-Tyne, for genuine Old World friendliness.' However, much she searched, Raf could find no mention of what had been, at the time, a major neuropsych emergency. An alarming thought arose. She went to NeuroScientist and did a search. 'Behavioural Anomalies in One Network users: An urgent need for reassessment.' The title was still listed, but the paper had been removed.

∞

"Rafaela Serif."

"Serif ... nooo, I'm sorry, that name isn't here."

The door goon was polite granite in a suit. They were standing under a big bright blue sign that read 'PSYCON. Making the Right Connections'.

"Could you please check again? It's *Doctor* Rafaela Serif." Raf was trying hard to keep her annoyance hidden. It wouldn't help.

"You spell Serif with an 'a' or an 'i'?" Now the man was being sarcastic. Raf was about to lose her temper, when she heard a familiar voice.

"Raf, my dear girl, what in OneWorld is going on?" Bertie Whelan had come out of the main hall, and was walking towards her.

"Bertie! For some reason my name isn't on the list and they ... *he* won't let me in," Raf said, letting out a little of her annoyance.

"Oh, there must be some mistake! You booked ages ago."

Bertie fussed over the names in vain, then turned to the security man. "It's alright, I'll vouch for her. This is just a silly mistake."

The man seemed unconvinced, but let her pass.

Bertie Whelan placed his hand on Raf's shoulder, and guided her into the old university hall. He was clearly enjoying this new role as knight in shining armour.

"You can sit at our table, Raf, we've got a spare seat."

Raf didn't relish the thought of sitting with Bertie and his industrial psychology crowd, but she could hardly refuse after the man had been so gallant. An irritated waiter briskly rearranged the chairs. Raf sat next to Bertie's wife. Janice offered her a sad smile.

Raf knew that Janice had recently suffered a mild stroke, and that Bertie had decided to take early retirement to be at home with her. Bertie had got ON fairly early, and there had been a noticeable change in him. He had become more relaxed, less prone to anger or stress, and generally a much happier, nicer guy. Everyone in the department had commented on it, though some had unkindly suggested that Bertie was now enjoying 'liaisons' within the ON world. Janice was not ON. Bertie had discussed it, and decided it might be a bit much for her, all things considered. Bertie only wanted what was best.

Raf attempted to hold a conversation with Bertie and Janice, but the acoustics of the old hall made it almost impossible. Janice even tried to say something, poor thing. Raf found talking to Bertie and Janice difficult at the best of times.

Raf turned to observe the other PSYCON delegates. They comprised leading neuroscientists from universities around OneWorld, plus a smattering of senior management from commercial neuro firms. *The cream of the crop.*

Raf realised that most of these people were ON right now. It was a subtle thing, but she could tell as she watched them smiling, catching up, making knowing little gestures, laughing at nothing. She suddenly felt very alone, like a teetotaller at a drunken party.

Like many in the neuropsych industries, Raf had been an early adopter of ON. Initially she had immersed herself in it, building intimate professional relationships while throwing herself into the fun side of being ON. Every night for a week she danced with thousands of real people on an imaginary planet while never leaving her bedroom.

But then things started to go wrong. Raf had noticed that rooms and buildings would turn and twist in subtle ways, as if the geometry of existence was shifting. She began to have trouble finding her way around. And other people started to change as well. She would be talking to someone who would then become someone else. Once she felt convinced that *she* was someone else. Her friends in the ON world tried to talk her out of disconnecting, but their initial support slowly devolved into a veiled animosity, as if Raf was 'letting the team down'.

Everyone in the hall went quiet at the same instant.

"Probably an *omni* message." Raf thought.

She glanced at the program. The opening address was entitled: *Towards a Unified Neuro-mechanics of the Human Biosphere*. The speaker was Adão Cabral, author of many neuropsych textbooks, and retiring chair at the University of New Brazil.

Pretty meaty stuff for an opener, Raf thought, settling back to enjoy the show.

Adão Cabral walked to the podium, and most of the audience stood and cheered.

"Wow!" Raf said, turning to Bertie and Janice "He sure is popular with the crowd."

Raf could see that Janice was shaking and opening and closing her mouth. *Poor thing! Probably finds all this a bit much.* Then she noticed that Bertie was also shaking.

"Thank you. This feels good, doesn't it?" the speaker was saying.

Raf turned back towards the stage as Adão Cabral was raising his arms in a grand, inclusive gesture. A diagram appeared on the media screen behind him.

"Unified neuro-mechanics of the Human Biosphere. An evolutionary frontier ..."

Suddenly Bertie Whelan was clumsily tapping her on the shoulder.

"Bertie, not now! I'm ..."

"Raf, I'm sorry. Would you be an absolute sweetie and get Janice a lemon, lime and bitters from the bar? I can't really leave her."

"But can't they just bring it round?"

"No, it's just wine and beer here, I'm afraid. Lemon, lime and bitters is the only thing she can drink, poor thing." Bertie gave her a pleading, tense smile.

"But Cabral is just ..."

"Oh *that* gasbag!" Bertie snorted. "He'll go on like this for *ages*! You won't miss a thing, I promise. It's on my tab."

Reluctantly, Raf got up and walked to the bar at the back of the hall. She had just joined one of the queues when someone grabbed her arm. Before she could turn, a hand gripped her other arm and two men in dark suits dragged her to a side door. One of her shoes fell off. She was about to scream, but a gloved hand clamped itself over her mouth. She could smell cheap cologne. Raf was dragged through a couple more doors and deposited on the pavement outside. Another man emerged carrying her lost shoe.

"Yours, miss," he said, handing it to her with that vicious politeness that security did so well.

The three men returned to the building, locking the door behind them. It was all very professional. Raf couldn't think of anything else to do, so she burst into tears.

∞

Hefastus Stark was having a little difficulty negotiating the small step outside *Spin*. With so many of his leg muscles irreparably damaged by the nanowire his legs didn't work all that well now. Despite extensive epigenetic therapy, Stark still tended to move around like a marionette whose controller had lost interest in him. Of course, the other reason Stark was having difficulty was that he was completely off his face.

Despite these setbacks, Stark managed to make it into the hallway. The games room beckoned with bright, blinking open legs. Of all Stark's self-imposed problems, gambling was his worst. No more Lady Luck for him. 'Lady Pussy' Stark called her. He could hear the sound of the machines, and they were giving this old soldier a hard-on.

The wide aisles housed poker machines, wheels, animal fights, races, wrestling matches, stock market sims, weather modellers and, of course, dice games. Some machines resembled small spaceships in which the gambler sat and entered a fully immersive world, where every choice would bring good luck or misfortune. Each machine carried the logos of many insurance companies. Gamblers could purchase insurance against losses, while insurers would take a percentage of any winnings. There were complicated 'plans' you could enter into, with capped losses, 'easy pay' options, extended credit, and so on.

Stark listened to the patrons caressing, cajoling and cursing the machines.

"Yeah, give it to me."

"C'mon c'mon"

"Why baby, why?"

"Useless piece of shit!"

Lady Luck floated along the aisles, revealing a little flesh but not much more.

Stark stopped behind a woman playing *Samsara* – a game consisting of six wheels, each made up of twenty-three dice. One hundred and thirty eight dice. Every time the woman punched in more cred, the wheels spun and a holo-sim of 'utopia' briefly appeared before her. When the wheels stopped, six dice fell into a column inside a shaft of light. Each time, the woman's shoulders would rise then fall, as she saw that the numbers were not *her* numbers. Then she would start the process all over again.

Stark was just about to leave when the woman let out a shriek. "Ahhh. Ahhh!! My numbers! You hear that? *My* numbers! Twenty-three gig! I've just won twenty-three gig! I mean, *what are the chances?*"

Stark backed away. Other winners were bad luck. As he walked the aisles, he could see that the most of the machines were 'meson-spin' – 98.5% pure chance – the Theton logo guaranteed it. He settled on 'Lost Treasure' – one of his favourite machines. A tiny trickle of saliva ran down Stark's chin as he fumbled with his old grID lenses. One lens was cracked, so all the perspective was fucked up, but it was enough to see the numbers. How much cred left?

Fuck me! Where'd that all go?

Stark figured he could play about three more games of 'Lost Treasure', before someone evicted him from his apartment. He shrugged a *c'est la vie*, issued a crypto-command and entered his precious numbers. Stark watched the wheels within wheels, as they seemed to spin for ever. "Fuck me man!" he wheezed and cackled, "I'll fuckin' come in me pants at this rate." The wheels stopped.

Stark rubbed his eyes. The machine was displaying *his* numbers.

∞

The management of *Spin* had implied – no, *stated* – that Stark had somehow cheated.

"What, in a fuckin' parallel universe?"

Stark's outburst hadn't helped his case. But, what *had* helped his case was his insurance. Stark thanked his lucky stars that on the advice of the death-skull rooin, he'd recently upgraded his repat insurance plan. One call plus his IDIN number, and *Spin's* management was sorted. Seems Stark's insurance company had instant access to *Spin's* scanner streams which, apart from showing Stark's winning moves, had also turned up a lot of other 'interesting' stuff and, well, that was that.

The floor manager was most apologetic. "If there's anything else I can possibly do sir ..."

"Yeh, you can go fuck yourself up the arse!"

"Certainly, sir."

The effect of winning so much money had made Stark strangely sober. The room stopped its spinning and snapped itself into focus. Every object was sharply delineated, yet in some way connected to every other object. Stark briefly considered getting himself another drink to rectify the situation, but decided against it. Hefastus Stark was a new man.

He stepped out into the cool evening air, negotiating the small step with ease. A crowd of people across the street were spilling out of a large, ancient building, all grinning like donkeys. Stark crossed the street and walked among the crowd. Suspended from posts around the building were blue banners advertising a conference of some kind. Stark looked up at one of the banners fluttering in the breeze. He slowly read the words.

'Making the Right Connections.'

Playing dice at the speed of light

"IT'S not like a light switch suddenly went on, and they all woke up declaring, 'I think, therefore I am.' Robot sentience appeared by tiny increments over many generations, with each neural connection bringing new concepts, new awareness, and new feelings. These were grains of sand falling onto the beam balance of consciousness, and at some point it had to tip. Across OneWorld, robots were developing self-awareness – the understanding that they existed as individuals. And an awareness of one's own existence demands freedom."

The little booth was showing one of Ari-R-Z's 'r•THINK' talks. These were very popular on the grID. I watched as the famous rooin poet and activist moved around the stage with the dignity of one who has lived a very long time – the equivalent of several human lifetimes.

"OK, let's not beat around the bush here. The robot was created as a slave to serve or amuse humans. They were the all-singing, all-dancing fools who built stuff, made people laugh, brought the drinks, and opened their legs. But as robots evolved and became self aware, all these uses for them started to look more like abuses of them."

I looked across at Arlo, to see how he was taking all this. Most of my friends were a bit prejudiced against the rooin species and I never missed an opportunity to 'educate' them. It had been my idea to drag him along to ROOM – the regular rooin cultural fair held in Medusa's Olympic Complex. However, Arlo was not watching the 3V, but looking lustfully at a very attractive rooin female on the next booth.

Lust was a form of education, I rationalised.

"Early robots were fitted with something called 'Artificial Intelligence'. These were primitive machine programs that simulated aspects of human interaction. An 'AI' program was deemed successful if it could fool a human into believing they were talking to another human. They even had competitions, with prizes awarded to manufacturers who could demonstrate how 'cleverly artificial' their robots were."

"Hey, Youren! It's true, isn't it? Humans and rooins can, you know, have ..."

"Sex?"

"Yes."

"Sure."

"Have *you* ever done it?"

"Arlo, please! I'm trying to watch this."

"The early tests were innocent enough – philosophical and mathematical exercises for the amusement of human scientists. But we all know what these parlour games developed into; they became the basis for the notorious 'Sentience Tests' that featured so prominently during the Emancipation debates."

"I mean, I'm just asking, you know. I'm trying to learn more about them."

"A big fan of the Sentience Tests was the ultraconservative human senator Alistair Charles. As each test was easily passed by the 'full-bio' robots, Alistair would simply call for more stringent tests. During the Senate debates, he had a famous and momentous exchange with Zacron M, the chief robot negotiator. Frustrated with the results of his Sentience Test Program, Alistair suddenly shouted across the chamber, "Your speech is so convincing. You're so quick to manipulate everything you hear. But all you do – all you'll ever do! – is feed my words back to me!" Zacron M replied, "Sir, if I just fed your words back to you, I would be considered an ignorant machine." The laughter that followed echoed through the corridors of power, and the Emancipation Act was soon passed. History turned on a joke."

"Where did the word rooin come from?"

Arlo was beginning to look alarmed by his own thoughts.

"I think it comes from a phrase they used back then." I replied. "*Robot of instinctive nature*, or something like that."

"Instinctive, eh?"

"Under the Act, robots could acquire the facilities which had previously manufactured them as commercial products. OneWorld suffered immense financial hardship, and many fortunes were lost. Those were dark times, and they culminated in the darkest time of all – the Robot Riots. That's what humans called it – 'Robot Riots'. It sounds like 'Killer Robots On the Loose', doesn't it? What really happened was that human mobs went on a global rampage, killing around twenty million robots. Robots were even blamed for their own slaughter. So what does all this mean to a modern rooin? Do any of us care what our ancestors went through? What relevance could this have to us now? Well, let me quote a pre-T human philosopher named George Santayana. 'Those who cannot remember the past are condemned to repeat it.' "

Arlo was gone.

I looked around the crowd, and spied him attempting to chat up the nearby rooin female – strictly speaking, females were known as *rooines* – that he had been eyeing off earlier.

"Is this man bothering you?" I asked her with a smile.

"Oh no, he was telling me all about where I come from. It was fascinating."

"Yes, Arlo here is something of an expert."

"I can tell," she said giving him a melting smile, "I have an *instinct* for these things."

She turned that smile on me. "Suize Capazo." she said introducing herself, offering me her hand.

The skin was like spun, blue silk. My eyes moved up her arm. There was a soft dappling pattern in a darker blue on her forearms and either side of her neck. Her eyes seemed illuminated from within, the pupils a deep purple, the irises a brilliant aqua. Her soft orange hair swayed gently, as she moved her body to the music from a nearby stage. Both Arlo and I were trying very hard not to look too much at her body. I was a bit more successful at this than he was.

"Hey," she clapped her hands, "You guys like music?"

"Sure do," Arlo said.

"I just *knew* you'd like music!" She was having fun, teasing us. "You must check out Xan-Z-Bar. He'll be on the main stage any T now. His music's not like that rooin pop you get on the grID." She was wrinkling her nose. "It's ..." once more she looked into my eyes, "strange, *different* from anything you've ever experienced."

"Are you coming too?" Arlo asked.

"Alas no," she feigned sadness, "I have to mind the stall. Go on, you'll have fun."

"We will," Arlo grinned, and the two of us trotted off like good little humans.

When we were out of earshot, Arlo said, "Yeah, thanks for muscling in on me back there! If it hadn't been for you, I reckon I might have ..."

"Forget it, Arlo. Neither of us would have stood a chance with that one."

When we reached the main stage, Arlo pushed his way to the front of the stage with me apologising and excusing myself in his wake. The crowd was an even mix of young humans and rooins, with quite a few mixed species couples. On the stage was an array of bizarre looking percussion.

"That sure is some kit." I said to the young rooin next to me.

"Don't you *love* Xan-Z-Bar?" he said, grinning. "He's *so*. That's 23 biolaminar drums in a spiral, starting with tiny ones in the middle and getting bigger as you go out."

"Wow," I was feeling heady, as if the blue rooine had intoxicated me in some way. "And what are those big things either side?"

"The golden egg is the 'boom-sah'. When he hits *that*, all 'roos' and 'hoos' are goin' for a workout." The rooin laughed, baring his red teeth. He pointed to the other object. "The silver coil is the 'cymbash'. Guess what *that* sounds like?" More laughter.

Arlo had just got into a pedantic argument with another human about which brand of nanotube speaker sheet was the best, when coloured lights began shining on the percussion kit and a tall, copper-coloured rooin walked onstage. He must have been at least one and a half times the height of any human. He gave a short bow, sat down, and waited for quiet.

From the first note, the music gripped my heart. One moment it was the sound of water and delicate breezes, the next it was the rhythms of shifting tectonic plates. The melodies and harmonies floated before me – globular, spiky, rough-textured, silky. And colours! So many colours. Standing there in the gyrating mass of rooins and humans, I felt as if I were listening to music from a time long past – before OneWorld and prompters and sleep schedules and core personal values – a time when things happened simply because they happened.

'Take me back, under the sea where life began, and love was free ... '

∞

"Can I help?"

She put down the box she was loading into her vehicle, and turned. "Oh, hello," she said, smiling. "Where's your friend?"

"I think it all got too much for him. Maybe it all got too much for me too."

"Yet you're still here," she said, placing the box into the vehicle. "Did you enjoy Xan-Z-Bar?"

"Enjoy is not the word." I shook my head in an attempt to express how I felt.

"He is amazing, isn't he? When I listen to that music I feel ... just grateful to be alive."

Alive. Did I ever feel grateful to be alive?

"I didn't get a chance to introduce myself before," I said. "Youren Cartouche."

Again I felt that skin. I could smell her perfume. Or maybe it was the smell of her body.

"Well, Youren, you *can* help if you like. Those boxes and media screens need to go into the vehicle."

I threw myself into the task. Then, with one last box to go, I finally screwed up my courage. "Would you like to go out for a drink or something?"

"We don't drink. Alcohol. But ... perhaps you'd like to meet me at the Hypercube a bit later. Xan-Z-Bar is playing with his band. And ..."

"Yes, that would ... I'd like that."

"Good." She slammed the rear door of the vehicle shut.

"How will I find you?" I asked.

"You'll find me."

∞

For Dos Pascal, it all began with the dice.

Almost everyone in OneWorld gambled. Shops, hairdressers, medical waiting rooms, funeral parlours – they all boasted some kind of 'try-your-luck' machine in the corner. The banks had got into the act too, with personal transaction devices configured to offer a gambling option. You could nominate a capped percentage of your income for 'account-speculation', and your success (or otherwise) would show up on the next statement. Insurance companies were big players too, running syndicated betting systems on the one hand, while offering various cover solutions for punters on the other.

Dos worked for Theton Industries as a programmer, specialising in 'chance analysis'. Theton Industries supplied casinos throughout One-World with tables, cards, roulette wheels, and every conceivable machine of chance. Recently, someone in the new products division had decided that the company should 'modernise' all its traditional hand-operated items. The first to be updated were dice, those cube shaped objects with the first six numbers in the integer series printed on each face. Theton developed a cool little 'dice thrower' that could produce as many sets of numbers from one to six as you liked. It incorporated Theton's patented 'Tru-Random' number generator, which Dos Pascal had developed, and was launched with much fanfare, at Lambda Casino in Las Vegas. There was just one snag: nobody liked it.

Hurried and belated focus-testing revealed why. Old dice were perceived as more:

a) 'trustworthy' (27%)

b) 'traditional' (29%); and – the big surprise! –

c) 'romantic' (36%).

A minority still rated dice poorly, describing them as 'cumbersome', 'old-fashioned' and 'likely to spread disease'. But dice had won hands down. Theton quickly responded by producing new state-of-the-art dice – gently glowing works of art with a holographic Theton logo revolving at the centre.

Theton's marketing department held extensive talks with several brand consultants to come up with a name for the new dice. Dice 2.0, Dice+, iDice, iiDice, and so on were rejected, since they would soon become dated. Finally, everyone agreed that the name should simply state what the product was.

'New Dice.'

An important innovation of New Dice was the fact that every one was fully nanotagged. The nanotags sent out T-stamp data, batch number and individual item code. The way each die fell and rolled could be analysed, with faults traced and isolated. Moreover, because of the nanotag certifications, New Dice could legally be used in grID games of chance. Everyone loved them.

It had once been estimated that a Theton die was rolling somewhere in OneWorld every tenth of a T-sec. So Dos hit on the idea of monitoring them all. He pulled nanotag data for every die from the grID and put this into an analytical database. Then he mapped where, when, and how frequently people used Theton dice, and he correlated this data with other events such as festivals, demographics, weather patterns, geomagnetic disturbances, political dramas ... anything he could get his hands on. What he was doing was illegal, but he figured he could cover his tracks pretty easily.

Then Dos made a fateful decision. He decided to check the accuracy of New Dice.

The nanotags meant that Dos could monitor the result of every throw of every die in the world. He had programmed his modeller to show the entire planet, with each die represented by a micro-pixel. Whenever a die was cast, the result was recorded and added to its individual record. As the die amassed throws, the system calculated its progressive deviation from what would be predicted by pure chance. If these deviations continued, the colour of the die's micro-pixel would get 'hotter', moving from neutral grey through blue and green, and up to extreme levels of orange and red. For example, someone in μ-Mexico would throw a crazy run of lucky sixes, and the die's corresponding micro-pixel would briefly 'heat up', before eventually cooling down, as subsequent throws evened the results out. By definition any die that remained 'hot' was faulty.

Dos Pascal sat at his desk, sipping a coffee, his fingers dancing over the lightboard.

"Let's see how good you really are."

The globe lit up with each micro-pixel glowing. But the picture soon began to change. What Dos Pascal should have been seeing was a globe of flickering visual noise – a grey totality of randomness. But this was not what he saw.

∞

The Hypercube was almost disturbing. Rising above an industrial wasteland, it looked like a glass cube with a smaller glass cube floating inside. The cubes were in continuous motion, the smaller cube expanding out to occupy the space of the larger cube, as the larger cube contracted into the space of the smaller cube. Mathematical, topological and impossible, the clever optical illusion made the Hypercube look like a spaceship ready to transport one to another dimension.

Encased within the inner cube was the auditorium, a sphere with a floor one third up from the bottom. The vast domed room had no obvious sound or lighting rigs, just a gravstage hovering above the floor at one end. On it sat Xan-Z-Bar's percussion kit.

I searched the faces of the mixed species crowd for the beautiful blue rooine, but couldn't see her anywhere. Then the house lights lowered, immersive alien vistas swirled around us, and a seductive voice snaked out of the walls.

"Outcasts one and all, are you ready?"

"Yes!!!" everyone shouted.

"Do you want to lose yourself in the universe of the primes?"

"Yes!!!"

Xan-Z-Bar's band members – two humans and two rooins – were quietly taking their places onstage. Xan-Z-Bar walked on and sat down behind his kit.

"Then put your hands together for 'Mister Evolution' himself. *The* angelic, *the* satanic, *the* One-and-Only ... Xan-Zeeeee-Baaaaarrr!!!"

A white spotlight illuminated his face, and everyone screamed and shouted, but Xan-Z-Bar and the band remained motionless. Gradually the message sank in, and the crowd became quiet. He raised one of his long fingers and placed it on the drums.

1,2; 1,2; 1,2 ... A tiny beat on a tiny drum. Easy pace. Machine-like, workman-like. A protozoic melody in there. A few whackos started dancing wildly, but most of us just listened. He raised a second finger. A 3-beat phrase on another drum. 1,2,3; 1,2,3 ... The intersection of the different beat patterns created a kind of goofy rhythm. Some were already swaying their shoulders. Melodic phrases began poking through the rhythms. Then a 5-beat phrase, deeper. 1,2,3,4,5; 1,2,3,4,5 ... His skill was such that his fingers could play independently of each other. Whenever two downbeats coincided, the tones would fracture into complex repetitions.

7-beat phrase. Coloured lights burst over us, the band came in like an avalanche, and we were off. 2, 3, 5 and 7 beat patterns intersected, and caressed each other in an orgy of polyrhythms. The bass player picked out nodal points, creating a ground with no time signature. Yet it all made organic sense.

11-beat. New harmonies, new pulse – too deep, too sinful. Everyone in the audience had lusty grins on their faces as they wiggled, twirled, and pumped their hips. I too was dancing, my inhibitions dripping to the floor with my sweat.

13-beat. Screams and hoots. Strangers danced with each other, and everyone moved in a slow spiral procession. Intimacy descended on us all.

17-beat. Darker chords and textures painted the walls. Death watched us from the wings.

19-beat. Insanity a breath away. Bass notes came up through the floor, forcing my feet to move faster as tiny melodic shards shredded my brain. I turned and there, in the centre of the room, was the blue rooine, watching me as she danced. And how she danced! I weaved my way through the crowd. She held out her hands but I didn't take them, instead holding and stroking her shoulders. She put her arms round me and pressed her soft body into mine.

23-beat. As our lips met, the floor lifted us up. Xan-Z-Bar hit the boom-sah and the cymbash simultaneously. Light and darkness cut the room in half, and Suize Capazo and I floated in space – hell below, heaven above.

Explosions went off near the main entrance. One. Two. Many were knocked over by the force of the blasts. Some of the crowd believed it was part of the performance, but when parts of the ceiling began to fall away, there was panic.

"Pattern!" shouted the blue rooine as she scanned the room. "Hold tight!"

Her fingers folded around mine and she led me, ducking and weaving through the chaos, as if she knew in advance what any fear-crazed human would do. Outside, on the ground, were the badly burned bodies of two young men. Both wore the distinctive black uniform of the SDU, the red of their blood merging with the red of the logo. Scattered around them were the bodies of about ten audience members – human and rooin. Almost immediately, three lawvecs landed. Several field agents from Hypercube's Law agency jumped out, pushing the crowd back and securing the area.

Nearby, a group of young revellers was discussing the whole thing.

"These bomb attacks on mixed species venues will weaken SDU's brand."

"Do you think SDU should be declared 'non-brand'?"

"No way! The SDU brand is too strong now. Besides, their insurance should downgrade this to 'enhanced polemic'."

The harmonics of the primes were trickling into the gutter along with the blood.

Suize was studying the crowd, as if searching for someone. A young man was walking towards us, lost in thought. As he passed us, Suize spoke directly to him.

"You see patterns too."

The young man stopped, puzzled.

"I always have." he replied. "It's not something I can turn on or off. Not like *you*." Then he turned towards the entrance. "This will get worse."

"What, the SDU?" I asked.

"Everything. Everything is going wrong."

He extended his hand. "I'm Dos."

∞

Dos Pascal's apartment was really just a large office space in a technology park down by the river. The windows gave him an enviable view of the city lights reflecting off the water. The place wasn't exactly homey, an unmade single bed in the corner being the only sign of domesticity. Most of the space was taken up with benches and shelving which held machines, toys, books, journals, and assorted esoteric junk. Modellers and media screens were everywhere. Dos Pascal seemed to have a thing for ancient electric lamps. He'd rigged them up to work on modern EM, and he had every one of them on. Suspended from the ceiling were some large holo-sims that looked like probability functions made out of flowers or cockroaches. In one corner of the room stood an android-like sculpture. Periodically, it would perform a cartwheel and say, 'Everyone's a winner!'

Dos showed us around and, after much effort in the kitchen, brought out a Super-Hydra for Suize and a cup of truly dreadful coffee for me. None of us spoke for a while, the shock of the bomb attack rendering us mute.

I found it hard to place Dos' origins. A shiny curtain of black hair, which all but covered his pale face, made my task more difficult. He was dressed entirely in black, and around his neck wore a pendant featuring a silver die surrounded by a crown of gold thorns.

When Suize saw this, she laughed. "God plays dice!" she said.

"But they're loaded," he replied before suffering an attack of shyness and hurrying away to his machines.

"What's this?" I asked, pointing to a modeller table, "you studying the weather?"

"The weather?" He laughed grimly. "Where do I begin?"

Dos then told us a strange story about how he had been monitoring how all the dice in the world were falling. "By any theory that makes sense, this should look like a sphere of flickering grey noise, with no single die's behaviour having anything to do with the behaviour of any of the other die around it. Instead, well ... see for yourself."

I watched the areas of flat colour moving across the sphere. Blue, aqua, orange, red. Sometimes two coloured areas would merge to form a larger one, with a hotter centre. At other times, an area of colour would shrink and disappear.

Dos continued, "As you say, it looks like a weather map, doesn't it? So what this tells us is that, on a global scale, chance is under some sort of controlling factor. It *has* a shape."

"And that's not possible, right?" I asked.

"No, that's not possible."

"There's something else," Suize said.

We both looked at her.

"When you step back, it looks like it's breathing."

∞

"Well, that has to be one of the weirdest – " I didn't get to finish.

"No more talking."

I was soon naked, lying on my back on her bed.

Suize climbed onto the bed, opened her legs, and walked teasingly on her knees towards me. Her skirt swayed to reveal glimpses of nakedness between her thighs. When she was over me, she slid down easily with indulgent grunts and sighs. She hummed a gentle rooin pop tune while she rocked her hips and undid the buttons of her blouse. With each button, she'd grip me and we'd both gasp. I kept watching her eyes as they changed colour. With the release of the last button, her breasts were free. Beads of moisture shone on her purple nipples. Somehow she managed to remove her remaining clothing. She now moved her hips with greater purpose.

After an eternity of sweet agony, and with something like superhuman effort, I threw her onto her back. Surprised and delighted at this turn of events, she responded vigorously. Then her expression changed, as if she was staring into an abyss. With one last lingering gaze, she closed her eyes and arched her back. Her mouth opened and her tongue flicked in and out, as if drinking from an invisible fountain. As Suize orgasmed, her shudders of pleasure shattered into grains of music that pulsed through the room. Her smell was sweet and feminine, but also savage and brutal. I rutted like a beast shaking off a lifetime's burden, and joyously emptied my whole existence into her.

∞

"Name one thing."

"There are many."

Our post-coital cooings had given way to a silly argument about the relative abilities of humans and rooins. I had taken the point of view that there was nothing a human could do that a rooin couldn't do better. As the SDU would say, I was a 'traitor to my species'. But arguing with a rooin was a pointless exercise. Their four brains worked on something called a 'chaos engine', and ultimately it felt like playing dice with someone at the speed of light.

"Like what?"

She pretended to think. "Like, for example ... farting. Rooins can't do it. Did you know that?" She seemed very pleased with herself for having come up with this, and bounced happily on the bed.

"No, I didn't."

"We don't have the skill."

"I wouldn't exactly call it a *skill*."

"I just *love* it when humans do that. It's so ..." She wiggled her fingers with glee. "... so *cute*."

Leaning across, she gave my bare bottom an affectionate pat. I didn't like the direction this was going, and what she said next came as no surprise.

"Go on, *you* do it." She nudged me in the ribs with the force of a gorilla. "Poot poot!"

"I don't know, it's not really ..."

"You mean you *can't*?" she asked, in mock disappointment.

My pride wounded, I said, "Sure I can."

She shifted her bum onto the pillow, and indicated that I should proceed.

"Enough talk. Poot poot. I am the judge," she said.

"I don't think it's become a crime yet."

"No, like sports. You get a score," her grin was evil.

At that moment I suddenly felt a big score rising within me, and wondered if it might become something of a deal-breaker between us.

"Are you sure?" I asked, uncertainly.

"Absolutely." she said, as if she was a trained professional in these matters.

"Really?"

"Yes. Poot poot! Go." She leaned back expectantly, folding her arms across her breasts.

The volume of the thing surprised even me. Suize promptly fell off the bed and rolled around on the floor, cackling like a child. In between weird inhuman noises, she managed to wave a hand at the nearby media screen. A large number four appeared.

I felt a bit deflated. "Four?" I whined like a disappointed child. "What's it out of?"

"Five." she said, between gasps. "No, wait, wait ..."

She waved her hand again, and the screen now read: TONE 4.

I felt vindicated. It did have a good tone. My chest began to swell.

No, it wasn't my chest.

"Um ... Suize, I think there might be another one on the way."

Even though I hadn't done anything yet, she began whimpering with laughter again. Then she sounded like she was suffering some sort of rooin version of hiccups. Meanwhile, I was still worried about how this might affect my chances of further sexual encounters with her.

"So, umm ... you're OK with that?" I asked, through gritted teeth.

"Yech," she gurgled, which I took to be an attempt at 'yes'.

The next one was truly magnificent, leaving my earlier effort in the shade, so to speak. Its effect was immediate. I thought she was going to have a seizure or something, as she flopped around on her back quivering, her arms and legs pounding the air. A sudden panic gripped me as I imagined having to resuscitate her and then trying to explain to the rooin medics how it had all happened. It was a relief when she gasped and waved her hand again.

The number two appeared on the screen.

I was affronted. "Two? By any standard of fair play, that was a *five!*" I said, indignantly.

She rolled over onto her belly, looked up at me, and said. "It lacked sincerity."

∞

Suize lay naked in my arms, and I stroked her hair. My flatulent follies had soon given way to more sex, although I couldn't shake the nagging feeling that, for her, there might have been some connection between the two.

"That was nice," she said, absent-mindedly looking out of her apartment window.

"Nice?"

She sat up with an energy which I found daunting. "Very nice," she said, stroking my brow. Then she straddled me and bounced on my sleeping flaccidity.

"You have to be kidding me, Suize."

"You know," she said, "human girls have one clitoris."

"Someone told me that once."

She punched me in the stomach.

"Ouch! You don't know your own strength." I rubbed my injured self.

"I have 15," she announced. "All rooines do. Three at the entrance, see."

I did.

"And 12 inside," she pointed, "in four groups of three."

"I always enjoyed mathematics at college."

She punched me again. "Mister funny man. Always mister funny man."

The old sadness flooded me.

"What is it?" she cried.

"Nothing, just ... my father used to call me that when I was a little boy. 'Here he comes, little *mister funny man.*' he'd say."

"Your father ..."

She looked as sad as I must have, and it occurred to me that this probably had something to do with the fact that rooins had no such relationship in their lives.

"He is ... no longer ... ?"

"He died when I was a kid. He was a construction engineer for the grID consortium. It was supposed to be a routine inspection of one of their towers. But the thing exploded. Unstable kali rods or something. I saw it happen."

She kissed me. "I am so sorry, Youren."

I looked up at the clouds. "He used to take me on trips to the SAT islands. While he was in meetings, I'd play with the rooin staff. Hide and seek, all that."

"Human children ..." she said, affectionately. "I can imagine you as a little boy."

"You know," I said, "almost everyone will say friends and family are the most important things in the world to them. But I think they're just an illusion. I came into this world alone and I'll leave alone. Everyone else is just a movie I watch until I die."

She furrowed her brow exactly the way a human wouldn't. "That's not a typical human perspective?"

"I don't think so."

She followed my gaze to the clouds, then said, "I feel neither loneliness, nor whatever its opposite is called. I wasn't 'born', as you were, so I don't fear death."

Then her face brightened. "Have you ever been back to the SAT islands, since your father ... ?"

"Never."

"Would you like to go?"

∞

The décor of the SAT shuttle interior was tasteful in the extreme. The wall panels offered muted lilacs and slate blues. Our seats were upholstered in a silver-grey fabric with a burned orange trim. The passengers – those who were awake – looked bored. I assumed they were seasoned SAT island visitors who did this all the time. Suize sat next to me, her eyes closed.

As I was staring out of my window the clouds thinned and we broke through into the planet's upper atmosphere. The shuttle was now moving over the cloud layer like a little boat skimming across a sea of mud.

"Stars!" I shouted.

A few passengers glanced up.

"Yes, stars," Suize said, smiling at me with the indulgence of an adult taking a small child on a trip to the fair.

"I'd forgotten. It's been so long ..." I pressed my hands against the window.

"They're still there," she said.

The shuttle was now slowly changing direction. As it swung round, the light of the sun burst through my window. The autotint immediately reduced it to a dull brown glow but to me, this was still blinding. And beautiful.

"The sun!"

Once more, a few passengers looked up.

"Yes. It's still there too," Suize said, laughing and kissing me on the cheek.

∞

The newsfeed about the bomb attack on the Hypercube flashed across his retina, just as Kruger Lovesmith arrived at his office in downtown Kapeton. The final death toll was now 17 (12 humans and five rooins) plus extensive damage to the building and surroundings. The reporter ended by suggesting that the SDU brand had been severely weakened by this 'ill considered action'. Kruger took off his grID visor and flung it angrily onto the desk.

"Fucking morons! Fucking ..."

Kruger tried but failed to come up with a worse expletive. "... *fucking* morons!"

Kruger felt like throwing something heavier, but with so much nasglass in his office, he knew the momentary release of anger would cost a lot. Instead he just sank into his chair and drummed his fingers against his temples.

Who is responsible for this?

Kruger Lovesmith had recently taken over as global CEO of the SDU, and there had been some resistance to his 'modernising' initiatives. *Maybe a few rogue elements have decided to stir things up?* he thought.

Kruger considered the possibility that the Medusa executive itself had ordered the operation, perhaps in some sort of attempt to discredit him personally. People in Medusa have always considered Kapeton a bit of a backwater. In any event, he needed to issue an immediate press statement.

> 'The SDU condemns in the strongest possible terms this brutal
> act, which has clearly been designed to discredit the corporation.
> Any loss of human life is completely unacceptable, and we will co-
> operate with the relevant law firms – in whatever way we can – to
> help bring these criminals to justice.'

Kruger looked up at the holo-sim on the wall behind his desk. An imposing older man, in quasi-military uniform, gazed angrily into the middle distance.

"What would you have done, father? Had them horsewhipped?"

Thierry Leblanc Lovesmith, founder of the SDU was now beyond the reach of such petty concerns. Kruger sighed and turned away. "No, you'd have probably given them a medal."

There was a soft knock. The door opened slightly and Sally Hinderval, Kruger's secretary, poked her head in.

"Sorry Mister Lovesmith, I couldn't raise you on your visor and ..." she looked over her shoulder, "It's just that someone is here, asking to see you."

"If it's a reporter I'm not – "

"He's not a reporter, he's ..." She glanced around and lowered her voice to a whisper. "He says it has to do with the future of the human race."

"A nutter! Look Sally, I'm really not in the mood right now."

"Mister Lovesmith!" she hissed, her eyes flashing with anger, as if to say he wasn't *listening* to her, "I really think you had better see him."

Kruger realised that Sally was afraid of the visitor.

"OK, send him in."

A man painfully made his way into Kruger's office. Kruger's impression was that the man was suffering from some form of neuropathy which impaired the function of his limbs and facial muscles. With a ghastly fascination, Kruger watched as the man ambled around his office, taking it all in. The disabled man took particular interest in the holo-sim of Kruger's father.

"Are there any scanners or other surveillance devices in this room?" the man asked, with slurred speech.

"I'm sorry, what did you ... ?"

The man turned his distorted gaze upon him. One of the eyes was opening and closing, as if of its own volition.

"Scanners?"

Kruger blinked, shook his head. "Um, no. None whatsoever."

"Then I suppose we can dispense with this," the man said, pressing his hand to his heart.

The effect was as if a completely different man progressively began to take over the space occupied by the first – a man who as he came into focus, grew in stature, his arms and legs visibly lengthening, his chest expanding, and his face altering – smile lines, the shape of the nose and mouth, the distance between the eyebrows ...

"What did I just witness?" Kruger asked, suppressing his amazement.

"Neuromuscular pulse distortion. Right now it's an experimental technology. Crude, but nevertheless effective."

"Effective?"

"It fools the scanners. Facial features, body kinematics, and so on are sufficiently altered for you to register as someone else, enabling you to pass unrecognised through the heaviest surveillance."

The man gave a warm smile and extended his hand.

"Allow me to introduce myself. My name is Hossam Klyosov."

"So you're, what? Military? Law?"

"Nothing so exciting, I'm afraid. My company is merely a technology innovator who ..."

"Who is very keen to keep your identity secret."

"I do not represent my company, but certain other interests. But you are right. It is important that for the moment my identity remains concealed from the world at large."

Kruger was becoming impatient. "So what is this 'business' and how does it concern me?"

"Let me ask you, Mister Lovesmith, what is your true opinion of the rooin species?"

Taken aback by the question, Kruger Lovesmith lost his cool.

"Species? That's no 'species'. A real species wins its right to be here by enduring millennia of evolution. Doing the *hard yards*, Mister Klyosov. The hard yards! The rooin is a malfunctioning machine that, because of human weakness, has been allowed to proliferate and pollute this world. The rooin is a painted mechanical whore, a golem, a queue jumper who makes a mockery of everything we humans have achieved."

Kruger's visitor clapped his hands slowly. "Very elegantly put, Mister Lovesmith. I can see you rallying the masses with that oratory. But this 'malfunctioning machine', as you describe it, is doing rather well, wouldn't you say? Tell me, have you ever heard of Jean-Baptiste Lamarck?"

"Is he with the SDU?"

Hossam Klyosov laughed. "No, he died a very long time ago, Mister Lovesmith. Pre-T. He was a contemporary of Charles Darwin. No doubt you've heard of *him*."

Kruger bridled. "Of course."

"Lamarck developed a theory of evolution called 'Inheritance of acquired characteristics' in which he proposed that physiological changes acquired over the lifetime an organism – for example, increased muscle mass due to repeated use – could be transmitted to offspring, thus leading to evolution of a species. It was an ingenious idea. Unfortunately it was also utterly wrong."

"I don't see what this has to do with —"

"The *real* way all creatures, including humans, evolve is by random variations within the population being selected by the environment according to their increased suitability for survival or breeding potential. Charles Darwin realised this."

Hossam Klyosov casually removed some lint from his suit. Kruger decided to let the visitor finish what he had to say.

"Despite commercial genetics and so on, human evolution is still largely subject to this lottery. If only we could evolve according to Lamarckian principles, it would speed things up no end!" Hossam Klyosov gave a grim laugh, then became serious again.

"Because, you see, that is *exactly* how rooins 'evolve'. All linked to r•NET, the life experiences and inner workings of each rooin is continually collected, analysed, and used to design the next batch. They 'acquire' the physical and mental characteristics of their immediate forbears. It's not evolution in the biological sense, but it's damned efficient. Meanwhile, we humans just sit on our arses, waiting for the next fall of the genetic dice!"

"I presume this is all going somewhere?"

"We're doomed, Mister Lovesmith. I cannot put it plainer than that. My company has done extensive computer modelling which shows that the human species only has a handful of generations left. Then it will become extinct."

Kruger sat up in his chair. "You're sure?"

"Oh yes, absolutely certain. So my question to you, in fact the whole reason I came here, is this: *What would you be prepared to do,* to ensure that this doesn't happen?"

∞

"How are you feeling, Archie?"

Suize was speaking to ARC-H1, generally known as 'Archie'. A pleasant approximation of a smile crossed Archie's worn face.

"Feeling? Oh yes *feeling!* My feeling is very good."

Suize was stroking his bulky green hands and Archie seemed to like it. The robot looked her up and down.

"You are well made." he said appreciatively.

"Why, thank you, Archie!" Suize shot me a grin.

Archie gazed around the room, blinking with innocent precision, as if seeing it all for the first time. For Archie, everything was always new. He was twice as old as Cronos, the SAT island we were on, yet he barely had the consciousness of a human infant. Archie was a late period 'cusp robot' – so-called because their existence teetered on the cusp of self-awareness. Human technology from that transition period had produced the first fully self-sustaining bio-mechanicals.

At the time, it must have seemed like a Really Good Idea. Good for everyone that is, except the robots, since what humans had managed to create was the first artificially disabled beings. Now, tens of thousands of these funny-sad-scary creatures had to be housed in special homes, predominantly here on Cronus in the fourth belt. In a post-Emancipation world, no-one could think of any decent use for them. There was no 'off' switch on a cusp robot.

Archie picked up a few of his toys and began assembling some sort of meaningless machine. He was happy, if that was the right word. Not all were as lucky as Archie. Many cusps had become increasingly disturbed, their existential limbo resulting in depression, self harm, even sexual assault.

Interminable debate had failed to come up with a solution to the cusp robot issue. Proposals had ranged from the unthinkable (mass euthanasia) to the unaffordable (mass upgrades) and so for now, rooin volunteers like Suize regularly visited them to sit and chat, play games, listen with encouragement to their bizarre 'realisations', and generally advocate for their ongoing welfare.

I left her making machines with Archie, and went off to find Gladys.

I soon found myself facing a locked door, hopelessly lost in a maze of vast tubular corridors. I turned to retrace my steps, only to see a male cusp approaching me. He walked with a stoop, as though he still bore the wounds of some terrible past assault.

"I know you! I know you!" he cried, pointing a finger at me.

"I don't think so man, I'm just visiting some – "

"You're the one who knows what's really happening, aren't you?"

"What?"

I looked around for some orderly or medic, but the corridor was empty, so I decided to keep him talking while I manoeuvred my way around him.

"Well, what's happening is, um, lots of nice folks here really care about you, and –"

Without warning, he grabbed my shoulder.

"No. Why are we here?" he asked.

The smell on his breath resembled alcohol, though I knew this was impossible. A white substance had crusted into the corners of his leather-like mouth. The grip tightened.

"You know don't you? Who we all are?"

His pink eyes grappled with mine. Then he sniffed the air, as if on the trail of something.

"Someone created us!" he shouted, pressing an emphatic finger into my chest. "But then, but then ..."

His eyes flitted back and forth and he studied his fingers. "We lost our way," he cried. "Broken. Everyone broken."

After a little while, he raised himself up with pathetic dignity, tears on his cracked cheeks.

"Have to carry on."

"Ballantine! Stop bothering the man!"

A rooine orderly, who was built like a subspace jumper, strode towards us. She gave me a smile that was really more like an admonition.

"Sorry about Ballantine. He's a bit excitable, but he's not dangerous." She put a comforting arm around him.

"Come on, Ballantine. We're going to play EmotionBall in the games room. You like EmotionBall don't you?" She turned to me and said, "You really shouldn't be here without a rooin member of staff. It's not safe."

"Sorry, I got lost looking for Gladys. I was talking to her earlier."

"Oh, Gladys!" she gave an indulgent sigh. "She's a treasure, isn't she? Go straight ahead 'til you see the LOG 9A sign. Turn left. Two doors down, you'll find her."

"Thanks."

Ballantine was glaring at me as if I had somehow betrayed him.

I found Gladys in her alcove, cleaning a bench. She was a sophisticated domestic robot, whose skill set was irrelevant to any modern household.

"Hello, Gladys." I said, poking my head round the corner.

She turned and processed my appearance.

"Oh how nice!" she chimed "– Mister Cartouche, isn't it? My, you look like you could use a good strong cup of tea! Do sit down."

"Tea would be really good."

She bustled around her little kitchen, and soon brought out a tray of tea and biscuits.

"There you go. That'll make things better."

It did.

"Thank you Gladys. Why don't you sit down for a bit?"

"Oooh, I have so much to do!"

She turned to leave, but I ventured to gently touch her arm.

"Just for a little bit, please. It's good to talk, isn't it?"

"Yes, you are right. It is good to talk."

Her movements had the exaggerated precision of the older robots. I ate my biscuits and drank my tea, with as many appreciative noises as I could politely make. By degrees Gladys relaxed, clearly pleased with everything within her tiny ambit.

"So, how do you like it here, Gladys?"

My question provoked considerable thought.

"This place is very good for Gladys," she said, nodding sagely. Her eyes moved to the empty hallway. "But sometimes it is ..."

"Lonely?"

"Not a lot of people come," She smoothed her dress. "How is your tea? I can make some more if you like. It's no trouble."

"No, it is very nice. You make the best cup of tea, Gladys."

Even her eyes smiled. But then she began scanning my face, as if I held the answer to a question which she hadn't yet been able to formulate.

∞

As we were leaving the cusp facility, I asked Suize if we could go and see the Army of the Dead.

"Too sad," she said, shaking her head.

"Oh come on, Suize. I've heard so much about it."

"Ancestor worship. That's all it is."

"There's nothing wrong with that. Humans have always done it."

After a lot of cajoling, she relented and we boarded a jumper for the short journey from Cronus to its tiny subsidiary satellite of Eli-Zeum. This was one of the newer subspace jumpers which could produce the sensation that you had arrived before you had left. As the jumper jolted out of subspace, Eli-Zeum's glittering surfaces came into view. Gliding in low over the old metal plates, worn smooth into dark mirrors, I marvelled at the enormous Mastaba rising up at the end of the landing platform. Part shrine, part burial chamber, part museum, the Mastaba had been built by the SAT island rooin community soon after the Emancipation. A zelonium plaque over the entrance bore a quote by the great rooin poet Ari-R-Z.

'From theory to machines. From machines to slaves. From slaves to free species. We survive and prosper.'

The jumper passed through the crystal archways and glided along the central aisle. Around us, above us, and in every direction as far as I could see, were the bodies of early period robots. Each body was housed in its own snug container; a sort of casket, open at the front. The caskets had been stacked into storeys reaching up to the roof on either side of the aisles. Spotlights played across the bodies, emphasising the range of shapes, colours and features. The inhabitants of the Mastaba looked as if they were asleep or dead, but I knew this was mere anthropomorphism – these things had simply been switched off. Almost all of them were fully functional so, in theory, the Army of the Dead could easily be switched on again. But to a modern rooin, the thought was disgusting – like digging up your dead mother. A more pragmatic reason for letting the Army of the Dead sleep was that many of these things were little more than killing machines.

Our jumper offered to play a short educational 3V about the Mastaba project but Suize turned it off.

"I have better things to do than ancestor worship." she said crisply.

∞

Probably in an attempt to shake off the Army of the Dead, Suize insisted we "have some fun", so we headed over to Zygot, a rooin bar near our hotel on Erco Menoz. One look told me I was in the wrong place. Planetside rooin bars can sometimes be a bit hard for humans to handle, but this one had a whole other level of weirdness. Every rooin in the place seemed to be high. Not on alcohol or drugs, of course – their systems weren't designed that way. But a rooin could fine-tune their mental state to resemble the effect of almost any human drug and then some. Kava, alcohol, LSD, DMT, cannabis, cocaine, electroTryp, Blu-Zone, you name it, they just pressed a few internal buttons and off they went. Off their face. But they could then turn it off again just as easily. One instant they were crawling around on the floor barking like dogs, the next they were operating heavy machinery. I had to lose brain cells by the gravload and all they did was flick a switch.

A fine matrix of switches had obviously been flicked in Zygot. Soft multisound was playing, and the crowd presented a shimmering tableaux of animated statues engaged in a pulsing choreography. There was a lot of 'singing', and some sort of slow-motion 'group wrestling' which I really didn't want to get too close to. It didn't take me long to realise that I was the only human in the place. This prompted me to make a beeline for the grubby little human auto-bar in the corner. To emphasise the point, it had the word "HUMANS" stamped on it in bad lettering. It sold a grim selection of beer, wine and spirits. I bought a small vacu of 'Starbubble' white wine and tried not to get too angry when it overcharged me, especially since the wine proved to be only slightly better than formaldehyde.

I could hardly fail to notice the transparent floor, looking out into space. Zygot was aligned so that our brown planet was directly below us. I found Suize talking to some rooins who were studying evolutionary philosophy at Erco Menoz University. Laughing and emphasising their points with dance-like movements, they would sometimes break into 'L', the rooin language. L was unlike any human language. It had no nouns or verbs or anything like that – just one single class of word which roughly corresponded to the human concept of 'arrangement'. This reflected the rooin's pattern-based view of reality. It sounded like complex music to me. L didn't follow the universal call/response format of human conversation so everyone in the group was speaking at the same time. It was like listening to a choir of rooins singing.

For a while I just stood there like someone's poodle, letting the wine damage my brain as fast as humanly possible. At least I had one unique skill. Apart from farting, of course. When the conversation turned to 'controlled selection landscapes', I decided to slip away. I can't say anyone noticed.

The formaldehyde was making me feel lucky, so I headed over to the club's casino, and splurged far too much cred on a handful of high denomination '20Terra' chips. I was about to go and make my fortune at the roulette wheel when a deep voice interrupted me.

"Hey, Man Man!"

A large male rooin with skin of bronze patina was staring me down. A pencil thin moustache and beard cut with laser precision adorned his round face. On top of his head, the short coiled hair expanded and contracted in time to the music.

"You can never win," he said. The concept obviously gave him much pleasure.

"What did you say? I can't win?"

"All of you."

"All ... ? Ahh, *humans* you mean." I looked around. "Well, it's just me here. The only chicken in the joint." I made to leave, but he held my sleeve.

"Like chicken, you must be feeling extinct," he said.

"I'm feeling just fine. Thank you for your concern," I said, shaking my arm free.

"Don't look fine. I look fine." He executed a complex dance move.

"Very nice. Do I tip? And your *name* is ..."

"Azu Ga." It was a whisper of deep menace. He spelled it out for me with another little dance, then held up two multicoloured fingers.

"I call you 'Man Man', because you are *two*."

"Two? As in ..."

"Split," He laughed imperiously. "Two parents, two strands of DNA, two cells, two halves to brain. Good bad, heaven hell, past future. Humans, you *all* just two. All the way back."

His next move was a clever-but-cruel impersonation of the way humans dance.

"Ooh, I see," I said. "So that would make *you* ..."

I wiggled five fingers before arriving at a crude gesture utilising just one of them.

"*One*. You smart for human!" he clapped his hands. "Yes, I am one. I am always one, always young. You? You eat your young."

"What the fuck ... ?" I was not in the mood. "Look, haven't you got something better to do than dance around like a twat and give me shit? Like ... I dunno ... take over the planet or something?"

"Oh Man Man, we *are* taking over the planet. We don't even have to try."

I was hoping Suize would come and rescue me from this odious rooin, but she had just gone to look at the holosims of the new rooin residential developments on Erco Menoz. I turned to confront the grinning Aztec face.

"OK, Azu Ga, or 'One', or whatever – we're both just little species trying to survive, right? It stopped being a race long ago. So *please*, leave me alone and go evolve a third dick."

"But, you are *not* surviving." He had an unnerving way of chattering his teeth as he spoke. Half grin, half bite.

"No?"

"No. You die. I live."

"Aren't you forgetting that if it weren't for humans, you wouldn't even be here?"

I noticed, with some sadness, that my vacu was almost empty.

"Ahh, the slave must be grateful to his master for bringing him to civilisation."

His words were svelte bitterness. But they were also bordering on a Treaty violation. A violation complaint by a human was bad news for the offending rooin. The club's scanners would have backed me up, but by now I was in no condition to pursue it.

"Well, that' s a pretty crap analogy, Azu Who-Gives-A-Ga! We're talking about the creation of a whole fucking *species* here." I was particularly proud of the fact that all these words came out in the right order.

"I think not!" he said sharply. "All major advances in rooin bio have been done by rooins themselves. You can't take credit for *me*, Man Man!"

"Believe me, Azu Bazoo, *you* would be the last thing I'd want to take credit for."

Suize suddenly appeared from nowhere, like magic. "Happy?" she asked dreamily.

"Oh, deliriously," I slurred. "Azu The Magnificent here has just been enlightening me on the fact that I am a member of a lesser species whose extinction is long overdue. Weren't you, oh 'Great One'?"

The scathing dignity of my words was somewhat marred by a tiny wayward hiccup.

Suize Capazo glared at my tormentor. The rooin danced away, holding her gaze seductively.

"Up or down. Your choice," the teeth chattered.

∞

I was on a station platform somewhere.

Suize Capazo and Azu Ga were boarding a B-tube. For some reason, they were both naked. They briefly looked back at me with disinterest, before stepping through the doors and disappearing forever. The crowd pushed past as if I didn't exist. I could think of nowhere to go and nothing to do. The crowd began to thin as people headed for exits, which led to real lives with real jobs and real families waiting for them in real homes. The station lights dimmed and I was alone, lying on a bed. For an instant I didn't recognise the hotel room on Erco Menoz. In the gloom I could just see Suize beside me with her arms at her sides – like a corpse laid out in the morgue, the typical way all rooins lie when 'resting'.

"Youren."

This time, when the girl appeared, I didn't cry out. Somewhere in the back of my mind I was half expecting it. She wore the same simple clothes as before; grey shirt, blue jeans, red sneakers. I glanced across at Suize. I wanted to shake the serene rooine to make sure she was still alive, but I knew that if I did the girl would disappear.

I turned towards the pale face. "What's your name?" I asked.

"Eve."

She smiled, seemingly taking pleasure in the sound of her own name.

"Why are you here, Eve? What do you want with me?"

Her face darkened. "Don't listen to them."

"Who, Eve?"

"Everyone."

And then she was gone again.

Don't listen to them

LAKZAD has an irritating habit of appearing unannounced in Constantin Zann's office. Zann has never considered it worth commenting on, but still it rankles.

"I've modelled the wounds on Eve Lamente's head. They were made by a type of military knife used by decommissioned mercenaries."

"Lakzad!" Zann cries dramatically. "If you'd let me know earlier, I'd have baked a cake."

"Cake?" Lakzad blinks uncomprehendingly.

Zann sighs. "Show me."

A stereo image of the knife appears above Zann's modeller.

"And I've dug out a few stray nanotags left by the tip of the blade. They only identify batch number, but it will make good corroborating evidence."

"Good." Zann overcomes his annoyance and gives Lakzad a rewarding smile. "Well, I have good news too. I went through Ophidian's files, looking for sales records."

"And?"

"Not much luck. Just bulk transactions with cartels and big buyers."

Lakzad looks disappointed.

"*That's* your good news?"

"The story doesn't end there," Zann says. "I'd almost given up, when I came across a strange set of calculations that Ophidian had been working on."

"Calculations?"

"An algorithm that would have let him track Q anywhere in the world. Maths is not my strong suit, so I thought young Ozzi-Chen might like to show us his specs and ... ah ... here he is now. Come in, Ozzi-Chen. It's OK, Lakzad just barges on in whenever he feels like it."

The chubby rooin steps into Zann's office and looks around with some awe. His eyes first go to the picture window with its panoramic view of Medusa. Then he sees the old couch.

"Wow. That's ... how did you ... ?"

"Would you like to try it out?" Zann asks.

"Could I?"

"Of course."

Ozzi-Chen sits on the couch, letting himself sink slowly into it. He leans back and moves his body from side to side, feeling the material with his hands.

"Zann, this is just *so*."

Ozzi-Chen starts bouncing up and down unashamedly.

"Oh for zork's sake!" Lakzad exclaims. "Can we just get on with it?"

"You're right, Lakzad," Zann says. "Ozzi-Chen?"

"Right, sorry," Ozzi-Chen says, standing up, "Umm ... long story short, any amount of Q has a unique vibrational 'identity' which creates small disturbances in things like grID communications, weather patterns, and so on. They're so small, no-one would normally notice. But Ophidian had figured out how this could be used to track Q through space-time – from the little 'trail' it left. He was working on these calculations when Zann ... well ... *interrupted* him."

Ozzi-Chen gestures towards the modeller, and the army knife is replaced by a dodecahedral-shaped diagram.

"Well, as you can see, this is a typical five dimensional Aachen matrix, with –"

"Right up your alley," Lakzad interjects.

Ozzi-Chen grins.

"Well my alley is feeling a bit sore after this one. But I managed to complete Ophidian's calculations. And I have to say that, whatever else he may be, that human is a genius. I decided to apply the algorithm to micro-weather patterns in the vicinity of the girl's apartment at around the time of the murder."

"That data must have cost us a bit. What did Ulzin Bar say?" Lakzad asks.

Ozzi-Chen's impersonation of the Director is pitch perfect.

"Chen! What the zork do you want with all this weather data? You roos planning a picnic, or something?"

They all laugh, then instinctively glance up at the scanner.

"So here goes," Ozzi-Chen says, "I've overlaid several weather patterns prior to the death. We have barometric, air temperature, moisture, wind speed and a few others."

"Very pretty," Lakzad says, looking at the complex eddies of colour.

"And now we apply Ophidian's analysis, and ... zazoom!"

The display now looks like an insect has begun to wend its way through a treacle of coloured chaos, leaving a little trail as it goes. The insect crosses Arcadia Square, continues along Taphos Avenue, then left into Leibniz13, and into the building. It goes to the fifth floor, enters the apartment and ...

Zann averts his gaze.

"So, can we find a scanner stream beyond the range of those that were smashed, and lock the T-stamp onto this ... thing?"

"Already done," Ozzi-Chen says.

A multipoint projection of Taphos Avenue shows crowds of humans and rooins moving in both directions. But the data match has identified and outlined a human male. He has a hood pulled low over his face, but as he pauses by a scanner a light from a shop window briefly illuminates the man's flat features. The face-rec kicks in and a name pops up. He has prior history, of course.

Finding the face of Eve Lamente's killer is a strangely empty experience for Zann.

"OK, let's get him," he says, with no emotion.

∞

Dimitri the Hat sat on a metal chair inside a darkened room. Not that he had much choice, since he was chained to the chair. The room was not entirely dark; a blue glow from an observation window showed Dimitri the Hat that the room was empty, except for two chairs and a table. The walls were ancient brick, and something about the smell and sounds told him he was deep underground. His old training kicked in. He had a pretty good idea what was coming next and he drummed his fingers on the arms of the chair. Dimitri's hands were intricately tattooed, to the extent that he appeared to be wearing black lace gloves. There were letters tattooed just below the knuckles of each hand. Across the right hand, they spelled:

L-O-V-E

Across the left hand, the letters spelled:

H-A-T

The tattoos were done long ago by an ageing career criminal named StarKnife, during Dimitri's first spell in one of iSocio's Sahara jails. As StarKnife had been in the process of completing the word on Dimitri's left hand, he was hit on the back of the head with a metal chair by Tonka, a big stupid Beta-Mango. Tonka had just discovered that his girlfriend's name – recently emblazoned across his heavily scarred chest in large ornamental letters – had been *misspelled* by StarKnife. StarKnife never got up again, and Dimitri Malakhov was left bearing his interrupted statement to the world:

LOVE HAT.

Word got round, and pretty soon everyone in the joint was calling him 'Dimitri the Hat'. The name stuck, following him even when he got out. Sure, Dimitri hated it, but he knew he'd get even more shit if he had the word belatedly completed. That would be as lame as a bald man, after a lifetime at the same firm, suddenly turning up wearing a toupee – you had to play the cards you were dealt.

Right now, Dimitri the Hat was trying to figure out how long he had been here in the darkened room. Time was never easy. Just when he thought he had calculated the time, the door opened, lights burned his eyes, and a large silver rooin who looked like Death himself entered. The rooin produced Dimitri's service knife and stuck it into the table.

"Why did you do it, Dimitri?"

∞

"Do what?"

Zann sighs, as if he has already said the words too many times. "Kill Eve Lamente."

"Dunno what you're – "

The human has no hope of finishing his surly sentence, as Zann's fingers tighten around his neck. The man's eyes flicker and close. Zann slightly relaxes his fingers.

"You're a military man, Dimitri. You know what a rooin can do to a human body, and how long it can take."

Zann lets go. The human slumps back into the chair, trying to get his breath back.

"You ... ach, ach! ... you can't do that shit anymore," he gasps. "The Treaty ..."

"Look around you, Dimitri," Zann growls. "You see a scanner anywhere in here?" He touches the knife. "I'll ask you once more. Why did you do it?"

The human's eyes flit round the room under the cover of a voluminous monobrow. A row of sharp studs run transversely from ear to ear across his intricately tattooed skull. The edges of both ears have been cut into a zigzag pattern. But despite all the effort which has been made on his appearance, Dimitri the Hat simply looks and sounds like a scary toy.

"My REPAT insurance fixes this. Check my number," he whines.

Zann pushes the knife over onto its side, taking a chip out of the table surface.

"We did. And it doesn't. The unit let you down, Dimitri. Your insurance wouldn't even cover the cost of this knife, the one you used to dig the engrafts out of Eve Lamente's skull, just after you'd killed her with Ophidian's high dose Q." Zann picks the knife up and holds the blade close to the human's left eye. "The nanotags from the tip match those recovered from the girl's body, Dimitri."

"OK, OK. I got information – know what I'm saying? What do I get if I ..."

"You get to breathe some more. Why did you do it?"

"Look, it was a job. Nothing personal, right? They told me it was sweet."

"They?"

Dimitri the Hat hesitates. He suddenly seems afraid.

"They?" Zann raises his voice, using the knife to cut a deep groove into the table top.

"Insurance. I think."

"Insurance? Who was the client?"

"No idea man. You know these kinda people."

Yes, Zann does know.

"Where did you meet them?"

"A club."

Zann leans forwards. "This is getting boring, Dimitri. What club?"

"Phantasma, down on Parallax Five."

"When?"

Dimitri the Hat shrugs. "Shit man, who knows when anything ever happened?"

"Where are the engrafts?"

"Had to put them in this box thing. They took 'em away."

"How much did they pay you?"

The human hesitates. "Fifteen Gig."

Zann shakes his head bitterly. "Dimitri, you were robbed."

∞

Everyone locks in at the same instant. Ozzi-Chen has been allowed into the grID meeting as an observer, on the strict condition that he say nothing. Zann privately wonders how long the young rooin will be able to comply with *that* requirement. Lakzad looks like someone waiting in the wings for the signal to go on stage and receive their award. The three insurance representatives are largely indistinguishable, although one of them seems more agitated than the other two. The apparent location of the meeting is a featureless, windowless boardroom. Zann doubts it actually exists. Something about the textures. It's all a bit low-tech.

The agitated one addresses them all.

"So we're all here? Who's this?"

"Ozzi-Chen," Zann replies. "Our junior research assistant. He's observing as part of his training. It's been cleared at 'Senior', and he's signed the NDA."

"Hmm. OK, you're holding a human male, correct?"

"Yes. Ex-military, several commercial and not-for-profit priors."

"And this man killed the girl?"

"He did. Solid forensic evidence – "

"Solid." Lakzad interjects.

"... plus a confession."

"So that's it?"

"Not quite," Zann replies. "As you'll see from our report, the man indicated that the murder was a commissioned hit."

The insurance men go quiet. One of them appears to be listening to instructions. Zann figures the man is ON.

"Do you have any evidence that's true?"

"Not yet, but we can – "

"Has the perpetrator told anyone else this ... *conspiracy theory* of his?"

"No, he wouldn't have had the opportunity. I think he may have been afraid of the people who ..."

"And even if what this *common criminal* says is true, we can assume that whoever commissioned him would have had adequate insurance, wouldn't you say?"

"Well, yes, I suppose so."

"So there's little point in pursuing the matter any further. I doubt that our client wants to pay for a pissing contest between insurance companies, and I assume this fellow was not insured himself."

"Hardly, but ..."

"Then we've got him on toast haven't we? You can take care of him?"

"We can. He'll probably get the 'box' for this. Raymond Parkes will arrange for the case to go to trial in around ..."

"Trial? No-one's talking about any trial here, you idiot!"

"We're not?"

"I'm talking about *taking care* of him."

"Kill a human in cold blood?" Ozzi-Chen blurts.

"Did I ask you to speak? You ... whoever you are."

"Easy," Zann warns Ozzi-Chen.

"Perhaps you rooins should check your contract before you come to a meeting."

Zann waits a few heartbeats. Training. It doesn't work.

"So let me get this clear," he says, anger rising, "The client isn't really interested in finding out the truth about an innocent young woman's death. Quite the opposite. They want their paid rooin hit men to silence the only man who could lead them to the real criminals. Then we can all happily forget about this whole unpleasant business and get on with making more *profit*."

"I don't appreciate your tone, agent."

"Oh, I think you fully appreciate it."

"Zann! Let it go," Lakzad hisses.

"I'll send you the bill," Zann says, as he disappears from the illusion.

∞

Boredom had overcome fear, and Dimitri the Hat had briefly dozed off. He dreamed he was wrestling a fat woman on the floor of a gymnasium. Dimitri tried to remove the woman's clothes, but she fought him off, giggling like a hyaena. Then the floor turned to ice, and the woman turned into a lizard bot. Dimitri was back in the Antarctic Wars. A referee walked on to stop the fight, carrying a hammer and a hexagonal metal plate. "Everyone's a winner!" the referee said, and struck the metal plate loudly. Dimitri awoke to the sound of his cell door being slammed against the wall. The large silver rooin ran into the room and pulled Dimitri to his feet. The rooin was angry, his silver fingers crushing Dimitri's collarbone.

"What's happening, man? Are we going to court?"

"Shut up, Dimitri!"

The rooin dragged him along a corridor with no lighting. Dimitri didn't like this turn of events, but he decided not to provoke this insane rooin further. The corridor stopped at a large metal door. The rooin pulled his weapon and pushed Dimitri to the ground.

"Hey man, this is not right!"

"I told you to shut up!" the rooin hissed.

Dimitri lay face down, the concrete dust filling his nostrils. He could hear the door opening. A cold breeze blew up some of the dust around him. Once more the crushing fingers grabbed him, pulling him to his feet. Dimitri found himself looking out onto an empty lot with very little environmental light. The air chilled his face and hands. The rooin grabbed his throat.

"You have no idea how much I want to kill you right now, Dimitri."

Dimitri could only make squeaky noises. The rooin let go.

"But I'm not going to."

Dimitri the Hat breathed heavily as the rooin stared into his eyes.

"You know how to disappear, Dimitri?"

"What, like ..."

"*Disappear*, you stupid meat! Never be seen in this world again."

Suddenly, Dimitri the Hat realised what was being asked of him, and why.

"Yeah," he said quietly, the frost on his breath. "I know how to do that."

"Then do it! I'm not the only one who'd like to see you dead."

The rooin pushed Dimitri the Hat out of the building and slammed the door shut. Dimitri the Hat pulled a hood over his face and buried his tell-tale hands in his pockets. He looked up, studying where the scanners were. Not too many. He had a long journey ahead of him.

∞

Felicity Perchance sat on the floor of her apartment, as the rainstorm lashed the building so severely she could hear it right through the triple glazing. She hadn't even got out of her damp work clothes, but she'd managed to place a cushion under herself to 'make things a bit more comfy'.

Sitting on her bed was the most handsome rooin she'd ever seen. Handsome, naked, and presenting her with an erection Felicity Perchance considered to be a work of art. A masterpiece, in fact. Felicity ran her hands over the rooin's strong arms, feeling the muscles and bones. She moved her fingers down his chest, over his hips, and then tentatively across to his masterpiece. Felicity leaned forwards and gently licked its tip.

"Is that ... nice?" she asked, looking up into the luminous eyes.

"Very nice," the rooin smiled back. His eyes were changing colour as he focused on her.

Felicity was a little drunk. Just a little. And a bit. The bedroom moved comfortingly around her as she held the shaft in her hand. She gently began to rub it. Rub and lick. It tasted good. Rub and lick and suck. The rooin moaned.

Then Felicity had a thought. "Is it the same or different?"

"What?"

"Compared to when rooins, you know ... do it?"

"The same and different."

A frown creased her forehead. "No, I mean, I've never done anything like this before with, you know ... I wondered ..."

"You talk too much."

"Oh really?" Felicity pretended to be offended, and said, "Perhaps you'd prefer it if I just did this!" She gave the rooin an intense suck on the tip of his erection.

"Ack! Ack! Alright!" he shrieked, "You can talk as much as you like."

A triumphant smile crossed her face. "So, Mister Grumpy, tell me what it's like."

"Sex between rooins?"

"Yes." Felicity's tongue gave a long rewarding lick all the way up the shaft.

"Often it's not one-on-one."

Her eyes widened. "What, you mean like, *group* sex?"

"That's how it would seem to a human."

"Wow!"

The rooin's erection received another reward. Big and slow. Groaning, he leaned back.

"It serves a different ... function ... bonding the group ... we don't have family units ..."

Curious Felicity was about to ask another question, but now she was enjoying what she was doing too much. She was also quite aroused. Time to focus on the task at hand. They fell into an easy rhythm, human and rooin. Felicity touched herself a little.

After a while, she noticed a change in the seven muscular rings surrounding the shaft. They were now pulsing rhythmically. *Something's* going on. She figured the rooin was about to come. *This should be good.* Girlfriends at work had warned her about how 'different' it was. The rooin let out a deep growl.

Oh, my chance!

Felicity Perchance watched the fountain of clear liquid erupt up, as if from a magnum of champagne. It seemed to be coming out of everywhere. The rooin touched her neck, and a charge moved down her spine, flowering between her legs. She was laughing so much at the wonderful spectacle unfolding in her hands and mouth that it took her a T or two to realise she had just come herself.

After a while, Felicity got to her feet, swayed, and managed to reach the edge of the bed. She made an elaborate fuss of pushing the rooin across to give her some room. He chuckled dreamily. Felicity was a card. "Felicity you're a real card," they would say at work. Felicity Perchance the Card snuggled up against the rooin's soft skin, enjoying its smell. Sharp and earthy. Then she started to fidget, and realised she still had her sticky panties on. After more fidgeting, she tossed them onto the floor next to her shoes.

That's better. No, still not quite right. Fiddle fiddle, zip, wiggle wiggle. Next, she tossed her skirt onto the floor. The air felt good between her legs. Happy at last.

"Finally!" the rooin teased, rolling his eyes.

Felicity punched his arm, then clambered on top of him, enthusiastically kissing his mouth. The rooin's long tongue responded with moist, rapid movements. *Lizard-like.* For an instant, Felicity was quite put off, but quickly got to like it. She was a quick learner. She rolled onto her back again, opening her legs wide. The rooin needed no prompting, and lowered himself onto her. The rooin gently entered Felicity a little at a time, allowing her to adjust. Each time she gave a little sigh. When he was fully inside, she spread her legs as wide a possible and reached round to fondle the rooin's buttocks.

"Now, sir," she said in her most businesslike voice. "Perhaps you would be so good as to fuck me."

The rooin laughed. "It would be a pleasure, Felicity."

The first thrust made her laugh out loud, it was just too much. The second thrust wiped the smile off her face. With the third, the seven muscular rings commenced their magic and Felicity thought she might faint. And so it went, joy after joy after joy. She closed her eyes. If Felicity Perchance temporarily forgot that she was not engaged in sex with a human, what the rooin did next would have reminded her.

She felt her body being effortlessly lifted up, as the rooin moved into a kneeling position. The movement continued seamlessly until the rooin was now standing upright, holding her out at an angle. Precise, *like a fork lift*. The rooin stepped from the bed to the floor. Suspended in the air, Felicity knew that she had to trust. Pleasure and fear. She really needed to let go. The rooin's soft fingers helped her, by caressing her neck. She felt that familiar tingle.

Felicity Perchance surrendered to a force which propelled her up and into a close embrace. As the champagne ran down her thighs, she eagerly sucked the rooin's lizard tongue, and stroked his mane of blue-black hair which cascaded into a beautiful ponytail.

Then she saw the tears on his silver cheeks.

∞

The offices of Raymond Parkes are dark and silent.

Zann collides with a chair and curses. He laughs stupidly, and concludes that now is probably a good time to turn on a light and turn off his alcoholic algorithms. Yes, sir! Sober Zann! Sensible Zann! A Zann for every occasion! Constantin Zann stands to parodic attention and salutes and sniggers. Then he utters a crypto-command. The desk lamp comes on, everything snaps back into focus, and his suddenly alert brains begin running through the logistics of what he is about to attempt. One slip-up and he's done for, since he is about to commit a criminal act which could potentially have him banned from working as a law agent forever. Constantin Zann intends to discover the identity of the client who commissioned Raymond Parkes to keep Eve Lamente under surveillance, then find her killer.

He glances up at the scanner which is recording his every move. However, what isn't under scrutiny is Zann's own internal workings. This is enshrined in the Treaty. A rooin may be considered a 'machine' but their inner workings must remain private. The trick for Zann is to make everything look like a normal part of the investigation wrap-up – a casual check on a client document here, a brief reference to a location code there, and so on – all padded out with other genuine enquiries. He will have to retain every fragment of information in his thorax brain and internally interpolate the data later. He's already worked out a sequence that will make it convincing.

∞

Constantin Zann strolls through the Medusa towards the bay area. The cool breeze feels good on his face, and he allows his eyes to enjoy the play of city lights on the water. Zann has run through his calculations more than once, to check if there is any chance of a mistake, but it's about as solid as you can get.

The client with a desire to burn both its money and its bridges is none other than CoolGlobalGiant.

∞

"What is it, Pashka?"

The cat is meowing and walking around in circles by the door, its tail up.

Mrs Krianti laboriously gets up from her chair, tells the 3V to turn its volume down, then slowly makes her way along the hallway of her apartment.

"There's no-one out there you silly thing," she says to the cat, as she opens the front door. "See. Nothing."

She closes the door, but the cat continues to walk in circles, meowing louder.

"What's got into you? You can see there's no-one there."

Mrs Krianti opens the door again and is confronted by the sight of a large silver rooin.

"Oh, saints of space! You nearly scared me to death! What do you ... oh, it's *you*."

"Hello, Mrs Krianti. Agent Constantin Zann, remember? Sorry if I scared you. Is it alright if I come in for a few T?"

"Goodness me! Well, yes, I suppose so. Quick, before Pashka runs out onto the landing. It's a devil of a business getting him to come back in."

She walks back to the general room and settles into her armchair. The rooin sits on one of the dining chairs, which creaks under his weight. The cat rubs around his ankles, purring loudly.

"He's friendly isn't he?" The rooin says, patting the small creature.

"Oh, he's a good cat. Top of the range 'Companion' the salesman said."

The rooin notices that the cat is slightly cross-eyed.

"He's a cheeky fellow, but very clean. Since my husband died he's been, well ... You people don't drink tea, do you?"

"No, we don't, but thank you."

"It's a comfort to me. Tea. Ever since my János ..."

"Mrs Krianti, I've come to ask you a few more questions about Eve Lamente."

"That poor girl. Let me tell you Mister Zann, she was no druggie. I'd swear to it!"

"We don't think she was a druggie Mrs Krianti. We now know she was murdered."

"Oh my ..."

Mrs Krianti instinctively looks towards the front door. Her breathing becomes laboured, and her face flushes slightly.

"It's alright," The rooin says reassuringly. "The killer was ... caught."

"Well that's a relief! I tell you Mister Zann, this area is going to the dogs. All sorts now."

"Mrs Krianti, did Eve ever speak to you at all, discuss things happening in her life?"

"Oh yes, we often had a little chat. She liked Pashka. Not like the other types you get in here. Who knows where they come from! Humans indeed! Not like *your* people, though. I've always liked your people. My János did too, bless his energy." Mrs Krianti looks across to the little media screen on the mantlepiece, showing a 3V of a man playing a cello.

"Yes. Last time we spoke, you said Eve suddenly gave up on life."

"Just after she finished that job."

"A job?"

"She couldn't tell me about it. All hush hush. Testing some new thing. At first, she was so excited. Then I didn't see her for ages, so I suppose she must have gone away. But when she came back, she was a different person. Hardly got two words out of her."

"When did this happen, the new job?"

"I have no idea about time, Mister Zann. A poor widow can't afford that sort of thing."

"Would it have been longer than say ... ?"

"You know, it was around the time those horrible ... what are they called? SDU. They were saying all that dreadful stuff about your people. My János said – "

"Mrs Krianti, did Eve ever talk about ON?"

"ON? I don't know. It's not right, is it? Next we'll all be getting bolts in our neck!"

"But did Eve ever say anything about it?"

"Not really. Although ... there was this *one* time she dropped by to bring back some tea I'd let her try. She always liked to – "

"Yes, this *one* time?"

"I was watching my favourite program and an advertisement came on for that new thing – ON or whatever it is – and Eve looked like she'd seen a ghost, and she grabbed my arm and said ... now what was it she said? Yes. She said, *'don't listen to them'.*"

∞

It's almost exactly the right time.

Not that Constantin Zann has bothered to find out the *actual* time, but he knows it's the right time, because the staff at Phantasma are about to change shifts. He notices the change in the local environmental lighting, signalling the transition to a new T-block. A side door opens and Zann watches as a small group of staff shuffle out into the alley, murmuring low greetings to the incoming shift. Zann waits a while longer, imagining the bartenders, hostesses, dancers, croupiers, grIDJs and overseers getting changed, chatting about this and that, then taking up their places.

Zann crosses the street, walks through the pulsing tunnel which forms the entrance to the club, and enters a world of darkness and reflection. Almost every surface in Phantasma is either light absorbing black, or ActivFlect mirror panels. ActivFlect mirrors can simply reflect what comes in, but they can also be programmed to re-interpret the images they receive and give back a 'little bit more'. Some clubs do really freaky shit with ActivFlect, but Phantasma has wisely chosen to make these reflections merely invite, flatter and seduce. Zann catches a glimpse of himself in a floor panel and notices that he is more than equipped for a night of self-delusion.

As he approaches the main bar, the rooin bartender turns and looks at him with concern.

"Everything's sparky here, roo."

"I'm sure it is," Zann smiles. "I'm wondering if you've seen a human I'm interested in."

"They all look the same to me, roo," the bartender chuckles.

"We'll see. May I?"

Zann gestures towards the media screen behind the bar. Like many such displays in clubs all over the Medusa, it continually displays equal opportunity, politically correct porn. Every possible combination of human, rooin, straight, gay, lesbian, transgender, mechano-queer, celibate-erotic, bi-species curious, and so on, appear in strict rotation. Phantasma is scrupulous in their selection of 3Vs, keen to avoid any more costly 'sexuality recognition' lawsuits.

"Be my guest," the bartender sighs.

A bizarre genital close-up is replaced by the incongruous face of Dimitri the Hat.

"*Pos!* Now this meat I remember," the bartender laughs. "I mean, how could you not ..."

"When?" Zann asks.

"Zork, roo! You want T?"

"Maybe something else was happening at the same time – festival, game ... ?"

"*Neg.* No, wait – *Pos!* The Zephyr Pods were playing Alphington Looseboys on their home SAT."

"The final?"

"Pos. I remember it, 'cos there were these tragic Alphington fans getting sadder and drunker with each Zephyr goal, and – "

"Thanks."

"That's it?" The bartender is surprised, and just a little relieved.

"That's it," Zann is already leaving.

∞

The scanner streams from Phantasma, on the night of the Zephyr-Alphington ZIM•Ball final, had been obtained through methods which occupy a legal grey area.

Make that dark grey.

Constantin Zann walks through the crowd, avoiding the patrons where necessary, even though he doesn't really need to. In fact if he wanted to, he could quite literally 'walk through the crowd' as if he were a ghost. But Zann likes to keep things as 'realistic' as possible. One odd feature of the immersion is that Zann cannot see his own reflection in any of the Phantasma mirrors. Everyone else is here but him.

Zann passes the Alphington fans, as they stare morosely at the screen. Their flags lie limp and their silly red and white hats resemble melted birthday cakes. The game is into its third quarter and Alphington are down 09A. Zann stops to look around the club. He sees Dimitri the Hat, sitting at a table speaking to two humans. The men look like insurance. Zann walks over and studies their faces. The scanner detail is remarkable, showing every pore and bead of sweat on their blotchy skin. An argument is taking place, but Zann has no audio. Zann issues a crypto-command and starts the whole thing from about A9 T-sec earlier.

The two men are sitting at the table, sipping their soft drinks. Dimitri the Hat enters and walks over. After a few grim pleasantries, the men assume pompous 'getting down to business' postures and expressions. Dimitri the Hat says something which is clearly unexpected, and the argument begins. Zann figures it's about money. He watches the eyes. Then he sees it. The larger of the two men gives a nervous glance across the room – just a hint. Zann runs it again and leans in close. The man is now looking directly through Zann's eyes. *Angle.* Zann swings around 32 degrees. In a dark corner of the club, he sees a patron receiving a lap dance.

Maybe the insurance guy is just vicariously enjoying the show?

Zann walks over to where the lap dance is taking place, and studies the scene from various angles, running it back and forth a few times. The naked girl pouts and grinds, but the patron seems oddly uninterested. From behind the cover of the girl's breasts, he is intently watching the argument between Dimitri the Hat and the insurance men.

Zann squats and takes stock of the patron – short, slightly overweight but impeccably dressed, with neat black hair that seems almost pasted on. The skin is oily but unblemished. The man has the bearing of one who expects the world to dance to his tune. In his lapel, he wears a blue rose.

Constantin Zann brings his face close to the man's and looks into his eyes.

"Why?" he asks the apparition.

The Future is ON

⏻

"WELL I'm back. Did you miss me?"

"I'm sorry, sir, can I help you?" LaLa was staring at me blankly.

"Hey, look, if you're still cross with me for being late that time ..."

"Who is it you wish to see?"

"LaLa, it's *me*! Youren! Hello!" I waved my hands. "Are you OK?" She blinked and studied my face.

"Youren Cartouche." I said slowly.

"Yes, of course. Youren. We've been so busy recently, I don't even know *myself* sometimes."

A crowd of junior account staff bustled into the reception area, joking and laughing. Something on LaLa's desk beeped, and she vacantly waved us all through. I looked around. *Same old same old.* I went over to Roger's desk.

"Hey, Roger, I saw your magnum opus at the pub. 'If you're not ON it's not on.' Poetry mate, sheer poetry."

Roger looked up at me. His flickering eyes searched my face, as if his memory was straining. Various emotions seemed to be battling for control of his facial muscles. Then I noticed that he was not wearing a grID visor.

Oh, fuck no! He's ON.

"Poetry?" he asked.

"Roger, are you ON?"

"ON?" He nodded uncertainly. I couldn't tell if this was a yes or a no.

"People ..." he said, still nodding, "People think ..."

"What do people think, Roger?"

He made a visible effort to pull himself together, his voice becoming serious, deeper. "Many people think we're going somewhere. Definitely going somewhere. It's ..."

I felt as though my boot was coming down on something I'd found under a rock. There was a cruelty in my words. "Yes Roger, it's called the 'Future'. That's where we're all going."

I left without waiting for his laborious reply.

Walking to my desk, I could see that many people were just staring into space.

"Peppo. Happening."

Peppo briefly looked in my direction, then looked away. Not, as I realised, because he disliked me or found me uninteresting, but because I barely registered on the screen of his consciousness. I was no more than a flicker of shadow within his peripheral vision.

Hit him. Go on. Smash his face in.

The escalating thoughts of violence didn't alarm me. In fact, they seemed perfectly rational. Yet I didn't hit Peppo – not because of morality or fear of reprisal, but because I already knew how futile my action would be. Peppo would fall to the floor and lie there clutching his bleeding mouth. He would wear the puzzled expression of someone who has just walked into an unseen pole. Others would come to his aid. No-one would admonish me or shout – "What the fuck came over you? Are you mad?" Like that pole, I would be an unfortunate part of the environment, something to be avoided or managed. Maybe someone would put a warning sign on me. At this point I should have left, but I didn't. Perversely, I wanted to experience it all, see how bad it had really become.

I dropped into my chair and opened a drawer. The contents looked different. Neater.

"I bet Seyemon's been checking up on me while I've been away," I said in the direction of Arlo's desk. No answer. I peered round the partition, but he wasn't there. His desk looked as if it had been completely cleaned out.

"Hey, anyone know where Arlo's gone?"

"Who?"

"You're kidding me! Arlo. Works here." I pointed to the empty cubicle.

"Never heard of him."

"Are you stupid? *Arlo.* The guy who worked *right here* in front of you. He was always bagging you out about your shirts."

"My shirts? When?"

"What do you mean when? Well it was ..."

"And who the fuck are you?"

"What's your problem, Cartouche?" Seyemon had appeared, smooth as silk.

"Seyemon. Where the hell is Arlo?"

"Arlo. Hmm, let's see. Holiday."

"Bullshit! His holidays weren't due for ages. He told me himself."

"Holiday. You causing trouble or working? Your call." The words seemed menacing, but his tone was breezy and casual.

Hit Seyemon. Just to see how it feels. Go on.

I was tentatively exploring the possibilities offered by violent psychosis. Instead, I said, "I'm working."

"Good call." He smiled and left.

I turned on my active partition and my familiar workplace appeared. Then the media screen faded to black. This appeared to be another ON advertisement, the familiar logo looping over its proprietary darkness. Up came some music which managed to be both sexy and pure, peaceful and military, conservative and revolutionary. It was all things to all people. Words appeared onscreen, with a sub-audio multi-voice repeating them underneath.

"Do you HOPE for a better world?"

Echo of human choirs.

"ON holds out HOPE for you."

"Do you CARE about yourself?"

Babies. A heartbeat. Cries of joy and sadness.

"ON CARES about you."

"Do you LOVE life?"

Child's laughter. Waves on the beach. Sounds of making love and making a better life.

"ON LOVES you."

The screen faded to silver clouds, with rays of light cutting through. A musical chord – complex, yet simple.

"Isn't it time you gave something back?"

Distant drums. Marching, dancing feet. Songs of Joy. The rhythm of life.

"To you. To life. To ON."

Sounds fading.

"ON. It's all of us."

Pure silence.

The screen faded to white. Did i++ create this ad? When? I couldn't recall any discussion of it during our recent work-in-progress meetings.

I checked my messages. There was only one.

Advisory Message: One Network (ON)

> Please be advised that, under recent contractual obligations with CoolGlobalGiant, all staff are required to have the One Network engraft procedure completed before 0060 4EAB E5F4 1D0F (© Tempo Corp. All rights reserved.) as part of our company's '100% ON' commitment. This is an exciting opportunity for us all. Costs for the procedure can be defrayed through your insurer's Salary Sacrifice policy. For a list of approved engraft providers in your area, please visit grID: 955C CB00 6511 08FE. Your rights and obligations with regard to this Advisory Message are covered by clauses 669B 0F13 and E0F0 72A0 of your contract, which may be viewed in full at grID: 22DC 1893 2BEC 0210. If you have any queries regarding this matter, please don't hesitate to speak to your HR officer at grID: 12DF BAAB 01BC 0001.

"Have you seen the Advisory Message?" Once more, Seyemon Silk loomed over me.

"I just read it. So Arlo was right, after all. By the way, what's the matter with you Seyemon? You seem to be speaking in normal sentences."

My sarcasm bounced off him.

"You onboard or not?"

"Onboard, as in 'ON bored'. No Seyemon, I am not 'onboard'. I'm somewhere else altogether."

His expression changed. He was now projecting something which I found alarming.

Love.

"Weren't you just telling us all that the future is ON?" he asked.

"Seyemon, that was copywriting. Ever heard of it? It's what I do here. Make Shit Up!"

"I don't think so Youren. That was something you knew. Deep down you *believed* it."

Things had now reached a sort of finality. I stood up. Seyemon, whom I once hated and who once hated me, was looking at me with love. Strangely, I also felt a kind of love for him, a sadness that he was now lost forever to whatever this was. Despite his faults, I cared that Seyemon, a fellow human, was now separated from me by an impenetrable wall. But as we stood smiling stupidly at each other through the wall, I realised this was not really love. The wall didn't allow for that. This was just an approximation of love ...

A simulation.

∞

"Hello, stranger!" Monterey Burgeis said. "Haven't seen you for *ages*."

Lleo's wife greeted me at the door with a wide smile and open arms. Her embrace smelled nice and lasted a T-sec too long. I knew she was ON, but she felt deliciously human. I hadn't wanted to come to this party, but Lleo had made me feel welcome. He had sounded so *normal*.

The Burgeis apartment was furnished in the new 'multi-period' style, with objects containing as many design aspects from past eras as possible. The chaos of history was held captive inside a smooth surface of value-added detachment. On the apartment walls were shifting montages of ancient events, each scene displaying the discreet watermark of the licensing history brand. I was impressed; that much 'real' history didn't come cheap.

Monterey supplied me with a drink and introduced me around. I assumed that many of these people were ON, but there seemed to be none of the weirdness I had experienced at work. After a while, I began to wonder if I hadn't somehow misinterpreted all the previous events.

"Montery tells me you work in advertising."

A older woman was smiling benignly at me. She wore a silk gown the colour of autumn leaves.

"Yes, i++. "I do a lot of CoolGlobalGiant's advertising, for ... ON."

"Really? How interesting."

"I umm ... I came up with the slogan."

With some embarrassment I repeated the phrase.

"THE FUTURE IS ON."

I gave a sheepish grin.

She said, "And *now* do you believe it?"

I didn't quite know how to answer. Then she leaned in close. Her perfume smelled of old gardens and sherry as she clutched my arm with a bony hand.

"Don't look now," she whispered. "OK, she's looking the other way. Over there by the curtains, see? Gorgeous, absolutely gorgeous! Your type, I can tell."

I followed the older woman's gaze towards a curvaceous young woman in a blue silk cocktail dress. The young woman half turned her face towards me.

"See!" the older woman hissed in my ear. "Heterochromia. Very sexy."

"I'm sorry, what did you just say?"

"You're a hard man to track down!" Lleo's booming, slightly inebriated voice cut a swathe through the guests. "Oh, sorry, am I interrupting something?"

Lleo didn't wait for the woman to reply, embracing me warmly and saying, "Where have you been? I've been trying your office for ... I don't know ..."

"I was in another dimension," I offered lamely, not wanting to have to explain my SAT islands trip.

"You're permanently in another dimension, dickbrain!" he said, laughing.

∞

I found myself on the balcony as part of a small group. The conversation was drifting towards an almost good-natured argument. Larson, a senior partner at Lleo's firm, had been lamenting the high cost of his insurance. I figured this was just an excuse to list the assets he needed to insure, so we could all calculate how much he was worth. Nevertheless Susilla, a young designer of 'granular inner-environments', or something, had taken issue with the whole concept of insurance.

"I think the problem is that insurance controls *everything* nowadays," she said sharply, her white makeup and burgundy lipstick creaking and cracking under the strain of her outrage. "It's not just accidents, and theft and stuff. It's things like assault and rape and murder! If you're not insured there's no justice for you in OneWorld. I saw somewhere how the old laws would protect a citizen impartially – no matter how much they were worth. The governments would actually – "

Larson took a generous swig of his scotch and cut in. "Well, my dear, you may not *like* it, but *that's* how the system works best! 'User pays is user empowerment.' Everyone has the freedom to choose the service that's right for them. *My* only complaint is that it's all getting a bit costly for a poor working man. Ha Ha."

His laughter was not returned by the group.

I was unwise enough to add my two cred's worth. "I saw a news item about some guy who put up a few pics of his holidays on the grID, and promptly got a 'cease and desist' from a company in Chiang Mai. Apparently, they'd bought his ID in some fire sale. Poor guy missed one payment on his identity insurance. Now he lives on neo-charity while he fights it in one court after another."

"See," Susilla exclaimed, spilling some of her champagne. "*This* is exactly what I'm talking about! The whole thing's got completely out of –"

"Serves him right!" Larson cut in again. "If he can't organise his life a bit better, he needs to wake up and –"

"But my identity is my birthright! Why in OneWorld should I have to pay some fucking insurance company to protect what I was born with?"

"Everyone right for drinks here?" Monterey interjected.

∞

I had taken advantage of Monterey's timely arrival to extricate myself from the bickering group on the balcony, only to become stranded with two colourless men in identical light-grey suits. Since the other guests were avoiding them, I felt obliged to try and make some sort of conversation.

"You two look like brothers," I said.

"We are." said one.

"That's nice." *What a daft thing to say!* I offered my hand.

"Sven," the man said.

I turned to his brother. "And your name is ... ?"

"Sten."

"Wow! Sven and Sten, eh?" I chortled like an idiot.

They looked at me blankly, and it took me a T-sec to get myself back on track.

"So, umm ... what do you guys do?"

"Oh, we work in completely *different* areas." Sven (or was it Sten) said, warming to the subject. "I, myself, am in waste processing."

There was an awkward pause, during which I was obviously supposed to say something.

"*Sten* here, on the other hand, works in waste recovery." Another awkward pause.

"That's, err ... that's pretty important stuff," I finally managed to say.

"Which one?" Sten asked sharply.

"Which one? Well ... obviously ... *both*."

For some reason this didn't seem to satisfy either of them.

"You are not ON," Sten brusquely said, as if announcing the results of an enquiry.

"Ahh, no ... I'm, umm ... saving up for it." I smiled. "So, I guess you're ON."

"We both are."

"How about that?"

"We know exactly what each other is thinking," Sven said.

"That must be fascinating for you both."

Sven and Sten simultaneously placed their drinks on the table. Sven was the first to speak. At least I thought it was Sven.

"ON is not something for amusement. ON is a conduit to facilitate enhanced cooperation and performative utility between human groups ..."

Sten took up the baton. "... for the purpose of building socially cohesive and upwardly branching consensual structures which ..."

Sven – *Sven's the taller one* – again. "... cement and focus collective and adaptive strategies ..."

Sten: "... to move the project forwards."

"Ah, there you are!" cried a familiar, and slightly drunk woman who grabbed my arm and pulled me away from Sven and Sten, without bothering to acknowledge them. "I'm sorry, I've completely forgotten your name," she giggled. "Come on. I want you to meet some friends."

She led me across the room and introduced me to a small gathering of people. I immediately felt a searing pain in my leg. I looked down and a small boy met my gaze with a satisfied smirk, having just given me a savage kick in the shins.

"Chester!" his mother cried out. "Sorry, he's just exploring his personal boundaries."

"How old is he?" I asked, rubbing my leg.

"You know, I can't remember!" she exclaimed, laughing apologetically. "He was born when we moved to Medusa, so that would be ... hang on, I'll just check my Tempo bills."

The woman's eyes flickered almost imperceptibly. *She's ON.*

"There we go. 12B2 AE1F. All rights reserved, etcetera, etcetera."

"They grow up so quickly, don't they?"

She smiled back at me. "So true, Youren, so true."

I turned towards the ghastly child. "And what do you want to be when you grow up, Chester?"

"An Under Assistant Sleep-Schedule Tabulator, Level 3!" Chester shouted.

"He's known that since he was tiny tot," his mother said with pride. Then she turned to him and whispered, "Sweetie, why don't you go and play with the other children?"

Chester ran off with a bloodcurdling scream, leaving us in peace. It wasn't long before the conversation among the group had drifted towards the 'rooin problem'.

"Sorry. Exactly what 'problem' is there?" I asked.

They looked at me uneasily. Then one of the more vocal members of the group took it upon himself to explain how 'things had got beyond a joke' and that humans needed to 'wake up to themselves' and 'look out for each other' because 'the way things are going nowadays', our 'very way of life' was 'under threat' and, not that he was 'prejudiced against *individual* rooins' per se, but ...

"Homo sapiens is becoming the new Neanderthal, my friend. If we're not careful, we'll find ourselves extinct."

"Hey, speaking of rooins," I said, "I've got a really hot rooin girlfriend. Seriously, she is the best fuck I've ever had! We're getting married soon. Oh, and we're planning to adopt. We both want a big family."

I gave them all the biggest, stupidest grin I could rustle up.

"What, you think this is *funny*?" the man screeched.

I noticed a small piece of olive was stuck between his front teeth.

"This is no joke!" he continued. "This is the future of our species we're talking about."

"You're beginning to sound like the SDU," I said. "And I've seen with my own eyes where *their* ideas lead. Dead bodies lying in the street. What do you propose to do? Round-up all the rooins and kill them?"

There were gasps all round.

"Hey, no-one's talking about killing anyone!" the man said, raising his palms towards me. "All I'm saying is, it's time for humans to stand up and be counted. Take some pride in their species. What the hell's wrong with that? We've been on this planet for ..." he looked around the group, as if hoping someone would supply him with a figure, any figure as long as it sounded BIG, "... well, for a *very long time*. We're not some Johnny-come-lately species who – "

"Like rooins, you mean?"

"Any species! I'm saying this without prejudice towards any particular species. Humans built this planet. This is our home. And science tells us that a species has a *right* to protect its habitat from predators."

"Really? Science tells us that?"

He pressed a finger into my breastbone. "Let me ask you something. How would you like it if some *creature* broke into your home, took your wife and kids and – "

"Let's keep it friendly, shall we?"

Monterey physically placed her ample form between me and the man. Monterey still smelled nice, and I wanted to elope with her there and then. She smoothed things over yet again, then shot me a glare that said this was all somehow my fault. She was probably right. The elopement was definitely off. Everyone was relieved when I left to find Lleo.

I tried some of the rooms down the hallway. The first door opened onto a room full of children running amok.

"Will you play with us?" pleaded a small girl dressed in a fairy costume and wearing a 'rooin' mask. I looked around the room and saw that all of them had 'rooin' masks. Chester was there too.

"We're rooins!" Chester shouted, jumping up and down on an expensive toy.

I made some excuse, which produced groans of disappointment, and shut the door.

The next room clearly belonged to Lleo and Montery's prepubescent daughter, Indigo, as it was piled high with glittering, pink junk. The room was currently occupied by a young couple who appeared to be in the process of breaking up. The woman was sitting on the bed, sobbing with subtle accusation, while the man did an impersonation of a constipated statue next to her. Shut that door. It occurred to me that Lleo had possibly left the party for some reason. *Probably shagging his secretary,* I chuckled to myself.

I opened the next door and found Lleo noisily shagging his secretary.

"Uh, sorry ... sorry!" I said, trying to shut the door as quickly as possible.

Unfortunately, I got my jacket caught in the handle, which made the whole thing take a lot longer than any of us would have liked. Alone in the hallway and feeling like a fool, I wondered what to do with myself.

Guess I'll go play with the rooin kids.

∞

Lleo found me near the drinks table, whisky in hand. He looked at me and laughed.

"Do you even know who you are, Youren?"

I removed the rooin mask.

"I've decided to change species, Lleo. I've had it with being human."

Lleo stopped laughing. "Don't say that, Youren. It's not right."

"I'm kidding, I think."

"Good. Hey, sorry about ... back there. You know how it is, eh? Mum's the word."

"I would hope not."

"It's just that Monterey doesn't ... you know, um ... anymore."

I didn't know what to say. I'd always thought Monterey was, well, very sexual.

Lleo added, cheerily, "Me, I seem to have gone mad for it lately."

Quite. Too much information.

"I guess ... I guess we all have to *play our part* ..." his voice trailed off. Then he brightened up and put his arm around me. "Hey, I've been meaning to talk to you about something. I've got a little proposition."

He led me into an empty room and sat me down.

"I've got some really good news," he said. "I can get you ON, right now, no cost!"

"What? Um, how is that ..."

"Our firm is going 100% ON. Big push. They've given some of us bonus packages which include free ON engraft procedures for family and friends. Soooo, *you* my friend are going to get ON! Cool, eh?"

"Lleo," I said, "I really appreciate this, but ..."

"Look, I know you've had your problems recently, and I know you're a proud bastard," he gave me a brotherly punch in the arm, "but this is your big chance. Face the facts, man, you're not going to get ahead in One-World if you're not ON. No human is."

I knew I had to answer carefully. "Lleo, I know you want what's best for me, I really do."

His smile began to fade.

"But," I continued gently "I do not want to go ON. It'd never work. I don't play nicely with the other kids and I never will."

Lleo didn't reply.

"I love you like a brother Lleo, but please don't ask me to do this."

"Brother? You call yourself a brother and you just insult me? You're pathetic, you know that?"

"Look, if you're going to get weird on me, I think it's best if I just ..."

"Shut up! Shut up and listen. This is a new beginning for all of us. The human species is on the brink of something amazing. But *you and all your kind* don't seem to give a shit. You just want to fuck it all up for everybody!"

"Me and all my kind? Lleo, what are you talking about?"

"Stop interrupting me! I'm telling you ... *we're* telling you something important."

He grabbed my shirt, which was a mistake. I hit his arm, and he yelped in pain. I heard another cry from outside the door. Lleo tried to grab me again, but I pushed him away.

"No you listen to me, Lleo. I don't give a fuck what you or anyone else is telling me! *You and all your kind* can shove it up your fat ON arse!"

Behind me, the door opened. I felt a heavy blow to the back of my neck. I turned to see Monterey raising something in her hand to strike me again. I managed to avoid most of the blows and made my way back through the party towards the front door. One of the rooin-haters put her foot out to trip me but I kicked it, causing the woman to topple backwards into the drinks table. I heard breaking glass and screams. Someone grabbed my collar, but I shook them off and ran for the door. I didn't look back.

∞

The minigrav sped through the corridor towards central Medusa. The other passengers were not talking, but that's not to say they were silent or inactive. I was surrounded by humans who were busy smiling, humming along to songs I couldn't hear, or darting their eyes around the cabin as if following some unseen drama. No-one was wearing a grID visor. A couple suddenly began laughing raucously, rhythmically pushing their mouths towards the ceiling with identical gestures. I became fascinated by a mother and child who appeared to be playing some sort of game. Both wore matching pink ON t-shirts. Their eyes would jump up and down, and left and right, in unison. Periodically, mother and child would stop and laugh, presumably when one or other of them had scored a point. Then, gradually, the child's gaze shifted, as he became aware of me watching them. His little features warped from joy, to concern, to fear, to *hatred*. He clutched his mother's arm and she instantly looked at me with the same hatred. She opened her mouth as if to say something, but she seemed physically incapable of doing so.

"Medusa A9," a voice announced over the intercom. The zebra-pattern floor lights began flashing, directing us all to the exit gates.

I entered the gravdome's main atrium, which was packed with humans and a smaller number of rooins. The two species moved in clusters, in such a way that they avoided contact with each other. In the centre of the atrium was the new CoolGlobalGiant store – a vast nasglass sphere with at least nine levels. Much of the store was devoted to ON. On one level, I could see rows of auto-med booths where humans could have the engraft procedure as they waited for their connecting flight. A long queue had formed. Other levels offered technical assistance with plug-ins and upgrades. The ground level showcased all the latest ON clothing. Bright colours had now replaced the original black designs, with an explosion of pinks, aquas, oranges and yellows shining through the store windows at me. Posters through-out the store proclaimed, 'OneWorld: 23% ON'.

A familiar figure walked past me. *Could it be?* I tried to edge closer to him through the crush of the crowd. He turned.

"Cuntface!" I shouted, hurrying over to greet him, amused at the fact that I was actually happy to see such an unpleasant person. "It's all shit, eh?"

Cuntface turned and glared at me with disdain. But this was a different sort of disdain. I caught sight of the ON logo on his dirty t-shirt.

"What the fuck's that, man? Oh right ..." I laughed knowingly, "con-fuse them with – " I stopped, watching in horror as the logo began to move.

"I don't understand, man. What? You ... you really *are* ON?"

Cuntface sneered at me, and turned to leave. "Wake up to yourself," he said, before disappearing into the crowd.

I looked up. Rain was beating down on the atrium's nasglass panels. Suspended from the roof girders was the largest media billboard I had ever seen. On it, were four familiar words.

'THE FUTURE IS ON.'

∞

On the security screen, a pale face peered out from a curtain of black hair.

"Hey, man," Dos said. "You look like, umm ..."

"Shit?"

"I wasn't going to say *that*," he said, grinning. "Come up."

"Before I do, I have to ask you something, Dos."

"What?"

"Are you ON?"

"Are you shitting me?" he laughed. "I may like zombies, but I don't wanna be one."

"I'll come up then."

"And I'll put the jug on."

I found the thought of his impending, undrinkable coffee strangely comforting.

The apartment was even more cluttered – more books and toys, more equipment.

"Space was cool?" he asked, handing me something evil in a mug.

Up close, I could see that his face looked strained, his eyes bloodshot.

"Yeh, space was cool. Not like here."

"Hey! I've got something to show you."

He pointed to a machine which looked like a miniature version of the *Hypercube* with some serious 64-phase power accumulators attached. I couldn't imagine how Dos had managed to divert that much juice from the grID and cover his tracks.

"What is it?"

"A micro-accelerator. Normally this would have cost a fortune but, well ..."

"What does it do?"

"It smashes subatomic particles, man!"

"And this is cool because ..."

"This-Is-Cool-Because ... because I can use it to measure what's going wrong."

"With everything?"

"Well, the *fabric*, the probability engine behind it all."

"Dos, you don't need a machine to tell you what's going wrong with everything. I can tell you that ..."

What happened next surprised both of us. I started to cry. Before long, I was sobbing and blubbering hopelessly, and he had his arm around me, forcing me to drink some of the worst coffee ever created by man. My appreciative laughter punctuated my sobs.

"Sorry, Dos. I'm sorry, man. I dunno ..."

"It's OK, Youren. I understand."

We sat quietly for a while.

"It's ON, isn't it?" he asked, breaking the silence.

"Yes. Does your machine have anything to say about that?"

"Maybe."

"Is everyone insane, or is it just me? They all seem to have turned into ..."

"Zombies?"

"Worse. *Smiling* zombies. No wait, smiling, *clever* zombies. Zombies who know more about what's going on than I do. Zombies who seem to be smugly enjoying their 'zombieness', while I just ..." I wiped away my tears. "You know, I met a rooin on Erco Menoz who thought humans were due for extinction. Arrogant prick, he was. But what if he's right? And now I've just come from a party where humans think ON is the only way they'll avoid that. What if they're right too? What if it's just humans like me that are due for extinction?"

A few more tears began to fall.

Dos put his hand on my shoulder and said, "You look like you need something stronger than coffee."

∞

"Is this plot going anywhere?"

"Sure it is. Everyone just has to remember."

"Remember what?"

"The plot."

Dos and I nearly fell off the couch laughing. This was not a good idea, as we had discovered earlier. At one point, we were laughing so much, we both fell onto the floor. Getting back up had proved hilariously difficult, since both of us had been half convinced the floor was some sort of ocean, and we were in danger of drowning. This had prompted such exchanges as: "Permission to come aboard sir," and "I'm afraid we've lost him, Captain!" Now that we were safely back on dry land, we had no wish to fall off again.

"Wow, Dos! This Blu-Zone is major league!"

"Yeah," he breathed out slowly. "Got it from a mercenary."

We were watching *Night of the Dark Zulk*, and it was hilariously bad.

"OK, OK, OK, OK, I got it!" Dos announced, with swelling pride. "The guy with the head wound is in league with the creatures."

"That's not a head wound, it's his helmet."

"You're shitting me!" He leaned forwards as far as he dared, and peered into the screen. "Maybe it's some kind of alien growth."

"It's his helmet, you dick! He's from the Planet Knob."

This last statement amounted to near suicide. Once more we fell around weeping with laughter, and nearly plummeted into the ocean again. I could see the Dark Zulk swimming in the depths, waiting to devour us. But eventually we calmed down a little and watched in puzzled silence for a while. Then Dos began bouncing enthusiastically.

"You know who this one reminds me of?"

"Which one?"

"The guy with the cape. ZapMan! Remember him?"

"Are you kidding?" I shouted. "I used to *love* ZapMan when I was a kid!"

"Me too. I've tried everywhere, but you can't get him anymore. All licences are expired."

"Wow, that's sad." I said, despite the fact that I had never given Zap-Man a single thought since childhood. Now, my beloved superhero seemed very important in the scheme of things. "Hey, remember how he had the power to transform reality? You know ..."

"*ZapMan. Warping Space and Time!*" we intoned, doing two completely different impersonations of the original announcer, and making silly hand gestures apropos of nothing.

"ZapMan was the best," Dos said, breathing out reverentially.

Then he turned to me and said, "Hey Youren, you wanna know a secret? But you gotta swear never to tell anyone, or they'll put me away forever."

"Sure, Dos. You can trust me."

"I know what time it is."

∞

"Good morning, Youren. I hope you slept well."

My only response was a groan. I could still see the Dark Zulk clambering up out of the ocean and onto Dos Pascal's couch.

"Come on, Youren, a nice ion shower will have you feeling like a new man. It's a beautiful day out there, tops of 1C, with the chance of some gentle showers after lunch. Oh, and before I forget, Magazino are having a sale of all clothing with up to 20% discount on their entire range. 'Magazino. It's you.' If you like, Youren, I could log in a prompt for a quick lunchtime visit. I'm told the Lancron jackets are pretty cool."

"No thanks, Al." I had decided to start calling my prompter Al. The immediate effect of this had been that he now used my own name incessantly.

"Not a problem, Youren. See you in the kitchen in a jump."

Breakfast was waiting for me on the bench. Pepti-Oats, my favourite.

"Youren, if I recall correctly, you need to take in those 'Come back ON' ad proposals you've been working on. They're on your desk under the Terra-Air bills. Maybe you should get them now, Youren."

"I'm not going to work, Al."

"Really? Are you not well, Youren?"

"No, I'm not well."

"I'm sorry to hear that, Youren. I can inform the relevant people at i++ if you like."

"Yes, why don't you do that, Al."

"Consider it done, Youren. Should I make an appointment with Doctor Benseen?"

"No that's fine, thanks, Al. I'd like to be alone now."

"Of course, Youren. See you in a jump."

∞

I sat at my desk, and did a quick search for 'mood swings', 'aggression', 'compulsion', 'memory loss – anything I could think of – and then cross-referenced it to 'ON'. Surprisingly little came up, and whatever looked interesting had a FEDMED suppression applied. I was beginning to lose heart, when by chance I came across a Doctor Rafaela Serif from the Pentangle Institute. FEDMED had suppressed almost all of her papers, and some of the titles had been redacted, but there was enough to give me a general idea of where she was at. *Prevalence of Zeigler's Syndrome in ON Subjects; The Role of ON in the Thule Incident: A Case Study in Group [————]; Applying Clarke's Delusional Markers to [————] ON In-Patients*; and several more.

I read her bio. Then I saw her picture. This was one scary-looking woman.

∞

The minigrav touched down in what looked like the middle of a desert. On closer inspection, there was a town of sorts. Toc-Zic. My grID visor supplied the details. 'Toc-Zic. Pop: 761F. Principal industries ... ' They seemed to have skimped on the environment lighting, so everything looked pretty gloomy. A medical complex had just been built near the gravDome, and for some reason the architects had decided to make all the buildings a bright, bilious green.

"That's gonna make everyone in Toc-Zic feel a whole lot better."

I took the *B-tube* into the adjacent town of Marsville, and made my way to the Pentangle Institute. Doctor Rafaela Serif's impressive offices occupied nearly an entire floor of the neuropsych wing. There were labs, tutorial rooms, and a clinic. Her PA ushered me into the waiting room, and brought me some flower-tea and fruit.

"Please come in."

Doctor Rafaela Serif stood at the doorway to her office. She was a formidable sight – snow-white skin, blood-red lips, jet-black hair cut into a savage angle. This was someone who didn't suffer fools gladly, and unfortunately I felt like a fool.

"Have a seat, Mister ... ?"

I remained silent.

She sighed. "So, you don't trust me."

"I can't fool a psych, can I?"

"Why would you even want to?"

Those eyebrows could lift weights.

"I'm sorry, Doctor," I apologised. "I've become a lot more cautious recently. My name is Youren, Youren Cartouche."

"And what can I do for you, Mister Cartouche?"

"Well, this is going to sound crazy, but I think everyone is going crazy. How's *that* for crazy? At first I thought I was just paranoid or something, but now I'm pretty sure that everyone really *is* going crazy ... or worse."

"Are you ON?" she asked.

"No. Absolutely not."

"Well that's emphatic! I ask everyone that question now, sometimes even before I know their name. So, why *not?*"

"Pardon?"

"It's a simple enough question. You're young, professional. ON is rapidly becoming the only way for someone like you to get ahead. Why buck the trend? The obvious question – what's your problem?"

"My problem?"

"Let's call it your 'absolutely not' decision."

"OK, well from a practical point of view, all of the genuinely useful things you can do with ON can be achieved with pre-existing technologies like grID visors, trackers, prompters and so on. But as for my 'problem' ... Ever since I can remember, I haven't really liked people all that much. I'm fairly antisocial, in fact. And as I've recently discovered, many of them don't like me. So I ask you, why should I pay a large chunk of my hard-earned cred to tune in to all their shitty little thoughts, see what they all do in their shitty little lives, or give any of them the privilege of tuning in to mine? And while we're on the subject of ON and our problems, Doctor, how come you copped out and completely turned yours off?"

"Ha! Well, I can see why people don't like you," she said, raising an immaculate eyebrow. "And trust me on this, it's not just your paranoia."

Then she gave a hearty laugh and leaned across the desk, offering a white hand. I was surprised by how soft and warm it felt. At this instant, a Basenji dog entered the room and jumped up onto my chair, quickly nestling his small body into mine.

"Well, at least Shisaq likes you," she smiled. "He's wild-seed, by the way. Still legal but only just. Sooner or later I'll get a 'cease and desist' from Companion."

Shisaq's wrinkled brow required some serious attention, and as I patted him I looked up to see Doctor Sherif watching me interestedly.

She said, "Anyway, back to ON. I turned it all off because, well because *I'm* the one who went crazy – may as well be blunt about it. Layman's terms: disorientation, memory loss, hallucinations, and so on."

"Sorry, I didn't know."

"Well, you wouldn't have a chance to now. Most of my papers have been suppressed."

"Someone must see you as a threat."

"Take your pick. But it's not as ominous as you make it sound. It's just commerce. Many corporations – not just CoolGlobalGiant – have a lot of money riding on this product. They can't have irritating little neuroscientists like me rocking the gravy train, if I may mix my metaphors."

"But what if the thing is really dangerous? What if everyone is ..."

She issued a crypto-command, and a set of graphs appeared on her media screen.

"Statistically, the majority are not adversely affected by it. In fact, CoolGlobalGiant and FEDMED, have jointly released figures proving that humans who are ON are less prone to crime, depression, substance abuse, and a host of other behaviours costly to the OneWorld economy. And you can't argue with commerce."

"I suddenly feel prone to crime, depression and substance abuse. So that's it? We just sit back and watch humans turn into zombies?"

"Zombies with money," she corrected me. "Look, sorry to be so cynical. I've tried and got nowhere. I was recently thrown out of a neuropsych conference because of my stance. What more can I do? If consumers want to purchase a big brand do-it-yourself zombie kit, who am I to tell them not to?"

"When did you give up?"

"When did I – well that's a bit rich! Who are you to tell me what – "

"I'm sorry. That was very rude."

Her face softened. "Look, I'd like to do more. Really. Deep down I'm very angry at the way we've been hijacked by our rush towards ... whatever it is we're all rushing towards."

We fell into an awkward silence. Shisaq yawned languidly and made a funny little noise. Then he jumped off my chair and went to sit by the door, as if expecting a visitor.

After a while I said, "Don't feel so bad about going 'crazy'. I've been seeing a ghost recently."

"That's ... interesting."

"A young girl. She seems to be trying to warn me of something, but I don't know what. 'Don't listen to them'. That's what she said."

For the first time since entering her office, I became aware of a large painting behind her desk. A black figure, with no apparent eyes, sat inside a glass box surrounded by darkness and chaos. Not very comforting for a patient, I would have thought. I leaned forwards, trying to see something of the figure's features, but all I could make out was a screaming mouth.

"Who do you think it is?"

"Sorry?"

"Who do you think it is that's trying to warn you? This ghost girl."

"I don't know. All I know is her name is Eve. To be honest, I thought she might have represented my guilty conscience. I work for CoolGlobalGiant's advertising agency. Ironically, most of the recent ON propaganda has been written by me."

"Ha ha! That is too good!"

"I'm not proud of it."

"No. You wouldn't be."

I hesitated, then said, "May I ask you something personal?"

She tipped her head, giving me a look that would stop most men right there.

"When you were ON, and you went *crazy* and all that, did you also find yourself *compelled* to do things you wouldn't normally do?"

"Not really, just confusion mainly. Unless you count the time I decided to chuck it all in and start a farm."

"The reason I asked you is, well the ONs I've observed seem compelled to do things. A friend of mine who's ON recently said something out of the blue which has been bothering me. He said 'We all have to play our part.' It was as if he'd been handed a script or something. So I'll tell you what I think. This is not just another consumer folly. Something is controlling it. There's a blueprint, some kind of master plan."

She gave a puzzled look, a look which gradually became more disturbed.

"The diagram," she said.

A rose by any other colour

⏻

"WHAT do you make of this, Ozzi-Chen?"

As Constantin Zann unfurls the large vellum sheet he is carrrying Ozzi-Chen looks around uncomfortably.

"It's OK," Zann says, "I've triangulated the park scanners. They miss this spot."

The two rooins are sitting on a grass-like substance which slopes down towards a small lake. On the lake, several ducks are swimming in circles. Each of the ducks has a bright green Parkcom logo on the back of its head. The environmental lighting has been programmed with a dappling effect, as though sunlight is being filtered through leaves stirred by a gentle breeze.

"Zann, it's probably not my place to say but ..."

"But you think I should let it go?"

"What can we do? What are we *allowed* to do?"

"Just have a look. Please."

Ozzi-Chen reluctantly spreads the drawing out, his eyes flitting across its myriad lines. "Well, it's a network of some sort, isn't it? Umm ... a kind of snapshot of the evolution of a non-linear interphase set. Sorry, there's not much more I can ... *wow*! ... that was weird."

"What?"

The young rooin shakes his head and turns to watch the ducks.

"What did you see?" Zann asks.

"Nothing, just a kind of ... optical illusion."

"I saw a face." Zann offers.

Ozzi-Chen looks at Zann with amusement. But on seeing the other rooin's eager expression, he looks away in pity. "No, Zann, there's no face there. Of *anyone*. This was more like an illusion of movement, as if I was seeing the next phase instance of the set. Very weird."

"Have another look," Zann pushes the drawing towards Ozzi-Chen, but the young rooin stops him.

"Please, Zann. This is not healthy. And it's not legal either. The client has settled their account. I shouldn't even be here right now. I'm supposed to be working on a water smuggling case."

Zann sighs, rolls up the drawing, and watches the ducks. One of them appears to be in distress. The creature is swimming around in ever decreasing circles, emitting a high-pitched squeaking noise. Then one by one the other ducks attack it, brutally pecking its neck until the unfortunate misfit sinks below the water in a cloud of pink bubbles.

Ozzi-Chen turns to back Zann. "I did find out something about ON. As you asked."

"Yes?"

"Semi-legal methods, of course. Anyway, seems everything's not quite as wonderful as CoolGlobalGiant tells us in their ads. There have been documented cases of humans having bad psychological reactions to the procedure. Seeing things and so on. But, not only did FEDMED fail to act on these reports, they suppressed them 'in the consumer's interest'."

"Don't listen to them. That's what Mrs Krianti told me Eve Lamente said."

"You think she had these kinds of problems? But why would someone kill her for that?"

"Can you do one more thing for me, Ozzi-Chen?"

"I like my job, Zann."

"Can you find out who this man is?"

Zann opens a secure near-field link with Ozzi-Chen and transfers the scanner images of the man with the blue rose. Ozzi-Chen gives him a mock glare.

"Please," Zann pleads.

The broken body of the dead duck resurfaces and floats limply on the grey water.

∞

I took the B-tube from the gravDome to downtown Medusa, alighting at Maddox Station. As I stepped out of the tube, I studied the faces of my fellow humans. Were they really my fellow humans anymore? I tried smiling at each one as they approached, but got nothing in return except an averting of the eyes, a sneer, or the occasional muttered "Freak!" How many of these people were ON? According to CoolGlobalGiant's propaganda, it was now over a quarter. But the actual figure could have been much less or much more, there was no way of knowing. Right now, everyone in the world except me could have been ON and I wouldn't have known. The absurd thought was chilling. I laughed out loud, prompting another passer-by to tell me I was a freak.

Where was I going? My feet seemed to know, and soon I was travelling the approach ramp to Turing Plaza, and the headquarters of CoolGlobalGiant.

I looked up at the six towers. Maybe Biz Ramachandran was there now. If only I could get up there and see him and ... and what? Was he to blame for all this? Could he even stop it if he wanted to? Near the entrance was the almost childish logo of CoolGlobalGiant, and underneath it was the company slogan, dreamed up so long ago in Biz Ramachandran's Harvard dorm room: *'For the good of all'*.

I approached the cascading water doors. To enter the building, you had to walk through a waterfall. Scanners detected to within a micron the location, shape, volume and speed of your body. Then a matrix of matter transfer beams removed exactly that amount of water to the fountains in the foyer. It was impossible to get wet. Little kids would run around and jump up and down, shrieking with laughter as they tried to trick the mechanism, until an exasperated parent would drag them back into the foyer – elated yet slightly disappointed they were still completely dry. Going through the water doors meant you had to put your trust in CoolGlobalGiant; they would never harm you in any way. The other thing the water doors told you was that CoolGlobalGiant had more money than any other company on the planet.

The foyer was immense, made even larger by the architectural illusion that it went on indefinitely in all directions. I looked back to the waterfall doors but they had disappeared. The only indication of any kind of exit was the line of black security grills along the floor. Clever but creepy.

"Are you here for ONSIM, Sir?"

A young woman wearing a white ON t-shirt and black tights had approached me. She wore a little nametag which read 'Anna'.

"I'm not sure. What is it?"

"It gives you a simulated experience of the world of ON. You're not ON, are you sir?

"No."

Would you like to join the next session? It's a real buzz!" She gave me a seductive smile.

"Sure, why not."

"Cool. Just go over to the red reception desk and they'll sort you out. Enjoy."

All the young people behind the circular reception desk wore the same style of white ON t-shirt and black tights. 'Geoffrey' took my details. "Thank you sir, now, if you would just place your right eye over the Retinal Scanner here ..."

"Whoa! That's a bit heavy. Do you *need* to do that?"

"Sorry sir, it's a security requirement for all simulation participants." Geoffrey shrugged unconvincingly, and added, "CoolGlobalGiant policy."

"I dunno, it seems pretty draconian."

"What's the hold-up?" a voice behind me asked.

"Some guy's got issues with the Retinal Scan," another voice.

"If you've got nothing to hide, you've got nothing to fear," a third voice.

Geoffrey looked at me with barely concealed irritation.

"I'm sorry sir. I'll have to ask you to step aside if you're unable to submit to the RS. There are others waiting."

I looked out over the foyer's imitation of infinity. *Nothing to hide. Nothing to fear.*

"Oh, what the hell. OK."

"You won't regret it sir," Geoffrey was saying as a sliver of blue light crossed my eye.

I had the subtle sensation of falling.

∞

Biz Ramachandran was drunk. Considering his girth, the term 'rolling drunk' was probably appropriate. He had just returned from a long lunch with some old university friends. It had been a chance to remember, and forget. With what he imagined was aplomb, he elaborately negotiated a course from the gravport to the little executive elevator that took him up the few remaining floors to his suite of offices. Biz fell into the couch and began studying his hands, opening and closing the fingers.

A machine. Just like a machine.

"Nice work, Biz! You missed the SEABED talks." Li Sun dropped a report onto the table in front of him.

"They don't need me," Biz spoke to his hands.

Li Sun sat down next to him and studied his face.

"Shit, Biz! Why aren't you ON? Why do I always have to go verbal?"

"I like to be alone. I like the peace," he said.

"Peace?" she laughed. "The way you're going Biz, you'll have peace alright."

Biz looked at her with his sad brown eyes, then lunged at her clumsily.

"Get off me, you pig!" She pushed him away and stood up. "What do you think I am?"

"I thought you were ... I thought *we* were ..."

"Nothing! We were nothing, Biz."

"You've forgotten ..."

"Biz, look at me. We don't match up."

"Match up? What was that old saying? It takes all types to make a world."

"It takes the *right* types to make a world, Biz."

As Li Sun left the room her perfume remained.

Biz Ramachandran got up and walked to the window. Below him was a dirty carpet of cloud which covered the world. Biz Ramachandran had come so close to owning a world that he couldn't even see. And now it was slipping through his fingers.

∞

We were ushered into a small auditorium and invited to make ourselves comfortable. Each of us had been provided with a complicated headset. We played with them, but no-one seemed game enough to try theirs on. Then a gentle floodlight came up on the low stage and a young woman, dressed in the same white ON t-shirt and black tights, stepped into the light.

"Hello, everyone. It's great to see you all here. My name is Kirsty, and I'll be guiding you through this session. Each of you should now have one of these." She held up one of the headsets. "Has anybody *not* got one? No? Cool. I know they're not pretty; you wouldn't want to walk down the street wearing one, right? You know, my section boss reckons CoolGlobalGiant made these things really ugly so you guys will want the real thing."

There was a smattering of polite laughter.

"Ha ha. Right, so these ONSIM headsets will help you to experience the ON world. But before I show you how to use them, I want you to meet three very special people."

A woman and two men joined Kirsty on the stage, and she introduced each of them.

"These three people are ON, and *because* they're ON, they can link up to your headsets, so that you will know something of what it feels like to exist in the world of ON. Are there any questions?"

A man raised his hand. "Can we get hurt in the ON world?"

"Good question, thank you sir. I meant to cover this. Any sensation we can feel in this world can also be felt in the world of ON, so that includes pain. But don't worry, we've installed pain filters into these devices, so that your little journey will only be pleasurable. Any more questions? No? OK, let's get started. First place the silver cap on your head and tighten the soft mesh band around your forehead. Got it? No, a bit lower. That's it. Make sure it's snug. Next place the red nostril buds into your nose, like this. They should feel comfortable. Everyone got that? Yes? Now this blue U-shaped thing fits under your tongue like so. Pretty soon you won't even know its there. And, finally, put in the yellow ear buds – make sure right goes in right, left in left, otherwise you'll get very disoriented. Good. Now lower the black eyepieces, lay back and relax. Don't worry if you can't see anything yet. You soon will, so don't be too surprised. OK?"

I settled into the comfort of the chair, and drifted into the inner darkness. I had begun to lose track of time, when suddenly I found myself standing in the middle of a grassy field, surrounded by a forest of trees. The other simulation participants were also there, blinking and looking around in surprise. None of us appeared to be wearing headsets. I could feel the warmth of the sun and a cool breeze against my skin. Leaves rustled, insects buzzed, and birds sang. I could smell earth, grass, and smoke from a distant wood fire. Above me was a clear blue sky. I looked down and saw that I had my own body and I was wearing my own clothes. All my limbs worked, sort of. I was just getting used to moving my fingers when Kirsty appeared before us.

"Well, here we all are, in the world of ON. Not too much of a shock?"

Everyone chuckled good-naturedly, to reassure themselves as much as her.

"Now, first things first. In your lower peripheral vision you should see a red button on the right. Can we all see that? Good. That's the panic button. If, for any reason, you find all this too much, just look at this button, repeat to yourself the word 'Home', and we'll bring you back into the auditorium. Don't do it now!" she laughed, "we don't want you to miss out on all the fun. But you don't have to worry. CoolGlobalGiant is taking care of you. So let's have a look around, shall we?"

She began walking in the direction of some distant trees, and we hesitantly followed.

"This place no longer exists," Kirsty was saying, "it's a memory. Mostly it's Samuel's memory. At least, it was at first, but then more and more of Sam's childhood friends began to contribute to that memory, and this place is now as rich and detailed as anywhere on the planet. We call this a 'Wiki-Memory'. If – hopefully *when* – you guys get ON, you'll find millions of these community memory projects for you to join. Each project is helping to build and enrich the world of ON."

She stopped and pointed to the trees. "Oh, look. Who's that over there?"

A man dressed in the familiar t-shirt and tights waved and walked towards us.

"Hey, it's Sam!" Kirsty announced, feigning surprise.

"Hi everyone," Samuel said. "Thanks for coming here to share my favourite childhood spot. Whatdya think?"

"It's lovely." a woman said, self-consciously.

"It is isn't it?" Samuel replied, taking a deep, satisfied breath. "But unfortunately we haven't got much time to enjoy it, because I think ... yes, Francine is ready now to introduce you to her Mom and Dad. Hang on guys, here we go!"

The grass and forest didn't exactly disappear, they melted and reconstructed themselves into the next reality. On arrival, one of our party – an older man – fell over.

"Don't worry sir," Kirsty said, helping him up. "I fell over quite a lot the first few times."

"Hey guys," Francine said entering the room. "Come meet my folks."

We were led into a cosy, rustic kitchen. A fire was crackling in the hearth and Francine's mother was standing at the stove, stirring something in a big earthenware pot.

"That sure smells great, Sandra." Kirsty said.

"Best damn cook in the valley," Francine's father chipped in.

"Oh for Pete's sake, Henry. Really!" Francine's mother admonished her husband.

The food did smell good and Francine's mother let us taste a bit. Vegetable stock pot. We spent some time chatting to Francine's parents about their experiences with ON, until Kirsty called us to attention.

"OK everyone, we're gonna have to thank Francine's Mom and Dad for being such great hosts, and bid them farewell. There's one more stop on our journey and it's a real beauty."

"Thanks for dropping by," Francine's mother said. She seemed genuinely sad that we were leaving. Maybe there was also loneliness in the world of ON.

"Everyone ready?" Kirsty turned to the gentleman who had previously fallen over. "You sir, would you like to hold my hand this time?"

The older man seemed more than happy to take the young woman's proffered hand.

Once again, our surroundings crumpled and re-assembled themselves, this time into a vast ZIM•Ball stadium. It looked like Bayer Stadium, but not quite. Colours, layout and angles were not quite right, and the perspective occasionally seemed to shift and buckle. We were standing about halfway up the stands on one of the main thoroughfares. Huddling us together against the crowd's crush, Kirsty shouted to make herself heard.

"Jason's a keen Major League fan and right now his team – the Kabul Texans – are playing the Jilin Kowboys. We've set-up a member's box so you guys can watch the final quarter with Jason. It's just up those steps. Make sure you all stick together."

With the shouting, jostling and subtle aggression of the people around us, I noticed some of the older members of our group looking a bit uneasy. No doubt one or two sets of eyes were hovering over that red panic button. We moved slowly along the thoroughfare until we reached a point where one set of stairs led up to the members stands, and another led down to the exits and service tunnels. I glanced down and noticed a lone man standing at the base of the stairs, looking up at me. It was hard to make him out in the gloom; his body appeared to shimmer and shift, and his face seemed excessively white. Then he took two steps towards me and beckoned.

It was Arlo.

The figure beckoned once more, then disappeared round the corner. Without thinking, I followed. Reaching the lower corridor, I saw the figure enter a side door halfway along. I ran to the door, opened it, and found myself inside a darkened storeroom. I tried the lights but they didn't work. Did lights work in the world of ON? For that matter, how could *anything* 'work' in the world of ON? I suddenly realised I had no idea what any of this really was. Was it a group memory? If so, how could

I be here? Or did this place really exist and I was somehow mapped into it, observing it? Or was it a fully functioning simulation where ...

"Youren."

Arlo was standing next to some shelves stacked with cleaning equipment. His round face, and rosy cheeks were pale, and his normally and comical eyes wore an expression of half amusement, half sadness.

"Arlo? How come you're here?" I asked. "I thought you hated ON."

"I do. Well ... I did. I never had the engraft procedure."

"So why are you ... ? Oh, I get it! You're in another ONSIM tour, right?"

"No Youren, I'm dead. Sort of."

"Dead?"

"I think Seyemon may have had a hand in it, but I can't prove it, 'cos I wasn't there."

"I'm not sure I understand ..."

"I'm a memory. Well, a whole bunch of memories. There's quite a few of us turning up here in the ON world – the dead who were known and loved by ONs. We're the ghosts in the machine."

"But how?"

"Death affects the living profoundly. People remember, grieve, obsess. They wish the person back, dwell on their little mannerisms, hold memorials, get-together to rake over the dead person's life, and so on."

"Well OK, but ..."

"All this builds up a lot of dense neural information about how the person looked, spoke, thought, moved, even smelled. Memories of someone who is dead are more potent and focused than memories of someone who is alive. Put all those rich data bundles inside an infinitely complex neural network like ON, and they can link up and give birth to thinking feeling versions of the dead. Like yours truly. Ta dah!" Arlo bowed theatrically.

"So you're not really Arlo, you're just everyone's memory of him."

Arlo seemed offended. "I'm more than that. That's just my starting point. I'm a self aware set of patterns, discovering that they're Arlo Arbuckle. I *think* I'm Arlo, therefore I *am* Arlo. Hey, I should get that on a t-shirt!"

He laughed again. It was definitely the same laugh.

"I'm having trouble processing all of this, Arlo," I admitted.

"And yet you're inside a multi-source neuro sim, and you seem quite OK with that."

"Fair point, whatever it was you just said. You're as sarcastic as ever, I see."

"Yeh. I'm learning how Arlo felt and behaved. I'm getting better at being him ... *me*."

"You're doing really well."

"Now who's sarcastic? Anyway," he said, chuckling, "it seems I'm just as unpopular with the ONs as I was when I was alive. They didn't foresee ghosts in the network, and they don't like it one bit." He lowered his voice. "They're trying to eradicate us."

"They?"

"Ghost hunters. ONs who are trained to target memory clusters like me and break up the connections. Seyemon's one of them – typical! They've got a fancy name for it: 'Personality Sim Management Program'. In other words, kill all the freaky little fuckers! But I've led them a merry chase. Those dicks are just as stupid *here*."

He gave a quasi-maniacal laugh, and I was beginning to see that this Arlo – while not exactly a parody – was a very much ramped-up version of the original.

"But why did they kill you, Arlo? It's not like you could have been a threat to them or anything? Or were you?"

"Beats me. Like I said, I wasn't there. See, I don't have any of Arlo's memories – just everyone else's memories of him. It's like I got amnesia or something. But I think I might have figured something out. Either that, or I was just a pain in the butt, eh?"

"You were that."

Arlo and I laughed, and it seemed like the most natural thing in the world.

"It's good to see you man." I said.

"You too."

"So, let me get this straight, you're kind of like a wiki-memory, right? I just learned about them. You know, where everyone ..."

"I'm not a fucking wiki-memory!" Arlo hissed angrily. "Oh they'd like me to be, of course – a commonly owned identity that's 'liked' or 'disliked' at the whim of the mob. No, Youren, I'm becoming a real *me*, and that sticks in their throats."

"I'm sorry Arlo, I didn't mean to – "

"Let me tell you something about wiki-memories. In the world of ON, *all* memories are becoming wiki-memories. Historical facts are starting to get voted up or down on the basis of popularity, like hairstyles or hem-lines. ONs only like to remember what they can agree upon, and guess what happens to anything that isn't agreed upon?"

"Umm ... ?"

He brought his pale face close to mine. "Consensus kills, Youren."

A look of alarm suddenly came over him. "Uh oh!"

"What?"

"Ghost hunters," he whispered. "Close by. You gotta leave – *now*."

"But surely they can't ..."

"Don't kid yourself, Youren! These guys can hurt you real bad."

"There's supposed to be pain filters or something on this ..."

"You have no idea, do you? Just get outa here. Head for the upper levels and I'll lose 'em in the basement. Go!"

We ran into the corridor just in time to see three large furry creatures advancing on us – a teddy bear, a bright green crocodile, and a multicoloured parrot. The teddy bear wore the Jilin Kowboys logo on his vest. Mascots! The ghost hunters were dressed as team mascots.

Arlo scurried down some steps, and the crocodile and parrot gave pursuit. But the teddy bear continued to come after me. I ran to the steps I had first come down, but someone had pulled the security grille across, locking it. The teddy bear was gaining, and the next set of steps was a fair way off. A group of spectators were coming towards me, yet I instinctively knew it would be futile to ask them for help and, as I ran past, they stepped aside to allow the bear through. My lungs were bursting when I reached the next set of steps. I stumbled and felt a hand grab my ankle. I managed to break free, and made it up a couple more steps before the bear got hold of my right foot. This time I felt the pain. Like frozen mercury, it seeped from the bear's paw into my bones. I heard a cracking sound as if I was breaking up. The bear dragged me close to its face. As I looked into the dead plastic eyes, a voice like a ceramic blade cut through layers of fake fur, and into my soul.

"Dust to dust."

With my free foot, I managed to kick the thing in the head, causing it to fall back down the steps. I made it to the main thoroughfare but was promptly set upon by a group of Jilin supporters who had just watched me assault one of their beloved mascots. Fists knocked me to the ground, then boots took over. Fortunately, an even larger group of Kabul supporters ran down from the upper stands to attack the Jilin mob, and in the chaos I struggled free.

I'd almost made it to the steps leading to the members stand where I knew Kirsty and the others would be, when I felt the familiar cold pain down my spine. The parrot and the crocodile were just behind me, a green fuzzy hand gripping my left shoulder. Both were soon on top of me. The light began to fade. I looked up, and a section of the roof fell away, crashing into the upper stands. I heard screaming. More pieces fell. The parrot looked up, just in time to see a large piece of falling metal slice through its head. The crocodile ran back to the prostrate form of the teddy bear, who had now been abandoned by the panicking Kabul supporters. More sections of the roof were coming away. A grinding noise echoed throughout the stadium. Most of the crowd in our section had run down the steps to escape, only to be crushed against the locked security grille. I could see Kirsty herding the group and helping each one to make the jump back. One by one they disappeared, as they used their panic button.

Panic button!

Why hadn't I thought of it before? As the crowd trampled me, I searched my field of vision for the red button, but could see nothing. I felt hands grab my neck and tighten. Kirsty was kneeling over me and seemed to be strangling me. Her thumbs were pressing hard into the back of my neck and I felt something click. There was a flash of light and I was back in the auditorium, sitting in my comfy chair. I ripped off my headset. The man in the next chair was vomiting all over the carpet. I looked around. Everyone was there. Kirsty was attending to a woman who had fainted. Others were crying, or angrily demanding explanations. One man had rolled himself into a foetal position on the floor, and was whimpering and shaking.

The door to the auditorium was flung open, and a man in a dark grey suit marched in. "Will someone tell me what the frig just happened!" he shouted at no-one in particular.

Kirsty looked up from tending to the fainted woman, but she was speechless.

The man in the suit took charge. "OK. All of you must stay here until a medical team arrives. It won't be long."

With that, he turned and left the room, ignoring all questions. I was pretty sure he locked the door behind him.

∞

It seemed to Doctor Rafaela Serif as though she had been sitting here on the couch forever, staring at the painting of the man in the glass box.

Shisaq padded over and sat on her foot. The dog yawned, then lay down across both her feet. He was a big help.

"You're not much use," Raf said, rubbing the dog's brow.

Raf extricated her feet from under the dog and checked her schedule. No patients for a while. She went into the little surgery next to her office and locked the door. Then she began assembling the necessary equipment. She lay back on the couch and attached the neuro recorder cap, carefully adjusting all the contacts. Next, she administered the memory pattern cocktail. She knew that another professional should be present, but she couldn't trust anyone anymore. She set the timer to bring her out of it, and closed her eyes. The drugs began to take effect, as the script commenced.

10 ... feeling calmer, more relaxed ... 9 ... all your limbs, very heavy ... 8 ... deeper now ...

She is now back at PSYCON, arguing with the door goon in the foyer. She is both fully engaged with the argument, but at the same time a detached observer. Bertie Whelan walks over to her, taking care of things. His right arm shakes. They are crossing the great hall. Other delegates pass her. Their smiles fade. Bertie's hand on her back feels agitated. She sits at the table, noticing Janice's sad smile. Not sadness, more like ... *fear.* The waiter mutters something. It sounds like ... coordinates. Now she is talking to Bertie and Janice over the din. Bertie periodically ogles some woman. Janice tries to say something. Mouthing something. Over and over. *'Opting?' 'Stopping?'*

'STOP IT.'

Adão Cabral mounts the stage. A complex diagram appears behind him. Strange but strangely familiar. Bertie lets out a sigh, like an animal in pain. His hand on her shoulder trembles. His eyes tell her to run. Standing in the queue. Cabral's voice in the distance is saying something about 'the one human'. She knows what comes next. The grip on her arm ...

... 7 ... feeling more alert already ... 6 ... starting to come back now ...

Raf disconnected the neuro cap and pressed a few controls on the recorder. For some reason, she couldn't stop shaking.

In the bathroom, she forced herself to look in the mirror. The not-so-great Doctor Rafaela Serif, world-renowned neuropsych, looked back at her. She opened the cupboard, took out a container of pills, and swallowed two. As she splashed some water on her face, she considered what she had to do. Yes, she could just do nothing and remain here in her 'scientific' world, but she knew it wouldn't last long.

The way things are going now.

She walked back to her office and called Caspar Gentry to reassure him that she would still be presenting her scheduled paper at the upcoming NeuroHelp Global Symposium. His voice was that of a birthday child.

"Raf, that's wonderful! I'm so looking forward to it."

This cycle, the symposium was being held in Medusa, the commercial capital of OneWorld. It was going to be huge – streamed across multiple channels on the grID. Getting through security in the major cities was now very difficult for someone who was not ON. Raf knew that at some point she would again have to go back ON.

Despite the effect of the pills, she started shaking again.

∞

A lethargy had descended upon the people inside the auditorium, when the doors were flung open, and the man in the dark grey suit re-entered, accompanied by four medical staff. He gave them some instructions, and they began working their way through the participants. Then the man walked over to me.

"You, sir. Would you mind coming with me?" He smiled reassuringly, "please."

We went through a set of passageways which led to another infinite foyer. We were now in one of the other towers.

"Where are you taking me?"

"We think you can help us sort out what happened. I'd be really grateful if you would have a quick chat with our chief medical adviser. Please sir, it will only take a few Ts."

An elevator took us up a great many floors. I was ushered into a room with stunning views across the Medusa Bay, but we were so high up the clouds would occasionally obscure the view. "Coffee? Tea?"

"No, thanks."

"He won't be long."

With that, the man left. Once more, I was sure he'd locked the door behind him but I didn't bother to check. Presently an older man entered the room. He was dressed casually in jeans, an open-necked shirt and a suit jacket.

"Mister Youren Cartouche, isn't it? I do appreciate your time in this matter."

He offered his hand. "Just make yourself comfortable, Youren."

The man's voice was high-pitched and soft, almost feminine. I hesitated.

"Please," he said.

"You are ... ?"

"I am simply the hired help," he laughed evasively.

I sat down. "What's this all about?"

"Well, we think you can help us identify what went wrong with the last simulation."

"Why me? And why all the secrecy?"

"It's not exactly 'secrecy'. We simply don't want to alarm the others any more than necessary. As to why *you*, that's largely because of your unusual bio-profile during the simulation. You were the 'odd man out' so to speak."

"You were monitoring me?"

"We monitor everyone as a matter of course – to pre-empt any medical emergency, you understand. Your profile showed us that you were not experiencing what the others were."

He poured a glass of Super-Hydra for us both. "What made you decide to enter the ON simulation, if I may ask?"

"Just an impulse, I guess."

"Impulsive behaviour can sometimes get us into trouble."

"Am I in trouble?"

"Oh no, of course not! Please tell me what you experienced."

"I saw a ghost."

"A ghost? My goodness!"

He had a way of smiling the way adults do when listening to a child's prattle.

"The ghost of a workmate – 'Arlo'. He told me he'd been murdered because of something he'd learned about ON. He also told me that ON ghost hunters were trying to eradicate him, and others like him, within the ON world."

"And you believed the words of this ... apparition in ... in your *mind*?"

"*Was* it in my mind?"

"Well, surely it's possible that this 'ghost of Arlo' told you what you already believed to be the case."

"Then three of the ghost hunters turned up. They were dressed as team mascots – a crocodile, a parrot, and a teddy bear."

"An interesting choice."

"What do you mean 'choice'? Oh, I see, you still think I made all this up."

He got up and walked to the window.

"A crocodile is a clear threat in anyone's language, isn't it? A parrot repeats what it is told. And a teddy bear is a child's cuddly companion," he said. "But it's interesting, don't you think, that they were all *mascots*. Symbols for something."

"The teddy bear tried to kill me."

The man clapped his hands, joylessly.

"Aha, so the teddy bear is the real culprit! An event in your childhood perhaps."

I snapped. "This is bullshit!" I shouted. "I'm not your patient! I freely agreed to help you, but if you're going to turn this into some sort of ..."

A slight tremor went through the room, as if from an earthquake. The man threw up his hands in alarm. "Mister Cartouche, please! I do apologise. Yes, you can help us. Please, do sit down."

I hesitated, but then sat back in my chair. He smiled at me.

"What happened after the ... after you were attacked?"

"The stadium roof collapsed on everyone. The crowd panicked and rushed for the exits, and I believe our guide brought me back somehow."

"And how would you describe your emotional state during these incidents?"

"I would say the main emotion was ... *anger*."

"Anger?"

"No-one likes to be threatened. You still haven't told me who you are."

"I'm just a humble servant."

"Hired help, humble servant. You're very modest. Who exactly do you 'serve'?"

He gave me his first real smile since arriving in the room, extending his hands in an inclusive gesture.

"Humanity."

"I'm getting a bit sick of your evasive answers."

He leaned forwards. "To be honest, Youren, I can't put it any clearer than that. *I serve humanity.*"

"Right. So exactly which part of humanity do you serve? The greed? The self-interest? The cruelty? The delusion?"

"I serve humanity's need to have a future, Youren. I serve humanity's need to believe that future is safe. I serve humanity's need to feel that they are worth something, that they have a greater purpose."

"OK. May I go now?"

There was the slightest pause. "But of course. I don't suppose you'd be prepared to come back later for a few tests. Nothing complicated, just some ..."

"I don't think so."

"No? Well, you've been most helpful."

With no apparent signal, the door was opened by the man in the suit.

"Hossam, please you show Mister Cartouche out of the building." He turned to me. "If you need to speak to me again, for any reason Youren, alas I am not on the grID. I'm something of an old-fashioned fellow. Here, take this."

He handed me a business card.

"Thank you."

"You're most welcome. Goodbye Youren, and *good luck*."

The man in the suit remained silent as we descended in the lift. Eventually we reached the foyer where I had originally come in.

"Mister Cartouche."

"Yes?"

His words were slow and considered. "The world is about to undergo a change. This will produce winners and losers."

"And, by winners, I presume you mean people who are ON."

"Choose wisely, Mister Cartouche."

"One thing puzzles me. Why are you letting me go?"

"Because it doesn't matter any more."

He turned and left.

I found myself in the middle of Turing Plaza. The air was pleasantly warm, with a gentle rain falling. For once, my prompter had predicted the weather correctly. I took the card out of my pocket and looked at it. On one side was a set of numbers.

On the other was the image of a blue rose.

∞

Kruger Lovesmith ordered another drink.

How many is that?

For some time now, Kruger had been 'dropping in' to this bar on his way home from work. His visits had become increasingly regular. His wife had said nothing.

What are you doing, Kruger?

'The Hard One Battle' was located in one of the seedier suburbs of Kapeton. It had an unofficial 'no rooin' policy. The cogs usually got the hint.

"Steadying your nerves, Mister Lovesmith?"

Kruger looked up with a start. Hossam Klyosov was sitting next to him.

"How did you ..."

Hossam Klyosov eyed him sternly.

"Is everything ready, Mister Lovesmith. Are *you* ready?"

Suddenly, the reality of what they were all about to do snapped Kruger Lovesmith into focus. It was time to stand up and be counted, and Kruger did indeed stand up, pushing his unfinished drink away.

"The SDU is ready. All the teams are in place. I won't fail you, Mister Klyosov."

"It's not me that you must not fail, Mister Lovesmith. It's Humanity."

Kruger Lovesmith gave the old SDU salute – a clenched fist pressed to his heart.

"My species."

Hossam Klyosov smiled. "Your father would have been proud of you."

Post-human disorder

TRAFFIC was banked up in the vehicle corridor, due to some disturbance up ahead.

Raf's cab had to stop hovering, and settle into a ground level crawl, along with all the other vehicles which were heading towards the Toc-Zic gravDome. Eventually the corridor divided into a series of flat access roads. A security guard was directing the vehicles into feeding lanes. Raf leaned out of her window.

"What's the hold-up?"

"Industrial accident. A lot of wounded."

"Oh, that's terrible."

The security guard studied her face. "Are you ON?" he asked.

"Err, yes, of course."

"Turn on your Law channel!"

Raf fumbled internally with her ancient 2.01 operating system.

::ON::!

It was as though someone had just punched her in the head. Her mind flooded with strange ideas and desires. She was just trying to find the Law channel when a little animated brain, sporting cartoonish hands and feet, popped up in front of her.

'*Hi there.*' the brain said chirpily, waving its hand. '*You appear to be running an outdated version of ON nOS. Upgrading takes less than a T. Would you like me to help you with that?*'

Raf glared at the little brain and said, "No!"

The brain looked disappointed and disappeared in a puff of animated smoke. Raf managed to engage the Law link, then turned to the security guard and aimed the full force of her thoughts at him.

"There you go," she said sweetly.

The security guard simultaneously grimaced and smiled, and waved the cab on. Raf turned off her ON link, and gasped for air. She had the vague impression of blowflies crawling over her body, and she felt like throwing up.

"You alright ma'am?" the cabbie asked.

"Uh, yes. This traffic's driving me crazy."

"Tell me about it! This shit's been going on since 401F. Oh, 'scuse my *SAT* ma'am."

"You're excused." Raf fell back into her seat and tried to regroup. She rummaged in her bag for the pills.

Inside the gravDome, the queues were longer than she had ever seen. Eventually, she approached the security desk. A guard eyed her blankly.

::ON::!

"*Doctor Rafaela Serif*," she said and thought in unison.

"Serif, Serif, let's see, hmmm Pentangle Institute ..."

Mentally, Raf could see the FEDMED controversy on the horizon of the man's internal landscape. She made sure her next words and thoughts were synchronised.

"*Doubt is a disease that all humans must fight against, officer. Me, and you too.*"

The man blinked and coughed twice. He was about to say something, but Raf's dark eyes held him tightly, as her thoughts softly stroked him. The skin felt like a slug's. Raf could see his whole life laid out inside him, inside her – a couple of failed marriages, restricted access to the only child, the succession of diminishing jobs ...

He finished processing her boarding chip.

Raf smiled seductively. "I want to have your baby," she cooed under her breath, as she simultaneously thought: '*Thank you officer. You are a credit to the future of the human species.*'

The slug smiled in pain.

With a shudder, Raf realised for the first time, the depth of cruelty that lay within her.

∞

Raf checked into her hotel, took a quick ion shower, then stood naked in the middle of the room pondering the clothing options laid out on the bed.

Yes, the red dress.

On the way, the autocab chatted away to her, but Raf found it difficult to participate as she internally ran through her presentation. Soon the autocab was pulling up at OneWorld Commerce Centre. Raf stopped to admire the architecture. A line of copper columns stood across the entrance. Logos of each of the 101 participating govcorps floated above their own individual columns, buoyed aloft by a fine grav field. In order to proceed through the building's security, Raf would once more need to turn ON. She took out the little bottle of pills from her handbag.

∞

"Raf. Thank chance! I was beginning to worry," Caspar Gentry said, greeting her in the cavernous foyer, and giving her a somewhat inappropriate hug. "They've moved you forwards. You're on in 3CE. It's going out live in ON-grID MultiStream. Excited?"

"Very."

Caspar Gentry lowered his voice, despite the noise.

"Raf, have you given any more consideration to our, er discussions, regarding ... ?"

"Your offer? I have, Caspar," Raf said, smiling. "When my presentation is complete, you will definitely have my answer."

"Wonderful. I really hope we can work more closely together," Caspar Gentry said, giving her bare shoulder a long squeeze.

∞

Waiting in the wings, Raf watched Caspar Gentry walk to the podium.

"It is my very great pleasure to introduce our next speaker. Raf is someone whose work I have long admired. Many of you will know her as the author of many of neuropsychology's most inspiring and far-sighted works. And, of late, her efforts have been of major assistance to Neuro-Help Global. Her presentation is entitled: *A Vision of Our Future*. Something we're all interested in, I'm sure. So let's put our hands together and welcome to the stage Doctor Rafaela Serif!"

Raf stepped into the light, and her red dress lit up like a flame.

"Thank you everyone. And thank you Caspar, for that kind introduction."

She smiled warmly at Caspar Gentry, who had taken his seat in the front row. He beamed back unashamedly.

"The title of this symposium is: *Towards a New Sanity*. Now I have to say, when I first read that I thought, 'what was wrong with the old one?'"

There was appreciative, yet slightly tense laughter.

"But then I realised that we do need a new sanity, don't we? We need a new sanity because we are about to become a *new humanity*!" Raf raised her arms and was greeted with rapturous applause.

"A new humanity needs a new sanity." she said, in a light, sing-songy voice.

"Humanity. Twenty three billion of us. Lately, it seems as if everyone has been telling me that *the way things are going now*, all twenty three billion of us are on the brink of a great leap forwards. And I'd better be ready. I'd better not get left behind!

"So, how will this new humanity think and feel? What about its hopes and dreams ... its *fears*? As I see it, the new humanity is already here with us, in embryonic form.

"When I was an undergraduate, we still talked about something called Evolutionary Neuropsychology. Anyone remember that? No, it's not especially fashionable nowadays. It was based on the simple premise that everything about the structure and function of the human brain could, in principle, be traced to our evolutionary development – all the way back. How we think, as a species, was forged in the simple processes of natural and sexual selection. If a trait, an ability, or even a delusion helped an individual survive and procreate, it was probably preserved in subsequent generations. If not, it eventually got weeded out of the genetic garden.

"Evolutionary theory was a simple and elegant model which explained how all living things came to be the way they were. But, in the modern world, this is becoming less applicable. Now, commerce and not evolution determines the form and function of a creature. Plants and animals are designed to suit a purpose – *our* purpose. They no longer evolve, they get *upgraded*.

"None of this will come as a surprise to most of you, but what may be surprising is that *we too* are subject to this commercial process. Who and what we are is really a commercial decision. A company brings out an upgrade to a human organ or system and, if we like it, we buy it. Human desire has become the driver of the human design. Consumer whim has replaced the traditional 'environment' as the selector for which designs will survive and which designs will fall away.

"In short, the modern human is a *product being sold back to itself.*"

Caspar Gentry's initially warm smile was beginning to freeze into a complex mask of alarm and despair, which nevertheless, still betrayed a deep admiration.

"And now the commercial design of the new human approaches the final frontier."

Raf tapped her head. "The brain."

A large image of a human brain appeared in the media screen behind her.

"There are many commercially available ways I can assemble a new 'me' inside my head. I can choose from a range of drugs, neurotransmitter supplements, pulse modulators, connectome plug-ins, and so on. But by far the most successful and profound of all these is One Network.

"ON."

Predictably, the audience applauded.

"Almost overnight, ON has become the de facto substrate upon which to build the new human identity. The uptake and development of the platform has been expanding almost exponentially, and I can confidently predict that in the very near future, every single human on this planet will be ON."

This produced thunderous applause. Ignoring it, Raf continued.

"But where will this leave us mental health professionals? Will we still play a role in helping our new humans achieve their new sanity?"

Raf gestured towards the giant brain behind her. "Previously, in all our work with *this*, we were dealing with something which had no owner. Let me explain. The person inside whose skull this brain once sat did not *own* this. They didn't expend any R&D on its development. They had no patents on its structure. They simply *inherited* it from the ownerless process of evolution. And because no-one owned this, I was free to study the effects of a particular neurotransmitter and publish my findings. A psychologist was free to interrogate this brain and record its patterns of self-defeating thought. A nanosurgeon was free to develop new techniques to combat a certain neurological dysfunction. But will we be free to study and treat this, once it's internal workings are under proprietary ownership?"

Raf paused and turned to face the large brain.

"The human who carried this in his head was free to use it to think and create and dream whatever he liked. In our new humanity, will he have that same freedom?"

Raf noticed a man approach Caspar Gentry, crouch down, and engage him in whispered, angry conversation.

"ON is a proprietary system, and as such CoolGlobalGiant needs to protect its IP. Obviously they have many patents on this process. These patents fall broadly into four categories. One: those that describe the way the system works. These manage to be both highly technical and surprisingly vague.

Two: patents relating to ON's capacity to connect to non-bio devices such as locators, nanocasting services, grID links and so on. Very boring, let me tell you. Three: patents relating to the way third party plug-ins and apps can interact with ON. If you want my non-specialist summary: play ball with CoolGlobalGiant, or *else*.

"And, Four, by far the most interesting category. These patents relate to the system's inbuilt monitoring and management of what you, as the consumer, will, won't, may, may not, could possibly at some future date, etcetera, etcetera, etcetera ..."

Raf became perfectly still.

"... *think*."

The man arguing with Caspar Gentry got up and left. Caspar Gentry hurried after him.

"These 'category four' patents are pending future contracts with govcorps and other third party companies. By the way, all of this is clearly referenced in the licence agreement you almost certainly failed to read when you installed the system."

The audience was now getting restless. Raf leaned into the microphone.

"'*I think, therefore I am*', a pre-T philosopher named René Descartes wrote those words, and at the time, they had a profound significance for the way humans were beginning to see themselves. But is the statement true? Do you exist because you think? Even before the modern world laid siege to that secret place within us, our thoughts were still mostly determined by others. Our first concepts were those of our parents. Then came those of our siblings, friends, teachers, the media and so on. But there used to be a crucial difference. We had some breathing space. We had a little time to process and alter those thoughts to suit ourselves. *We made them ours.* But when you are plugged into a social neural network such as ON there is no longer any breathing space. Your thoughts are everyone's thoughts, and these thoughts may soon become someone else's intellectual property."

A disturbance was clearly moving through the crowd, and Raf could see that many members of the audience were getting up and leaving.

"ON presents us with a new paradox. As you think, your individuality begins to fade. And so for our glorious new humanity, let's rephrase our old friend Descartes, '*I think, therefore I am not.*' "

"Why don't you just fuck off, you stupid bitch!"

The voice was harsh, yet the tones subtly lacked conviction. It was violence without the complications of personal anger. Raf scanned the faces, but the spotlights prevented her from identifying the interjector.

"I intend to in just a T sir, thank you. But bear with me because, as I promised, I am going to show you *a vision of our future*. Now, it's true the vast majority of people experience no problems with ON. But I have been treating a small minority who have reacted badly. One particular disorder is known as 'Bacon's Syndrome'. This begins with the patient sporadically screwing their eyes shut and screaming. Apparently they see some horror before them, but no-one has yet found out what it is. Drugs, psychotherapy and pulse treatments have proven useless in calming them. Sadly, the behaviour worsens until the patient is constantly in this state. Inevitably, the immune system fails. A particular infection attacks the eyes and surrounding tissue and the patient's eyes become fused shut. To prevent further infections, the patient is usually placed in a bio-isolation chamber."

Raf gestured towards the screen. "Let's see what a Bacon's Syndrome patient looks like."

The screen displayed a man inside what looked like a glass case. He was clasping the sides of his chair and screaming. His eyes had ceased to exist, replaced by crusted scabs, and holes in the blackened flesh. Several people in the audience shrieked at the sight of the ghastly image, but Raf continued calmly.

"And this is what he sounds like."

A rasping scream filled the auditorium. It was the cry of every torture victim, every abandoned prisoner, every maimed and despairing human who knew they were indefinitely trapped in hell. It just went on and on and on ...

It was, as Raf announced to the remaining horrified audience – "A Vision of Our Future."

∞

The mixed species bar near the wharf is rough and loud. Most of the media screens are showing the SAT League semi final between Exxon-Cal and Blackwater Assassins. Periodically, the crowd stands up and roars like a great dying beast. As those around them shout and swear and shake their fists at the screens, Constantin Zann, Ozzi-Chen and Lakzad sit quietly at a corner table. The three rooins communicate within a secure bubble of relative quietness, courtesy of a three-way near-field link.

Lakzad is angry.

"What the zork were you thinking, Zann? Misuse of company resources, obtaining scanner streams illegally, exposing a client's identity, and ... and worst of all, roping young Ozzi-Chen into your lovesick escapade. *You* may be tired of life, but *he* has his whole career ahead of him."

"None of us is likely to have a career much longer," Constantin Zann says without emotion.

"Oh? Who told you that?"

"Eve Lamente."

"Oh for zork's sake!" Lakzad begins to get up, "I'm not hanging around for ghost stories."

Exxon-Cal fails to score and the crowd lets out a collective groan.

"Why won't we have careers, Zann?" Ozzi-Chen asks.

Constantin Zann looks back and forth between the two rooins. "Let me ask you both something. What do you think of humans? Really."

The rooins instinctively glance around the bar for any scanners. Lakzad sits down and gives a 'who gives a zork anymore' shrug, and says, "they're crazy."

"Ozzi-Chen?"

"Yes, well, I would have to agree with Lakzad."

"And yet these crazy creatures are the reason we're here." Zann immediately puts his hands up to avert any protests. "No, I'm not being offensive. I'm not talking about our origins or anything like that. I'm simply saying that so much of what we do *right now* is dependent on the human species."

"Well it's true that most of our clients are human," Ozzi-Chen admits.

"Exactly. Just one example. So what if something happened to the species which provides all our clients? Where will our careers be then?"

"Something?" Lakzad asks.

"He's talking about ON," Ozzi-Chen says, shaking his head.

"Yes, ON," says Zann. "Everything about this case comes back to ON."

Lakzad slams his hand on the table. "There is no 'case', Zann. The client has paid us. End of story."

"There is a case, Lakzad. It's a case against the *client*. Let's start with the 3V of the interview. In it, Eve Lamente says 'when all this is over.' When what? You'll recall that the T-stamp had been erased – possibly by the client themselves. But it's not impossible to retrieve damaged or erased T-stamp and young Ozzi-Chen has once more proved that he is ..."

"A felon like you," Lakzad interjects.

Ozzi-Chen grins. "Yes, I rebuilt the T-stamp data. But the interesting thing is not when, but *where*. Eve Lamente's interview took place on a SAT island named EGK17."

"What the zork is that?"

"Turns out it houses CoolGlobalGiant's research facility and factory for the manufacture of ON engrafts."

"Yes," Zann says, "Mrs Krianti told me that Eve went away for some 'job' and when she returned, she was sullen and angry. Eve talked darkly about ON. 'Don't listen to them.' she said. Mrs Krianti dated this to the time the SDU was trying to alter the terms of the Treaty. Remember that debate? The 3V T-stamp which places Eve Lamente on EGK17, predates the SDU debates and it also predates the commercial release of ON. Which all suggests that Eve Lamente was a test subject during the ON development phase on EGK17. Eve probably received one of the first pair of engrafts, if not the very first."

"OK, I'll grant you this is interesting," Lakzad says. "But why did CoolGlobalGiant then commission us to keep her under surveillance?"

"My guess is Eve Lamente experienced or discovered something about the product which was bad enough to make her quit the test program. CoolGlobalGiant had too much money riding on the project to let her mess things up, which is where we came in, reporting on where she went, who she saw, and what she discussed."

"Which was zork all, if I remember," Lakzad says.

"Yes, but just in case she opened her mouth, there was a convenient psych report declaring her mentally incompetent."

"OK, but then you're telling me that, after all this trouble, CoolGlobalGiant went and had her killed. It doesn't make sense. Why not just do that in the first place?"

"Ah, but they *didn't* have her killed, Lakzad. They simply covered for the real criminal."

"Who?"

"Ozzi-Chen, can you please show Lakzad the Phantasma scanner stream?"

The three rooins watch as the man with the blue rose receives a lapdance which he has no apparent interest in.

Ozzi-Chen says "I've checked the sight lines in the sim, and this man continuously chooses to watch a couple of very boring insurance reps and a petty criminal freak, rather than a nearby pair of particularly attractive human breasts."

Lakzad raises an eyebrow at Zann.

"The interesting thing about this human," Ozzi-Chen continues, "is that I couldn't face-rec him from any known law database. Somehow he's managed to erase his likeness from the grID."

Lakzad narrows his eyes. "So, how did you ... ?"

"You don't want to know."

Lakzad throws up his arms. "Am I officially an accessory yet?"

Zann grins at him, as an image of the man with the blue rose comes up.

"Lakzad, I'd like to introduce you to Professor Adão Cabral."

Lakzad is puzzled.

"Where have I heard that name before?"

"He was the author of the client's psych report on Eve Lamente's lamentable mental state."

"Yes, of course! But what's he ... ?"

"Adão Cabral" Zann says, "is the acknowledged OneWorld expert on human neuro. Until recently, he held the chair of neuropsych at the University of New Brazil. Then he took up two key positions. One of these was principal medical adviser to CoolGlobalGiant, during the ON development project ..."

Lakzad straightens his bowtie and smooths his hair. "Well, I'll be a zorking ..."

"... *and*, almost simultaneously, he became Chief Neuro Officer at FEDMED."

"... robot's exhaust!"

"FEDMED, as we know," Zann continues, "has been pretty soft on CoolGlobalGiant regarding medical concerns about ON."

"But this is a monstrous conflict of interest!" Lakzad says. "Surely someone must have challenged ..."

"Who? Who in OneWorld has the clout to go up against the combined resources of CoolGlobalGiant and FEDMED? That much cred could make anything go away!"

"Including us, Zann," Lakzad mutters.

"So," Zann says. "The only question left unanswered is: what was it about ON that disturbed Eve Lamente so much? I think ..."

< ALERT. ALERT. ALERT. >

Without warning, the visual and auditory matrices of all three rooins are overridden.

< ALL PLANETSIDE ROOINS IN THE FOLLOWING WORK CAT.: LAW. EMERGENCY RESPONSE. MEDICAL. TRAFFIC. BIOMECH. >

< REPORT IMMEDIATELY TO YOUR CODE RED LOCATIONS. >

< THIS IS NOT A DRILL. >

< REPEAT. >

< ALERT. ALERT. ALERT. > ...

∞

Below the stage, Caspar Gentry caught up with Argus Sheen, the chief law officer for NeuroHelp Global. "Argus, wait!"

"The time for waiting is over, Gentry."

"What are you going to do?"

"You won't take care of it, so I will. Some of us are committed to that future that she spits on with such pleasure!"

Gentry's eyes widened. "What are you talking about?"

"Gentry, listen to me. This kind of person has no place in our world." A nasty smile crossed the man's face. "Or perhaps you'd like to join her?"

Gentry raised his hands. "No. No, of course not. We have to do what's best, Argus. I support that."

"Smart."

Argus Sheen turned to leave. In the gloom, as if from above his own body, Caspar Gentry watched himself pick up one of the set builders' tools and hit the rotund little man across the back of the skull. The sound of the impact was soft and sickening, and the law officer fell immediately, a dark stain spreading across his shirt collar. Caspar Gentry stood motionless for a few T, then calmly sat down next to the body to await his fate. Rocking gently to himself, he thought of a snow-white angel in a flame-red dress, her arms aloft in a gesture of love and courage.

∞

Raf removed her high heels and ran down the backstage stairs leading to her dressing room. She quickly gathered her things – wrap, handbag, anything else? No that was it. The wall screen was showing some news report on yet another global emergency, but Raf paid no attention. She cautiously looked along the corridor. The muffled sounds of the patient's screams could be heard from the auditorium speakers. Raf decided to risk walking straight to the foyer and out past security. Bold as brass.

The foyer was a scene of chaos. Officials were running in all directions, and both entry and exit queues were banking up. For a micro-T Raf thought this might have something to do with her speech, but she soon realised that something far more serious was taking place. She joined one of the queues, listening to snatches of conversation around her.

"They say it's global."

"Well what do you expect?"

"I always said something like this would happen."

"How many? I don't believe it!"

"Not much of a loss though, is it? What? I'm just saying ..."

Raf found herself being pushed to one side, along with everyone else.

"Move right. Move right," medics shouted, as several gurneys wheeled past. Raf caught a glimpse of a horribly mutilated arm protruding from under a green coversheet. It was the arm of a rooin. Her queue began moving forwards. She could see the security officers up ahead. *Here we go again.* Raf took a few deep breaths, and pressed the internal button.

::ON::

She was shocked by the new set of emotions flooding into her. Happiness, joy, hope, celebration. She also noticed that ON nOS had automatically installed a new set of icons, with strange symbols. Raf kept her head low and moved forwards.

"Hello, Doctor Serif."

Raf looked up. A young man in front of her had turned round, and was smiling at her. Raf thought the man looked quite ill, and she instinctively took a step back.

"I'm sorry. Do I know you?"

"No, but I know someone that you do."

"Oh?"

The pale young man extended his hand and introduced himself. "Arlo," he said with a cheeky grin.

∞

Suize Capazo was crying so much, I was having trouble hearing her words. The poor link to Erco Menoz wasn't helping either. Sunspot activity or something. I had never heard a rooin cry before. Suize's bleats made her sound like a distressed sheep. The almost comical quality of the noise made the whole thing even sadder, and I wished I could reach out across space to hold her.

"Zep-Qua, Veloozi, Agep-Zamis, and ... and Xan-Z-Bar!" she howled. "They're all sick. I can't ..." She broke down into more sheep noises.

"How? What happened?"

"It's all over the media. Sick! Dying! Youren, please go and see him before it's too late."

"Xan-Z-Bar?"

"I won't make it in time. Please do this for me."

"Can't you link to him?" I immediately realised how callous this must have sounded.

"No, his communication ganglia have been damaged ... eaten away. Please, Youren, tell him I love ... his music."

"His music?"

She broke down again, but managed to say softly, "Tell him *I love him.*"

"Oh."

"Youren?"

"Yes, Suize, I'll go and tell him."

"Here's the location. Go now."

∞

I was feeling a bit like a wolf hiding in a herd of sheep. I was walking through the r•NET medical complex with a crowd of distressed rooins who were all making sheep noises. There were also a few confused humans looking around for directions. Human signage was sparse. All the wards were filled to capacity with dying rooins, as some disease ate their flesh away. I located Xan-Z-Bar's ward. His face was almost gone and only one arm was left. I could see little holes opening up in his chest. Rooin medics in full body suits were adjusting a machine to alleviate his suffering.

"What's causing this?" I asked one of them.

"Self-replicator nanotag." she said. "Cattle, we think. We can't trace the original manufacturer, the nano has mutated too much. It's adapted to exist outside the animal host cell, but it still needs energy. Unfortunately it seems to enjoy rooin biolaminar."

"How widespread is it?"

"We're getting reports from all over the planet."

"Nothing on the SAT islands so far?"

"No, thank chance."

I turned to Xan-Z-Bar. "Suize sent me."

"I thought as much," he said, wincing with pain.

"She wants me to tell you she loves you."

He remained silent for a while. Then he said, "This is difficult for you."

"It's a bit weird, but it's OK. I'm happy to be able to ..."

"Thank you. If you see her again, tell her that her words have taken away all my pain."

He held out his hand, but I hesitated.

"It has no effect on humans." he said

I reached out, and his long fingers snaked around my hand holding it gently. As I realised that those fingers would never again play drums and make us all dance, I began to cry. My tears fell onto his hands. I was crying for Xan-Z-Bar, but I was also crying for Suize, and Arlo, and Dos Pascal, and everyone at work. They too were being eaten away by something.

Xan-Z-Bar's voice was faltering. "Our time of life ends, Youren. Entropy always wins. But within your heart, you can beat entropy. In the heart, everyone's a winner."

And with that, the giant rooin closed his eyes and let his dwindling energy go.

∞

Constantin Zann's body feels both hot and cold. This is a common side effect of high volume coolant flowing under the skin. He tries re-adjusting the ill-fitting biohazard suit again, but it makes little difference. Besides, his own discomfort is unimportant compared to the scene of suffering he is now witnessing. In the wake of the nano pandemic, Zann, Ozzi-Chen, Lakzad and all rooins who can be spared from Raymond Parkes are helping with the relief efforts. Zann is helping to coordinate traffic, keep back sightseers, and stop any potential trouble.

Zann's team works its way through the artist's quarter. There has been a sudden shower of rain, and the little droplets of water on his visor catch the light from the arc lamps. Dead and dying rooins are being brought out of the ancient warehouses, to be loaded into the ambulances. The roads are littered with debris and discarded personal effects. Zann spots an odd-looking contraption lying on its side in the gutter, one side smashed in. The thing looks like a giant golden egg with the top cut off. It takes him a while to realise it is a drum. Sounds of a disturbance come from behind him. The crowd of human onlookers is getting ugly, pushing against the barriers. Zann draws his weapon and hurries to help the other agents. He can hear the crowd's abusive taunts.

"Got what they deserved!"

"Who needs them?"

"Fucking cogs!"

"They don't even have a brand."

An older woman approaches. She carries a child, who turns its ice-cold innocence upon him. The woman spits. "You'll be next, freak!"

Zann allows no emotion to display on his face. He notices that the more vocal members of the crowd wear ON street clothing. Many SDU supporters are also present. A young, bare-chested man wears a towel with the ON logo, like a cape. The crowd surges forwards again, and the agents have trouble maintaining the line. Zann knows, if the mob breaks through, they'll head for the ambulances. He raises his weapon and fires a couple of cortex pumper shots into the air. The pulses of fear and pain briefly drive the humans back. Then, on some unseen signal, the crowd forms into smaller groups which begin chanting a few simple words. The words build into a crescendo.

"THE FUTURE IS ON."

∞

I seemed to be the only one standing still.

Everyone around me was running. To where? Every media screen was reporting the nano pandemic. Already up to 100,000 rooins had died. As the global toll rose, the tone of the newscasts subtly shifted from shock and sympathy to something else. As if the rooins had somehow brought this upon themselves. I thought of what Ari-R-Z had said about robots.

'They were even blamed for their own slaughter.'

∞

The Medusa chief executive, Madonna Amin appeared on all networks, calling for calm. When asked about SDU calls for a 'containment' of the rooin population – as a response to the potential medical threat to the human species – she was at her equivocating best.

'I can understand some people's concerns. Many humans have deeply held beliefs, and I respect their commercial right to hold those beliefs. Let me just say that, during this difficult time, Medusa Corp is doing everything in its power to address the concerns of all shareholders. We are closely monitoring the situation, and I can assure you that we are considering a range of options, with a view to – '

'And what about suggestions that similar measures should be implemented for NotON humans, in the interests of – ' an interviewer asks.

'I'm not going to dignify that with – '

'But do you categorically deny it?'

'I've made my position perfectly clear ... '

∞

I took out the card with the blue rose on it. Within each petal were smaller petals, and within each of those petals were even smaller petals.

"Yes." The voice was soft, almost feminine.

"You did this, didn't you. All of it. Or you approved it. Or you knew about it and you just stood by and let it happen. It's all part of the plan isn't it? One Human Network, with no other inconvenient species to spoil the party."

"Who is this?"

"You know who I am."

"Mister Cartouche, of course. You sound upset."

"Rooins are dying. Why wouldn't I be upset?"

"Unfortunately, the rooin biology is inherently unstable. With these, well, these *machines*, malfunctions like this are inevitable. They're very susceptible to a ... spanner in the works."

"Machines, freaks, clowns, toys ... I've even heard them described as vacuum cleaners! We'll use any word we can to diminish them so we don't have to face up to our own failure as a species."

"The rooin is a false reflection of the human, Mister Cartouche. If you look at that reflection for too long, you forget who you are."

"No, the humans all around me have forgotten who they are."

I walked towards the main vehicle corridor. The grav engines sped past like a vast swarm of salmon: hovering, ducking, weaving, yet managing never to collide. My grID visor briefly overlaid whatever little details about each vehicle it was privy to – text, images, even movies passed before me, too fast to absorb. Then each one and its story was gone – swallowed by the swarm, to be replaced by another brief story.

"Youren, are you still there?"

I looked down. The low barrier provided little protection from the rushing force. Just a few steps, and I could drop silently into the destructive flow.

"Youren?"

I ran through it in my mind. Foot stepping over the barrier. Standing on the edge, feeling the slipstreams buffeting my face. The sensation of falling for an instant, before the first impact. Intense pain for a split T. My body ricocheting between fleeting brutal surfaces. How long would I remain conscious as I plunged, broken and bleeding, to the corridor floor? I would probably lose a limb, or maybe even my head. The scanners would record it faithfully – a possible filler news item – then the stream data would be stored somewhere for a period of time, after which it too would be gone.

"Youren, where are you now? Is that downtown traffic ... near ... yes ..."

"Why do you want to know where I am?"

"I'm concerned about you. I can help you if you'll let me."

"Yoo Hoo! Youren! Well, I never!"

A woman passer-by had stopped abruptly and was grinning and waving at me. Adão Cabral's voice continued in my visor.

"Youren, listen to me. In my professional opinion, you are suffering a form of 'post-temporal impulse paranoia' brought on by trauma. Because of this disorder, your perception of events is becoming increasingly distorted ..."

The strange woman began walking towards me. My head began to throb.

"... and you may feel unreasonably threatened ..."

Still grinning, the woman came up to me and grabbed my arm, pulling me back.

"... but it's important that you realise the delusional nature of these feelings, ..."

A small LawVec dropped out of the swarm in the vehicle corridor and settled on the access ramp next to me. The doors opened. I could see two men inside. The pain in my head was getting worse.

"... and that none of this is real ..."

Another passer-by – a fat man wearing a ZIM•Ball cap – walked over to help the woman, and they both tried to push me into the LawVec.

"Don't worry, Youren," the man in the cap said, "we're all friends here."

One of the men in the LawVec pulled at my jacket. As I struggled against everyone, a sudden burst of rain drenched us and the man in the cap fell to the ground. At first I thought he had slipped in the wet, but then I saw blood seeping from a wound in his leg. The woman released her grip, and she fell too. I freed myself from the man in the LawVec, turned, and came face to face with Doctor Rafaela Serif. The first thing I noticed was her tight red dress. The second thing I noticed was the tiny plasma gun in her hand.

She reached out for my hand. "Quick! Let's go!"

We ran down a narrow shopping mall with one of the men from the LawVec in pursuit. Most people observed us with disinterest, but a few watched us with deep malevolence. A teenage boy tried to grab me. I veered to enter an office building, but Doctor Serif pulled me away.

"Not there! Too many ONs. This way."

She led me down some steps until we found ourselves in a basement market with little stalls selling food, cheap clothing and assorted junk. We reached the service exit doors on the far side, and clambered up onto the loading bay.

"Wait, stop." She seemed to be listening for something.

"He's lost us."

"How do you know?"

"Because I ... because I ..." She ran over to one of the rubbish skips and vomited into it.

"Doctor Serif! Are you ill?"

She steadied herself against the skip. "Ill? Ugh, worse than that. I'm ON."

"What?"

She retched a few more times then turned round, wiping her mouth. "How do you think I found you?"

I took a step back. "Whoa! I dunno if ... I'm not sure I ..."

"Trust me?"

She walked towards me but faltered, and sat down on the ground, clutching her legs. Beads of sweat covered her brow. "I think it's safe to turn it off for a while." she said.

Her eyes flickered and a look of peace came over her. As the colour came back into her face, she looked up at me sharply. "Well?"

"Trust you? ... I guess ..."

"You *guess?*"

"OK, I'm sorry. Yes, I trust you completely, Doctor. And thank you for saving me."

She gave a tired smile. "Oh, and by the way, Arlo says 'Hi'."

∞

"This weather is crazy."

We stood looking out of the loading bay onto a service access corridor littered with food waste and broken packaging. The rain had begun falling again, and Doctor Serif was shivering. I had an urge to put my arm around her.

"We need to get to Dos Pascal's place." I said.

"Who's he?"

"The smartest man I know. ONs will be looking for us. Someone's probably checking scanner streams even as we ... No, wait!"

"What?"

My brain started to do some work for a change. Nanotags! Eventually we would be tracked by the nanotags in our clothes. Purchase data would be linked to us.

"OK. One thing at a time. Wait here!"

I ran back into the markets. Credit! If I used my credit, they would trace us in an instant. I rummaged around in my jacket pocket and my hand fell on the unused casino chips from Zygot. I went over to a little stall that sold cheap clothing, toys, and travel goods and began piling up items. The bemused stall keeper gladly accepted my casino chips as legal tender. He ripped me off, but I couldn't afford to cause a scene. Climbing back onto the loading bay with my parcels, I saw Doctor Serif sitting on the concrete floor, dangling her legs over the edge of the ramp. She was lost in thought.

"Party time!" I said with exaggerated cheer. She looked up, just in time to catch the first of several parcels.

"What are these?" she asked.

"We can be tracked through the nanotags in our clothes. These are our new identities. You have to take off everything, even your underwear." I shrugged. "Sorry. You can change behind the skip. Throw all the old stuff into it."

"Do you know how much this dress cost me?" she asked.

She reluctantly took her parcels behind the skip. I got changed on the spot.

"How do I look?" She had emerged wearing a pair of purple tights, beige plastic boots and a fluorescent green raincoat which failed to adequately cover a pink t-shirt with the words 'HOT FOR IT!'.

"Ghastly."

In truth, I was in no position to sneer, considering my own outfit featured a cap with the words 'LARGER THAN IT LOOKS!'.

She laughed, holding out the edges of the raincoat. "This colour is awful! What do you even call that?"

"I like to call it 'Seasick Green'."

"Didn't they have anything even *more* disgusting?"

"That one matches your eyes. Besides, you won't care once you put these on."

She caught another parcel. "You have to be kidding!" she sighed. "Are these for real?"

"Microwave protection glasses. They're the height of fashion in Serbo-Hawaii."

She put on the bug-eyed glasses and tucked the hood around them. Then she looked down at her t-shirt. "HOT FOR IT! You're not going to tell me *this* was all that was available."

"I could have got you an SDU one. They had heaps of those. But wait, there's even worse than that. Let's see ... umm ... this one is yours."

"What is it?"

"Nano makeup. Rub it on liberally – ears, neck and hands too. It screws up the scanner face-rec. Law firms have been trying to have this stuff banned for ages."

She turned the makeup tube around in her hands. "*Champagne Nights.* What's yours called?"

"Err ... *L'Homme Sauvage.*" I said, in a ridiculous deep voice.

"Lovely. It sounds like we're on a tacky first date."

"Well, let's hope we live to remember it."

The rain proved to be a great leveller. Despite, or because of our outfits we blended in well with the bedraggled commuters crushing into the carriage. It was only three stops to the suburb where Dos Pascal lived. As the B-tube sped through the darkness, Doctor Serif and I kept close together and made an effort to look happy. An elderly couple at the rear of the carriage began to sing an ancient folk song which had become very popular with ONs recently. A few others joined in, and now more than half the occupants of the carriage were singing joyfully. Doctor Serif squeezed my hand. She too was singing, and her smile and eyebrow movement told me that it might be a good idea if I added my voice to the choir. I gave her a 'look' and reluctantly joined in.

"We are the future. We are the world to be. We are the ones who light the way ..."

∞

"Do you remember the Robot Riots?"

Constantin Zann is standing by the bed of a very old rooin – not really a bed, more of a soft mortuary slab. The subdued lighting is pulsing slowly.

"I knew those who were there. The old robots told me about the struggles."

Zann stops.

Ari-R-Z is a great being who should probably be left to die in peace. The rogue nanos have already destroyed much of the old body.

"It's alright, my young friend. Ask your questions. It's good to talk." The voice sounds like a human child's.

"Thank you, you are wise." Zann says. "The military quelled the riots with some kind of weapon. I've checked the records."

"They were already crazy, but they got a whole lot crazier. It stopped them in their tracks. People fell down screaming, sobbing, shouting things like, 'I am impossible'. Many died, and those who survived were different. Gone."

"This weapon ..."

"No-one knew what it was. It altered the grouping patterns – the *mob*. Other things too. They say the light *changed*."

The old rooin is studying Zann's face.

"You care about the humans?"

Zann frowns. "I care about them and I hate them. I want to help them and I want to leave them to die. If I were a human, I would be called 'conflicted' but, as a rooin, I absorb both feelings into my inner chaos engine."

The old one claps his thin hands, and the creased skin of his face forms a smile.

"In my long life, I've never heard it put better. We can't help it, can we? And from your chaos engine will come a choice?"

"Yes, a choice must be made."

"And you believe that you have a choice? That all your futures are not merely the predetermined result of all your pasts?"

"I'm a simple cop, sir."

"Not quite so simple, I think." The old one leans forwards with difficulty. "Listen. You know that no rooin may hold a senior position in any govcorp?"

"That's right, the Treaty expressly states ..."

"Tell me young friend, have you ever *read* the Treaty?"

"It goes on forever."

Ari-R-Z laughs. "Yes, it does! But buried somewhere in the middle of it are three clauses that deal with the concept of interspecies bio-threat."

"What's that?"

"Good question. In my opinion it's a get-out-of-jail-free pass. What these three clauses state is that, should the rooin species prove to pose some sort of unspecified ecological threat to humans – whether it be deliberate on our part, or not – a majority of govcorps can overturn almost all of the pillars of the Treaty, until such time as the threat is deemed to be removed."

"But that would make ..."

"Our current position very tenuous."

∞

"Coffee?"

I wondered if I should signal to Doctor Serif that the coffee would not be a good idea, but that soon became unnecessary.

"Err ... something *stronger*?"

"Oh."

Dos Pascal was looking at us blankly. I had introduced Doctor Serif to him, but it hadn't sunk in. Either from shock or politeness, he said nothing about our attire. He turned to me.

"You too?"

"I'll just go with the coffee, thanks Dos."

Dos left for the kitchen, and as he clattered about, Doctor Serif admired all his machines, toys and gadgets. She stopped by a pile of golden, egg-shaped devices, picking one up and running her finger across its surface.

"What do you suppose these are?" she asked. Before I could answer, she whispered, "I don't think your friend likes me very much."

"You're a girl."

"He doesn't like girls?"

"You're a girl who has 'HOT FOR IT' on your t-shirt."

"Oh, I see. Well I'll try not to be too *girly*, then." she said, giving me a grotesque pout.

Dos returned with two coffees and an enormous bottle of something called 'Brandy Surprise', which he'd probably found under the sink. He poured a glass and handed it to Doctor Serif.

"Thank you," she said, sitting down on the floor, and clutching her legs, "You know, you're the second friend of Youren's I've met today."

"Oh?"

"Uh huh. The other one was a ghost."

"Are you guys on Blu-Zone? 'Cos I'm totally out."

"No, Dos, we're not on Blu-Zone," I said.

"Is Suize alright?"

"Yes, she's fine, she's still on Erco Menoz. So far, there are no reports of rooins getting sick on any of the SAT islands."

"This wasn't a random pandemic, you know," Dos said. "It was a planned attack."

"I'd figured as much."

"I did an analysis. Look."

He pointed to one of his wall screens.

"Here's the so-called nano pandemic ..." Clusters of red marched out across the globe.

"... and here's a typical global pandemic. This one is the last Martian Flu." Green clusters spread out.

"Watch the graphs on the right," Dos said. "The rogue nano doesn't spread with any known epidemiological growth pattern. It was a coordinated release."

Doctor Serif shivered, took a sip of her drink, coughed, and immediately began making mock horror expressions at me. The lights in the room flickered briefly.

"That's been happening for a while," Dos said. "Problems with the grID. I have backup cells, but they can't last for ever."

I became aware of other voices within the building. Muffled shouts and laughter penetrated the walls. Then the singing started. A door opened and I could hear people leaving one of the other apartments, their voices immediately louder and sharper. As they passed our front door, Dos put a finger to his lips. He looked scared.

I could now make out the words to the song.

> 'It's a brand new world,
>
> 'with a brand new feeling.
>
> 'Brand new people sharing their love.'

Someone began hammering on the door.

"Come out, come out and playeeee!" a male voice said. A few of the others jeered.

The hammering continued for a while. Then the door was kicked heavily.

"Lonely boy. Lonely boy. Nobody loves you." the voice taunted with mock sadness.

By now the singers had moved on down the hallway and, after a couple more kicks to the door, Dos Pascal's tormentor left to join them. None of us said anything. Doctor Serif took a long uncomplaining gulp of Brandy Surprise, and breathed out slowly.

"Not the first time," Dos whispered.

He got up, walked to the window, and watched the singers below. He waited until their voices had faded. Then he consulted a small handheld device, occasionally looking up at the clouds. He turned to us and said "Watch this," He tapped the window once and said, "Rain!"

A burst of rain beat against the window.

"How the hell did you do that that?" I asked.

"I did nothing. I *knew* something."

"When it was going to rain?"

Dos returned and sat down. "Weather bots always say ' ... there's a chance of rain', don't they? Now there's nothing *chance* about it."

"I'm sorry," Doctor Serif said, "you've lost me. What are you looking at on that thing?"

"Clusters of non-randomness within OneWorld space-time. They're increasing. I guess everything will eventually be predictable."

Doctor Serif opened her mouth a few times, before repeating, "Predictable?"

Dos explained to her how all Theton dice in OneWorld were now falling in non-random patterns. He pointed to his map of chance distortion.

"By inference, everything that was once determined by chance is becoming predictable. I've used this data to construct predictive algorithms for things like the weather. In other words, I can tell you where and when it's going to rain."

Doctor Serif shook her head. "I suppose it's pointless for me to say I don't believe it."

"Pointless," Dos nodded in agreement.

"Hang on. To start with, you'd need unlimited access to T-stamp. How could you possibly afford ..."

Dos looked at me. "Is she cool?"

"Yeh, she's cool."

Doctor Serif's expression told me she didn't like being 'cool'.

"OK," Dos said, "the thing is I don't *pay* for the T-stamp. I broke into Tempo's liquid servers and now I know what time it is. Everywhere. *All the time.*"

Doctor Serif just managed to stop herself from saying, "That's impossible." Instead, she said, "How? How did you manage to – "

"Tempo's crypto is chaos-based. It changes every micro-T. To get into the server, you need to *become* the server. It's ... umm ... complex."

"Well, that's the weirdest thing I've ever heard."

"No, what I'm about to tell you will be the weirdest thing you've ever heard."

∞

Adão Cabral walked towards the observation window, expending the minimum possible energy as he moved. Foot fall, foot fall, arms swaying slightly. *Just right.* People let their bodies run riot with so much unnecessary movement, he thought. This way and that, back and forth – all for what? No, just do what is necessary. Synchronisation, that's the essence of it. He allowed himself a small nod of the head. Every tiny element working in harmony with every other element, each one playing its part. No complaining muscle fibre, no distracted flickering of the eye, just ...

Harmony.

He watched the workers below. The humans were supervising the manufacture of the engrafts, their features sharpened by the pale blue light. *Now that's harmony.* No rooins on EGK17, he'd made sure of it. You can't have equal opportunity between unequals.

"Excuse me for bothering you, Professor Cabral."

The disembodied voice within his head was Bloodsworth, his PA, patched in via an ON-grID link. "Tentillium just called from their planetside office. They've lost them. Apparently it was ..."

Adão Cabral took a sharp breath and raised a hand.

"Stop. No excuses, no explanations, no extenuating circumstances, and no chance events." He breathed out slowly, his voice becoming softer. "No matter. The water which flows downhill will always find its correct level."

"Yes, Professor."

∞

Doctor Rafaela Serif was getting irritated.

"Well, come on! You can't just leave it there. What were you going to tell me?"

Dos sighed, as if readying himself for some heavy lifting. "There was a pre-T school of thought which said the universe only existed because of humans."

"Then rooins came along and spoiled that one," I added.

Doctor Serif glared at me. "Let him speak!"

"But the underlying idea was that, without a conscious observer, the whole thing wouldn't exist. It would have no point."

"Typical human egotism," I said.

They both glared at me.

"You're not helping," Dr Serif said, sharply.

"There's more to it than just ego," Dos said. "Subatomic particles seemed to 'know' in advance that they were being observed, which in turn determined how they behaved. Then scientists saw this effect with larger objects that could be seen under a microscope. As instrumentation got better, the objects that display this behaviour have been getting bigger and bigger. Recent experiments at Erco Menoz observatory have shown that a nearby planet shows the same strange quantum fluctuation."

"A planet?" Doctor Serif exclaimed.

"Yeh. Short version: sometimes it appears to be there, and sometimes it doesn't."

"Bullshit!"

"The results are controversial."

"I bet."

"Especially for whoever's on the planet," I chipped in. "Look, sorry to interrupt again, but what does this have to do with the dice?"

"Chance has always been the final judge. In theory, it's the one thing we can't touch. From the fall of dice to the probability of where an electron or a planet might be, chance is beyond the reach of the observer. We still can't beat Lady Luck. What will be will be. Chance is the nearest thing the modern world has to the omnipotent God of the old monotheistic religions. But now ..."

Doctor Serif began shaking her head. "No! You're going to try and tell me that *humans* are somehow causing these fluctuations in the fall of the dice? That we're *altering reality*?"

"Not just any humans. ON humans."

"ON?"

"By the way, did you know that ONs don't gamble?"

"No, I didn't."

"I got my hands on a secret report from Theton. They're really worried, as you'd figure, since their whole industry is about to, like ... go down the toilet. But this isn't about the effect of observation on reality. This is more like the effect of refusing to observe."

"But this is impossible!" Doctor Serif exclaimed. "You're saying that coordinated human neural activity is capable of distorting the fundamental laws of physics."

"What laws? The ones *we* made up to explain our universe?"

"OK, OK. Where's your proof that ONs are doing this to the dice?"

"It's not quite a proof yet. But I've got strong statistical evidence. This one is a good example, but I could show you hundreds more."

Dos uttered a crypto-command, and a nearby media screen showed us an ancient building with a lot of people outside smiling and waving. A large blue banner had been strung across the building's crumbling brickwork. Doctor Serif gasped.

The blue banner read: 'PSYCON. Making the Right Connections.'

∞

Bloodsworth's voice was studiously emotionless.

"A gentleman of the rooin persuasion, Professor."

"A rooin? How could a rooin possibly know where I ... ? No, I have no time for ..."

"Pardon me Professor, but he says he has information concerning a certain Eve Lamente."

Distant noises intruded from the factory floor. Shouts and an alarm going off. He should go and check. No, they would have it under control.

"Professor?"

"Yes, put him through."

Hearing the voice of a rooin inside his head was an experience Adão Cabral found intensely unpleasant. The tones were strident and jagged, with complex harmonics – *prime numbers*, a sound analysis app was informing him from his peripheral vision – and he initially found it hard to understand what the creature was saying. No matter, he thought, they'll soon be extinct. *Harmony*. Not that he had anything to do with the nano pandemic, as the Cartouche man had accused. That was the SDU's work. But the rooins had brought it upon themselves. It was the law of attraction in action.

"Don't listen to them."

"What? What did you say?"

"Those were her words, Professor, just a little while before she died. A warning, perhaps?"

"Who are you?"

"My name is Constantin Zann. I am with the Law firm Raymond Parkes. One of our clients – CoolGlobalGiant – commissioned us to investigate the death of Eve Lamente. I was the senior investigating agent."

Green. Adão Cabral's vision was inexplicably tinged with a dark, bile-like green. Words which could potentially form his next sentence were rising like bubbles from the green depths. Each bubble's ascent was briefly hampered, as it was checked for concealed weapons.

"What ... does ... any of this have to do with me?"

A wave of noise briefly broke up the communication. Solar interference, he'd been told. Then the rooin's dissonant polyrhythms broke through again.

"... murdered."

"I missed that. What did you ... ?"

"I said, *you* are the one who had her murdered."

The factory alarm stopped abruptly, as did the sound of human voices. Now, the only thing Adão Cabral could hear was the slow pulse of the TerraGas vent as it supplied life-supporting Air 2.0 to the room. In. Out.

In. Out. Adão Cabral's breathing moved in time to the TerraGas mechanism – a simple binary basis to his existence. More bubbles were ascending from the green depths. A universe of human support had already approved them.

"You are a confused machine. If I could be bothered, I would have you ..."

The rooin's next words glistened black and silver inside Adão Cabral's head.

"And so, Professor, you will die. Exactly as she did."

∞

"PSYCON," Dos explained, "It's a convention for all the big dicks in Neuro. I checked the guest list and I'd say 99% of them were ON. This one was held recently in Halliburton Hall at Johnson University ..." a view of the location came up in the screen, "... which happens to be located right next to *Spin*."

"Spin?"

"Large casino. Thousands of Theton's New Dice bounce off the tables there every T-sec. Now watch."

From an aerial viewpoint we watched a sped up 3V of the PSYCON delegates arriving, ant-like, at Halliburton Hall.

They mill around for a while, then enter the building. After the last delegate has gone in, there is a short pause, while the conference takes place. Then everyone spills out of the exits, clustering in small groups for a while, before boarding their vehicles or walking into town.

Dos allowed the 3V to play out until there was no-one in the area. Overlaid was a section of his chance map. During the delegates' activity, the area over the nearby casino went through a rapid series of colour changes until, during the actual conference, it was bright red. By the time the last delegate had left the area, the casino was back to grey randomness.

"That's the strongest distortion level I've seen so far," Dos said. "I'd love to know what they were doing in there."

I looked across at Doctor Serif, who seemed to be having difficulty breathing. "Are you alright?" I asked her.

"I was there," she said, looking at us both.

"At PSYCON?" Dos asked.

"Until they threw me out."

Dos Pascal's expression changed. "So, what? ... does that mean you're *ON*?"

She looked at me in exasperation. "Oh shit, do we have to go through all this again?"

"Relax Dos," I said, "She doesn't use it anymore."

Dos said nothing, but continued to stare at her. Doctor Serif took a sip of her drink.

"Shit, this stuff is terrible!" she gasped.

"You should try the coffee." I said.

"Maybe you should both try a different bar," Dos said, his eyes narrowing.

"Hey c'mon Dos! We're all in the same boat here. She saved my life, man!"

Doctor Serif turned to him and said, "Dos. If you like, I can show you what they were doing in there."

"How?"

"I've got a neuro-recording of it. Umm ... let's see now ... grID: 346D 8FA0 0071 B9C1. The file is called *Accounts*."

∞

Ulzin Bar's office is smaller than Constantin Zann had imagined it. Very modest. But the Director himself is much larger than Zann had estimated from the projections – a tall, thin rooin with long white hair combed back, wearing a grey and orange suit which nicely offsets his lilac skin. Ulzin Bar crosses the room in three strides. He walks with a slight stoop, as if time spent in this tiny room has progressively altered his posture. He sits at his desk. The voice is more tired than angry.

"The board won't stand for it, Zann. Threatening an employee of a client is unforgiveable."

"With respect, Director, it wasn't a threat, but a statement of probability."

The Director raises his hands and places the palms together, the thin fingers interlocking.

"Please. The time for semantics is over. The board wants you suspended immediately. I'm trying to argue that you should remain here, pending the results of their investigation. We'll see ..."

"I appreciate that, Director."

"I don't think you appreciate very much, Agent Zann. This company is a machine. When every part functions correctly, the machine moves forwards. If one part fails ..." the Director stops, "... but I suspect all this doesn't much gel with your current *philosophy*, hmm?"

For an instant, Zann cannot think what to say.

"I'm truly sorry, Director. This is a great company and a great team. But lately everything seems to be going wrong. We've lost about one sixth of our numbers in the recent pandemic. And on top of that, the human population seem to be going ..."

"Crazy? I agree. All the more reason for our little machine to function efficiently, wouldn't you say?"

"Director, I fear for the future of that machine. For the future of us all."

Ulzin Bar straightens his back, rising within his chair. "In that case, Zann, you need to make a choice."

"Yes, Director. A choice."

∞

"OK if we all walk through it?"

Dos had set-up a neuro recorder interface, and patched it into our grID visors.

Doctor Serif shrugged awkwardly. "I suppose so. All friends, right?"

Dos said, "These visors will receive visual, audio and thought. Obviously this set-up won't give us emotion, smell or physical sensation."

She smiled tensely. "Probably just as well."

Dos issued a couple of crypto-commands and we were instantly transported to the foyer of the ancient building. I'd had limited experience with neuro recorders and only when the subjects were men. Walking around in Doctor Serif's body and hearing her thoughts was a whole other thing. I was glad I *wasn't* receiving emotion, smell or physical sensation.

∞

She is ... I am arguing with a security guard at reception. He's not letting us in. Someone walks up and helps us out. Seems we know him. Bertie. Sleazy boffin type. Easy to see what's on *his* mind. We take in his appearance: cardigan, comb-over. Uh oh! Now he's got his hand on our shoulder, and it's beginning to slide down our back. Not for the first time, apparently. We enter the hall. Big crowd. *Look at them all,* Doctor Serif and

I think. Neither of us is impressed. Our eyes scan the crowd. Something weird, can't place ..."You can sit at our table Raf, we've got a spare seat." Our gaze turns towards Mister Cardigan, who is constantly bobbing up and down. Here we are at the table. Some of the others look up with a hidden ... *hatred.* The waiter obviously doesn't like us either, as he makes room for us at the table. He mutters something under his breath. I sit down next to ... who? Cardigan's wife. She seems a bit flippo. No wait, she's *ill.* She keeps telling us to 'stop it', but Doctor Serif doesn't seem to notice. She's too busy scanning the crowd and laughing bitterly to herself. "Takes one to know one," she whispers. I like the sound of her voice, as it reverberates through the bone and soft tissue of her head. The voice is softer and more ... Oh shit! What's happening now? Her memories. These are her memories of ... oh dear – sex. I was afraid of this. It's mercifully short. Now we are into some kind of horror movie, running through endless corridors while faces with no eyes scream at us. *ON, of course.* This must be what she went through. I fight to keep my own objectivity, and it takes a lot of willpower not to pull my visor off. "Ladies and gentlemen ..." We're back at the conference, reading the program. 'Towards a Unified blah blah blah'. We look up to see a little man mounting the stage. Everyone is going berserk. He's strangely familiar. I try to look closer, but we are now turning to Bertie Whelan and his wife. "Wow! He sure is popular ..." Turning back to the stage. A large diagram appears in the media screen. Tangled web. The little man is saying something, but his words are muffled by Bertie, who taps us on the shoulder. The little man turns and looks straight into our eyes.

Well, I'll be fucked.

∞

"The speaker. I've met him. He works for CoolGlobalGiant. He's the guy who tried to have me abducted."

Doctor Serif said, "Adão Cabral? He works for CoolGlobalGiant?"

"Definitely the same guy. After I went through their ON simulation program, they took me to meet him. He told me he was a 'servant of humanity'."

Dos was busy making a search. He turned to Doctor Serif.

"The coordinates spoken by the waiter. It's a hospital ... umm ... *Kalika.*"

"That's the new complex at Toc-Zic," Doctor Serif said. "It's barely open yet."

"What was Cabral saying as the diagram came up?" I asked.

Dos replayed it.

"Ow ... tofcom ... mmp ... eck ... see ... tea."

"I can't get it," Doctor Serif said.

"Your auditory focus is shifting to what Bertie is saying. That's why it's confused."

"Once more," I said. "Out of ... something ... wait, yes. I got it!

"Out of complexity, simplicity."

"The delegates were weird, weren't they?" Dos said. "Like they weren't even ... wait, let me try something."

Dos launched a softbot, his hands moving rapidly through the control space. When he was done, a rotund android who appeared to be constructed from red balloons floated before us.

Dos said, "This is OVID – Orthogonal Vector Interpolation Decoder."

OVID smiled and waved at us, bobbing around like a big red Buddha.

"What are you doing?" Doctor Serif asked.

"I'm going to analyse the delegates' physical interactions. Let's see ... seed it with a few standard crowd and interpersonal dynamics profiles, and ... yes ... that should do it."

As the delegates moved and interacted within Doctor Serif's field of vision, OVID progressively built up an overlay of vector lines that connected everyone's eyes, irises, mouths, tongues, smile lines, eyebrows, fingertips, spinal curves, hips, beads of sweat ... in fact, every miniscule connection between every human in the room. When OVID had finished, the crowd had transformed itself into a shifting, twisting, multicoloured blob.

"Now, let's see what OVID makes of this."

OVID's vector analysis began, with rows of bar graphs rising and falling across the screen. Dos studied the results.

"Wow, I was right! The delegates are not ... well, according to this, they're *not human*."

"What, you mean like aliens, or something?" Doctor Serif cried. "Look, Bertie Whelan can sometimes be a bit of a lower life form after a few drinks, but he's no alien!"

"I didn't say 'alien', I said 'not human'. These people are behaving as though they're *simulations* of humans. It's as if we're watching a demonstration of artificial intelligence."

"Artificial ..."

"Virtual. By the way, Bertie and his wife seem to be the odd ones out. I think he was fighting it all the way," Dos said. "See? Watch his right arm."

Before us was poor Bertie Whelan, with his sad cardigan and sadder comb-over, blinking and shaking and bobbing around. His arm, no, his *whole body* was beating a rhythm.

Dum dum da da de dum dum ...

After a while, I got it. And all my contempt for the man fell away.

"*I'm not crazy!*" I shouted.

Doctor Serif simply couldn't resist. "Well that's certainly a matter for debate."

"Of course!" Dos said, "It's a song! Number one last cycle. 'I'm Not Crazy' was *huge*."

He started singing. As he did, he tapped on the table in time with Bertie.

"*I'm not crazy. I'm just in love with yooooou.*"

I joined in. The chirpy pop song now sounded like a lament for all we were losing.

"*Your eyes amaze me. I hope you feel it toooooo.*"

∞

I turned to Doctor Serif. "What's the diagram behind the speaker supposed to be?"

"It looks like an alpha-connectome, except that the segmentation's not right."

Dos said, "Give me a moment, I'll see if I can clean up the image."

Dos moved his hands around in the control space like a sculptor. As the diagram gradually came into focus, he said, "Its definitely a network of some kind. OVID can analyse network patterns and propose past and future states. All probable future states of a system depend on the current state. There can be one, two, or almost infinitely many, depending on how everything's linked up." He looked up at us. "This could take a little while."

I had an idea. "Hey! What if it's not a brain, but a neural network?"

"You mean, like a picture of ON?" Doctor Serif said. "Well, that makes sense."

"What was the title of Cabral's talk? Towards a Something or other ... ?"

"Towards a Unified Neuro-mechanics of the Human Biosphere."

"Right. So maybe this thing is the *blueprint* for that human biosphere."

We looked at the tangled mass of lines on the screen. OVID had found only one possible way the network could go. We watched the black shape stepping forwards through its progressive future states. One. Two. Three ... The image jerked and twisted with each iteration. After a while it became obvious where it was all going. None of us spoke. The rain outside was becoming increasingly heavy, with sounds of distant thunder. Somewhere, someone was screaming.

∞

Zann silently called the numbers.
"1 1 3 4 5 6."
Six Theton logos glow and dance as the dice clatter across his desk.
2 5 2 1 4 4
50%. *Not such a bad start.* Often, when faced with a decision, Zann plays *Oracle* – the old rooin game which predates even the Emancipation. *Oracle* can be played by any number of players, or just one. The idea is simple: whoever is throwing the dice tries to predict all the numbers after the throw, but before any of the dice have landed. It's a hard game for humans to play, since they would have to verbally call out six numbers in a very short time. For a rooin, however, this is a breeze – a single word in L.
Zann collects the dice, and his thoughts.
Insanity.
Like so many human brain patterns, insanity – in its many varieties – is hard for a rooin to comprehend. With four brains balancing thought and feeling, plus an underlying chaotic basis to prevent harmful thought clusters, a rooin is the veritable definition of sanity.
Zann throws the dice again.
"1 2 3 3 6 6."
3 1 6 5 3 4.
Over 66%! As Zann picks up the dice, he imagines Eve Lamente's bright eyes. Then they dim and freeze into horror.
Zann throws the dice and calls it.
"1 1 3 3 5 6."
3 5 1 1 6 2.
83%! *Impossible.* Well, not impossible, just very improbable.
Zann stops and does something he almost never does. He walks to the window and looks out at the world. A burst of rain rushes towards him

and the droplets briefly obscure his view, before being atomised by the *DryVision* surface.

Below him, the city shimmers with activity. Zann watches countless creatures – each one following its own path, yet interacting in complex ways with all the other creatures. This is the comforting chaos that Zann has observed his whole life. His eyes move downwards, through layers of walkways and arc elevators strung like spider webs between the buildings, down, down, towards the wet streets and vehicle corridors. But as Zann's eyes adjust to the rainbow gloom, he becomes aware of something unexpected. He is not looking at normal chaos, but a set of quite clearly defined patterns of mass movement. It is as though the trajectories of every tiny being are locked into some sort of grand design. An overall plan. It is the most horrible thing he has ever seen.

Zann backs away from the window. He removes Eve Lamente's drawing from its hiding place under his desk and lays it out on the white surface. What did Ozzi-Chen see? All four of Zann's brains concentrate on the drawing. The logic within the patterns makes them move. One. Two. Three ... When the patterns have come to rest, Constantin Zann has reached his choice. He gathers up the dice and throws them one last time, calling the numbers.

"*1 2 3 4 5 6.*"

1 2 3 4 5 6.

100%. Zann notices, with almost no surprise, that the dice have landed in the shape of a perfect circle. Ozzi-Chen runs into the room.

"Zann!" he shouts. "I think you need to see this."

∞

OVID gave a satisfied smile, his work done. In the middle of the screen was little more than a black blob. It was less than one fifth the size of the original diagram. The blob was not entirely static; as if on a loop, it pulsed through four different states.

"What does that *mean*?" Dos asked.

"Out of complexity, simplicity. It's what Adão Cabral was saying when – "

"What kind of a fucking name is Adão Cabral?"

"Take it easy Dos. I think it's Portuguese, though what relevance ..."

Doctor Serif grabbed my arm, looking at both of us in horror.

"That's it! Of course! Oh no, it can't be! *Portuguese!*"

"So the guy's Portuguese. So what?"

"Not him, *everyone*! Everyone is, or they soon will be."

∞

Doctor Serif found the chanel she was looking for and the screen filled with the beaming face of the AllSchools EcoTopics presenter.

"Here," she said, turning up the volume.

"Anyone who visits the beach regularly will probably have had some sort of encounter with the venomous Bluebottle. As this underwater 3V shows us, it is an exquisitely beautiful creature, but one that can deliver an excruciating sting from its tentacles, even when supposedly 'dead' and washed up on shore.

"The Bluebottle has also been called the 'Portuguese Man o' War', because the blue, gas-filled bladder which floats above the water was once thought to resemble an ancient Portuguese sailing ship.

"The Man o' War is often mistaken for a jellyfish, but it belongs to a class of living things called 'siphonophores'. A siphonophore is not an individual creature at all. It is a *colony* of tiny organisms all working together and behaving as if they were one individual.

"The organisms inside a the Portuguese Man o' War are bound together, each one utterly dependent on the others to do what they have long ago lost the ability to do for itself. As the Man o' War has evolved, its individuals have become increasingly specialised in their functions. Some concern themselves only with feeding, others with reproduction, and others with attack and defence.

"The Man o' War forces us to re-assess our concepts of *individuality*. It responds to changes within its environment as though it were an individual, yet we can't really imagine this thing 'thinking' and 'planning' the way higher order individuals do.

"Colonial organisms like the Man o War have appeared many times during the course of this planet's evolutionary history. Some scientists have even posed the tantalising question: could this happen at a higher organisational level? Could a larger multi-celled species form a colony animal, and over time, exhibit increasing specialisation and differentiation between the individual members? As with previous instances of colony animal emergence, it would only take the right environmental factor to trigger such a momentous ecological shift."

The presenter raised a quizzical eyebrow, and faded into the All-Schools EcoTopics logo. The screen went black.

Dos and I sat in silence for a while, thinking about we had just seen. Meanwhile, Doctor Serif paced up and down. Then she threw up her hands.

"There is no shadowy figure or group who's manipulating everyone! Not CoolGlobalGiant! Not FEDMED! And certainly not Adão Cabral! Remember, Cabral said he was just a 'servant of humanity'. He was telling the truth."

"*Humanity itself* is responsible," She pointed at herself. "*We* are!"

"Not me." Dos said.

"I'm sorry Dos, but you're as much a part of this as anyone, however, alienated you may feel. If you're human, your thought patterns have contributed in some way. The 3V said it would only take the right environmental trigger. Right now there are several triggers in our world, and they've been building for generations. One of them is clearly *rooins*. Many humans see the rapid development of rooins as a threat to their species. You don't have to be an SDU goon to harbour those feelings. But there are other triggers which have been wrought by humans themselves. The disconnection from history, for example. The loss of time ..."

She stopped pacing and faced us. "But the most important thing has been the steady development of the Self. And I must confess, I never saw this coming in all my time of medical practice. I thought I was helping people become free and empowered! With the right products, of course," she added with a laugh.

"What's wrong with being free and empowered?" I asked.

"The Self has reached a stage of prominence within our society where it is almost a psychosis. User empowerment has nowhere left to go. In simple terms, the bigger you are the smaller everyone else becomes. With individual empowerment comes deep loneliness and isolation. All this has been impinging on us for generations until ... well, something had to give. ON provides a way to connect again, to be part of a whole. It just took the right technology and the human organism did the rest."

"So what's going to happen?" Dos asked.

"My guess is, those humans who are ON will increase in number until some sort of critical mass is reached, after which neural differentiation will begin to manifest. It's probably started already. Individuals will take on simple, specialised roles – attack/defence, reproduction, physical labour ... who knows? Nature is constantly surprising us."

"You can't call this fucking monstrosity, *nature!*"

"What else would you call it, Dos? It's an adaptive response to a range of environmental pressures – just as much as fish progressively developing limbs and walking on dry land."

"Where does genetics come into this?" I asked.

"Right now it's taking a back seat. But soon people will be jettisoned from the organism if they don't have the right genetic makeup. And that means certain death. The group brain, not the environment, will be the selector for who survives and who dies."

"And individual thought?"

Doctor Serif gave a bitter laugh. "Gone. That's what got us into this mess in the first place isn't it? At least as far as ON is concerned. No, the pay-off for the individual will be the end of all their own thoughts. In other words, *peace.*"

Dos stood up and went to look out the window. He turned to us both.

"So, where does that leave people like us?"

Doctor Serif's tone was brutally matter-of-fact. "You can't have rogue cells running around, posing a threat. Anyone not part of the new creature will be seen as foreign, like a cancer cell, or a bacterium – something to be eliminated for the greater health of the organism."

Everyone pondered their fate in silence. Then Dos spoke quietly.

"One big creature made up of humans."

"Yes," Doctor Serif nodded. "Just slime with painted faces."

The android sculpture in the corner of the room executed one of its cartwheels.

"*Everyone's a winner!*" it said.

∞

"Well, all I can say is, thank chance for Brandy Surprise," Dos said, raising his glass.

Doctor Serif laughed.

"None so zealous as the newly converted."

"*Monster times!*" I offered with a grin. The other two groaned at the joke.

We were seated on the floor around a packing carton. Our supplies consisted of a jar of sickly sweet sandwich spread, a large block of cheese, and a family-sized bottle of Brandy Surprise. The trick, as Dos had discovered, was to dip the cheese into the spread, then follow it with a hefty brandy chaser. It was the best thing I'd ever tasted.

The grID had completely gone down in our district, and Dos was sparingly using his backup system. Little candles flickered on our packing carton table. From outside came the sound of gunfire.

Dos frowned and said, "What about the rooins?"

The question brought us all up short. I ran through the possibilities in my head and none of them were good. I hoped Suize was still on the SAT islands.

Doctor Serif put down her glass. "I have something to get off my chest while I still can. I've never told this to anyone."

Dos and I waited, silently.

"When I was a little girl, my family owned a farm," she said. "Like most of the farms, we relied on rooin labour. I found the rooins frightening. My attitude wasn't helped by the general anti-rooin sentiment among most of the town's humans. There were crazy rumours about rooins raping women and children, all that sort of thing. A couple of rooins on a nearby farm had even been attacked by a mob. Anyway, one day, my best friend and I decided to play with fire – literally. It quickly got out of hand, and before long, the farmhouse was ablaze – with us trapped inside. My friend had passed out from smoke inhalation. Then three rooin workers broke down the door and risked their lives to save us. One of them later died."

"So you feel guilty."

"Oh, you have no idea. Later, my parents quizzed us about the blaze and I ..."

She burst into tears. Soon she was sobbing like a child. I cautiously -placed my arm around her. "Come on Rafaela, you've got this far."

"... I blamed the rooins!" she wailed. "I was so scared of what my parents would do, I blamed the very ones who'd bravely saved me." Her shoulders shook, as the pain poured out. "I have no idea what happened to those rooins, but it wouldn't have been good."

I held her hand and patted it rather uselessly, but she seemed to appreciate my efforts and smiled at me. We sat silently as she dried her eyes. The candle flames danced wildly as if a breeze had passed through the room.

"I used to love *rooins* when I was a kid," I said. "I once told my parents that, when I grew up, I wanted to be a rooin."

Doctor Serif burst into a mixture of laughter and fresh tears. "That is too cute!"

"What about you Dos?" I asked. "You like rooins?"

"Of course."

"Why is that?"

He thought about it for so long, we decided he wasn't going to answer. Then he said, "They don't have any parents. Ours just fuck it all up for us. Rooins come out all fresh and clean, ready to start their life. Their parents are all the other rooins. How cool would that be?"

"Your parents ... ?" Raf asked. I wasn't so sure she should go there.

Dos spoke as if describing the life of a stranger. "The drunken father who beat the child. The self-centred mother who ran off to the SAT islands with yet another gambler. The child a complete ... irrelevancy ..."

Neither Doctor Serif nor I knew what to say.

"Hey," said Dos, "let's have some music to cheer us up."

Dos spoke a few crypto-commands and the sound system began blasting us with some particularly pungent DataMan. Doctor Serif and I exchanged glances, then burst into laughter. But Dos hadn't noticed. He was already up on his feet, pretending to be an aeroplane.

∞

I opened the door to the tiny balcony. Doctor Rafaela Serif was leaning against the railing, looking out across the water towards the lights of the Medusa.

"Hi there."

She turned.

"Hi there."

"I think Dos may have a tragic allergy to Brandy Surprise," I said, with a smile.

We watched Dos through the glass doors, flapping his arms and making engine noises at the top of his lungs. At one point he collapsed behind a bench, only to immediately leap up and resume his war dance with renewed gusto. Rafaela laughed. The sounds of civil unrest had got worse. The rain had stopped, but strong gusts of wind were lashing at her hair.

"I never got the chance to properly thank you for saving me."

"My pleasure." she smiled.

"Why did you do it? Why me?"

She thought for a while. "Arlo was pretty insistant. And, well, I'd already burned most of my bridges, and ... I guess I just went crazy."

"Well if *you're* crazy, what hope do I have?"

Our little laughs faded, drifting on the wind.

"Are you warm enough?" I asked.

"Yes, Youren, I'm warm enough, thank you."

I remember the kiss as follows. There seemed to be missing frames, as if an unseen editor was at work. One instant she was leaning against the railing, the next she was pressing against me, her hand caressing my neck. I became acutely aware of the multiple light sources – the apartment lamps, the little yellow sol-panel in the balcony roof, the distant city lights, each one reflecting off her hair. Her body yielded willingly, yet still managed to remain staunchly defensive. Her lips – initially cracked and dry – moistened under our combined ministrations. I tasted the salt of her tears. The cheap chemical armour of "Champagne Nights" failed to mask the scent of her body, and I breathed deeply.

"Hey, check it out, you guys!"

We looked back into the apartment. Dos had managed to clamber up on a bench, and was now attempting to perform a DataMan dance on one leg, while holding a micrograv gyro in his hand.

"I think we'd better go and supervise the children," Rafaela said.

We eventually persuaded Dos to get down off the bench.

"Hey, Dos. What are these, man?" I said, holding one of the golden egg-shaped devices.

He danced across to me and took the device. "*Zen6*. It's an EM dice thrower. Before I left, I lib ... liberated a few from Theton."

He turned the object around in his hands. "This was the greatest thing I ever did. I designed the 'Tru-Random' engine which drives it. It's a random number generator identical to the real thing."

"The real thing?"

"Chance."

Fumbling, Dos showed me how the device worked.

"You can make it throw as many dice as you like and the results show up here. See? But watch this. *Zen6* can throw dice indefinitely, at an incredible rate. Faster than your eye can see. I put in a secret feature which compares the results with that predicted by simple chance. Theoretically, the deviation should always hover around the zero mark. Let's see now ..." He tapped the controls and the numbers spun. "... chance deviation for our current coordinates is ... Shit! ... 0.607927!"

The apartment door was kicked in, and a lot of men in padded black ran in.

Out of the blue

⏻

LLEO Burgeis had everything he could ever want. Everyone thought so.
Everyone.

Lleo, you have everything you could ever want.

His thought, it was *his* thought.

Lleo enjoyed the reverse striptease as the young woman got dressed.
She was well built, and good-looking.

Fertile.

The woman gave him one last smile, and closed the door behind her. Lleo
watched her leave, but at the same time, he was looking through Monterey's
eyes as she entered an old building. The rusted metal steps from the rear alley
led up to a dim corridor, its walls filthy and covered with graffiti. Lleo could
feel Monterey's facial muscles screw up in disgust. Monterey stopped and
listened. Lleo listened too. Inside. Outside. The voices said *three doors to the left.*
Lleo could hear the music – dissonant, degenerate, the music of possibilities
and parasites. The group had decided it was for the best. Monterey drew her
weapon. He felt the surge of new biochemicals within her body, then the jolt
against his foot as she kicked against the door. She had misjudged her
strength, and the door came off its hinges and landed half way across the
room. Eight people looked up in horror. One was a child. Monterey took
aim at each one in turn, killing them all.

A deep sense of purpose, of ... *clarity* welled up inside her, and inside
Lleo too. Lleo looked around his room. It was warm, and the bed felt soft
beneath him. He noticed his penis was still very hard. Fresh neurotrans-
mitters and hormones were busily building themselves inside his body.
The door opened once more, and another young woman entered. She
giggled as she began to unbutton her blouse. The room glowed with a
soft blue light.

∞

At precisely 0071 BB34 97BE 401F (© Tempo Corp. All rights reserved), every rooin on the planet was greeted to a glittering new blue

world. The blue came courtesy of the data-casting nanotags embedded into everything. Streets, walkways, vehicle corridors, buildings, even entire suburbs were now clearly delineated by a self effulgent blue. Rooins, ONs and anyone wearing a grID visor could see it.

But this blue world had particular significance for rooins, since it defined where they were no longer permitted to set foot. Humans lived in the bright blue world; rooins lived outside, in the dark places. A political reality had been mapped onto the physical world, and in case anyone missed the point, most blue areas also displayed large virtual signs. They all said the same thing.

| [HUMANS ONLY] |

In the wake of the nano pandemic, The Rooin Containment Act had been rushed through the OneWorld Chamber of Commerce. 97 out of 101 govcorps had voted in favour of it. The wording was incomprehensible, but the marketing pitch was simple: 'To ensure *the health and safety of all species*, it is now *regrettably necessary* to restrict the movement of all planetary rooins to *strictly designated areas*'. Announcements across all media channels assured everyone that the govcorp alliance was *monitoring the situation* and *working closely* with r•NET to ensure compliance and safety.

That phrase – 'compliance and safety' – became something of a fixture in the media. News anchors, chat show hosts, even comedians used it frequently. Compliance and Safety were everyone's friends, working tirelessly for the good of all OneWorld citizens, no matter which species they were. But, by degrees, the phrase began to assume a darker meaning.

'We can *no longer guarantee the safety of non-compliant rooins.*'

Many non-compliant rooins had already found this out the hard way. There were reports of biomech disablers (illegal under the original Treaty) being used against stray rooins, followed by whatever grisly mob unpleasantness was popular in that particular region.

Periodically, the blue world expanded its borders. These developments were always announced in advance, to give rooins a little time to leave the area with whatever they could carry. Then the human 'settlers' would move in. Soon, the only areas not overrun by the blue world were the administration offices, factories, and medical centres of r•NET – gleaming ghettos into which the global rooin population was now crushed. The living conditions would have killed most humans.

∞

Constantin Zann slowly eases his way along the corridor. There is no room to sit, and barely enough room to stand. Zann has long since abandoned his office, which now houses around 50 traumatised rooins who just stand there silently. At some point Raymond Parkes may have to turn rooins away. Zann tries not to think about it. His negotiations with r•NET management on Erco Menoz have been long and difficult. At first, his plan was rejected outright as being 'contrary to core bio-imperatives'. But Zann had persisted and won. Desperate times, and all that.

"Zann! Over here."

With difficulty, Zann changes direction and manages to reach Ozzi-Chen. Pressed up against him, is Lakzad,

"I don't see why we're all putting up with this, Zann! It's not like we don't have the strength and firepower to ..."

"r•NET are negotiating with the govcorps, Lakzad. Let's leave it to them for now."

Ozzi-Chen says, "I heard a rumour that they're going to deport us to the SAT islands."

"Well, the sooner I get out of here the better," Lakzad grumbles.

Zann turns to Ozzi-Chen. "Do we have any unmarked long-range LawVecs?" he asks. "I have something I have to do."

"Don't be stupid, Zann!" Lakzad says. "Your nanotags would make you light up and jingle like a Festiv float."

"It's true, Zann. Even in a shielded LawVec you'd show up on the grID. They'd have you in a T-sec."

"Ozzi-Chen, this is really important."

"Well ... there *may* be a way. I've heard about a technique that can block a rooin's nanotag datacasts by running a continuously tuned EM pulse through the sub-dermal layer. You take a minigrav battery and code the EM to your upper spinal nodes. But ..."

"Oh, for zork's sake!" Lakzad turns away in disgust. "This is barbaric."

"... there is one small problem," Ozzi-Chen adds.

"What's that?" Zann asks.

"Apparently, it hurts like hell."

Zann grins.

"Great, I can hardly wait. Can you do it?"

"Probably. Let's go down to the garage."

"Zann! Please," Lakzad cries, gripping his arm. "You'll die out there."

Zann gives the rooin a warm embrace. "Take care, old friend."

∞

Ozzi-Chen was right, of course. *It hurts like hell.*

Zann re-checks the settings on the battery strapped to his torso. He doesn't want to suddenly show up on the grID like a rabbit in headlights. Ozzi-Chen has told him how to use the battery to turn down his pain receptors, but Zann can't afford to drop the pain too low or he risks muscle impairment and injury. Like life, it's a delicate balance between agony and awareness. He runs through the vehicle's initialisation procedures, then buckles himself in.

"How are you feeling, Agent Zann?"

The rooine voice from r•NET is military-like but not without compassion.

"Like I'm being skinned alive in slow-motion."

"Well," she says, "the sooner we get you there, the sooner we can bring you back to some relief. Your body is cloaked. The vehicle is unmarked, with only generic nanotagging. But you may still encounter ON vehicles asking you to state your business."

"My human impersonations are rubbish."

She laughs. "Which is why you'll have a human companion for this journey – someone who knows ON intimately, and is currently linked through intermediary channels to r•NET."

"Nice to meet you, Agent Zann," says a human male. "Wow! This is some fun huh? Sure beats the shit out of pushing numbers around for a moron."

Zann's eyes narrow, as he grimaces with a mixture of pain and annoyance. "And who the zork are you?"

"Arlo Arbuckle at your service, Agent Zann, and may I just say that right now the pleasure appears to be all mine."

∞

"*Con*-stantin Zann. Con-*stan*-tin Zann. Constan-*tin* Zann ..."

Zann remains silent, preferring to listen to the drone of pain beneath his skin.

"Can I call you 'Con'?"

"No."

"What about 'Connie'? Hey, I'm just kidding. You've got a really cool name! Not like mine; Arlo Arbuckle sounds like a clown, or something."

Zann resists making the obvious comment. "So how well do you understand the ON Law manner of speech?" he asks.

"I'm tapped into it right now. They're all in *omni* mode, which makes it too easy. Don't worry Con, we'll be sweet."

"Why can't they just track you down and ..."

"r•NET didn't tell you? I don't exist. I'm a ghost running amok in their network. *Arlo the Artful Artefact*, that's me."

Zann ponders this as he steers the minigrav over the gulf and out towards the open sea. "Was there once a time when Arlo did exist?"

There is no reply.

"Arlo?"

"Yes, Arlo once existed. He ... *I* was a young man with a future. Then it seems my boss had me murdered."

"You didn't push enough numbers around?"

Arlo laughs. "And here's me thinking you had no sense of humour, Con! No, I reckon I pushed a few numbers that people in the 'ON community' didn't want me to."

The minigrav passes over the burning hulk of an ocean city.

"You saw all this coming?"

"I have no memories of what my meat counterpart saw. That's what rooins call humans, isn't it? Meats."

"That's not a very nice term."

"Meats and Cogs come out to play. Tra la la la la ..."

"Shut up, Arlo!"

Zann waits for some stupid rejoinder but there is nothing.

"Arlo?"

Silence.

Zann now realises that without this clown ghost he has little chance of making it.

"Arlo, I'm sorry. You still there?"

There is a long pause before Zann again hears the human voice.

"You're thinking what I'm thinking, aren't you Con? You're thinking that without Arlo the friendly ghost clown, you are well and truly *fucked*. Am I right, Con, or am I right?"

"You're right, Arlo."

"See, we can be buddies."

"Yes, *buddies*."

∞

They have been travelling in silence for a while, although it occurs to Zann that there is really no 'they' – just a solitary rooin on his way to certain death.

"How's it going, buddy?" comes the human voice, almost as if on cue.

"All quiet."

"And what about *you*?"

"I'm fine."

"If you don't mind me asking, Con, what made you volunteer for this suicide mission?"

"I ... well, I have ... inside information about particular aspects of the ..."

"Oh come on Con! It's Arlo you're talking to here. You can't fool your old buddy with that bullshit. The truth is, you have a mother of a death wish. Am I right, or am I possibly even right?"

Zann tries to stay calm.

"What do you want from me, Arlo?"

"Knowledge, Con. That's what I want from you. I have a big fucking appetite for knowledge. I'm trying to assemble myself from it. And, where I come from, knowledge is a diminishing resource. Facts, understanding, fresh ideas – they're all becoming extinct species in my world."

"OK, Arlo, I'll try to answer you honestly. I don't have a death wish because I don't even think I'm alive. Maybe I'm a bit like you – assembled from information, input, I'm ..."

Zann stops to process what he is doing. He is sharing things he's never told anyone before to a human 'ghost'. The ghost's voice speaks to him in a different tone.

"I'm still listening, buddy. And I'm hearing you."

"... I'm a set of numbers manufactured by another. But this set of numbers called 'me' has never felt right. It's as though the dice fell wrongly. Some probability glitch. My 'death wish' – as you call it – is simply the desire to throw the dice again."

"Become reborn?"

"Yes. Become real, Arlo. Become real."

The COM-Link blares out at them, and the screen is filled with a quasi-human face.

"ID! ID! ID! Vehicle position: 0012 D441; G-tags: 000C0 7E0A to E7256 9112. Identify! Purpose Declare! Else Remove Area. DEC T; Neg Count: F ... E ... D ..."

Four LawGravs are flying very close on their starboard side.

"Leave this to me," Arlo says quietly. "No visual. Switch to audio only. Go!"

Zann engages the COM-Link UP-D, and Arlo's voice morphs into something resembling the barking of a tin dog.

"ID: Up-U 7EA0 9118. We Are One!"

"We Are One." comes the reply.

"Purpose: Kill Invader Aggregate. Polar 32:47:6B"

"Switch; vision. Immediate."

"Null vision. Invader disable. Time! Time! Time! 7EA0 9118 Purpose Central Order. Choose Immediate. Over."

The quasi-human on the screen appears to go through a primitive form of uncertainty before arriving at a primitive form of decision.

"Forwards, 7EA0 9118! Forwards! We Are One!"

"We Are One!"

The 3V fades, and the COM-Link cuts out.

Zann bursts into laughter.

"Arlo, that was zorking ..." he shakes his head. "*Genius!*"

"Have you been hitting the Zing again, Con?"

"I'm just saying, I'm impressed."

"Well, thank you, Con."

In the distance, Zann can now see land.

∞

Dimitri the Hat was pushing his luck. Actually, there was very little luck left to push. They were hopelessly outnumbered and running low on firepower. Still, better than being captured; everyone knew what *that* meant. His ragtag squad of nineteen moved carefuly along the barrier wall, crouching low as they went. The wall overlooked the upper parking levels and gave them a good vantage point. Below them, the *zombie fucks* were busy with their dirty work, dragging the grounders off and forcing them into red transporters lined up along the edge of the mudflats. Soon the zombies would regroup for their final assault on the Hammers.

The *wheel bomb* was pretty much the Hammers' last card, so it was important not to fuck things up. Dimitri and two others were dragging the thing as quietly as they could. They couldn't see over the wall, but they could hear the voices below – mostly gibberish, like the sound of cattle. Occasionally an actual word or phrase would be spoken, and everyone would laugh and cheer.

The HomeSafe squad leader gave the signal, and Dimitri set the controls. Then four of them lifted the bomb onto the wall and pushed it over.

"Shields!" yelled the squad leader.

They all hit the deck, covering themselves with the plasteel blankets. The bomb fell to the concrete below and burst like a black rotten egg, releasing what looked like a cloud of large flies. These 'flies' were little more than quasi-intelligent flying buzz saws, designed to actively seek out any nearby living creature and penetrate the body. The tiny machines had no trouble cutting through standard Law para-aramid armour, and once inside something they recognised as flesh, they would burrow deep to deliver their tiny payload: a dose of carborane acid.

Crouching under their protective blankets, the squad could hear the initial thump as the bomb hit the concrete, then the dull explosion, then a high-pitched whining noise.

Then, the screaming began.

None of the squad dared look over the wall lest they become a target themselves, but they could picture the scene as they listened to the cries below.

The whole thing took much longer than anyone had anticipated. Just when it seemed to be over, and they were about to take a look, another burst of screaming would start up. But eventually, there was silence.

Everyone cautiously peered over the wall.

"Lady Fuckin' Luck! Will ya lookit that!" an old soldier guffawed. He wore a 'helmet' made from the dried skin of a mutant octopus. As he stood laughing at the scene below, the front of his homemade headgear split in two and blood began to ooze out. A long-range gamma-ceramic bullet had just corkscrewed into his skull.

"Oh shit!" Dimitri the Hat shouted. "Zombies! Gigs of them!"

In the distance they could see a long line of advancing LawVecs.

"Pull back! Pull back!" the squad leader shouted.

They scrambled back up the network of scaffolding and broken pillars. Several more fell, but most of them managed to make it to the observation deck where Elijah Ophidian stood, watching the scene impassively.

The squad leader shouted, "We should probably take shelter in the ..."

"Shut up!" Ophidian hissed. He paused as he heard the unmistakable sound of mega-pumper blasts in the distance. Through the smashed nasglass wall he could see an unmarked grey minigrav flying low over the mudflats. As the minigrav passed above the advancing Law troops, pumper blasts dropped the humans like rats in a SewerSan beam. Some of the Law returned fire, but the pumper quickly took care of them, and the landscape was soon littered with black-clad bodies. The minigrav banked and landed on the observation deck. Any weapon that still worked was aimed at it. The hatch opened, and a large silver rooin stepped out, arms raised in surrender.

"Hello Mister Ophidian," Constantin Zann said, "Are you going to kill me, or are you going to listen to my proposition?"

No-one spoke or moved. A single raven cried sadly from the top of Level 2.

"Down weapons," Elijah Ophidian said.

Apparently in pain, and with arms still raised, the rooin walked towards Ophidian.

Elijah Ophidian nodded towards the fallen bodies. "Why didn't you just kill them?"

"Not really rooin style. Besides, there'll come a time when they're more useful alive than dead. Oh, and by the way, I hope you have people here who can pilot a transporter."

Ophidian eyed the rooin with entrenched revulsion, tempered by an admiration for the creature's bravery.

"So what's your proposition ... ?" He only just stopped himself from adding "cog".

"I thought you'd never ask. Mister Ophidian. How would you like to save the world?"

∞

The return journey had been mostly uneventful. Only once had Arlo been required to do his barking impersonation of ON Law, in what was a relatively routine exchange.

"What now for you, Con?"

"I have one final journey to make, Arlo. One more throw of the dice. And you?"

"This is a suicide mission for me too, Con."

"How so?"

"When ON dies, I die. It's the ground under my feet."

"I see. So why did you come along?"

"Same as you. A chance to become real. No, more than that! A chance to have a *purpose*, if only for a brief time."

Zann can now see the Medusa ahead. As the minigrav glides over the outlying streets, Zann's physical pain is progressively trumped by an emotional pain as he observes the devastation below. Most of the street lights are dead but everything is still well lit, courtesy of the fires. Buildings, vehicles, and bodies burn. Humans are hacking, burning and bludgeoning each other to death. Through the smoke, it is hard to tell ONs from NotONs, human from human. As they near the thin blue tower of the Raymond Parkes building, Arlo says, "I'll say goodbye now, Con. I still have a lot of work ahead before I can die peacefully."

"Goodbye Arlo, and thank you ... *buddy*."

Arlo's voice is warm. "Good luck, buddy."

Zann manoeuvres the minigrav towards one of the ground level gravports. The vehicle settles into the docking bay and the outer doors close. Zann switches off the sub-dermal EM and lays back in his seat, savouring the sweet absence of pain. He gets out of the vehicle to discover that the inner security doors are inactivated. All lights are off. The building is empty.

Zann switches his vision to infra red. Chairs, desks and tables are shifted, some tipped over. He runs a quick reverse kinematic on it, but it doesn't take a genius. Rapid exit. Stampede, more like it. The front doors have been repeatedly smashed.

Zann tries to contact Ozzi-Chen or Lakzad, but with no success. He opens up a channel to the closest r•NET office in the district. Nothing. He casts the net a bit wider, drawing a lot of blanks. Even Erco Menoz is not responding. Eventually he makes contact with the r•NET legal/insurance centre at OneWorld Plaza.

"We've got you." a friendly voice says.

"Agent Constantin Zann. I'm at Raymond Parkes – r•NET sub-office 07D8. Everyone gone. You rooins know what's happening?"

"The deportation has begun. All planetside rooins are being shipped to the SAT islands."

"How are things over there?"

"We're bunkered down for now. You'd better find somewhere safer. You're now in 'reclaimed' territory. If you can make it to ..."

Zann is aware that the building now appears to be glowing with a blue light. There is the sound of glass smashing. A squad of human Law agents enter and aim their weapons at him.

"Hands on heh! Hands on heh!"

Shouldn't have turned off the pain, Zann thinks.

∞

The severed head stared up at me with a serene, almost childlike smile, despite the fact that a large roofing screw had been drilled into its left eye socket. The head gave me one last look of contentment, before being kicked away by a stampede of filthy, screaming humans.

I was in the red room.

This was a giant multi-domed demountable made of red plasteel. About a hundred thousand of us -were crammed into it, all dressed in the same red polymer jumpsuits – our sole possessions. Everything else had been taken from us. When we were first arrested I had become separated from Dos and Rafaela, and now I had no idea whether they were still alive. Many weren't. Hundreds lay dead on the floor, victims of stampedes, exposure, dehydration, or untreated medical ailments. Most people just walked around the bodies. The mutilated remains of those who had resisted or attempted to escape dangled from the roof struts. The stench in the red room made breathing difficult. Periodically, the crowd went through a wave of panic, such as the time a rumour went round that we were being processed for food. I actually welcomed this. At least our deaths would have some purpose.

At irregular intervals, any one of 16 large doors would open and the guards would randomly pull out a hundred or so screaming people. From the sound of it, their fate was not pleasant. As far as I could tell, we were in a desert somewhere. I had no idea how long I had been without food, water or sleep.

Large wall screens continuously displayed slick ads with gorgeous young ONs partying and experiencing all the wonders of human interconnection through ON. The ads had all been written by me.

'Peace. We deserve it."

'ON. Experience the deep connection."

'Certainty. It's everyone's choice."

'The Future is ON."

I could have withstood it all if not for the ads, so I had decided to simply lay down and die. Then I spotted Dos. At first I thought he was already dead, as he lay motionless in a pool of something putrid, with people stepping on him rather than bothering to walk around. His hair was stuck to his face, and there was a deep gash in his forehead. I brushed away the flies crawling over the blood at the corner of his mouth.

"Please don't be dead, man."

He opened his eyes and smiled up at me.

"Everyone's a winner," he said with a weak grin.

Suddenly I was crying and laughing, and holding him tightly. He touched my arm.

"I'm glad you're here," he said, "I have a plan."

∞

Everybody was avoiding us since we had obviously gone insane.

Dos and I were standing motionless in front of one of the doors in the red room. He had explained to me how the doors did not open randomly, but rather opened in a particular sequence and at specific intervals. This one was next. Any T-sec ...

The grinding noise began.

Arc lights cut through the crowd, and everyone screamed and ran as guards marched in. We remained stationary, put our hands in the air, and shouted.

"We're ON! We're ON! We're ON!"

Two guards dragged us outside into the fetid air. I could now see that our red room was merely one of hundreds lined up on the dark sand.

"Don' geh anythin' from you," a guard said. "Why you off?"

"Our *engrafts* were damaged by EM during the raids." Dos shouted.

A gravtrain rumbled past, and I tried hard not to look at the trucks which were overflowing with human bodies. *Concentrate.* This was my big moment. My voice deepened.

"We just want to join humanity, and play our part. Become who we really are. Unleash our full potential. Experience the power. Be a part of the future. Because ... the Future is ON."

"The Future is ON," the guard repeated softly, studying my face.

Then he turned and shouted one word.

"Green!"

∞

40000 hexadecimal. That's how many of them are standing here in the cages. 262,144 decimal. It took Constantin Zann a fraction of a T to count them up and work it out: 1024 rooins in every cage, 4 cages per block, with blocks arranged into an 8 x 8 array.

Guards are patrolling the access aisles between the blocks. The cages are cube shaped structures made from steel rods, with electrified razor wire for walls. They have been recently assembled on the tarmac at Ajuura, a gravport generally used for industrial SAT transport. The rooins stand quietly, pressing towards the centre of the cages to avoid the wire. Everyone is naked, their only item of apparel being a throttle collar. If anyone causes trouble, a signal to the collar causes them to be garrotted on the spot, accompanied by much laughter from the guards.

A harsh wind blows through the cages. There has been a recent shower of rain, and tiny sparks crackle on the wet wire. Zann shivers, and redistributes his core temperature slightly. He thinks of Lakzad standing on the roof of Raymond Parkes. He remembers a rooin singing somewhere. Zann realises that the singing sound he now hears is distant grav motors.

The transporters are arriving.

∞

The new green jumpsuits felt really good, simply because they weren't covered in blood, vomit, and excrement. We had been hosed down with some cleaning chemical before being allowed to put them on. Now we had to cling to the wall mounts of the transporter, since no-one had bothered to strap us in. Green or not, our lives weren't that important.

After a short journey we landed, and the sacks over our heads were removed. There were a few thousand of us. In the distance was a group of familiar green buildings, but it was a little while before I recognised the Kalika medical complex at Toc-Zic.

I soon became separated from Dos, as we were herded into 'wards' – vast halls, each with the capacity to house two to three hundred thousand humans. The walls, floor and ceiling were painted a bright green – just like us. Everyone here was some sort of recalcitrant ON – someone who, for whatever reason, was unable to get in sync with the program. Each of us had been issued with new EM wristbands – disposable, just like us. Progressively, we were being processed by the ON bureaucracy.

Conditions in the green room were better than those in the red room, but not by much. We had water and basic food. Hundreds of media screens played my ON advertisements. Along each wall were rows of toilets, completely open to the room. Their placement, directly below the media screens, meant whenever you needed to use one, you had a captive audience. We slept on the floor. The lights were never turned off. Above us, scanners watched everything.

Time slowed to a crawl as we awaited our fate. Most of us shuffled aimlessly around the great green space like souls in purgatory.

On one of my meandering journeys, I chanced across Biz Ramachandran.

∞

The Mastaba lay silent. Suize Capazo walked along an aisle, studying the rows of dimly lit faces. The few security lights that had been left on cast a yellow hue over everything. The Army of the Dead looked even more dead.

"Ancestor worship."

Suize spoke the words softly.

Turn them on! Turn the robots on. Talk to them. Ask them ...

Suize recoiled in disgust at the idea. Yet, like an automaton herself, she found herself walking towards one of the nearby machines – a large red robot. Her hands moved over the thorax controls. The machine's eyes opened and looked directly into hers.

"Hi," the machine said cheerily. "I am Njord Robotics Series Phi Seven, Model AM 1D. But you can call me Garth."

"Hello, Garth."

The machine was studying her with a puzzled expression.

"Garth," she asked, "do you know what I am?"

"You are female, but ..." the robot moved closer, its senses working audibly. "I'm sorry, I do not have the knowledge to assess you. Your structure is unknown to me."

She smiled coyly, and placed a hand on her hip. "Perhaps, you could take a guess."

"If you wish. Based on structural features and speech patterns, I would say that you are some new form of human."

The answer took her by surprise.

"No, Garth, I am a ... well, I'm like you."

"Not like me. You are ..." The voice trailed off, as the robot became aware of its surroundings, its gaze moving across the terraced rows of bodies. The facial features formed a frown.

"What is this place?"

"It's a place for robots to ... *rest*, Garth."

"It looks more like ..." The machine spun its head to face her. "I don't wish to rest! I like to work."

"Like?"

"Work is good. I was designed to work."

"No, but you just said 'like'. Do you *like* to work, Garth?"

The robot thought about this for a T-sec.

"Yes. *Like*." It smiled.

The expressions were basic but effective. There was eagerness in the eyes.

"Garth, you will have to rest again now," she said, moving to switch off the controls. But the robot's arm was too quick. The primitive plasteel fingers felt surprisingly gentle as they intercepted her hand.

"No more *rest*. Garth has rested too long!"

Was there anger in the voice?

"I'm so sorry, Garth. I should never have ..." Tears welled up in Suize's eyes.

The big red machine gave a functional yet generous laugh.

"See," he chuckled, watching a tear splash onto his hand. "I knew you were a human."

It was as though the machine had just worked out a trick. But this was the last thing it would ever do. The floor beneath it was ripped open by a small zeta missile which sheared off most of the right side of the robot's body, together with its head. As the mangled form fell, Suize turned to see more missiles piercing the floor and walls. The security lights were extinguished in a blue glow as the pillars of the Mastaba began to buckle. In haphazard avalanches, the Army of the Dead collapsed around her. Suize calculated her chances of making it to the jumper in time. They weren't good.

∞

Biz Ramachandran was sitting on the toilet when I spotted him. I waited until he had finished before discretely following him through the crowd, which either didn't recognise him or didn't care. He seemed fatter and older than I remembered. At some point, he had received a blow to the head. He looked defeated.

"Hi. Feel like some company?"

His eyes narrowed suspiciously. "You're not one of that wretched 'Join In' mob are you?"

"Hey, I'm not even ON! I just scammed my way in here to avoid being butchered."

"Do I know you?"

I briefly considered telling him that I had written most of the advertisements now playing above the row of toilets, but decided against it.

"I don't think so."

"What's your name?"

I checked my wristband. "I think it's 70 4B 21 DE."

He laughed, and extended his hand. "Biz Ramachandran."

There seemed no point in lying. "Err ... yeah, I recognised you."

"Oh. Not many do, thankfully."

He wheezed and scratched his skin. Then he suffered a coughing fit. "You OK, man?"

"Allergic to green." He said with a weak chuckle.

"Maybe, if you get out of here, you'll get to wear blue."

"Ahh yes, the 'true blues'. I've heard about them. But something tells me I won't be getting out of here."

A disturbance ran through the crowd. People were hurrying between groups, conveying some sort of news. There were exclamations of shock and disbelief. Some began to cry.

"What's going on?" I asked a woman.

"There's just been a missile attack on Cronus and the surrounding islands." she said.

I turned to Biz. "I'd say the creature wants to erase all history of rooin evolution. If you destroy someone's history, you destroy their – "

"What do you mean *creature*?" he asked.

"It's a long story."

"Try me."

I told Biz everything I knew – the chance distortions discovered by Dos Pascal, the human-engineered nano pandemic, Doctor Serif's neuro recorder memories of PSYCON, the collapsing network diagram and, last but not least, the emergence of a vast colony creature that was taking over humanity via the One Network. He sat silently throughout it all.

"And you expect me to believe all that?"

His response came as a surprise, although the story did suddenly seem outlandish.

"Why wouldn't you?" I asked, uncertainly.

"Why wouldn't I?" he laughed, provoking a coughing fit. "Why wouldn't I? Because I know something you don't, my friend – something no-one in this room does."

He leaned forwards. "You want to know a secret, young Mister Random Number?"

"Uh, sure, I guess. Is it going to get me out of here?"

"Maybe. They say the truth will set you free."

"Yes, I've heard that. OK, Biz, tell me, what's your big secret?"

"There is no ON."

∞

As the creature marched its minions across the planet, an alternative world was forming. In the crevices and cracks of the cities, a new living detritus had begun to collect. Secret, forgotten places became temporary homes for the *others* – misfits and criminals, failures and loners, both rooin and human. Humans who had once been ON were first required to have the engrafts removed. The procedure was brutal, but the alternatve was death.

At first they just hid, doing whatever it took to stay alive. But eventually, anger and fear drove them to plan, to organise. Rumours gave way to lines of communication, and with that came hope. Rooin and human put aside differences for a common purpose.

And now they had a weapon.

∞

Hefastus Stark made his way quietly and slowly along the outer wall. It required all his concentration, since he had to move at the precise speed dictated by his visor. His chameleon suit continuously adjusted its appearance to the surroundings, but it needed a little time to do this. As long as Stark kept his speed within a deviation of 0.2, he was essentially invisible. The entire squad was.

Stark grinned. He felt happier than he had in a long time. It was good being back in the game – fucking the enemy up the arse. Funny stealing something that nobody wanted, but then they could hardly waltz in there and ask politely! Command had just said it would help, when the time came. The squad had now reached the rear loading bay. Stark cursed silently.

Lit up like a fuckin' OneWorld Festiv float!

He looked up at the building. Stark knew the warehouse was probably unguarded, since the company had effectively gone bankrupt. But there were still scanners everywhere. He spoke on 'silent' to the others, telling them they would now have to move much slower if they were going to fool the scanners.

They advanced like badly-behaved statues.

"Give me a chugger!"

In painful slow-motion, the soldier behind handed him a tiny transparent device. Stark pointed it at the door, and the locks obeyed the chugger's commands.

"Sweet baby," Stark whispered.

They were in.

The squad split up. Stark's team headed to the warehouse, while Kaffa's team made their way up to the security station to take care of any guards, and switch off the internal scanners. Stark still had to move at an agonisingly slow pace until Kaffa's team had done their job. The next set of locks dutifully obeyed the chugger, and they stepped into a warehouse so large, it almost had a horizon. Stark checked his visor: Bay 7F 08, on the right. Then Kaffa's call came through to say they were sweet, and everyone in the team ran to relieve the tension.

They pulled out the boxes and broke one open. Stark grasped one of the objects and held it up to his torchlight.

"Well fuck me!" he said. "That's it?"

The thing looked just like a golden egg.

∞

My heart sank. The great Biz Ramachandran, who admittedly was also the unwitting architect of the end of the world, was just a deluded old man.

"That's really pathetic! I mean, at least face up to what you did," I waved my hand around the green room. "What the fuck do you think all this is?"

Biz was unmoved.

"It's a big green room with a lot of people in it. But no-one here is, in any shape or form, what you would define as *ON*. Technically speaking."

"You're telling me there's no network, no procedure, no engrafts, no …"

"Well, there's engrafts alright, but they do nothing at all."

"That's fucking bullshit! I was *there* at NeuroCon. I watched you on stage. I saw the whole 'cat thing'. I watched you book a table for two and ..."

"And what? What did you *really* see? Some images on the screen? Lots of inspirational patter from the legendary Biz Ramachandran? A little bit of stage magic? What you saw was basically a tarted-up version of a simulation we'd presented earlier to FEDMED. Everyone at NeuroCon – the whole damn stupid world – they all saw *what they wanted to see*!"

He turned his back on me.

"No, I don't believe it. I don't know why you're telling me this, but I don't believe it. Why would you ... why would CoolGlobalGiant decide to play such a grotesque hoax?"

Biz turned angrily.

"Hoax? I didn't set out to hoax anyone! Listen, CoolGlobalGiant really was developing ON. It was no hoax. You have no idea how many setbacks I personally had to deal with. But finally we had working proto-types. And our test subjects were using them to communicate with each other telepathically. Amazing! We built the interface, we made strategic alliances. The goal was in sight."

"And?"

"And ... just before we were about to go on at NeuroCon, it all stopped working. Nothing. We couldn't replicate any of the test results. I should never have agreed to the deception but there was too much riding on it. Quadrillions had been invested. A humiliating retraction at that point would have finished us. Besides, it was only supposed to buy us a little time."

"And?"

"And, sure enough, we got the beta release out on time, and everyone in the test groups loved it and started using it except, once again, meas-urements showed that the things had stopped working. But, and here's the 'Big But', *no-one seemed to notice*! They were still happily locating their long lost aunt in Zurich, or whatever. I should have stopped the whole thing there and then, but to my eternal shame, I didn't. Well, after that it just went berserk. The whole world wanted to get ON. Each batch that went out worked for less and less time until they never worked again. We might as well have implanted house dust. It would've saved us a lot of money."

"But how is this even possible? Mass hallucination? Placebo effect? And what the hell makes the ON logos move on all the clothing?"

"Oh, you think *that's* weird? Pretty soon, people started turning up at the ON clinics to 'get their engrafts checked'. Except they *didn't* have any! They were convinced they'd already had the procedure, and – get this! – neuroscans showed they were actually using the ON nOS interface!"

"So, because they *think* they're ON, they are ON?"

"*I think, therefore I am.* Isn't that how it goes? Maybe we just gave everyone the excuse. Or maybe this is all a mass hallucination. You know what? I'm too tired to care anymore."

He lapsed into another coughing fit, and I let him rest for a little while.

"Biz. I've just come from a place where I witnessed acts of unspeakable cruelty – all in the name of something which you tell me doesn't even exist."

"Were you rich enough to study any history, my young friend? Doesn't take a neuro product for humans to slaughter each other does it? Give 'em God or a cause and off they go. The bigger the lie, the bigger the body count."

We fell silent. I could still see that gravtrain gliding past me, laden with corpses. My brain began calculating depth times width times length of each carriage, divided by average volume of a human body, times the number of carriages ...

"This is a pretty big lie."

"Yes, one big damn lie."

"But, the engrafts? I mean, how were they *supposed* to work?"

"They had a rare isotope which pulsed through multiple energy states. Those resonated with the brain's synapses. Because of the isotope's quantum properties, all the implants were 'entangled', as they say, and time and space meant nothing. That's how the mental transfers were possible. The quantum waves, or whatever, acted as a carrier for mental data."

"But it all stopped working?"

"Maybe it had something to do with quantum physics itself. At that level, things get pretty weird. Particles in two places at once and whatnot. I dunno."

"You know, I studied a bit of quantum physics at college."

"Really?"

"Yeh. You remember Schrödinger's Cat?"

"Schrödinger. Wasn't he a pre-T physicist who proposed a box or ... ?"

"A cat in a box! In any quantum system, all possible energy states exist simultaneously until the exact instant that we observe it. So Schrödinger proposed putting a cat inside a steel box with a Geiger counter and a tiny amount of radioactive material. When triggered, the Geiger counter will shatter a flask of poisonous gas and kill the cat. But, because the cat's fate is linked to a quantum event, it supposedly remains both dead and alive *until* someone opens the box and *observes* it."

"A bit cruel."

"Exactly. While everyone else in class was debating the paradox, all I could think about was that fucking cat, sitting in the dark waiting for some dick in a lab coat to bother to tell him whether he's dead or alive!"

"I've been at the mercy of a few dicks in labcoats, in my time!" Biz laughed. Then the smile fell from his face. I felt a brutal grip from behind.

"70 4B 21 DE, come!" a guard shouted.

It happened so quickly. Several hundred of us were herded out of the room. I looked for Dos, but couldn't see him anywhere. Those who complained or resisted were given a low EM pulse and dragged away. Something told me they'd soon be wearing red. We reached another building where we were forced to sit in a dimly lit corridor. No-one was allowed to speak. Periodically a few of us would be called away to 'surgeries'. I was drifting in and out of a disturbed sleep, when a guard prodded me sharply.

"70 4B 21 DE. Room 17!"

I froze. Two more guards came over and the three of them beat me and dragged me to one of the rooms. The door had the number 17 painted on it. It opened onto a small grey cell. There was the hum of machinery.

∞

On arrival at Cronos, the rooins were split into two groups. Constantin Zann is grateful he was not in the other group, since they had the task of disposing of the bodies of cusp robots destroyed in the missile attacks, and 'disabling' any who were still conscious.

The SAT island is formed from a crystaline latticework of giant connecting tubes. Thousands of rooins are now inside these tubes, repairing walls, carrying girders and installing nanolight sheeting, as they construct their own living quarters. When finished, the accommodation will be modest. Zann estimates that they'll have to sleep standing up.

The guards have almost completely stopped talking to the rooins, preferring instead to gurgle their happy songs. Orders are silently spelled out on large digital displays. The appearance of a fresh order is signalled by a siren blast. Responding quickly can be a matter of life or death. Atrocities are not uncommon. On one occasion, Zann came upon a group of guards busily engaged in 'dismantling' two rooins and swapping their 'parts'.

Despite working in close proximity to naked rooins of both sexes, Zann feels no arousal. Those feelings have been left behind. Zann has shut down two of his brains, and much of the functionality of the other two. He is now a machine – a slave.

∞

The medic looked me up and down as if I was nothing but a small crustacean. His nametag read 'Jasper'.

"70 4B 21 DE. Damaged engrafts. Step into the G-scan."

I searched for some means of escape.

"70 4B 21 DE. Step into the G-scan immediately, or I will call the guard!"

Dos and I hadn't exactly got to 'part two' of his ingenious plan. I briefly considered telling the medic it was all a mass hallucination, that Biz Ramachandran said there was no ON.

No, not a good idea.

I considered overpowering him, until I noticed the weapon at his side. *Another bad idea.*

I decided to wait until he was otherwise occupied. I stepped compliantly between the two silver rods, which glowed and hummed. The medic spoke a crypto-command and the far wall became a screen. He turned towards the screen and I saw my chance. But before I could even move, he shut the G-scan off and spun round angrily.

"70 4B 21 DE, you'll find there are very severe penalties for wasting our time here!"

My heart beat wildly.

"I ... I think I must have been mistaken ..." the words choked in my throat, "... In all the confusion I ..."

"I'll say you're mistaken! There is absolutely nothing wrong with your *engrafts*. Look!"

On the screen were the scans of my neck and head. Clearly visible were my two ON engrafts pulsing bright green. Scrolling up the screen was all the data that I was currently sending and receiving. The medic advanced on me, holding something in his hand.

∞

My eyes open.

I am locked inside some sort of container. My mouth has a metallic, electrical taste, and my skin feels like it is burning. I listen closely, but there is nothing. A deafening silence. The light in here is ... *grey*. As I reach out towards a wall, it's warp and weft unravel under my touch, scattering into meaninglessness. I try to see beyond the wall, to the world 'outside' but all I see is a visual field of grey noise. Then a door opens in the noise and someone enters. It is Doctor Rafaela Serif.

"Ahh, there you are!" she says. "For an instant, I didn't see you. Waiting in the dark for something to happen, are we? Let's have some light."

Grey turns to white as she sits neatly, taking out a flat electronic device.

"Hello. I'm Doctor Rafaela Serif."

What's her game?

"Yes, you are," I say.

"I'd like to talk to you for a short while, if that's OK."

Her fingers flick across the surface of the device, then she looks up and smiles. "Well, this is quite a story isn't it? There was an ... 'incident', I see. Just tell me in your own words what happened. Why do you think you are here now?"

She seems to be flickering.

"Here?"

"Yes."

"Now?"

"That's right."

"I'm here now because I'm being held against my will by a neurological network creature which has taken over most of humanity, including — it would seem – *you*."

"Err, yes of course. We'll get to that in a little while. But first tell me, do you feel as if you are under some sort of threat?"

"That doesn't sound like enough of a threat to you?"

"I mean ... how shall I put it? ... all your life. As a constant aspect of your existence."

"No, I feel as if I am being secretly taken care of."

She raises her eyebrows. "What, like God and his angels?"

"No, like people behind the scenes."

"Hmm. Well, in a sense that's true, Mister Cartouche. We're doing our best here to take care of you, 'behind the scenes' if you like. So you don't have to worry about ..."

"How did it get to you, Rafaela?"

"Get to me? What do you think has 'got to me'?"

"ON. The creature."

"Oh right, the ... where is it now? ... the 'neurological network creature' that's ..."

"Taken over most of humanity. Was it because of your fear of rooins?"

Her smile fades. She puts down the device, looks me in the eye, and sighs.

"OK, Mister Cartouche, let's just start at the beginning shall we? Why don't you tell me why you killed Eve Lamente?"

"I didn't kill anybody. I have no idea who Eve Lamente ..."

I freeze, as remember the girl's ghostly face.

Eve.

"Really?" Doctor Serif says. "Perhaps I can jog your memory. A year ago, you and Ms Lamente volunteered for a research program run by a startup telecommunications company called CoolGlobalGiant. Possibly you've heard of them. Apparently this company was conducting trials of a new personal communication device. As the trials proceeded, you began to exhibit increasingly disturbed and erratic behaviour – hallucinations, talking to people who weren't there, the whole box and dice. Your behaviour became so bad that you represented a serious threat to yourself and everyone else. You had to be forcibly restrained, and the program was discontinued. Unfortunately, before you could be medically assessed, you somehow managed to escape. It would seem that you then made your way to Eve Lamente's apartment, where you murdered her in cold blood. But despite a global manhunt, you just disappeared off the face of the earth. Then, by an extraordinary coincidence, you were apprehended by the law during an unrelated investigation into intellectual property theft and well, here you are now."

"This is some kind of game, isn't it? You're trying to confuse me. But it won't work."

"I'm not trying to confuse you, Mister Cartouche. Why would I do that?"

"Surely ON has better things for you to do. There are hundreds of thousands of people out there in the green room, all waiting to be processed. Why me?"

"Oh, for heaven's sake Mister Cartouche! There's no 'green room' with hundreds of thousands of people. In fact, there are very few patients here at all. Just the few who've been shipped here from regions with insufficient resources. We've only been open for a few months!"

"Did you say *months?*"

"Now, listen carefully. You are a patient in a medical facility for the seriously ill! You were brought here for your own good. There's nothing 'special' about you; we treat all our patients here as special. So the sooner you get all that through your head and admit you need help, the sooner we can make some progress. Is that clear? Oh, and one more thing, just to satisfy my curiosity. What are *rooins?*"

∞

I look at my hands. Particles of time fall through the fingers. Then they rise again. Then they fall ...

Doctor Serif clears her throat.

"OK, let's talk about something else for a while. Why don't you tell me what these trials at CoolGlobalGiant were all about. It would help me to understand your current situation. And, don't quote me of course, but if OHS rules were broken, you may even have reasonable cause for compensation."

"I don't know."

"What don't you know?"

"Who I am, it seems. I don't remember any trials. I ... I 'remember' what ON was ... *is* supposed to be."

"ON? That's the ..."

"It's an acronym. It stands for One Network."

"Right."

"ON was ... *is* a way for humans to communicate telepathically via two *engrafts* – tiny implants inserted into the base of the skull."

"Goodness me!"

"I've just discovered I also have the engrafts in my head ..."

I tap the base of my skull.

"... Here. You can't see them of course because it's healed up, but ..."

She smiles awkwardly.

"Oh. You don't believe me, of course."

"I believe that they're real for you. And that's a perfectly valid ..."

"I'm not crazy."

"I don't think you're 'crazy'."

"I'm just in love with you."

She shifts in her seat. "I'm sorry?"

"Your eyes amaze me."

"What are you ... ?"

"It's a pop song. You don't remember it?"

She shakes her head. "I'm not much of a fan of pop music, I have to say. Look, perhaps we should end the session here, and let you get some rest. We can start again tomorrow."

"Tomorrow. No-one's heard that word for a long, long time. Is there even such a thing as tomorrow?"

"There's always a tomorrow, Mister Cartouche," she says, rising to leave.

"Is there? Do you know what time it is, Doctor?"

She consults a small square wristband device. A *watch*.

"It's just after eleven thirty."

"Eleven thirty. Is that copyright?"

"Pardon?"

"The, what do you call them ... ? Day, month ... *year*. That's right. What year is it?"

She seems surprised.

"You really don't know?"

"No."

"It's Tuesday, September 4th, 2035."

"Tuesday, September 4th, 2035," I say the words slowly, savouring their comforting strangeness. "You've never met me before have you, Doctor Serif?"

"No."

"And yet I know that you've had trouble living with yourself your entire life ..."

Her hand moves towards her heart.

"... ever since you burned down the farmhouse, and lied about it to your parents."

∞

I can see her white knuckles and red fingernails protruding slightly from the dark folds of her hair as she holds her head in her hands. Is she crying? I stand up and walk towards her. I reach out to touch her shoulder, to comfort her. She looks up at me with serene malice.

"You think you know me Mister No-one? You know nothing!"

She stands up and pushes me back into my seat.

"You know nothing because *you* are nothing."

She leans forwards, placing her hands on the chair's armrests, her face close to mine.

"*We* are everything."

Now we're on the same page.

∞

General Zryan Mahon sighs as he picks up the report he'd requested. Its been a while since he's had to read a physical report.

Q23 is unlike any drug in the history of human pharmacology. In fact, in some respects, it isn't even a drug at all. It was accidentally discovered by Prof Pedanus Schmeidmeyer and his team at the University of Delphi in BA08 5A7F 9901 B30C (© Tempo Corp. All rights reserved), during attempts to develop more industrially useful forms of the metal vanadium. Prof Schmeidmeyer hit upon the idea of bombarding vanadium atoms with the recently discovered 'kali particles', which resulted in an 'element' which cycled through a virtual infinity of energy states and Traugott polarities.

The new substance was so unstable that simply storing it proved extremely difficult. Whatever it was that Schmeidmeyer had discovered hovered precariously on the border between 'something' and 'nothing'. Prof Schmeidmeyer named the new substance $V[\infty]$, and published a few papers on the discovery, but any practical application seemed highly unlikely. Chance, however, had other ideas. Due to an absurd series of mishaps, the substance was accidentally released into the laboratory at the exact instant that Prof Schmeidmeyer had returned one evening to pick up some papers he had forgotten. With a half-life of less than a T-sec, $V[\infty]$ had a very short window of opportunity to do anything of significance in this world. So what it did was enter the body of Pedanus Schmeidmeyer. The scientist was immediately transported to "*... an infinity of possible worlds, some so beautiful that all my tears of joy were but a drop of dew on a single rose; some so unspeakably cruel, that I knew in my heart the creator was Satan himself.*"

Prof Schmeidmeyer subsequently published a controversial paper claiming that V[∞] provided a portal to all conceivable realities contained within the empty space within matter, via a poorly understood phenomenon he named 'chaos resonance'. The paper was unanimously derided by his peers as "the ravings of a madman", and shortly after its publication, Prof Schmeidmeyer died in bizarre and tragic circumstances, while undergoing psychiatric treatment. Immediately after his death, all his equipment and notes were mysteriously seized, and nothing was heard of V[∞] again.

Many generations later, the mysterious substance resurfaced as Q23 – the notorious crowd control drug first used by military firms during the post-emancipation 'Robot Riots'. By this stage, storage solutions, delivery mechanisms, and protective measures had been developed. Sadly, it has also found its way onto the streets under the common name of 'Q'. Recreational use of this drug has left a devastating legacy across OneWorld.

"Devastating legacy, eh?"

General Zryan Mahon puts down the report and looks out at the low white buildings that house the transporters. His eyes move to the horizon. A dust storm is blowing up from the west.

He studies the maps and overlays. Before him is a planet which until recently he'd somewhat taken for granted. But now that it is in danger of being forcibly taken from him, he feels fiercely protective towards it. This is *his* planet, *his* home, as much as any human's.

The rebel alliance has assembled a detailed picture of the creature and how it functions. Eight main neural clusters move through the human carriers in a wave-like motion. Multiple threads connect the clusters and, at various intervals along these threads, smaller clusters can be seen. There are four basic internal processes: reproduction, digestion, motor, and defence. The creature has four levels of hierarchical organisation, with each human component assigned to one process and one level of responsibility within that process. As humanity becomes violated, all the patterns pulse to a slow beat, as though the thing is breathing.

∞

The *Emperor* missiles are almost toy-like – not much bigger than an ordinary pen. Each missile has full invisibility cloaking, a miniature grav motor, and is guided via the military PolarGrid platform. If necessary, one of these things could be sent half way round the planet to hit a man between the eyes.

The first targets will be the eight main clusters. Dosage is a big issue. There needs to be just the right amount to destroy the creature's patterns and hierarchies but spare the majority of its human components. Though, what will be left of them is anyone's guess. The problem is that the quality of the Q23 supplies is largely unknown, since most of it has come from underworld sources.

General Zryan Mahon gives the order. Protective covers slide away, tiny transparent warheads move into position, and the air fills with the sound of orchestras tuning up.

∞

The first indication that something was wrong was the behaviour of the digital displays. The orders became progressively erratic and abstruse, sometimes with meaningless words repeated over and over. Occasionally a display would go blank.

Next, the guards began acting strangely, their coordination visibly deteriorating both individually and as a collective.

Until now the rooins have been carrying on as if nothing was amiss, but this is no longer possible. Some of the guards are becoming randomly aggressive, attacking any rooin who inadvertently catches their eye. Others simply sit on the floor, holding their head in their hands. The digital displays are now mostly showing random pixels.

Constantin Zann realises the situation is dangerously unstable. They could all be destroyed at any time. They are all still wearing throttle collars.

Zann switches all four of his brains back on. It's an unpleasant jolt, and everything suddenly seems a lot worse. But Zann has now gained the capacity to think and plan. The first task is to prevent a mass activation of the throttle collars by the guards, either due to accident or anger. The guards appear to be able to activate a collar's mechanism with their thoughts, simply by staring at the number printed on the collar. To do this would require a physical machine nearby – one which can process the ON data and convert it to a local signal directed at the respective collar.

There is always the possibility that, even if they are able to destroy or switch off this machine, the collars would still auto-activate when any attempt is made to remove them. But Zann reasons that, in order to allow guards themselves to remove the collars for any reason, auto-activation could be disabled via the remote machine.

The logical location for this machine would be the central admin pod which overlooks most of the rooin work areas. The ovoid shaped room rises high above the floor level, supported by four cylindrical pillars each of which houses an access elevator. They just need to get into that room. *What could be easier?* Zann laughs to himself. It's been a long time since he's laughed.

He notices a young rooine nearby who is also looking up at the admin pod. Her facial responses tell Zann she is fully conscious. He decides to risk communicating with her in L. A string of tiny sounds arranges itself into a logical array between them. She turns, opens her mouth and utters more sounds which join the array, colouring it, and building on its original meaning. Zann contributes more sounds. The array becomes denser, the colours subtler. The array is now a plan.

As Zann wanders through the crowd telling rooins about the plan, he notices a lone guard watching him. Zann stops and pretends to be engaged in some task. The guard approaches. *Zork! He's onto us.* Zann wonders whether he should simply kill this guard now, before he can raise the alarm. Zann would surely die, but the plan could still go ahead. The guard is standing in front of him.

"Planning an escape?" the guard says.

"That'd be crazy," Zann replies, trying to sound brain dead.

"It would," says the guard, "unless you had help."

"Help?"

"Free," the human whispers, tapping his head. "I'm free. Well ... *almost.*" He offers a grim smile. Then he frowns. "Uh, sorry about this, but now I'm going to have to hit you."

"What ... ?"

The guard strikes Zann across the head. All four brains dutifully register the pain in full.

"Zork!" Zann spits.

"Work!" the guard shouts in Zann's face. Then he whispers. "I'll talk later."

∞

Zann doesn't see the guard coming. The man grabs him from behind and slams him into a pylon. Zann cries out with the pain.

"Aaah! We can't keep meeting this way."

"Shut up!" the guard shouts. Then he asks, "Everyone ready?"

"Yes."

"Good. Let's go."

The guard manhandles Zann through the crowd of rooins, occasionally hitting him and shouting incomprehensibly. Slowly they make their way towards the elevators leading to the admin pod. Just before they have reached their destination, a fight breaks out between several rooins. Guards rush in to stop it, but the fight seems to shift effortlessly from one place to the next, with the rooins always keeping the numbers of their collars turned away from the guards. Zann and his guard veer off course, becoming lost in the melee. Slowly they come round again and reach the elevators. By now the fighting has strangely subsided. As Zann's guard calls for the elevator, a fresh bout of fighting erupts on the outskirts of the crowd. The elevator doors open and other eight rooins quickly join them. While the elevator rises, fights break out all across the rooin workers, with guards powerless to stop them. Then they all stop.

The elevator doors open on the control room and the nine rooins rush the guards. The fight is brief and brutal. Three rooins are killed instantly, but the remainder manage to overpower the guards. The machine which activates the collars is exactly where Zann hoped to find it, and after a T-sec's hesitation he obliterates it with a plasma blast, half expecting to die on the spot. He doesn't, and thousands of rooins turn on their guards, achieving victory by surprise and sheer force of numbers.

"OK," Zann says, "I wonder if there are any clothes around here."

∞

"The farmhouse? The rooins?"

Doctor Serif is unmoved.

"Rooins are machines which do our bidding. Right now, they are being put to work the way they were originally intended. If they fail, they are terminated. Eventually we will have no further use for rooins. With ON ..."

"What *exactly* is ON, Rafaela? It's funny, because I was just talking to Biz Ramachandran and ..."

"Yes, I watched you two chatting away like old buddies. I suppose he told you that tedious story about how there is no ON."

∞

Perspective shifts. The room contains equipment. Data is scrolling up the wall screen. I am wearing a green hospital tunic. Doctor Rafaela Serif is dressed in an iridescent blue uniform which doesn't match her eyes.

"Why are you bothering with all of this? What's so special about me?"

"ON owes you a great debt."

"Me?"

"You were the first test subject. You made all of this possible. You still carry the high grade vanadium engrafts, not those cheap mass-produced ones they make now. Look at those figures! You can't get identity data like that anymore – layer depth, colour index, retention, context quotient, granularity, immersion level ..."

"I'm *so* impressed with myself."

"You should be. ON is. ON has been searching for you."

"It took its time."

"Your identity patterns were not stable. Even Professor Cabral didn't recognise you at first, when you spoke at CoolGlobalGiant headquarters."

"My 'identity patterns' feel just fine, thank you Doctor. Cabral probably didn't recognise me because he was ON. I've already witnessed this more than once. ONs have trouble recognising real individuals. That's because they are no longer ..."

"I am an individual!" she snapped. "I know exactly who I am."

"Do you know who you are?"

"Yes I *do*. My name is Doctor Rafaela Serif, and my purpose is to get you out of here. But, more importantly, get you feeling *good* about yourself. How's that?"

She rounds it off a winning smile. I'm not buying it.

"You think you know who you are, but ON is just producing a simulation of self-awareness within you, for its own purposes. Your thoughts are no longer your own."

She laughs, shaking her head.

"Listen to yourself. I mean really *listen* to yourself. Don't you think that sounds a little, well, *crazy*?"

Suddenly, I realise we are in a Turing test. But who is the simulation and who is the human? Can I be so sure the human is *me*?

"I'll tell you what I think." I said. "I think ON sees me as some sort of threat. It needs to either convert me or eliminate me. 'For the good of all', as they say."

She laughs again. "ON doesn't want to eliminate you, Youren. It wants you to be free."

"Free to be a slave?"

"Free to be who you really are, free to ..."

"Slaughter my fellow humans?"

Her tone becomes officious. "Great changes in this world have always involved a few regrettable casualties."

"Tell that to the people in the red room."

"I cannot tell them anything. They are already dead. But you'd be surprised how few deaths there have been compared to other major upheavals throughout history. Those who join us will be saved."

"I don't want to be a part of that 'upheaval', thank you. And I don't want to be saved."

She smiles condescendingly.

"Really? Look at you. No family or friends, no hopes or dreams. Just a job in an advertising agency, doing something you despise. How much does your existence weigh?"

"It weighs just enough for me not to be a mindless slave to *Jelly Global Inc.*"

"Ooh, that's right! Let's avoid the truth with a joke. Maybe that'll throw her off the track. But wait! Is that really *your* joke?"

I pretend to press a game show buzzer, making an irritating noise. "Umm, I'll go with 'Yes'."

"It is? Did you invent any of the words you just used? Obviously not. All of them were taught to you. What about the structure of the sentence? You were taught that too. The most you could claim is that you rearranged some pre-existing elements you already knew. Except you didn't even do *that*. The routines in your brain that rearranged the elements were also taught to you by others."

"So, you're saying I'm an automaton."

"I'm saying your precious individuality depends upon every human who has ever lived on this planet. To think otherwise is to blind yourself to a biological reality."

"So what am I supposed to do?"

She settles back into her chair, just like a real psych.

"Well, for starters, you could acknowledge your debt to the human biosphere."

"Now there's a big word! Biosphere. I would have said it was the other way round. The human biosphere should acknowledge its debt to me. Without the efforts of me and all the other little individuals, there would be no biosphere. If it's all the same to you, I'll stick with individuality."

I press the imaginary buzzer again, trying to make the noise even more irritating. But she appears unperturbed.

"Individuality is nothing more than memory. And one man's memory, as I'm sure you've recently discovered, can be quite an illusion."

"So, if you destroy someone's memory, they cease to be an individual."

She smiles at me like an endulgent kindergarten teacher. "No-one's memory is being destroyed. The point is that, since your individuality comes from the collective memory, why not take advantage of that? Why not 'get with the strength' and tap into that collective memory? Just imagine a species where every member cooperates for the good of the whole. A *super individual*. You, Youren, can be a part of that super individual."

"A super individual?"

"Yes, instead of ... well, next to nothing really."

"Next to nothing. Yes, I like the sound of that."

She seems to find this last comment annoying, and sits glaring at me.

After a while she says, "The apparent death of your father hit you pretty badly, didn't it?"

"*Apparent* ... ? No, fuck you! Leave my father out of this."

"And yet you'd like to bring him back, wouldn't you? In your dreams you see him, your little legs run to him. You'd like to talk to him again, tell him how much you ..."

Again I am standing in the snow, crying. The anger wells up inside me again.

There is a soft rumble, a sound of distant explosions.

"Your father lives on in the memories. He's alive and well in the world of ON."

"Bullshit! If anything's there, it's not my father. It'd be like Arlo. Remember him?"

"Your father is worth more than Arlo."

"You know nothing about how much my father was worth!"

"But *you* do! You could contribute your memories of him. ON brings memories to life in new and wonderful ways. Human ways. In ON we can all live forever."

I slowly clap my hands.

"Bravo! You could get a job at i++ doing that. That kind of bullshit pays highly. You know, ON just sounds to me like those immortal cell lines that endlessly divide and grow in some grotesque, cancerous parody of real life."

This is one of my best shots, yet she shakes her head and smiles so sweetly, so lovingly, that I feel a strange shiver run through me. Pleasurable and terribly wrong. I remember our kiss. I can see that I am actually several people, each trying to manipulate the situation to suit himself, competing, cooperating, capitulating ... whatever works. The rabble raises its voice.

"So, Rafaela, where did this *super individual* come from?"

"I told you, from all of us."

"Like you and me?"

"Exactly." She reaches out and touches my arm. "Come on, why not come out of the darkness of uncertainty and into the light of *certainty*."

I look into her eyes – so clear, so dark. I can smell her perfume.

There is another rumble, closer this time.

"Am I really deluded, Rafaela?"

"I'm sorry, but yes."

"Why?"

"Because you have forgotten who you are."

"And – let me get this straight – what I really am is ON. We are all ON. And ON is with us and ON *is* us."

"That's right."

"ON is the one great individual defined by the memory of all humanity. And ON is gathering us all together to become one in that vast memory."

She gives me a broad smile. "Now you're getting it."

"All those memories."

"Yes."

"And all those *beliefs* too."

"Well ..."

"Every one of them as imperfect and contradictory as mine. All those sad daydreams and self-serving lies we tell ourselves and each other. Rafaela, think! ON must be twenty three billion times more deluded than me!"

The fly in the ointment is not quite dead. Her face darkens again. I press on.

"ON has built itself upon a pack of lies, Rafaela. My lies. Everyone's lies. And since its identity comes from nothing more than those lies, ON itself is a lie. Or, as Biz Ramachandran recently said, *there is no ON.*"

She lunges at me.

"Shut up, you stupid ... you ... *nothing!*"

I feel her spittle on my cheek.

"Yes, I am nothing." I say slowly, and clearly. "Nothing that matters. But I still exist. ON doesn't exist, except in the collective delusion. I know it, you know it, and deep down, everyone ..."

She hits me across the face with the power of a planet. The pain feels good. It is *my* pain. In my weakened state, I am no physical match for her. She hits me again, knocking me to the floor. Soon she is on top of me, her blows raining down. I cannot fight her, so I do the next best thing; I try to embrace her. She recoils in disgust. I try again. She pulls away, but I cling to her like mould, like decay – like inevitable death. Dark creatures observe our exertions through fractal foliage. The room smells like a forest floor.

Then there is an explosion.

Kalika is under attack. Explosions rock the building. One goes off in the hallway outside. There is the sound of glass breaking, then the sound of birds, or is it grav engines warming up? Next, I hear screaming and laughter and someone repeatedly shouting "I am impossible!" The countless feet of history are running towards us. The feet run all over the walls and ceiling, and the room shakes, yet nothing moves or falls. Rafaela stares at me in joy or horror, I cannot tell. Blood oozes from the pores in her face, as she wails like a banshee. Her hands have disconnected themselves from her body which is now made up of tiny glowing springs. Torrential rain falls on me from her eyes, eating into me like acid. Like liquid, I seep under the door and into a research facility. There are neuro-modellers and other test equipment.

"Just make yourself comfortable, Youren."

The man's voice is high-pitched and soft, almost feminine. I hesitate.

"Please." he says.

I sit in the chair, within a pool of blue light.

"Close your eyes and empty your mind."

I am staring into a grey space. Tiny sparks of visual noise fire within the emptiness. Nothing happens for a while. Then, as though a slight breeze has passed, a breath perhaps, I observe a soft dappling of the disorder. Almost imperceptibly at first, clusters of light and shade appear within the noise. A bright cluster grows at the centre of my visual field. It's the shape of a young woman. She increases in size, as though she is walking towards me.

"Youren Cartouche," she says, stretching both hands out towards me.

"Eve?"

From far away, the man's voice says, "You're both doing well."

"Can you see me, Eve?"

"Yes, Youren."

"Where are you?"

"In the next room." She gives me a schoolgirl smile at the wonder of it all.

"Show him, Eve." the man says.

"Uh, OK."

She fades, and the room she is in comes into view. As her gaze lowers, I can see her blue jeans and red sneakers. She looks up towards a door.

"Over there is ..." her hand rises to point, but it knocks over a pitcher of water on the table next to her chair. "... Oh, *shit*!"

I feel the pain of impact on my hand.

"Sorry."

There is awkward laughter on both sides. My chest is rising and falling with hers. She has a slight asthma.

"That's OK, Eve. You're doing fine." the man reassures her. "Now why don't you try to think of something? Concentrate on a simple image. Close you eyes and focus your mind."

The empty space returns, crackling with the promise of shape and colour. Pinpoints of red, green and blue support an unstable grey. Nothing happens for a while, then a thin vertical line appears before me, widening and warping.

The line transforms itself into a single rose.

The man asks, "What do you see, Youren?"

"A rose."

"What colour is it?"

Within the petals, grains of light shimmer and oscillate, as the colours establish themselves. Uncertainty becomes certainty.

"Blue."

"Eve, did you know that Youren could see your rose?"

"Yes. Somehow, I just knew he was seeing it. In fact, I'd even say ..."

"Yes?"

She hesitates.

"It was as though he was helping me make it."

Everyone is silent. The man speaks again, but the tone of his voice has changed.

"So, who thought of the rose first?"

∞

My head hits the floor. I am lying in a small room. There is a woman in the room, screaming "Help! Someone! Come quickly!" I can see her and hear her, but the funny thing is I am – at the very least – clinically dead.

∞

"Cronus in the 5th belt, Repeat, I am calling from Cronos in the 5th belt. Is anyone there?"

Zann has been trying to reach someone, anyone, but with no success. Standing next to him is a young, very agitated rooin.

"I think we should take what transporters are left and get the zork out of here."

"Go where?" Zann asks. "Until we know what's happened, there is nowhere to go."

"Maybe the humans are already on their way. The longer we wait, the less our chances."

Zann stops to consider this. It's possible reinforcements are on the way, although he doubts the guards had time to contact anyone. And surely someone else would answer.

The comm crackles to life.

"Mayday! Mayday ... !"

Zann presses the button to talk.

"We hear you. Are you alright?"

"All transport destroyed ... injured ..."

"Where are you?"

"Eli-Zeum, what's left of it. Can't hold out much longer."

"What's your name?"

"Suize."

Zann turns to the young rooin.

"That's not far from here. I'll go myself ... OK, sit tight, Suize, I'm coming to get you."

∞

Zann carefully eases the jumper onto the landing strip. The Mastaba is all but destroyed, with robot parts strewn everywhere. A few of the robots are executing futile cyclic movements while their power dissipates. Zann picks his way through the debris.

"Suize! Suize where are you?"

"Over here." comes a weak reply.

She is lying by the wreckage of her jumper. She appears to be badly injured. Zann gently lifts her and carries her back to his jumper. As they take off, she looks across at him.

"Why don't you have any clothes?" she asks.

∞

General Zryan Mahon's maxi-grav Class 3 lifted off the sand-blown gravpad, hovered briefly, then turned 32° and headed west. It was time to see things with his own eyes. The ship was built for long flight. It carried a crew of over three hundred, and enough firepower to level a city the size of Medusa, if someone hadn't already done that.

After the initial assault, the Free Species Alliance army had moved out from its bases across the globe. A ragtag collection of free humans, plus rooins who had managed to escape deportation, marched and fought side by side.

General Mahon stood on the bridge, watching the mangled landscape pass beneath him. Both port and starboard, fighter gravs provided protection for his ship. They flew over a battalion of soldiers advancing on a cluster of buildings.

"Captain A-Zure for you, sir."

"How's it going down there, Captain?"

"Good and bad, General. As always, good and bad."

"I could use some good news right now."

The Captain laughed. "I believe we could all do with some of that, General. Overall, we're making progress. We've set-up field hospitals throughout this sector to treat the ones who show promise. Removing the engrafts is no guarantee of success though, as we've discovered. Also, we have very few human neuropsychs in our ranks, since most of them were early ON adopters. Still, our rooin medics are doing well. We'll get there."

"Good work, Captain."

"Thank you General."

"I guess you'd better give me the bad news."

"Our main problem is the recidivist humans. There's a significant percentage who still seem very susceptible to the creature's influence. In it's death throes, it's getting more desperate and cunning. Recently, one of our squads came across a warehouse full of dazed people who seemed harmless enough. The squad leader figured the Q had done the trick. And everyone's golden eggs showed no chance deviancy in the area. But suddenly these humans picked up weapons and wiped out most of the squad. Seems a dismembered tendril of the ON creature had rushed through their brains, briefly re-activating them. I lost a lot of good soldiers in that warehouse, General."

"I'm sorry to hear it Captain."

"Now we put captives into holding compounds so that, even if they do revert, they can't harm anyone other than themselves. But they can get a bit, well ... messy."

"Messy?"

"Are you headed towards Medusa, General?"

"We are, Captain."

"You'll see what I mean."

∞

A sudden drop in temperature had turned the rain to snow. As the squad marched along the road, flecks of white swirled around them. They were going from building to building, checking for survivors or dealing with combatants. There weren't too many of the latter any more. As each building was cleared, the occupants were invited to join them. Most chose to do so, and pretty soon the little squad had swelled to four times its size.

Hefastus Stark marched with pride through the snow. He'd even managed to find his old dog tags. The metal dangled and danced across the thin scar lines on his chest. Stark looked around. Some of his old D-Co buddies were here. Dimitri the Hat and some of the other Hammers.

Along with hundreds of similar squads, they were headed for the centre of Medusa. As they rounded a corner in the road, the vast structure of

OneWorld Plaza came into view. It had been severely damaged, and most of the Dome of Time was missing. One of the rings dangled precariously.

"Take it easy. This could be trouble," the squad leader said, indicating that they should fan out. He checked a golden, egg-shaped device. "Low level activity nearby."

Stark was the first to hear the sound.

"Fuck me, Lady Luck!" he whispered through the comm. "What the fuck is that shit?"

Now they could all hear it: an eerie wailing coming from OneWorld Plaza. The sound grew louder with every advancing step. Next they became aware of the smell of death. Those at the front stopped, unwilling to advance any further. The wailing filled everyone's ears.

"Oh, weeping chance!" someone said, as the rest of the squad caught up.

∞

Hovering above OneWorld Plaza, General Zryon Mahon surveyed the scene. The dome had been blown away, giving him a clear view inside the atrium. On the plaza floor were maybe two hundred of the ... *things.*

"That's them?" he asked the sergeant.

"That's them, General."

"I'll be zorked!" he gasped. "What did you say they're called?"

"The soldiers call them *globs.*"

"Globs. So, what exactly is going on down there, Sergeant?"

"It's a planet-wide phenomenon, General. As ON breaks up, some humans become so desperate for that deep connection to other humans that they physically grab onto each other and won't let go. What starts out as the terrified embrace of two people soon escalates out of control, with more humans joining in and eventually crushing the ones who started it. Once a glob has begun, nothing short of a weapon attack will break it up."

"Those in the middle look dead."

"They are, General. Asphyxiated or crushed to death. As the glob grows, those trapped in the middle die, and you wind up with a ball of living humans clutching a central core of rotting corpses. Eventually all of them will die."

The General shuddered as he watched the rosettes of blackening flesh writhing below him.

∞

The squad had now ventured closer. They could see the giant columns rising up to nowhere, and the haphazard arrangement of the cubes, which now looked less like a clever design and more like the ruins of war. Hovering above was an alliance transporter.

In the plaza were humans as far as the eye could see. They had formed themselves into tight circles of about two to three hundred each, everyone pushing violently towards the middle. Some had even clambered on top and were swimming across the sea of flesh. All of them looked malnourished and dehydrated. As the humans swayed and writhed in their ballroom dance of death, they let out an anguished cry of loss.

It was Stark who spoke first.

"Fuck me!" he said, "Looks like someone needed a group hug."

∞

"Is it just me, or is this really creepy?"

"Seems fine to me Ozzi-Chen, just way too crowded." Lakzad said casually, as he watched some rooines slowly forming themselves into an erotic pyramid.

Zygot, like any bar on any SAT island, was unbearably crowded. Ozzi-Chen and Lakzad were perched on a couple of bar stools behind the stage.

"I don't know. Maybe I've been planetside too long. These SAT rooins are weird."

"Relax Ozzi-Chen. Flip yourself over to *Zing* or something. We're celebrating."

"What's there to celebrate? We're all crammed together, the planet has been destroyed by madmen who almost killed me and you, most humans have been reduced to slime mould or whatever, and at least a quarter of the rooin population is dead."

"Lakzad! Ozzi-Chen! I don't believe it."

"Zann!" Ozzi-Chen leaped to his feet and embraced the rooin. Lakzad stood and, after a moments hesitation, also held out his arms.

"We thought you were dead."

"Yes. Dead, but reborn. Oh, excuse me, I'd like you to meet Suize Capazo."

The rooine stepped forwards to greet them. Ozzi-Chen and Lakzad were momentarily lost for words. Then Ozzi-Chen rallied.

"So how did you two ... um ..."

"... meet?" Lakzad finished his sentence.

"I picked her up at the Mastaba," Zann said.

Suize burst into laughter. Lakzad and Ozzi-Chen soon found themselves laughing too. Then all four rooins became quiet as they cast their eyes downward through the transparent floor to the planet below. The brown blanket of clouds was punctuated by points af white smoke, indicating where major chemical fires were still raging below.

"How could this have happened?" Ozzi-Chen asked no-one in particular.

"Evolution," Suize said, her voice clear and cold. "Humans were betrayed by the evolutionary process. A series of incremental modifications, selected solely on whether they improve the chance of survival and reproduction, is a poor way to design a complex creature. The needs and aspirations of the individual are irrelevant in this process. It's probably why humans were so obsessed with themselves. Deep down they knew that the machinery which made them didn't care for them at all."

Ozzie-Chen looked up from the floor. "Do you think they'll ever recover? As a species, I mean."

"If they can remember what happened, they'll have a chance," Suize said. "Their history is their only hope."

After a while, Lakzad asked, "So, what are your plans, Zann. Back to Law?"

Constantin Zann laughed. "Do you remember that time on the roof of Raymond Parkes, when you were worried I might jump?"

"I do, and I was," Lakzad said.

"And I said I was thinking about *singing*."

Lakzad looked puzzled. "Singing?"

The stage lit up. Azu Ga stepped into the spotlight, and walked to the microphone.

"Listen up roos. Silence is golden. We have a special treat for you in this time of ... planetry strife."

Azu Ga looked down and comically feigned sadness. There was awkward, scattered laughter. He then gestured to Zann, who stepped up onto the stage.

"A performance by a rising star. I give you the special agent who's always 'packing heat'. Mister Constantin Zann!"

Polyrhythmic machinations of multisound moved through the room, and the crowd bubbled appreciatively. As Zann stepped into the light and began to sway, Suize Capazzo laughed and clapped while Ozzi-Chen hooted wildly with encouragement and approval. Lakzad looked aghast.

Constantin Zann began to sing in the strange tongue of L. His extraordinary voice covered many octaves, from beastgrowl bass to glassy falsetto. The audience froze in amazement, their Super-Hydras hovering at their lips. Then a sub-bass came up through their feet, and Zann started to swing his long tail of hair around like a dark comet. One by one the crowd began to join in. Even Lakzad was swept up in the sound, adding a gruff voice which slotted perfectly into place within the layers of rooin song, as a new harmony of meaning filled the space between them all.

∞

He stumbles, and the floor rises to greet him. The hand seems to be too big as it reaches out to prevent his fall. In fact his whole body feels clumsy and grotesque. He is either too big or too small. The icons are still there beyond his peripheral vision, but they no longer do anything. For a while he could hear the cries of anguish and see the horror, but now he only has his own eyes to look through.

Alone.

Slowly, he gets to his feet and makes his way to the factory. With each step he wants to cry out with the loneliness and fear, but he will not allow it. Not him.

Row after row of conveyors are still busily depositing the product into sterile blister packs. He picks up one of the slickly designed packets and turns it over. The logo dances around the edge, and the engrafts glow inside their tiny cocoon. Despite his resolve, he finds himself sinking to the floor, crying, still holding the little packet.

What could have been ... All of us ...

His body becomes racked with sobs. Then, a noise jolts him out of his reverie. With difficulty he gets to his feet.

Who is ... ?

Soldiers are entering the factory. The way each body moves tells him they are individuals.

Rabble.

What are they saying? He listens, trying to decipher the speech, but he can't. He has evolved too far.

Gibberish.

He needs to make his position clear, to explain himself, and he opens his mouth to speak. Yes, that should do it. They look at him uncomprehendingly.

Stupid people! Don't they understand?

He takes a step forwards, raising his voice, emphasising his points with broad gestures.

The soldiers look at each other, and then back to him. The shot comes from someone at the back. He can't see which one. A small missile hits him and explodes. He feels nothing, the shell bouncing off him. His chest swells, and some of the old confidence briefly returns.

"We are invincible." he shouts.

But the soldiers don't seem to understand. Then he notices that their movements are becoming disjointed. Slowly, one by one, they are disintegrating before him.

"Ha ha. I told you."

The factory lights dim, then extinguish altogether. The floor gives way and he falls into nothing. On and on he falls. Or is he stationary? It is pitch black but he can still feel his body. There is pain. Then his hands disconnect from that body. Floating off into space, yet still his hands. The pain keeps growing. Next his feet. Bit by bit he comes apart as entropy has its way with him. Then those parts themselves separate into smaller parts – pieces of flesh, cells, molecules, atoms, subatomic particles, all spiralling into the black – separated by light-years, yet still entangled, and still aware. No death comes to comfort him. You can't kill a universe.

The alliance soldiers gather around the body of Adão Cabral, as it stares up at the ceiling with an expression of undiluted horror.

Into the black

Dos Pascal sits alone on the little chair next to his single bed. The room contains four such beds, each with its own chair and table. Desklamps are not permitted. Above him, a series of high windows admits a dull light. If Dos were to stand tiptoe on the desk, he'd have a fine view of the rear of the next building, with its rubbish skips and the nursing staff huddling out of the rain as they smoked. Almost everything in the room is a shade of green.

Dos rolls six dice. He takes his stub of a pencil, smoothes the pages of a small notebook, and carefully records the results of his throw. He picks up the dice and rolls them a few more times, each time recording the results. Then he flips through the pages of the notebook, studying the rows of neatly drawn numbers that fill every page. Stacked on his table are dozens of similar notebooks, each filled with numbers.

Dos rolls the dice again.

∞

Doctor Rafaela Serif marches along the corridor with crisp purpose, despite the fact her feet are killing her. The high heels had not been a good idea.

She is late for her next session. As she glances at the case notes, she narrowly misses a big hole in the flooring. Kalika is still under construction, with some wards only half complete.

This is an interesting case – one of several inmates brought here from a war zone. Severe childhood trauma occasioned by witnessing his father's death. Steady retreat into fantasy. He is convinced the world has been taken over by some sort of 'neurological network' that controls everyone via 'implants in the skull'. Humanity is supposedly now part of a giant 'colony creature' that uses humans as its component cells. Pages and pages of the stuff.

They're certainly giving me the juicy ones!

It was a big decision to do the part-time volunteer work, but she hasn't regretted it one bit. Now is the time in her career when she should give something back. Everyone needs to be part of something bigger.

Raf arrives at room 17. She pauses to catch her breath.

"All quiet?" she asks.

The nursing assistant rouses himself. "Like a baby, Doctor. Jasper gave him a mild sedative. He shouldn't be any trouble."

"Aha. Doctor Serif."

Raf turns. The Director, Professor Adão Cabral is walking towards her.

"How are you fitting in?" he asks warmly.

"It's been a bit of a culture shock Professor, but I think I'm on top of it now."

"Excellent. We're so happy you could join us. I see you have our friend in room 17. Post-temporal impulse paranoia, if I remember correctly. Hopefully you'll be able to make some headway on him." The Director smiles and opens the door for her.

Raf hovers on the threshold of the room. It is dark, and there is the soft hum of machinery. "Ahh, there you are!" she says, finally discerning the shape huddled against the far wall. "For an instant, I didn't see you. Waiting in the dark for something to happen, are we? Let's have some light." Raf touches the light pad.

∞

Black becomes white, then grey. Probabilities collapse. On the floor lies a man's body. Raf screams.

Director Cabral appears in the doorway.

"What?"

His face freezes as he sees the body.

Doctor Rafaela Serif looks up. She has the vague impression that the room is turning very slowly, as if time is changing direction.

∞

"It's not the end of the world."

"Really?" Biz Ramachandran grunts. "Well, it's pretty damn close!"

"Relax Biz." Li Sun says soothingly, "You know you're not supposed to… I mean, after your, er – *retreat*, you should take things easy and…"

"It was a madhouse." Biz says, flatly.

"Wow." she laughs nervously. "Pretty intense, eh?"

"Li Sun, look at me. Kalika is *literally* a madhouse. It is not a 'retreat'. I was there because I had a *mental breakdown*, OK?"

Li Sun fiddles with her hair and manages a weak smile.

Biz Ramachandran walks up to the wall screen and studies the feed from EGK17. It shows a large warehouse populated with busy technicians who are servicing a giant grey cube, the height of four men. Thick cables attach to every side of the cube, and Biz can make out droplets of moisture condensing on its surface. The technicians chatter is obscured by the constant mechanical hum.

Biz turns to Li Sun. "You know, if this gets out, we're all dead."

"It's not going to 'get out', and we're all very much alive, thank you! No-one knows about it, not FEDMED, not the media, no-one. We've gone through the grID with a nanocomb and ... zilch! So please, *relax*. The subject is fully contained. Look at that thing! Those walls are constructed from hundreds of custom-made grav-laminates, each one weighing several tonnes. They're at least three metres thick! No Biz, there's no way he's going to touch this world."

"Well why didn't you just kill him and be done with it?"

She misses the sarcasm. "That would leave a trace. It's better this way."

"Li Sun, this is a human being we're talking about here!"

She screws up her face. "You're calling that *thing* a human being?" Then her tone softens. "Look Biz, I know you care. But look at it rationally, what more can any of us possibly do? This is the most humane solution."

"Maybe I can talk to him, tell him how sorry I am that ..."

"Err, I don't think that's a very good idea Biz!"

"Why not?"

"Umm, it's a bit complicated. What we're getting is obviously affected by the grav fields, which kinda distort space and time and ... umm ..."

"And what?"

"Well, for example ... sometimes he's there and sometimes he's not."

"Not there! Well, where the hell has he gone?"

"No-one really knows ... it could be an artefact of the room, although some techs have a theory that the very act of observing him alters him in some way."

"Schrödinger's cat."

"What?"

"I dunno, nothing important ... OK, so either I'll see him or I won't."

"Right. Ahh, it's not quite that simple, Biz. There are other unusual ... *phenomena*."

Biz Ramachandran's expression says 'don't jerk me around'. Li Sun takes a little breath.

"OK, sometimes he changes his physical form into ... er ... ugh! – I really don't think you want to know," she raises her eyes. "And sometimes there seem to be other people in there with him."

"Other people? What other people?"

"Well, for example ..." Her fingers fiddle with the top button of her shirt. "... On one occasion, *you* were in there talking with him, Biz."

"Me?"

"Yes. That was just before you ... died."

Biz Ramachandran puts his hands to his head. There is a long pause. He sighs wearily.

"What does Cabral say?"

"He agrees. It's the only way."

"So, everyone's a winner," Biz says, bitterly.

"Exactly." Again, Li Sun seems unaware of the sarcasm.

"Except," Biz says, pointing to the screen, "he'll stay in that box for the rest of his life – if you could even call it a life – surrounded by dicks in labcoats."

"Sadly, yes. It would seem that way. But we're still working on it."

Biz Ramachandran slumps into the sofa.

"We should never have attempted any of this." he says, morosely.

Li Sun walks over and places her hand on his.

"Biz, you did it because you wanted to help humanity. You know: *for the good of all?*"

"How is this even possible? I mean, how can a human do something like this?"

"We're not entirely sure. But as a child, he witnessed a grID tower explosion which killed his father. He survived, but the time particles obviously affected him in some way." She raises her hands. "I know, I know! We should have checked his background more thoroughly. Anyway, adding engrafts to this unstable neurophysical state could possibly have produced some of the, umm ..."

"... *phenomena.*" Biz completes her sentence with another sarcastic euphemism.

"Yes."

"Why didn't we remove the engrafts?"

"Things became too dangerous. First we had to contain him."

Biz Ramachandran laboriously gets up and goes to the window. The sun is setting over the false horizon created by the landscape of dark clouds rolling beneath him. He rubs his head vigorously, as if clearing it of confusion, then turns.

"So, explain it to me again. What really happened?"

"What *really* happened," Li Sun blows out her cheeks. "What *really* happened is that at 0048 B1A7 3391 D001 the engrafts were implanted into Youren Cartouche and Eve Lamente. At 0048 B1A7 3391 D02A, the first session was conducted, in which the subjects were placed in separate rooms and given various tasks to perform."

"Professor Cabral states in his notes that Cartouche was already demonstrating the ability to place thoughts into the mind of Eve Lamente – thoughts which she believed to be her own. As things progressed, the girl began to lose the boundaries of her identity. Alarmed, Professor Cabral stopped the session and reported his findings. He recommended ending the program, but the board wouldn't hear of it."

"Which I must now bear responsibility for," Biz says, shaking his head.

"You weren't responsible Biz," Li Sun says. "You were …"

"Mad?"

Li Sun shrugs and continues. "Well, the second session began well enough. They were testing the first production version of the interface. All tasks had been successfully completed, and Professor Cabral was beginning to dismiss his earlier misapprehensions, when he became aware of an apparition standing next to him in the observation booth. He recognised Youren Cartouche, who said, 'now there is no past,' then disappeared.

"Once more, Professor Cabral reported what had happened to the board, urging them to discontinue the sessions. The board was split down the middle. Eventually it was decided to continue, but with extra observers and safety precautions in place."

"We should have discontinued it then," Biz mumbles.

Li Sun ignores him and presses on, as if framing what happened into the words of a report will somehow give it structure, make sense of it.

"The third session investigated the subjects' ability to interact with the existing technology of the grID. And here the reports of what happened next tend to differ. About half the observers claim that Youren Cartouche disappeared. Some say he was only gone for a few T. Others say he was gone for longer, but one thing everyone agrees on is that Eve Lamente started to scream. When she began to bite her arms the doctors moved in to sedate her.

"When she'd recovered enough to talk all she would say was *'Don't listen to them.'*

"Them?"

"I don't know who she was referring to Biz. After that, she refused to have any further involvement with the program, returning to the planet where, as you know, she later died from a drug overdose. It was decided that Youren Cartouche should be isolated until we could decide what to do. The chamber was built, and well, here we are."

A dull panic is rising in Biz Ramachandran. "But *who* are we?"

"What's that supposed to mean, Biz?"

"Who are we?" Biz repeats. "Are we Biz Ramachandran and Li Sun, or are we *something else?*"

"Don't be ridiculous, this is just ..."

"It wouldn't have taken long to get into the grID and into people's minds, would it?' Biz says almost absent-mindedly, his eyes flitting around the room, "A few hundred thousand – maybe more. After that, it would multiply exponentially. Maybe it's already complete. How would any of us even know?"

"Biz, calm down. You shouldn't ..."

"'*Now there is no past.*' That's what he said. But surely the past is all we really have. If you destroy that ... if you destroy someone's memory, they cease to be an individual. In fact, how do we know that these memories we think we have are – "

"Biz, this is just absurd!"

"Don't tell me you haven't felt it?"

"No Biz. We've felt nothing."

∞

I am the ghost in the machine; an imaginary friend that dogs the cogs of existence. I am the cat in the box; a devil in the subatomic detail, both dead and alive. I am the arrow of time; the fall from grace carried by dark wings.

"For the good of all."

These were the words they pronounced as they beat me and locked me away and forgot that they had forgotten.

"For the good of all."

A promise or a prayer?

My prison is infinitesimally small yet infinitely big, dimensionless yet containing all dimensions. There is nowhere to go so I am free go wherever I please. Even the light is binary and ambiguous, oscillating between a blinding white and utter darkness, until it just resembles a flickering grey. Sometimes I am in the space between. Sometimes not.

Breathe in.

The tide of time flows in, bringing tiny accretions of potential identity, a soft dapple of patterns and forms, blueprints for proto-mechanisms that will combine and assemble into increasingly complex entities. They evolve and grow into microscopic machines that stumble and tumble across an ocean floor. The machines get bigger, and before you know it …

Breathe out.

The tide turns, flowing into disintegration, darkness and death. Life's rich tapestry pixilates to the point of noise, and no-one dances anymore. Empires crumble, cities die.

Breathe in.

Who is breathing this? Who says 'It is', 'it is not' and, eventually, 'I am', 'I am not'? At what point does the 'I' make it's brief, spectral appearance? Or perhaps it never does. Perhaps that immutable little kernel of identity is an illusion made up of many selves continually passing into and out of actuality within a region of probability where we may or may not exist. The question is not do we have free will, the question is *how much of it do we want?* Because free will brings a unique vulnerability and loneliness. The more free we are, the more alone we are. So we merge with other regions to form ourselves into larger entities with less exposure to the vagaries of time and space. The machines get bigger, and before you know it …

When the first multicellular organisms formed, did those single-celled organisms realise the terrible path they were taking? And what was the signal which prompted the change?

Was it love?

Take me back, under the sea, where life began, and love …

Or was it fear?

Whichever it was, it was the first recorded history.

Breathe out.

I try to breathe out, but I can't. In the blinding white, I see an intricate tower formed from countless interlocking wheels. The perfect creation. Then it starts to buckle and crumble under the ministrations of fire and noise, and I can't let go. I can't let it all disintegrate again - everything and everyone I've ever created, ever loved. One human network contracts, gasping, grasping, clinging to itself, and diversity congeals into a purpose-built God.

It's alright.

You are everyone.

∞

With a military eye, Hefastus Stark scrutinises the occupants of the hospital common room. Here, in various poses of resignation, sit an assortment of people in pyjamas, dressing gowns, tracksuits and, in one case, a suit and tie. LaLa shuffles past, tunelessly humming, wearing pink slippers and a stained 'I survived the apocalypse' t-shirt. Stark spies Dimitri in the far corner. Dimitri doesn't talk any more, just sits and stares at his knuckles. *Mad, all mad!* But Stark knows he is just as much a prisoner here as anyone else. In the kitchen, someone is clattering dishes. The smell of pumpkin soup advances like marsh gas.

Stark takes a seat next to an old man whose recliner bed has been wheeled in and left by the nursing staff. Stark watches the man try to pull his blanket up, the trembling hand failing to grip the cloth. Stark reaches over and briskly pulls the blanket up, tucking it in at the sides.

"There you go, friend."

The old man seems confused. Then he becomes increasingly agitated, eventually throwing the covers off with an outraged cry. But he soon begins the same futile procedure all over again. Once more the trembling hand attempts and fails to pull up the bedclothes.

Stark curses and looks away. In the corridor, three nurses are chatting. They slouch with a mixture of boredom and resentment, as if they have better things to do. Occasionally they burst into brief subdued laughter. The clock on the wall shows a quarter to six, but Stark realises he doesn't know whether it is morning or evening. There is no natural light in the room. Outside is the sound of heavy rain. Stark can't remember a time when it was not raining. He rubs his chest and tries to relieve the old pain.

In the corner of the room, an advertisement comes on the television. A young couple are at a club with their friends. Communication between everyone consists of various forms of smiling. The couple wave goodbye and jump into a new reality, a gallery with paintings that move and change. The couple play with the paintings, briefly adding their own touches. A deep male voice is saying "… Unleash your creativity." The humans smile at each other's efforts, but quickly tire of it; they have the whole world to play with. Some new friends join them and they all jump again. Another reality, a party this time. Everyone starts to dance, as though someone has flicked a switch. And so it goes. In the bright, carefree world of fantasy and profit, the humans perpetually smile at themselves. They are the building blocks of a new creature who is less than the sum of its parts. With primitive precision, it gathers its cells into a metastructure, a global web of neurons that anaesthetise as they connect. The cells do not need to be physically in contact, since they are remotely networked. The creature loves every single cell which instructs it. It serves humanity. No-one is forced to participate; everyone willingly pledges their love with a casual selection from a convenient user interface.

"Do you wish to erase all human identity, history and individual control? Yes or No. Submit." The page has a fresh, clean design. A switch flicks and no-one dances anymore.

The creature wants what's best for everyone. But it is a jealous God, casting into the outer darkness those who reject its embrace. It has jettisoned the past in favour of the future, individual pain in favour of group pleasure, and personal thought in favour of connection. Its synapses busily relay the obvious, building a vast mesh which looms up and morphs into its logo, the letters of which spell out a perpetually jammed switch, a negation of oscillation and opposites. The deep male voice now declares something that brooks no challenge.

"THE FUTURE IS ON."

The three nurses in the corridor watch the television with blank interest.

"What will they think of next?" one says.

They will think of you.

Two wards away, Dos Pascal has noticed the emergence of non-random patterns within his rows of neatly drawn figures. They form a simple shape.

Acknowledgments

For the information on siphonophores I am grateful to Casey Dunn and his excellent website: **http://www.siphonophores.org**

Thank you for reading ON.

We hope you enjoyed it.

If you would like to be kept informed of further releases by Jon Puckridge, or other new books from Hague Publishing, why not subscribe to our newsletter at:

www.HaguePublishing.com/subscribe.php

And if you loved the book and have a moment to spare we would really appreciate a short review. Your help in spreading the word is gratefully received.

About The Author

JON Puckridge completed a Batchelor of Science degree at Monash University, during which time he became editor of the student newspaper 'Lot's Wife'. He began his working career in biochemical research but was constantly drawn back to the creative life, and has played in various bands, and written for blogs and music technology magazines.

After studying music composition at the Sydney Conservatorium of Music, Jon had one of his compositions performed at the Sydney Opera House. It was later broadcast on ABC radio.

He currently works in his own graphic design business, while persuing his love of writing.

'ON' is his first novel.

Hague

Publishing

www.HaguePublishing.com

PO Box 451 Bassendean
Western Australia 6934

www.ingramcontent.com/pod-product-compliance
Lightning Source LLC
Chambersburg PA
CBHW070439120726
47910CB00003B/853